Scotty Jackson Died... But Then He Got Better

Scotty Jackson Died... But Then He Got Better
© 2012 Mark A. Roeder

Cover Photo Credits: Soupstock (model), Lmphot (background), and Markobradich (casket) on Dreamstime.com.

Cover Design: Ken Clark

ISBN-13: 978-1481070140

ISBN-10: 1481070142

Printed in the United States of America

Acknowledgements

I'd like to thank Ken Clark and James Adkinson for all the work they put in proofreading this book. They spot the errors I miss. Jim provides a further and valuable service by pointing out the anachronisms that slip into my tales. I'd further like to thank Ken for creating the cover.

Dedication

This novel is dedicated to Tom Bridegroom. I wish I'd had the chance to get to know you better.

Dorian
Verona, Indiana
April 1983

I grinned at my boyfriend as he drove down Main Street. We were on our way to Shawn and Tim's apartment. Shawn was cooking supper and then we were all going to sit down and plan Scotty's funeral. I couldn't wait! It's not often you get to plan the funeral of one of your friends and I was looking forward to it. I was already thinking about what music to play. There would be none of that horrible organ music at Scotty's funeral. After all, it was the ultimate going away party and I knew Scotty would want to go out with a bang. I wanted to get Scotty the shiny, silver casket I'd spotted in Miller's Funeral Home. It was sweet! I just hoped the others would go along with my ideas. I figured I had a right to have the biggest input. It was my idea to kill Scotty after all. Without me there wouldn't even be a funeral. Sure, most of my friends helped kill him, but it was still my idea.

Okay, I'd probably better explain all this. I know the whole killing-one-of-your-friends thing might seem a bit odd to say the least, so here it goes.

It all started about a month ago...

Dorian
Verona, Indiana
March 1983

Last period drama was my favorite class of the day. Most of class was given over to working on scenes for the spring play, *Willy Wonka and the Chocolate Factory*. Yours truly had landed the lead role. That made two, count them, two lead roles in a row! In the fall production, I was Dorian Gray. Some of my friends joked that I only got the part because my first name was the same as that of the character, but I knew otherwise. This play had two lead roles. There was my part, Willy Wonka, and the other role was Charlie Bucket, the kid who finds the final golden ticket. I'd thought about trying out for Charlie, but Willy Wonka is a way cooler role and the costume was going to be fabulous! I love purple! Also totally cool was that Marc, my incredibly sexy boyfriend, was the understudy for Scotty Jackson, who had landed the role of Charlie. I convinced Marc to read for the part, or I should say I seduced him into it. I probably shouldn't say exactly how I seduced him into trying out for a role he didn't want, but it involved an alternative use of Marc's shower in his loft-bedroom.

I thought Mrs. Cook should have given Marc the role of Charlie, but I have to admit Scotty is fabulous! I wasn't surprised by his acting abilities. He'd played Basil in *The Picture of Dorian Gray* and had done a superb job. Scotty told me he was surprised he beat out Marc, so I'm not the only one who thinks my boyfriend has talent. Scotty said he thought he got the role because he wanted it more, just like Charlie found the last golden ticket because he wanted it more than anyone else. Scotty was probably right. Marc did a great job, but he didn't really want the part. It would likely have taken a good deal of convincing and some more seduction to get him to accept if Mrs. Cook had chosen him. Marc was Scotty's understudy and he was happy with that. Scotty was happy he landed a lead. I was happy that I was Willy Wonka and that Marc and I were able to spend a lot of time together during practices.

Tess Dupont, my best girl friend, landed the role of Veruca Salt. The role wasn't as large as Tess usually played, but then the play didn't have any big female roles. Tess was having a blast playing a bratty, spoiled girl. Marc said she was so good in the role because she only had to be herself, but he was just kidding. Tess was hilarious when she wailed "I want it now!!!!" and she had a great song.

I still couldn't believe we were doing a musical! I was soooooo excited! I had three songs! My favorite was "Pure Imagination."

Dane and Tim were also in last period drama and both of them had landed roles. Dane was Mike Teevee, the boy who is obsessed with television. Tim had the role of Augustus Gloop, which was kind of funny because Augustus is an overweight glutton and Tim is a football hunk with not an ounce of fat on him. I was surprised to see Tim and Dane in a drama class when the semester began, but I guess I'd talked about drama and the fall play so much at lunchtime that they thought they'd give it a try. I was not at all surprised that they were *both* in class. Tim and Dane were permanently joined at the lip.

I waved Scotty Jackson over to join Marc, Tim, Dane, and me as we waited for class to begin. Scotty had recently come out to me and, with his permission, I'd spread the word among all my gay friends. As far as everyone else knew, Scotty was a hetero, but we knew he was one of us. Oh yeah! Brandon and Jon knew about Scotty, too. They were heteros, but they were totally cool with the gay boys and even sat with us at lunch.

I hadn't even suspected Scotty was gay, but then it isn't as easy to identify sexual orientation as most people think. Just about all my classmates pegged me as a homo my very first day at Verona High School, but then with me it's obvious. I fit the stereotypes and that's fine with me because I'm *Fabulous* with a capital F!

I know I probably sound conceited, but I'm not. It's just that I enjoy being me. I'm not built like Shawn or Tim or even Marc. I'm not super-smart like Tristan. I'm not athletic like most of my friends. I'm not especially popular, except with the drama crowd. Marc says I'm the cutest boy he's ever seen, but then he's my boyfriend so he's probably a little biased. The point is that I'm not conceited, although I will admit I think I'm kind of cute and I love my long curly blond hair. Okay, maybe I'm just a little conceited, but not much. I swear on the shopping mall!

Scotty wasn't obvious at all. He was on the track team, which helped him to hide because a lot of people think jocks can't be gay.

I don't know why they think that, especially in Verona. My boyfriend is a kick-ass soccer player. Tim and his older brother Shawn are both gay and both football jocks, and, before you ask; No, Tim and Shawn don't do it with each other, at least as far as I know. Nathan's boyfriend, Ethan, who graduated last year, was the best wrestler around. He has the most incredible body! Wow! Casper's boyfriend, Brendan, graduated last year too. He was the quarterback and captain of the football team. Brendan is incredibly handsome and built. He plays football for Indiana University now. Boy, would I like to get a look in that locker room! Mmm. With all the gay jocks in VHS I don't see how anyone could think jocks can't be gay, but there it is.

Okay, I know I'm firing off a lot of names, but I have a lot of friends! You'll get to meet them all before we're finished.

Mrs. Cook called the class to order and we all focused on her. The whole class was pretty serious about drama, except maybe Trent Blackwell. He was there because his girlfriend, Tess, had talked him into or maybe seduced him into it. He was really uncomfortable in class at the beginning, but he'd mellowed out. He was playing the part of Mr. Salt, and since his girlfriend had the role of Veruca, that meant Trent was his girlfriend's father in the play. Kinky!

I liked Trent. He wasn't entirely comfortable with hanging around gay guys, but he didn't have a choice. Marc, Tim, Dane, Scotty, and I were all homos. Trent didn't know about Scotty, but he knew about the rest of us. Tess made him double date with Marc and me a few times. I had some fun with Trent now and then by pretending to be interested in him. At first it freaked him out, but now he mostly thinks it's funny, although it still makes him a little uncomfortable. He knows there is no way I'd cheat on Marc. I wondered what Trent would do if a gay boy really came onto him. I would pay to watch!

Mrs. Cook ran us through an unusual acting exercise. We began performing the scene where Charlie, Veruca, Violet, Mike, Augustus, and their guardians meet Willy Wonka for the first time. After a very short time, Mrs. Cook called out "switch" and each of us had to become the character to our right. This created confusion and some giggles as each actor tried to change positions a quickly as possible and then go on with the scene with as short a pause as we could manage. I had my part memorized already, but I had to keep an eye on the script because I didn't have all the

11

parts down. I didn't know who I'd be next! As we kept going, each switch went a little more smoothly. The actors became adept at jumping into position. Sometimes, there was no pause in the dialogue at all. Luckily, my voice is high enough that I could pull off Veruca and Violet's lines without much trouble. Trent's voice is a good deal lower and our classmates burst out laughing at Trent's attempt to sound like a girl. Trent almost lost it himself, but somehow managed to keep from laughing.

After a few minutes, Mrs. Cook had my group sit down and we were replaced by another. Marc was in the second group. He started out as Charlie, the character he was understudying. Marc and I had practiced a great deal together, so I was not surprised at his display of talent in portraying Charlie. He had nearly all of the lines down. What did make me gasp was his ability to move from character to character, only rarely looking at his script. I wished my boyfriend was more interested in acting. He had some real talent and it seemed a shame to waste it, but I wasn't about to try to change him. I liked Marc just as he was!

Marc is really hot! He's got this sweet skater look, which makes sense because he's a skater as well as a soccer player. He has blond hair with bangs that are forever falling over his blue eyes. He's slim, firm, and has just the right amount of muscle. I love the shape of his chest and abs and he has the hottest ass! Okay, maybe that's too much information and I'm definitely getting off topic, but I have a hot boyfriend so I like to think about him often.

When class ended, Marc, Scotty, and I walked out of the auditorium together for a short break. We hit the exit doors and headed for a bench off to one side where we wouldn't be bothered by the after-school exodus to the parking lot. Tim and Dane took off, no doubt to make out until it was time for play practice. Those two were worse than Marc and me!

I gave Marc a look as Scotty sat down beside us on the bench. Marc nodded.

"Why don't you come sit at our table tomorrow, Scotty? You know most of the guys. You might as well eat lunch with us."

Marc was referring to what was commonly known as "the homo table" even among those who sat there. Most of the out gay boys sat together every day at lunch.

12

"I don't know. Someone from my church might see me and my little brother would start asking questions."

Scotty's church... it was one of those churches that preached that being gay was a sin, which is total bullshit. I had never understood how the very places that should be spreading acceptance and love spewed hatred and violence instead. It was such churches that had once preached the women were inferior, that slavery was God's will, and that interracial marriage was a sin. Some of them still did preach that crap, except probably the slavery part, but who knew? People that nasty might even want to bring back slavery! Don't even get me started!

"Brandon and Jon sit with us and they aren't gay," Marc said

"Yeah, but they don't go to my church and they have girlfriends. Plus, they are major soccer jocks. The jocks can get away with anything. If I start sitting with you guys a lot of people will assume I'm gay and I'm not ready to be out yet. I don't think I'll ever be ready. My parents would freak out and the congregation at my church..."

"Why do you even go to that church?" Marc asked.

"I have no choice. My parents make Justin and me go everyday Sunday. It sucks!"

"Well, we'd really like to have you sit with us. You're always welcome," Marc said.

"Thanks. I appreciate the offer, but I need to keep on the Q T. You know? It's not you guys. You're all really cool, but I've taken about all the risk I dare by signing up for this drama class. Dad almost wouldn't let me try out for a part, but Mom said it would be good for me to get involved with another extra-curricular activity."

"You had a part last fall. You were great by the way," I said.

"Yeah. That was one of Dad's arguments. He said I'd wasted enough time. I finally sold Dad on letting me be in another play by convincing him it would look good on my college applications. I didn't tell him I'd already sent most of them out."

Marc looked at me and shrugged his shoulders apologetically. I smiled back. He'd tried.

"If you ever need to talk, Scotty, I'm here for you. I'm sure the whole gang is too." Marc leaned in close and whispered. "We homos stick together."

Scotty laughed.

I felt really sorry for Scotty. It had to suck having to hide like that. I had never even tried. In the beginning, I thought everyone was like me. Being out didn't take courage until I figured out I was different. I caught onto that in Kindergarten, but no one hassled me much until the second or third grade. That's when being myself started to take courage and it took more and more as I grew older. By then, I was so used to being me that I never thought of backing down, even when things got rough. Then, I moved to Verona. Things were much better for gays here, although obviously not for everyone. I sighed. I wished I could make everything better for Scotty.

Scotty's younger brother, Justin, walked past with some of his friends and eyed the three of us. Scotty stiffened slightly, but being seen with us wasn't overly suspicious. The three of us did share last period drama and had play practice soon. Why shouldn't we spend some time together? It made perfect sense, especially since Scotty and I had the leads.

Soon, it was back to the auditorium. Mrs. Cook had me sing "Pure Imagination" then Tess sang "I Want it Now," which was hilarious. Next, we got down to the business of running through scenes. It was much like class, only we didn't switch. Marc was helping paint the scenery along with other cast members who were understudies or had minor roles. He could hear and see everything, which probably helped him memorize it all. I secretly hoped Scotty would have to miss one performance so Marc and I could act together on the stage in front of an auditorium full of people. I was sure Marc didn't share my secret hope. I didn't want to take away Scotty's spotlight either. He deserved this and maybe he needed it too. It wasn't likely he'd miss a performance, but in theatre anything was possible. My understudy very nearly had to go on for me in *The Picture of Dorian Gray*, but that's a whole other story and one you probably wouldn't believe anyway.

Dane made a great Mike Teevee, even though Mike had dark hair in the movie and Dane has sort of long and most definitely curly blond hair. His last name is Haakonson and his ancestors were from Scandinavia so that will give you an idea of what he looks like. Dane has ice blue eyes and is very sexy in a dangerous-looking sort of way.

Tim pulled off Augustus Gloop well. During our very first practices there was some giggling as Tim practiced the part because, like I said before, Augustus is an overweight glutton and Tim is a football stud with zero body fat. He even has abs! The magic of theatre makes anything possible and Tim because Augustus as we ran through the scenes.

After practice, Marc asked Scotty if he wanted a ride home, but he declined. I guess being seen in a car full of gay boys was too much for him. Marc gave Tim and Dane a ride most days, unless they just wanted to walk home, which was often. He gave me a ride too, of course. After all, I *am* his boyfriend!

As we drove away from VHS Tim and Dane made out in the back seat, as usual. I don't think their lips parted once from school to Dane's house where we let them out. Dane had a really cool home. He lived in what had once been Verona High School. It was much smaller than the current VHS, but it was still two stories tall and had its own gymnasium! How cool is that?

Marc and I did some making out of our own as we sat in the car in front of my house. We weren't worried about my parents catching us because they knew we made out. Marc was Mom and Dad's hero, but that's part of that other story I mentioned. All that matters is that my parents loved my boyfriend so we could make out all we wanted. I'm not sure what they would have thought of all the other things we did. They probably suspected or even assumed we did a lot more, but we didn't talk about that. I think they just didn't want to know. That was fine with me because I didn't want to talk about my sex life either. Marc and I could do whatever we wanted because he had his own little apartment in the loft of his parent's barn. They probably assumed we got it on too, but they didn't try to stop us. I had one sweet life and Marc.... he was sooo hot!

"Pick me up in the morning?" I asked as I gave Marc one last peck on the lips.

"You know it."

I giggled and stepped out of the car. Marc drove away and I headed inside.

I was sooooo lucky. I had a sexy boyfriend who was kind and handsome and wouldn't even think about cheating on me. I had parents who were completely at ease with the fact I liked boys. I lived in what was probably one of the most accepting towns ever. I had lots of gay friends and lots of friends period. Verona wasn't a paradise where nothing bad ever happened, but it was a big step up from where I'd lived before. Did I mention I have a sexy boyfriend? The coolest thing about Marc isn't his good looks, but that he likes me just as I am.

I wished that everyone could have as cool of a life as me. I kept thinking about Scotty. He couldn't be himself at home. He was even afraid to sit with the gay crowd at school because his brother or someone from his church might see him. What kind of church made people feel bad for being themselves? It was horrible that Scotty was forced to go somewhere every week where people told him there was something wrong with him. They didn't say it to his face because they didn't know he was gay, but they were saying it to him just the same. If someone did that to me I'd get in their face and give them a piece of my mind, but Scotty couldn't. There had to be some way I could help him, but I didn't know how.

"How was play practice?" Mom asked when I walked into the kitchen.

"Great! I pretty much have all my lines down. I just need to practice tumbling."

"Tumbling?"

"Yeah. Willy Wonka comes out walking with a cane like he's crippled, but when he gets right up to the crowd he sticks his cane in the ground, leans forward like he's going to fall, but then turns it into a roll and jumps up to his feet. Gene Wilder did it in the movie. It makes the audience wonder if Willy Wonka can be trusted."

"I guess that gymnastics class you took when you were little will come in handy."

"Oh yeah! I can do the roll easy. It's turning a stumble into a roll at the last moment that's tricky. Need any help with supper?"

"Could you do the biscuits, dear? I'm making biscuits & gravy and bacon for supper. You know how your father loves it. The can is on the counter."

"Sure!"

Mom used to make biscuits from scratch, but Dad likes the biscuits from a can better. I set the oven to pre-heat, pulled out a baking sheet, and then picked up the can of biscuits. This was the part that made me uneasy. I knew it was going to happen, but the can always startled me when it popped open. Sometimes, it didn't open when I pulled off the foil wrapper. Then, I had to press down on the seam until it popped. It was the not knowing when it was going to happen that got to me.

I carefully pulled back the foil cover from the can. Slowly, more and more of the cardboard underneath was exposed. I tried to calm myself, but my heart beat faster. No matter how many times I opened a can of biscuits, the pop still took me by surprise. I peeled back more and more of the foil and then BAM!

I squealed as the can popped open with unusually violent force. One of the biscuits actually sailed into the air, but I managed to catch it.

"I guess I shouldn't have set the can out so early," Mom said, then began laughing at the expression on my face, which was somewhere between shocked and terrified. In moments, I was laughing too.

"I think I just had a near-death experience," I said. "I was almost killed by a biscuit!"

Mom smiled and hugged me.

"Next time, let's leave the can out even longer and then let Dad open it," I said.

Mom laughed some more.

"Good idea."

"What's a good idea?"

I turned around. Dad had just slipped in.

"Making biscuits and gravy more often," Mom said without hesitation.

"That is a good idea."

"Yeah, and next time you get to make the biscuits," I said.

Dad eyed us both. He had learned over the years to be just a little suspicious. Sometimes Mom and I teamed up on him. One time, we turned the volume down on the TV when he went out of the room and then pretended we could hear it when he came back. When he asked us why the sound was out, we mouthed our answers so he'd think he'd gone deaf. Our joke didn't last long. Mom and I both started laughing.

"Oh no. That's what I have a wife and son for," Dad said. He hugged me. I giggled, but then I grew sad.

"Is something wrong, Dorian?" Dad asked.

"I was just thinking about Scotty. He's a boy at my school. He's gay and his family is religious. He can't be himself around his parents or his brother. It made me sad just now because I don't think his dad will ever hug him like you just did me. His parents might even kick him out if they find out about him."

"I've never understood how people can be like that," Dad said. "Family should be loved unconditionally. You tell your friend Scotty that if he needs a place to come and stay he's welcome here."

"Thanks, Dad."

I turned my attention to putting the biscuits on the baking sheet. The oven had pre-heated by the time I finished, so I put the biscuits in, and set the timer.

Everything was ready about fifteen minutes later. Dad loved biscuits & gravy and I loved them almost as much. Mom fried the bacon perfectly. It was chewy without being undercooked. I hated crisp bacon and undercooked bacon was even worse. Yuck!

After supper, I went to my room. I pulled out the script and turned to the very end. I didn't quite have Willy Wonka's tirade down like I wanted it. At the end of the tour of the chocolate factory, Willy Wonka goes off on Charlie and Grandpa Joe. He really lets them have it. I wanted to recapture what Gene Wilder had done in the film, but it wasn't easy.

After working on my delivery and my lines I turned my attention to homework. I couldn't decide if homework was easier my senior year or if I was getting smarter. Perhaps I was just getting more organized. Whatever the cause, homework took less time than it had my previous years in school.

I wasn't sure if I was ready for college, but ready or not I was beginning at IU in the fall. And!!! Marc was going with me!!!! Yes!!! We had already applied and been accepted. If everything worked out we were even going to be roommates. Mmm.

I remembered the day we talked about college. Deciding to go to the same school took no discussion at all. Then, when we brought up the choice of school, we both said, "I want to go to IU in Bloomington." We said it at the exact same time! After hearing Brendan talk about IU and Bloomington there was nowhere else I wanted to go. Brendan was nearing the end of his freshman year at IU and he loved it. If Marc had his heart set on another school I would've gone with him, but I didn't have to worry about that.

Brendan had turned all the homos at VHS onto IU. Not only were Marc and I going, but Nathan was going too. Those who weren't graduating this year had expressed interest. Brandon and Jon, who were honorary homos, were going as well. In the fall, Marc, Nathan, Brandon, Jon, and I would join Brendan. The rest of the crowd would probably be along in a year or two, which the exception of Ethan. He was taking some classes at Purdue and running the Selby Farm with his uncle Jack. I guess that made him the enemy, only Ethan could never be an enemy.

It was Thursday so I watched *Mama's Family* on TV. I loved that show, but my favorites were on Saturday night; *Love Boat* and *Fantasy Island*. I thought that maybe I could even work on a cruise ship someday. I could perform in shows and live onboard while the ship sailed from one exotic destination to another. I wondered if it would be like the *Love Boat*. Probably not, but it would be fun. I wished I could travel to *Fantasy Island*, but then I didn't have a fantasy to act out. Having a boyfriend like Marc was my fantasy, so I had no need of Mr. Roarke, but it would have been cool to hear Tattoo yelling "De Plane! De Plane!"

I read for a while after watching TV and then stripped and climbed into bed. I lay there, giving some thought to how I could pull Scotty into my group of friends. He needed other gay guys to talk to and hang out with. He was able to spend some time with Marc, Dane, Tim, and me before and after play practices, but that wasn't enough. Once the play was over he wouldn't have even that. I fell asleep without coming up with any good ideas.

Scotty

Justin, my younger brother, walked into our shared bedroom.

"Mom says supper is almost ready."

"Okay."

I put my script away and climbed up off the bed. I walked into the dining room where we ate supper every night after Dad came home from work. I wished we could eat in the kitchen like most people. The dining room felt too formal. We had a house with only two bedrooms so I had to share, but had a dining room we didn't even need. I could have had my own bedroom if Dad would have given up his study, but I knew I could forget about that. I could not wait to move out and get away from my family!

Dad was sitting down as I entered the dining room. Mom had just finished setting out a platter of pork chops and bowls of mashed potatoes and cooked apples. We each had a salad too. Mom was big on making us eat green stuff.

"Will you ask the blessing, Justin?" Dad asked.

We always gave thanks before we ate, which was truly embarrassing in restaurants. I was all for being thankful, but I didn't think there was any need to make a big production out of it. I believed in God and all that, but my parents took everything to the extreme. When I was smaller, and sometimes even now, Mom told me to ask Jesus for forgiveness if I did something like track mud on the carpet or if I got home an hour late. I figured Jesus wasn't worried about our carpet and didn't really care what time I got home. He had bigger problems to deal with; like wars and husbands who liked to beat their wives. Instead of asking for forgiveness, I asked Jesus if he could get my mom to stop asking me to ask him for forgiveness. She doesn't do it much anymore, so I guess my prayer was answered.

Justin gave thanks and we passed the bowls around. Mom was a good cook. She fixed breakfast every morning and I'm not talking about a bowl of cereal or a couple of Pop Tarts. She made bacon and eggs, pancakes, and stuff like that. We were allowed to eat breakfast in the kitchen, mainly because Dad was always in a big rush in the mornings. He just grabbed some juice or coffee and was gone.

Mom stayed home and did housework. I felt sorry for her. I thought she'd be happier with a part-time job in a little bookstore or flower shop. I didn't think I'd like to stay home all day and clean and do laundry. It was like she was a mom from one of those old TV shows like *Leave it to Beaver* or *Dennis the Menace* where all moms were housewives and didn't have lives of their own.

"Do you have your homework done?" Dad asked. It was a predictable question.

"No, I don't have much. I plan to do it after supper," I said.

"He was reading his script instead," Justin said. Justin loved to rat on me. It was his way of making himself look better.

Dad gave me a stern look.

"Schoolwork comes first."

"I was memorizing lines. It is schoolwork."

"Don't argue with me. You do your schoolwork first, and then you can memorize your script. I still don't see why you should be wasting time..."

"We discussed this dear. It will help round out his college applications."

"Well, be that as it may, mind my words."

"Yes, sir."

That was the best thing to say to my dad. Arguing was a big mistake. He would just get louder and more demanding.

"Scotty was sitting with the faggots after school."

"Justin, I've told you before you are not to use that word in this house!" Mom said.

"Sorry, I mean Scotty was sitting with the homos."

Dad speared me with a stern look. I swallowed hard.

"I was sitting with Dorian and Marc. We were going over our lines in the play. Dorian is playing Willy Wonka and Marc is my understudy."

"Do you see the kind of people he's hanging out with?" Dad asked, looking at Mom.

"I don't hang out with them. We were just trying to work out a problem with our parts. We're in the same drama class last period and play practice is right after."

"This whole play thing is just a bad idea. You know the theatre world is crawling with homos."

I flinched. What would my father do if he found out I was gay? I wondered if he'd kick me out and if he'd still love me.

"I won't talk to them outside of class or practice," I said.

Dad looked at me. He seemed appeased. I breathed a sigh of relief. I knew Dad had been building up to making me quit the play. *Willy Wonka* was the best thing I had going in my life. When I was up on that stage I didn't have to think about how my family would react if they found out I was gay. I didn't have to think about the fact that I might be living on the streets soon or that my parents wouldn't love me anymore. I didn't have to think about being forced to go to church. I didn't have to think about any of the bad stuff in my life. I could just be Charlie, the boy who miraculously found a golden ticket. It gave me hope that maybe I'd find my own miracle and that everything would be okay.

"I already did my homework," Justin said.

When our parents weren't looking I rubbed my fist on my nose. Justin glared at me. He was a brownnoser. I didn't know why he bothered. Dad liked him best anyway. Justin played soccer. A "real sport" as my dad put it. I was only on the track team. My little brother was a jock. He was just the kind of son my parents wanted, unlike me. I wished things were the way they were when we were kids. Justin and I used to be friends. Now, we just coexisted in our shared bedroom.

I concentrated on supper. The worse things got, the more I tried to focus on whatever was pleasant. The pork chops, mashed potatoes, apples, and even the salad were all delicious. Later, after I finished my homework, I could read my script some more. I looked forward to that. I loved being in the play. I still could not believe I landed one of the leads!

I wished I could study something like theatre in college. I wasn't really sure what I wanted to study yet. At least I had another entire year to think about it since I was a junior. Dad was determined I'd go to a business school, but I didn't want to sit in an office and think about making money all day. I wanted to do something creative. Theatre was kind of a long shot. Most actors didn't make it, but there were other jobs. Lately I'd given some thought to producing. It would be cool to be the guy who put it all together. Maybe I could even connect that to the business career

Dad wanted me to pursue. Producers probably did have to know quite a bit about business. I wasn't sure what I wanted to do with my life. Dad said I lacked direction. He was probably right about that.

After supper, I went to my room and studied. Justin came in and pulled out one of his motorcycle magazines. Justin didn't even like motorcycles, but I knew why he had those magazines; next to just about every bike was a scantily clad girl. Justin knew he would be murdered if he dared have a *Playboy* or *Penthouse* around. Even the swimsuit issue of *Sports Illustrated* was pushing it. Justin has a subscription and I noticed that every issue disappears soon after he reads it, except for the swimsuit issue. More than once I've seen him whacking it while staring at his magazines, but I pretended not to see. I figure what he does in his bed is his business. I have been tempted to tease him about it and I'm not entirely sure why I haven't since he can be a jerk.

Justin isn't all bad. I like him, mostly. I just don't trust him to keep his mouth shut. That's why I don't dare to keep any magazines with hot guys in them around. I did get my hands on an Undergear catalog. I hid it in the trash after a couple of days because I was afraid Justin would find it and how was I going to explain it? It's not like there was any underwear in there I could actually wear. Some of it was so small that wearing it would be like wearing nothing! One was just this little pouch in front with nothing but a string between the butt-cheeks in the back! I could just imagine putting that in the wash. I can almost picture the horrified look on Mom's face.

Sometimes, I wished Justin was gay too. Then I wouldn't feel so outnumbered. As it is it's three against one. If my brother was gay at least things would be equal. I could probably keep a few magazines hidden then, especially if I bribed Justin by letting him borrow them. Tim was so lucky to have a gay brother.

There was no use thinking about it. Justin was about as far from gay as he could get. I was sure he would fake being straight if he was gay, but he was way too interested in his magazines when he thought no one was looking. I'd also seen him pop boners while watching girls on TV.

I was the only gay in my immediate family. As far as I knew, I was the only gay in the family period. My cousin Scott did get caught wearing a dress when he was fifteen, but he was nineteen now, married, and had a kid. His son was born seven months after his wedding so there was little question about why he got married. The thing is, that was just fine with my family. He was married and producing kids. That was the way it was supposed to be according to my parents. I doubted Scott was gay. There is that whole wearing a dress thing to consider, but I didn't think that meant anything. I was gay and I didn't want to wear a dress. I didn't get why any guy would want to wear one. I wasn't going to judge. If some dude wanted to put on a dress he could go for it as far as I was concerned.

I finished off my homework with no trouble at all. Dad didn't need to make a big deal about me doing my homework first. I always got it done. He just didn't like that I was in drama. He hated it when he didn't get his way. He was a control freak.

At least I could spend the rest of my evening and night with my script. There were certain lines that were giving me fits. I don't know why I could remember some lines with ease and others I just could not get. I practiced the tough lines in my head. I only practiced out loud if no one was around. I didn't want to do anything to rock the boat at home. If I did I'd probably lose the play and then what would I have going on that was fun?

I actually fell asleep reading. I had this dream that I was Charlie. Dorian, as Willy Wonka, took me to this secret room that was made entirely of chocolate. Dorian started kissing me and it was okay, because he wasn't Dorian cheating on his boyfriend. He was Willy Wonka. We began undressing each other and then there was a lot of feeling and groping. We didn't do anything specific, but there was lots of moaning. It was the best dream I'd had in a long time.

I actually remembered the dream when I woke up. I did that sometimes, but most of the time I couldn't remember my dreams at all. Maybe I didn't dream most nights. If that was true maybe I remembered all my dreams. I don't know. I figured I dreamed every night and just didn't remember. It was kind of cool—like a secret life I lived out that even I didn't know about when I was awake. I was glad I could remember the dream about Dorian, but I felt a little guilty. He did have a boyfriend. Then again, it was just a dream. We didn't actually do any of that stuff so how could it be cheating?

"Dude, you were moaning in your sleep last night," Justin said as he got up and pulled on his clothes.

"I was not."

"Oh yeah you were and I know what you were dreaming about!"

I was actually frightened for a moment, but there was no way Justin could know what I'd dreamed.

"I heard you going *unh, unh, unh*! You were having a sex dream!"

"Yeah, well. I know what you do in the shower. I've heard you moaning in there."

Justin's eyes widened. I was making it up. I hadn't heard him moaning, but I figured it was a good bet that he jerked off in the shower. Justin shut up about my dream.

After breakfast, Justin and I headed out to the car.

"I want to drive today," Justin said.

"You almost ran off the road waving to those girls last time."

"I did not!"

"I had to grab the wheel to keep us from going on the sidewalk."

"Oh, come on, Scotty."

"Okay, you can drive, but I'm driving home. If I'm going to get killed in an auto accident, I want it to be on the way to school."

Justin stuck out his tongue, but I tossed him the keys anyway.

Justin started the car up and turned on the radio. He checked his hair in the mirror and then pointed at his reflection and winked at himself. I swear I'm not making it up. Justin thinks he's really good looking. He's not bad looking. We look a lot alike, in fact, but I'm not a hottie and neither is he. I'm sure Justin doesn't agree. I made a mental note to buy him a mirror for his birthday.

Justin checked himself out as he drove. He readjusted the mirrors and his seat. He gazed at the gauges. He did about everything but watch the road.

"Dude! Pay attention!"

"I have the cruise control on."

"The cruise control does not drive the car! It's not an autopilot. It only controls the speed!"

"You sound like Mom. She's always screaming at me when I drive her somewhere."

"That's because you suck at driving."

"I do not!"

"Your eyes are everywhere but on the road."

"We're in town and the speed limit is 30."

"You still have to watch where you're going. What if someone steps out in front of you?"

"Oh, they're not..."

"Justin!"

Justin hit the brakes, narrowly missing the car that had pulled out when it should not have.

"See?"

"That wasn't a pedestrian."

"It doesn't matter. Pay attention or you're not driving when I'm in the car anymore."

"You can't do that!"

"I can if I tell Dad how you drive."

Justin glared at me, but he knew I had the upper hand. I had a reputation as a good driver and Justin had already been warned he had to shape up or else.

"You wouldn't really tell Dad, would you?"

"I should after you ratted me out for sitting with Dorian and Marc."

"They're faggots!"

"We're in the play together! So what if we were sitting together? We were talking about Willy Wonka."

"They will probably try to recruit you."

"They're gay. They don't belong to a cult."

"You won't really tell dad, will you?"

"I won't if you start paying attention to where you're going!"

Justin scowled, but kept his eyes on the road more. I was amazed he hadn't had an accident yet. I have no idea how he passed driver's education or how he managed to get a license. Justin was only a year younger than me, but sometimes he acted like he was twelve, no, make that eight.

We arrived at school without mishap. For the rest of the trip Justin had actually paid attention to driving the car instead of fiddling with the radio and flirting with girls. When he began to hand me the keys I held up my hand.

"Keep them. You can have the car this afternoon. I'll catch a ride with someone after practice or just walk."

"Really?"

"Consider it a reward for not driving like an idiot. If you pay attention to the road while you're driving I'll let you drive more often. If you don't, you won't be driving at all."

"Thanks, Scotty."

We climbed out of the car and Justin quickly disappeared. By giving Justin the keys, I wasn't so much being nice as I was insuring my own safety. Maybe I could bribe him into paying attention so he wouldn't get us both killed.

I spotted Tim and Dane climbing out of the back of Shawn's car. They were holding hands, talking, and laughing. Shawn and Tristan walked along together, talking more quietly and smiling at each other. I wanted that. I wanted a boyfriend. I wanted someone I could talk to about things I couldn't talk to anyone else about.

Inside, I spotted Dorian and Marc pulling their books out of a locker. They were so busy talking to each other they didn't even see me. I was glad I wasn't as obviously gay as Dorian. My dad would have killed me. Well, I don't mean that literally, but Dorian was the kind of guy who infuriated dad. He thought guys should be masculine and Dorian was anything but that. I didn't agree. I thought everyone should be just as they were and not try to be something they weren't. I admired Dorian for being himself. I wished I could do the same. I wasn't feminine like Dorian, but I couldn't be me. I couldn't have a boyfriend or even let my family know I was gay. I felt like a fake, but what else could I do but pretend to be straight?

At lunchtime I walked by the homo table. They were talking and laughing and joking around. I wanted to sit by Dorian, Marc, and all the others so bad I actually thought about doing it. I knew what would happen if I did. Justin would probably see me and tell dad. If Justin didn't see me, Devon or one of the other kids from my church would spot me. They'd spread rumors that I was a homo. I couldn't let that happen. I felt so sad as I walked on that I wanted to cry, but I couldn't do that either. I had to pretend that all was well in my fake straight world.

Dorian

Marc picked me up for school as usual. I climbed in the car and gave him a kiss before we took off.

"I was almost killed by a biscuit last night," I announced. "It was horrible! I think it was premeditated."

Marc raised one blond eyebrow.

"Premeditated? So... this biscuit planned your murder in advance?"

"Well, no, but it still tried to kill me!"

I told Marc the entire story of the murderous biscuit can and my near death experience.

"Do not tell that story at lunch or Brandon and Jon will make fun of you for weeks."

I laughed.

"True."

Marc and I made out in the car for a while after we arrived at school. It was our morning ritual. We both jumped when someone smacked the side of the car. We looked out the window to see Brandon mouthing "homos" and then waving. Marc flipped him off, we laughed, and went right back to making out.

We reluctantly parted our lips and climbed out of the car a few minutes later. Devon scowled at us as we passed him getting out of his car. Devon was Verona's resident homo-hater, but he wasn't all bad. Okay, he was mostly bad, but he, as well as a ton of others, had joined the search when I was missing last fall. I was kidnapped and held captive and no I'm not making it up. That's one of those other stories that I don't have time to get into. The point is that even though Devon hated homos, he was out searching for me, a homo, so he wasn't all bad. I felt sorry for him. He didn't have many friends. Worse still, I think he hated himself. What kind of life was that?

Marc and I parted at our lockers after a quick kiss. I headed for my first class of the day, waving and calling out to my friends. A lot of people liked me at VHS. I wasn't quite popular, but I was well liked. Maybe that was because I liked everyone else. My almost-popularity was evidence that Verona was an accepting place. I was out and I fit the gay stereotype exactly; my voice was high for a boy, I tended to squeal when I was excited, I was always superbly dressed, and I talked with my hands. I was what some would call "obviously gay" and yet most people liked me.

Of course, there were a lot of people who disliked me for my "gay" traits. Some hated me for it. Every day I walked past them, knowing they hated me. Like I said, Verona wasn't paradise. It was way better than most places and I would not let the haters get me down. I was determined to be me!

I couldn't believe this was my senior year. Considering that it had been my senior year since last August I'd had plenty of time to grasp the fact, but it just didn't seem real. A part of me felt like my high school life would just go on and on. It figured that high school was coming to an end just as I was truly beginning to enjoy it. Maybe my inability to grasp the fact I was a senior was a form of denial.

My morning classes passed quickly and soon it was time for lunch. I looked forward to lunch each day, not only because I sat beside my boyfriend, but because almost all the out gay boys in VHS, plus the honorary homos Brandon and Jon, sat together. When I graduated, I was going to miss sitting with the gang at lunch more than anything else.

Marc met me at my locker and we walked down to the cafeteria together as usual. When we came out of the line with our trays, Shawn, Tristan, Tim, Dane, Nathan, Casper, and Casey were already seated. Casey was the only girl at our table, but she fit in perfectly. Marc and I joined the others. I was starved and lunch looked especially good; grilled cheese, chili, salad, and apple crisp.

"She was looking at *me*," Brandon said as he sat down with his tray.

"No. She was looking at *me*. Why would she look at you?" Jon asked as he sat down across from Brandon at the end of the table.

"Because I'm freaking hot, that's why!"

"We discussed this before Brandon. There's reality and there's fantasy. You keep getting the two confused."

"Well, there was no way she was looking at you. I hate to be the one to break this to you, Jon, but you are fugly."

"Ha! I should be on the cover of a magazine!"

"Which one? *Dog Enthusiast?*"

"Playgirl."

"Now who can't separate fantasy from reality?"

"I know you fantasize when you look at *Playgirl*, Brandon."

"That's not what I meant!"

"I think that's why you like sitting at the homo table. You have homosexual tendencies. Not that there's anything wrong with that," Jon said, looking in the direction of the rest of us for a moment.

"You're the one with tendencies. You're dying to touch my hot bod!"

"Now, you're truly fantasizing. If I wanted to experiment with a guy you'd be my *last* choice. I'd do it with every guy at this table before I would with you because they're all hotter."

"Slut."

"Closet case."

"Can't you just feel the love," I said.

"Who asked for your input, homo," Brandon said.

"Really!" Jon added. "It's so hard to have a private conversation without someone butting in."

I laughed. I loved these guys. One of the best parts of lunch was listening to them go off on each other. They didn't sound like it, but they were best friends. They were also the most accepting hetero guys at VHS. That's why they could get away with throwing around words like "homo" and "fag." Coming from them it meant nothing.

"I do agree with Jon on at least one thing," I said.

"Not that I care, but what thing?" Brandon asked.

"Marc is way hotter than you, Brandon. Jon is correct in preferring him over you."

"I thought homos were supposed to have good taste. You're clearly delusional. Marc isn't half as hot as me. Just look at him!"

"He's adorable, isn't he?" I said. I hugged Marc and kissed his cheek.

"Save me! I think I'm going to choke on the sweetness," Brandon said.

"He's sooo sexy," I said.

Marc turned slightly red. Everyone grinned at his embarrassment.

"I'll admit, Marc isn't fugly like Jon, but I am *way* hotter!" Brandon said.

"Keep telling yourself that, Brandon, and maybe you'll start to believe it," Jon said.

"I hate you," Brandon said with complete insincerity.

Scotty passed with his tray. He glanced in our direction. He looked so very sad. I wished he could join us. He knew he was welcome, but I understood why he felt he couldn't sit with us.

"What's wrong, Dorian?" Tristan asked, gazing at me with his beautiful brown eyes. Tristan was so sexy with his long black hair. I loved the small, round glasses he wore.

"I'm sad that Scotty can't sit with us."

"Scotty?"

"Scotty Jackson," I said. I leaned in closer and so did everyone else. "I invited him to sit with us, but he's afraid."

"See, Jon. I told you that your foul body-odor was scaring people away," Brandon said.

Jon flipped Brandon off.

"Why is he afraid?" Shawn asked.

"His family is religious," Tim said, rolling his eyes.

"That doesn't mean they won't be accepting. My grandparents are very religious and they love it when I bring my girlfriend with me when I visit," Casey said.

"Scotty's family is bad-religious. They are Anti-Christians."

"Anti-Christians?" Jon asked.

"Yeah, those who say they are Christians, but then do the opposite. You know the type—they go to church and then go home and beat their wife and kids, they talk big about understanding and kindness and then rant and rave because a black family moves in down the street, they go on about love and family values and then kick their kid out on the street because he's gay. Anti-Christians. Hypocrites."

"I hate people like that," Brandon said.

"That's the kind of church-people Scotty's parents are—holier than thou, hypocrites, that would do who knows what if they found out about him," Tim said.

"I want to help him but I don't know how," I said

"Scotty sits with us during play practices. He's not afraid to be with us. He's just afraid to be seen with us when he doesn't have a good reason," Dane said. "Let's all do something and invite him. Maybe he can't sit with us at lunch, but we can make him a part of things."

"Party at Dane's house!" Brandon and Jon said and gave each other a high-five.

"Actually... we did all get together and play dodge ball at my place that one time. We could do that again," Dane said.

"Or basketball," Brandon said. "You are the only person I know who has an entire gymnasium, complete with a basketball court in his house."

"That's because I'm the only one who lives in an old school," Dane said, grinning.

"I hate basketball," I said.

"You hate every sport, except wrestling with Marc," Jon said.

"Hey! I like soccer! At least I like watching Marc play soccer. He's sooo sexy in his uniform."

"I think you've got a little drool running down your chin there, Dorian," Nathan said, then grinned. "We could do something on the farm."

"Oh, no!" Brandon said. "I know that trick. We'll end up shucking corn or slopping horses or whatever."

"Slopping horses?" Casper asked, then laughed. "I can promise you that you will not have to slop a horse."

Nathan and Casper both lived on the Selby Farm just outside of town. Nathan's boyfriend, Ethan, lived there too. Actually, Ethan owned the farm. His Uncle Jack had given it to him as a graduation present. Nathan had told me all about it. Talk about an extravagant gift!"

35

"I know! We can have an orgy! Oh, wait. There wouldn't be any girls there," Brandon said.

"I'll be there," Casey said.

"You don't count."

"Why not?"

"Because you don't think I'm the hottest guy at the table. You have bad taste."

"Who said I don't think you're the hottest?"

"Tell me more," said Brandon. Everyone turned and stared at him. "Okay! Okay! Let's get back to the problem at hand. Geesh!"

"If Dane and his parents don't mind, we could have a little party at Dane's place," Marc said. "Or we could have a party in my loft."

"We could use our loft too," Shawn said, "although we don't have as much room as Marc and no one has as much room as Dane."

"I think dodge ball at Dane's house would be the best way to include Scotty," Tim said.

"Oh! Oh! Instead of dodge ball we could play capture the flag!" Marc said.

"I'd be up for capture the fag. We can all chase Marc," Brandon said.

"I said capture the *flag*, Brandon."

"Okay, that won't be quite as fun, but I'm up for it."

"Me too!" I said.

There was soon general agreement on capture the flag.

"We could all bring a little something to eat, just chips and dip type stuff," Tristan said.

"I'll bring the dip. I don't mind giving Brandon a ride," Jon said.

"Ha. Ha," Brandon said. "Idiot."

Jon stuck his tongue out.

"It will be fine with Mom and Dad I'm sure. We can use the old cafeteria for eating and the gym for capture the flag."

"Or the other way around!" Brandon said.

"Yeah, that would be great, Brandon," Casper said. "Are all hetero boys that dumb?" he asked the rest of us.

"Hey!" Brandon yelled.

"Be quiet and I'll bake chocolate chip cookies, with M&Ms," Casey said.

Brandon immediately closed his mouth. Everyone looked at each other and nodded.

"How about this evening?" Dane said.

"If Scotty can make it," Tristan said.

"I'll go ask him now," Jon said.

"I knew having a hetero around would be useful someday," Nathan said.

"He is good eye-candy too," I said.

Brandon cleared his throat.

"Yes, you too, Brandon," I added.

Jon went on his undercover mission and soon he was back.

"We're on," Jon said. "Scotty said he'd meet us there. I told him seven. Is that cool?"

Everyone nodded. I grinned. Scotty's family and his church wouldn't support him, but we would.

"Thanks, guys," I said.

"We're always willing to help you out, Dorian," Brandon said standing up and walking over to me. "You're our pet." Brandon hugged me and petted my hair. "Good kitty."

"Rawrr," I said, then hissed.

"You guys are so strange," Casey said.

"Brandon is just trying to cover up his lust for Dorian so Marc won't get mad," Jon said.

"My lust? What about yours? You always checked out Marc's ass in the showers during soccer season."

"How could you notice what I was looking at when you were so busy checking out his front?" Jon shot back.

I shook my head. I'd heard that Brandon and Jon had been going at each other since grade school. I had the feeling they'd keep it up for the rest of their lives.

The remainder of the school day passed slowly until my last period drama class. Why did a class like government feel as if it lasted for two hours when drama seemed to zip by in ten minutes? I had my own theory that time actually did slow down or speed up depending on what I was doing. If I enjoyed something, time quickened its pace. If I didn't like something, time slowed down. The scientifically minded would argue the point I'm sure. They would probably point to a clock and say that time was consistent, but if time did change speeds wouldn't a clock be caught up in the change too? There was no way to prove or disprove my theory. Time felt as if it speeded up and slowed down so for all practical purposes it did.

Just about everyone in last period drama was also in the play. Class wasn't exactly like practice, but it was Willy Wonka oriented. Today, we did impromptu scenes as the various characters. In groups of three we drew the names of characters out of a bowl and then we selected one card out of another bowl. The cards in the second bowl said things like "Charlie celebrates his one-hundredth birthday" or "Willy Wonka becomes a used car salesman." Occasionally, the card referred to a character name that hadn't been drawn, but then we just drew another card.

When my turn came, I drew the character Veruca. Scotty drew Charlie, which almost wasn't fair because that was his character in the play. Trent drew Willy Wonka. The card we drew from the second bowl read, "Veruca gets everything she wants."

When Mrs. Cook said "begin" I ran around pretending I was admiring diamonds and tiaras and cars. I became more and more intense, screaming with glee, as I raced from one of my new possessions to another. First Scotty, then Trent, began trying to calm me down, but no matter what they did I turned up the intensity of my excitement. Soon, they were chasing me around as I screamed and jumped up and down. Scotty grasped me around the waist and then we acted as if he couldn't stop me. I pulled him around as I continued to go on and on about ice cream and stereos and a pony. Trent kept offering me candy if only I stand still for a moment. I'd pretend to be interested, then run off in another direction ohhing and ahhing over something. Soon, Trent pretended he was trying to tackle me, but couldn't never quite catch me. All the while I was still dragging Scotty around the room. The rest of the class was howling with laughter.

Finally, Scotty and Trent took me down together. They held me pinned to the floor while I continued shouting about pearl necklaces and motorcycles. Our classmates laughed the loudest when I yelled out something ridiculous like "pickles!" or "wax lips!"

We ended our skit by Trent and Charlie pretending to knock me unconscious for my own good.

I have to say that I think our skit was the best. It was fun to watch the others as they tried to act out a scene on the spot. It was good practice for when things went wrong on the stage. I had been in enough productions to know that mishaps occurred often. Every actor had to be prepared to make up something on the spot so that the play could go on.

Class was a blast, but a moment I had eagerly anticipated arrived later during play practice. Mrs. Cook announced that my costume was ready for fitting. Yes! I couldn't wait to try it on!

While other cast members ran through scenes that didn't include me, I went backstage to where Mrs. Cole, Tristan's mom, was waiting. She had volunteered to make my costume. The Coles were an artistic family. Tristan had created the painting used in the fall play, *The Picture of Dorian Gray*, and it was magnificent! The painting now hung in my boyfriend's loft. Tristan's mom was just as artistically talented, especially with anything that involved sewing.

"It's beautiful!" I said when Mrs. Cole pulled the plastic covering off my costume.

The long coat was soft; deep purple, and looked just like the one Gene Wilder wore in the movie. There was a pair of lavender pants and a lavender shirt with a pattern of little candies in every color. The costume was completed with a top hat in a slightly darker shade of purple than the coat.

Mrs. Cole handed me the costume and I stepped behind a dressing screen. I had no problem stripping down to my bikini-briefs in front of others, but I knew from experience that it made women Mrs. Cole's age nervous. I stripped behind the screen and then dressed.

As I stepped out I really felt like Willy Wonka. The costume was gorgeous and the shoes Mrs. Cook had provided, funky looking black and white dress shoes, matched perfectly.

Tristan's mom pulled out her pincushion and pinned up the pants so they'd be exactly the right length with the shoes. The costume fit perfectly otherwise, no doubt due to Mrs. Cole's skill at working with measurements. She had measured me up for the costume the very day I'd landed the role.

"I'll drop these off next Monday or have Tristan bring them in," Mrs. Cole said

"That will be great. This costume is fabulous, Mrs. Cole! I love it!"

Tristan's mom smiled. She was so beautiful. I could see where Tristan got his looks.

I changed back into my jeans and polo and handed the Willy Wonka pants to Mrs. Cole. The rest of the costume we put away. I couldn't wait for dress rehearsals!

I was on stage for most of the remainder of practice. Willy Wonka appeared in most of the scenes, except those at the beginning that involved Charlie in the candy shop and at home with his mother and bedridden grandparents. Scotty was really coming along in his portrayal of Charlie. I wondered if his family would show up for a performance. My parents had come to every production I was in, even when I had only a minor role.

No one from Scotty's church was in the cast so Scotty sat with the rest of the gay boys when he wasn't needed on stage, which wasn't often. Charlie actually had more scenes than me. We talked on the way to the parking lot after practice. Scotty kept looking around and seemed nervous, but almost everyone had gone home already. I didn't think he needed to worry. If anyone nosey saw us together they'd assume we were walking together only because we were in the same play. I suggested to Scotty that he use that excuse for sitting with us at lunch, but he shook his head. I wished he could sit with us every day, but at least he was meeting us at Dane's place soon!

Marc offered Scotty a ride, but he said he'd rather walk and practice his lines. He had his script out so maybe he was telling the truth, but I think he was scared that someone would see him in Marc's car. I hated that Scotty had to live in such fear. It wasn't fair!

It was already a bit past six, so Marc dropped Dane and Tim off at Dane's house and then Marc and I headed for the grocery. We were in charge of drinks and ice, so we picked up some two-liters of Coke and a big bag of ice. We had a little time to spare, so we made out in Marc's car in the parking lot. Our hands began to roam and I found myself wishing we could go to Marc's place instead of Dane's, but this evening was important. Besides, it was Friday and Marc and I could get together on the weekend for some naked fun.

Marc parked his Camaro in front of Dane's place just before seven and we climbed out of the car lugging drinks and ice. I looked up at the old school for a moment. It was two stories, red brick, and had lots of large windows. The cornerstone said it was built in 1874.

"This is a really cool building for a house," I said.

"Yeah. You haven't been inside yet, have you?" Marc asked.

"Nope."

"It's even cooler inside."

"It's big, but it's a lot smaller than VHS."

"The town was probably smaller back then and there were fewer kids. The class of 1954 was the last to graduate from here, so this place hasn't been used as a school for almost thirty years."

Shawn's old Cutlass pulled up and Shawn and Tristan climbed out with Tupperware containers and grocery bags. We all walked to the front doors together and were greeted by Dane and Tim.

"Just take everything to the cafeteria. I'm staying here to let everyone in. It's hard to hear anyone knocking on the door in this place."

"I bet. It's huge," I said.

Tim stayed behind with Dane. There was no surprise there. I knew what those two did while they waited at the door. I'd seen them making out as we'd walked up the steps.

Our footsteps echoed on the wooden floors as we walked down the entrance hallway and then turned right. There were doors on our right that must have led into old classrooms. Each door was wooden, with a large pane of frosted glass. There was a number painted in black on each window. As we came to the end of the hallway there was a door marked "Library."

We turned left. To the left there was only one door and there were none to the right. At the end of the hall were double-doors marked "Gymnasium." We didn't go that far. Instead, we went through the door marked "Cafeteria."

Casey and her girlfriend, Sandy, were already there, helping Dane's mom organize plates, glasses, silverware and such. We added our contributions to our little party and then I had a look around.

The old cafeteria gave me a slightly eerie feeling because it still looked like a cafeteria. There were long tables with attached benches that filled most of the room. The old serving line was still there and there were even old school posters on the walls. The whole place looked as if it was ready for students the next day, but there had been no students in almost thirty years. Marc put his hand on my shoulder and I jumped.

"Sorry."

"It's okay. This place is just a little spooky."

"We will liven it up soon enough. Until then, I want to show you something."

"Yeah? Mmm."

"Not *that*." Marc laughed. "Come on."

Marc pulled me out of the old cafeteria and back the way we came. We neared the entrance hallway and I thought he was going to take me up the wide, worn wooden stairs, but he turned to a door on the right just before we reached the stairs.

We entered to find an old classroom, looking just as it must have when the school was in use.

"Are all the rooms like this?" I asked.

"No. Just this one. It was left intact. Dane showed it to me once."

I looked around. There were old school desks looking as if they were just waiting for the class to arrive. There were large portraits of Abraham Lincoln and George Washington on the walls. One wall was mostly windows and the other three had chalkboards. There were books on shelves and an old overhead projector sitting in the corner. Above one of the chalkboards was the alphabet in cursive. I remembered practicing handwriting in grade school. I could never quite get the capital T.

"My grade school had desks like this. I remember thinking they were really old," I said.

"Isn't this cool?" Marc asked.

"Yeah, but it is a little creepy."

"Maybe there are ghost students here—kids who never left."

My eyes widened. I swallowed hard and grasped Marc's arm.

"Maybe there's one right behind you," he said.

I grabbed Marc and he wrapped his arms around me.

"You're scaring me," I said.

"Sorry. I thought it might be a good way to get you in my arms."

"All you had to do is ask," I said. I grinned at Marc and kissed him.

I could tell by the look in Marc's eyes that he wanted to keep kissing as much as I did, but we needed to get back. If we kept kissing we'd lose track of time and who knew what we'd end up doing in the empty classroom? I moaned at the thought, but then I imagined Brandon walking in on us. We would never hear the end of it.

"Come on. Let's go back," I said.

I took Marc's hand and pulled him out of the room. We returned to the cafeteria.

In short order, Casper, Ethan, Nathan, and Nathan's little brother Dave arrived. Scotty was next, escorted to the cafeteria by Tim, who instantly disappeared again. Scotty had been at the Halloween party at the Selby's last fall so he knew the whole gang. He also worked at Ofarim's some evenings. Everyone went to Ofarim's. It was the number one burger and hangout for the younger crowd. Scotty was immediately welcomed and I could tell he felt at ease.

Brandon and Jon arrived just a little late. They were loaded down with bags of chips.

"No girlfriends?" Shawn asked.

"Girls can't play capture the flag. It's a man's game," Brandon said.

"Hey!" Casey yelled. "I will mop up the floor with you, boy."

Brandon grinned. He loved taunting Casey.

"Yeah. Yeah. I don't remember you doing so well last time."

"That's because we didn't play capture the flag last time, but then you probably aren't bright enough to remember," Casey said.

"Ohhh! Score one for Casey!" Jon said.

Casey and Jon gave each other a high five.

"I seem to remember that Dave kicked everyone's butt when we played dodge ball," Tristan said. "Can I have him on my team?"

"Oh no! We get Dave!" Brandon said loudly.

"We don't even have teams yet," Nathan pointed out. "Since Dave is my little brother I think he should be on my team."

"No way! Dave should be on whatever team I am!" Shawn said.

Dave giggled. He was about twelve so he was the youngest of the group. He loved everyone fighting over him.

"We will draw for teams," Casey said. "Otherwise you guys will bicker over who gets Dave so long there won't be any time to play."

That settled that.

We all attacked the little buffet we'd sat up. There were bologna salad sandwiches, Doritos, barbeque potato chips, macaroni & cheese, chocolate chip cookies, and brownies. It was a great little feast.

"You guys all have to come see the play!" I said between bites.

"Why? Will you by paying us to go?" Jon asked.

"As if! No! Because Scotty is magnificent and my costume is fabulous! Your mom did a great job, Tristan. She's incredible."

"And hot," Brandon said.

Tristan gave Brandon an evil look, which was funny to see.

"I'm just saying," Brandon said.

Jon laughed. "What if Brandon was dating Tristan's mom? That would be hilarious."

"Hey, it could happen," Brandon said.

"Yeah, right!" Marc said. "Like Tristan's mom doesn't have way better taste than that."

"Maybe I should ask her out," Brandon said.

"Do not go there," Tristan said.

"I promise you won't have to call me daddy."

"You seem to forget you already have a girlfriend," Sandy said.

"Oh yeah!" Brandon said.

"Don't worry, Tristan. Even if Brandon did have the courage to ask your mom out there is zero chance she would say yes. Marc is right. Your mom has way better taste than that *and* more class," Ethan said. "I do agree with Brandon on one thing. Your mom is very attractive."

"Just like her son," Shawn said. He hugged Tristan close.

"Hey, remember when we played dodge ball, when Nate London was here?" Jon asked. "Shawn kept trying to kill him with the ball because he was jealous."

"I wasn't jealous."

"Yeah right!" Brandon said. "You thought he had a thing going with Tristan and you couldn't stand it."

"Okay, maybe I was a little jealous. He did show up with my future boyfriend."

"You were a lot jealous. It was so cute," Casey said.

"Can we talk about something else now?" Shawn asked.

"Yeah, like how incredibly hot I am!" Brandon said.

"Let's stick to reality," Nathan said.

"What?! You know I'm hot. I'm the hottest guy..."

"This could go on for hours," Tristan said. "Let me handle this. Brandon, you are the hottest guy who has ever lived. No one will ever come close to being as hot as you are right now."

"Finally! Someone understands! Sorry, Shawn. Tristan obviously thinks I'm hotter than you, but I'm sure you can understand that. You must have some other qualities he likes."

Shawn just grinned.

"I know what Tristan likes about Shawn," Tim said mischievously. "I heard Tristan moaning it the last time he was alone with Shawn in his bedroom. He said..."

Tristan shoved a sandwich in Tim's mouth to shut him up.

"It was all a dream, Tim, all a dream," Tristan said.

"Ha! It wasn't a dream!" Jon said. "It was a fantasy! Shawn and Tristan were acting out some extreme sexual role-play. What was it guys—master and slave boy? Football player and his tutor? Or..."

"Hey, these cookies are great, Casey!" Tristan said, trying to change the subject.

"Look at Tristan turning red. I must be close to the truth. Tell us, Tim, just what were Shawn and Tristan doing in his bedroom?" Jon asked.

Tim started to speak, but Shawn got him in a headlock, and held his hand over Tim's mouth.

"Tim can't talk right now. He's being threatened," Shawn said.

Shawn whispered something to Tim and released him. Tim sat up straight and didn't say a word.

"Come on, Tim, spill it," Brandon said.

"I didn't hear anything," Tim said.

"Shawn must have some great blackmail material," Jon said. "It's okay. We all know the truth. It's the quiet ones like Tristan who are wild. It's probably best if we don't know the details."

"Are you sorry you came yet?" I asked Scotty.

"No way, you guys are hilarious."

"It's like this every day at lunch," Casey said. "I keep thinking about switching to a better table."

"There is no better table because no other table has me," Brandon said.

"We have to spend a good deal of our time massaging Brandon's ego," Casey said.

"You want to massage my what?" Brandon asked.

"Keep dreaming," Casey said.

Scotty laughed.

"I wish I could sit with you guys at lunch," Scotty said.

"You're always welcome to join us," Tristan said.

"Thanks for inviting me this evening. I feel like I can be myself here."

"Everyone can, although we don't encourage Brandon to be himself," Casey said.

"Hey!" Brandon yelled.

"I know what it feels like to be alone," Casper said. "Before Brendan came along I didn't have anyone like me to talk to and it was sad, lonely, and depressing."

"Yeah, that's why drama class and play practices have been so great. I don't have to hide so much when I'm there and I don't feel like anyone is out to get me."

"I'd watch my back," Jon said. "Homos are like piranha when they see a sexy guy."

"Did you just say Scotty is sexy?" Brandon asked.

"Yeah. Wanna make something of it?"

"Nah, he is sexy. If I was a homo I'd go for him. Of course, I'd prefer a guy who looked like me."

"Brandon is Narcissus reincarnated," Tristan said.

"You think I don't get that but I do, Tristan Graham Cole," Brandon said.

"You sound like my grandmother." Tristan laughed.

"Good. That's what I was going for."

Scotty had turned slightly red while the guys were talking about him being sexy, but I could tell he liked it. It was such a pity he couldn't live his life as I lived mine and as so many of us lived ours. No one should have to hide. No one!

We talked and ate and laughed. We talked all together and in little groups. I kept an eye on Scotty, but he was mixing in well.

47

He wasn't shy. I saw him having what looked like a serious discussion with Brandon and Jon. Later, he was laughing with Ethan, Nathan, and Dave.

After we ate, I followed the others down the hallway to the gymnasium. When we entered the doors I stopped and gazed at the gym for a while. So did Scotty. He had never seen it before either. It wasn't as big as the VHS gymnasium, but it was big. There was a basketball court with a wooden floor and old wooden bleachers on three sides. At the far end was a small stage with old blue curtains. I guessed that the gym had also doubled as the auditorium in the old days when this was VHS.

There were old team photos still on the walls. Signs reading "Boys" and "Girls" were on the open doorways on either side of the stage.

"It's like time stands still here," I said.

"Yeah," Dane said. "Not much has changed since it was a school. The old boy's locker room is my bathroom. I shower in there every morning."

"Probably having fantasies about all the hot naked guys who have showered there before," Brandon said.

"Mostly, I just remember what Tim and I have done in those showers and in the locker room." Dane grinned and then he and Tim kissed.

"Let's get a game going before Dane and Tim start making out," Brandon said.

Casey stepped forward.

"I've written down everyone's name and put them in this cup. We will let Dave draw out names. The first seven he draws out will be one team. Everyone not drawn will be on the other."

"I don't know about Dave drawing names. The kid is sneaky," Jon said.

"Yeah, definitely can't be trusted," Brandon said.

Dave laughed and began drawing names. Soon, Tim, Dane, Scotty, Shawn, Tristan, Casper, Ethan, and Dave's names were pulled out and read. That meant that the team I was on included Marc, Nathan, Casey, Sandy, Brandon, and Jon.

"What do we use for flags?" I asked.

"How about my socks?" Brandon said.

"Like anyone wants to touch that," Ethan said.

"I brought some red cloth napkins from the cafeteria," Dane said.

Hiding the flag wasn't much of an option in a gymnasium, so each team just placed theirs as far away from the opposing team as possible. Ours was on the bleachers directly behind us. The other team put theirs on the stage.

We all took our places and the game began. The centerline divided our territories. Brandon dashed over, but was soon chased back by Ethan. Marc, Dave, and I dove in at once, forcing the other team to scatter and come after us. I wasn't good at sports, but I could run and, more importantly, I could change directions fast. Every time someone thought they had me I angled off in a new direction.

There was too much movement to keep track of it all. Everyone was running everywhere trying to get the other team's flag and protect their own. We captured Dane, but soon lost Casey and Jon. The game was mostly a blur, but it was a blast! We kept it up for a good twenty minutes before I raced after Casper only to hear cheering behind me. Scotty had captured our flag and made it back across the line. I hadn't even seen him in all the confusion.

We played a second game that was just as wild and chaotic. It was mostly a lot of running and laughing. At one point, Tristan and Scotty were about to catch me as I ran back towards our side so I dove and slid across the floor to escape. Dave liked that move was soon using it.

Our team won the second game when Dave raced back to our side with the flag. Ethan, Tim, and Shawn were right on top of him and I didn't think he was going to make it, but he faked a dive and then sprinted.

We decided to leave our score tied and headed back to the cafeteria because we were all panting and hungry.

We attacked our buffet again, talked, and laughed. We split up into smaller groups and played cards. Marc, Scotty, Dave, and I got up a game of bullshit. It's a card game where players sometimes try to bullshit and lay down cards that aren't allowed. If no one calls them on their bullshit, they get away with it. If someone does they have to pick up the entire discard pile. Calling bullshit on someone is risky because if they aren't bullshitting then you have to pick up the entire discard pile. I was sure Dave was bullshitting when he said he was laying down three eights, but when I called bullshit and he turned the cards over they were all eights! Dave thought that was hilarious because the discard pile was huge by then.

Scotty had a great time, which was the most important thing. I wished I knew a gay boy I could hook him up with. What he really needed was a boyfriend. At least he knew he had friends, gay friends he could talk to about whatever was troubling him.

Casper was having a good time too and that was also important because his boyfriend, Brendan, was off at IU. Casper had been getting along well, but I knew he had to miss Brendan something terrible. He was probably wishing Brendan could have joined us for the evening. I wish he could have too because it would have made Casper happy, but Casper was having fun even without his boyfriend.

I was glad Marc and I were about the same age and were both seniors. I don't think I could have handled Marc going off to college while I was still in high school. Poor Casper was only a sophomore when Brendan graduated so he had a long wait before he could join him. I guess that was the disadvantage of dating an older man.

We didn't wrap things up until nearly midnight. We helped clean up and then everyone headed out. Marc drove me home and we sat in the car holding hands for a while before I went in.

"I think tonight was a success," I said.

"Yeah, everyone likes Scotty and he fits right in. He's funny too. He has an edge of sadness than never quit goes away, but I didn't see him look truly unhappy once tonight. We need to remember to invite him to anything we do as a group. The two of us could even include him sometime."

"Yeah, although right now I want to be alone with you."

I pulled Marc toward me and kissed him. We began to make out. I hungered for Marc so much I couldn't stand it. Our tongues entwined and our hands roamed. Soon, things went further. Buttons were unbuttoned and zippers unzipped. We squirmed out of our pants and used our hands and mouths to bring each other intense pleasure. The car was filled with moans even as the windows steamed up.

Ten minutes later, I gave Marc one last lingering kiss and stepped out of the car. I was feeling mellow and content. Making love with Marc, even if it was only a quickie, always left me feeling relaxed. People who were uptight about sex were ignorant. It was a physical need. I was certain of that. The way my body felt at the moment told me as much. All the stress and tension was gone. I was willing to bet that the anti-Christians wouldn't be so mean and nasty if they'd get it on now and then.

Scotty

I couldn't remember when I'd had such a good time. Friday night at Dane's was a blast. What I liked best about it is that I didn't have to pretend to be straight. I didn't have to watch what I said, or did, or how I looked at another guy. I didn't have to have my guard up.

I don't think I'd had fun like that since I first realized I was gay. I'm not sure when it really hit me that I liked boys instead of girls, but I'm guessing maybe twelve. I was attracted to guys before that, but I didn't understand what it meant. It had been a long time since I could just cut loose and have fun.

The guys said they would invite me to join them whenever they got together away from prying eyes. I could hardly wait. It was a shame that all of them were taken. Maybe it's wrong, but I wanted to fool around with another guy. Seeing Tim and Dane kiss or Dorian and Marc start touching each other made me yearn to be with another boy. I tried not to do so, but I kept imagining what they did together when they were alone. The mental images of naked guys together made me want to hook up even more.

I had never done anything sexual with another guy. I'd heard that even straight boys often mess around when they're young, but I hadn't even done that. The opportunity had never presented itself. Even if it had I likely wouldn't have done anything because all I ever heard about sex was that it was bad outside of marriage. As I grew older, I began to question that and finally decided it was a bunch of crap, but when I was at the age where boys messed around I would have felt as if I was committing a horrible sin.

I knew a few gay boys now, but none of them was available. It might have felt strange getting naked with one of them even if they were available, but then again probably not if they were single. I was just used to seeing them all paired up. Even before I knew them I'd seen the out gay boys going around as couples. They weren't obvious about it, but I could just tell. I hoped to find a boyfriend someday, maybe in college. A boyfriend was an impossibility now.

I slept in until a little after nine on Saturday. It was the only day of the week I could sleep in. I had to get up for school through the week and for church on Sunday. Getting up for school wasn't too bad, but getting up for church sucked. I had to be up by seven on Sunday just to dress in uncomfortable clothes and go somewhere I did not want to be.

My parents would have been horrified by my ideas, but I didn't think the people who went to our church were very good people. Every sermon was against the evils of something or other and what we should all be doing to combat it. There were lots of what I called "anti-committees." I could remember several of them in the recent past. There was a committee to pressure the local government to make the county dry (anti-alcohol). There was a committee to lobby the state and local government to make English the official language of the U.S. (anti-everyone who doesn't speak English). There was a committee to pressure the school board into not allowing any mention of evolution in the schools (anti-reality). There was a committee to make sure that "the right people" purchased homes in the neighborhood (anti-minority; especially anti-black and anti-Hispanic). I couldn't remember any group formed to lobby for a homeless shelter, to form a soup kitchen, or gather clothes for the needy. No groups were formed to raise funds to help those who couldn't pay their heating bills in the winter. No groups were proposed to raise money for anyone hit by huge medical bills. Everything my church did was to fight something or to force others to do what the members of my church wanted. They were a bunch of ignorant, bigoted, control freaks. It was no wonder my dad was a devout member.

Grr! I did not want to think about church. My mind went off on little rants sometimes. I didn't like it, but the thoughts were difficult to shut down. I distracted myself by imagining what Ethan looked like without a shirt. Even with a shirt it was obvious he had some serious muscles. Nathan was so lucky! I couldn't even imagine having a boyfriend who was that hot! Yeah, I know. There are other things more important than hotness, but at the moment I was trying to keep myself from thinking unpleasant thoughts and the easiest way to do it was to think about sexy, shirtless boys. Mmm.

Mom offered to fix me some breakfast, but I told her I'd just have a bowl of cereal. She fixed breakfast every day of the week except Saturday because Justin and I didn't get up at our usual time. Dad even slept in sometimes. Mom always offered to fix me something when I first walked into the kitchen on Saturdays, but I always declined. I figured she spent too much time in the kitchen anyway.

I hurried through breakfast because I wanted to get out of the house. I never had any privacy when I was home. I had to share my room with my brother and even in the bathroom I was always aware that someone could knock on the door at any moment. This morning when I got up Justin was still asleep. It was kind of like having the room to myself, but not quite because he could wake up at any moment.

I stepped outside of the house and experienced freedom. True, I could be seen by others, but I doubted I was of any special interest. When I was home I felt like I was being watched. I know that's not quite the way it was, but that's how it felt.

I liked to walk and think. I especially liked to go places others were not likely to be. It's not that I'm anti-social, not at all; it's just that sometimes I like to be where no one else can see me.

Today, I brought along the biography of Eleanor Roosevelt I was reading for my U.S. History class. We had to do one report each semester. I had picked Thomas Jefferson in the spring semester. I wrote about the contradictions in his life. He wrote the Declaration of Independence that was all about freedom, and yet he owned slaves. That was a pretty big contradiction. I didn't understand how anyone could own a slave and not feel like they were committing a horrible sin. I think Jefferson was conflicted. From reading about him I got the sense that he didn't think it was right to own slaves, but without his slaves he had no means of support. He was trapped in a bad situation. It was easy enough for me to judge because slavery had never been a part of my life. I wondered if I would have thought differently if I lived in the eighteenth century and inherited slaves like Jefferson.

I liked reading about Eleanor Roosevelt better. She was a great lady. I have to admit I picked her partly to impress Mr. Hahn, my teacher, because he was an Eleanor Roosevelt fan. There was even a big poster of her in the classroom. As I began reading about her, I became more and more interested. She was the first First Lady who really went out and did things. She obviously cared about people and tried to make a difference. She could have just stayed in the White House and thrown parties, but instead she traveled around, visited coal mines and WPA camps and reported back to her husband. Even after he died and she was no longer First Lady she kept right on going. She spent her life trying to make life better for others.

Without deciding to walk there, I ended up in the cemetery. I spent quite a bit of time there. That might sound a bit ghoulish, but it's not like I dug up graves. There usually wasn't anyone around and if there was someone there they kept to themselves. The graveyard was kind of like a large park, only with headstones. I loved the green grass and the stately old trees. In the oldest part of the cemetery were graves dating back to the early 1800s. There were huge cedar trees that were probably planted as little saplings over a hundred years ago.

I had a special place I liked to sit. There was a bench under a large oak tree next to couple of graves. Two boys I had sort of known were buried there. I didn't know either of them well, but I felt a connection to them because they were gay like me. Their very presence as out gay boys had created uproar in my church. They were labeled a danger to society. I think that's when my church became seriously against gays, although it was already anti-gay. My church was anti just about everything except for telling other people how to live and what they could do and not do.

Some of my new friends were really close to the boys in the graves. Brandon was Mark's best friend. Tristan was Taylor's cousin. I didn't know Mark and Taylor well, but I had spoken to them and I liked them. I felt horrible when they died. Taylor killed himself because a lot of people were so nasty to him. I began to truly hate my church then. The congregation thought it was wonderful that Taylor was driven to suicide by bullying and abuse. They even said he'd go to Hell. I knew then for sure what kind of people went to my church. Mark killed himself because he loved Taylor so much he couldn't live without him. It was a Romeo & Juliet story. Their deaths made most people stop and think about how they treated gays. That's why things were so much better for gay boys in Verona now. The members of my church learned nothing. They just kept on hating and encouraging others to hate.

Mark and Taylor's graves were sad and yet they weren't. A peony bush grew right between them as if connecting them. Daffodils had sprung up there too and grew all over their graves. I had heard that no one planted the peony or the daffodils. They just appeared. I didn't know if that was true or not, but when I was sitting on the bench by the graves I felt as if Mark and Taylor were watching over me and protecting me. I felt a sense of companionship. I loved to sit there and read, then glance up and look at the bright yellow daffodils and smell their wonderful scent. That scent lingered in the air now. The peony had not yet bloomed, but the shoots were beginning to emerge from the earth.

I sat back and began reading about Eleanor Roosevelt. I lost myself in her world. From time to time I'd look up and take in the scenery around me, then go right back to reading. I'd brought my notebook with me too. When I came to something I wanted to put in my report I stopped and wrote it down because I knew I'd forget it if I didn't. It was so pleasant reading and taking notes in the cemetery that I stayed there until past noon. I was amazed when I looked at the time.

My stomach rumbled. I decided to head for Ofarim's. I didn't often eat there because I worked there part-time. Spending time inside was kind of like working when I wasn't working, but I was in the mood for a burger. Shawn was working there today and I liked being around Shawn. I like being reminded that I was not the only gay boy in Verona.

I put in my bookmark, picked up my notebook, and walked through the cemetery. It was a gorgeous spring day, perfect for hanging outside just as I'd been doing. I thought that after lunch I might go for a walk in the woods behind the school or maybe just hang out in the park. The woods would probably be better because there wouldn't be anyone around. Then again, someone cool might be in the park. I decided to choose my destination after I finished lunch.

Shawn smiled as I entered Ofarim's.

"You've come in early to take over so I can go outside and enjoy the weather, right?" Shawn said.

"Not a chance. You are stuck here until your shift is over. I'm not coming in a minute early on a day like this."

"It was worth a try. Are you just visiting or are you here to eat?"

"I'm starved. Get me a triple cheeseburger with lettuce, pickle, and onion, large fries, a Coke, and a chocolate milkshake."

"Coming right up."

I took a seat in a booth. Shawn brought my Coke right out. Shawn was really handsome and had a hot body. I knew him mostly from working in Ofarim's together, although we weren't both there at the same time all that often. Usually one of us worked while the other was off.

My food was ready soon, so soon that I knew Agnes was running the kitchen. Agnes owned Ofarim's. Those of us who worked here did the cooking sometimes as well as waiting on tables and cleaning up, but no one could cook as fast as Agnes. Her burgers were always just a little bit better too.

I bit into my burger. Yeah, it was an Agnes burger—delicious. I had eaten a lot of burgers in Ofarim's. Whenever I was working, meals were free. When I wasn't working, my employee discount was 50%. I guess I really should eat at Ofarim's more often, but hanging out where I work generally isn't my idea of a good time.

Shawn and I exchanged a few words now and then as I ate, but mostly he was busy. I didn't mind. I finished off my burger and fries as I watched the others in the restaurant. It wasn't crowded. There were two couples and two others there by themselves like me.

I was sitting in the booth, sipping my milkshake when Blake York entered. I knew his last name because I'd seen his picture in the Plymouth newspaper. He was a football player. I learned his first name by hearing Shawn speak it. Blake hadn't come in much after Shawn began dating Tristan, but he'd been in often before. I'd overheard enough to know that Shawn and Blake had hooked up a few times. I watched with interest as Blake talked with Shawn at the counter. Unfortunately, I couldn't hear what they were saying, but I saw Blake touch Shawn's arm. Shawn drew his arm back quickly so I had a good idea of what was going on. Blake was coming on to Shawn and Shawn wasn't having any of it.

I wished Blake was coming on to me. His chest and biceps stretched his shirt, revealing his muscles even through the cloth. He was facing away from me at the moment. His shoulders were broad and tapered to a narrow waist. Blake had the hottest ass! I wanted to walk up behind him and grope his butt. I'd never have the courage for such a thing, but that didn't stop me from fantasizing about it. I wanted to run my fingers through his black hair and all over his body. I was getting hard just sitting there looking at him.

Blake left. I sat there for a few seconds in indecision, and then I got up, paid the check at the counter, and walked outside. I looked up and down the street, but didn't see him. Then, I spotted a red Camaro. The windows were rolled down and I thought the driver had black hair. I walked toward it. As I came even with the car I looked inside. It was Blake.

"Hey," I said before I lost my courage.

Blake looked in my direction.

"Hey."

"What's up?" I asked. I leaned on the passenger side door.

"You work in Ofarim's don't you?" Blake asked.

"Yeah, usually when Shawn isn't there. Sweet car."

"Like it?"

"I love it. It's hot."

I could not believe I was leaning in Blake York's window checking him out. I was not that brave. I was that aroused. I wanted him so bad I was ready to pounce on him. I guess sexual attraction made up for courage.

"Want to take a ride?"

"Hell yeah!"

I climbed in. My mind was spinning. I almost couldn't believe what was happening. If I awakened to find it was only a dream I was going to be furious.

"Damn, it's hot in here," Blake said.

Blake stripped off his shirt. I just stared. His chest was smooth, muscular, and perfectly proportioned. Gazing at the ridges of his abdomen made me breathe harder. He had an eight pack! I looked up into Blake's sexy blue eyes and he grinned at me mischievously.

"I thought so," he said.

I would have feared Blake was going to kick my ass, but I knew he'd messed around with Shawn. I was almost positive he had taken off his shirt to find out if I was hot for him or not. He had his answer.

Blake started the car and pulled away from the curb.

"So, have you and Shawn ever hooked up?" Blake asked.

I was shocked by the directness of his question.

"Uh, no. I've never..." I stopped. I'd said more than I wanted.

"You're a virgin? Are you kidding me?" What are you? Twelve?"

"Not so loud, man!"

Blake laughed and I realized I was being ridiculous. There was no way anyone could hear.

"I'm seventeen."

"That's so sad. You've really never done anything? No hand job with a friend? No messing around with a girl? Nothing?"

I shook my head.

"Wow, an actual virgin."

I frowned.

"Hey, I'm not making fun of you, man. I'm just surprised. I figured a sexy guy like you would have at least had some head or something." Blake York called me sexy. Yes! "Actually, the fact that you are a virgin turns me on. I love virgins."

Blake drove to the VHS parking lot and stopped the car. He turned in his seat and looked at me.

"Well?" he asked.

My eyes darted around and my palms were sweaty. I leaned in toward his lips.

"No," Blake said firmly. "I don't go in for that."

"Uh, okay."

I wasn't sure what to do. I had no idea how it worked between two guys. Blake grabbed my hand and put it on his chest. His muscles were so hard!

"Nice," I said.

I began to feel Blake's chest and I grew instantly rock hard.

"Use your tongue."

I did not have to be told twice. If Blake had told me to hand over all the cash in my wallet if I wanted to lick his chest I would have done so. I leaned over and licked him. I began to explore his torso with my lips and tongue. When my tongue raked across his right nipple he moaned and pushed my head hard against his pec. I tongued his nipple until he let up on the pressure. I immediately moved to his left nipple. I got off on making Blake moan.

Blake pushed my head down so I moved to his abs. I had wanted to touch another guy for so long and at last it was happening! I was breathing hard and my cock was throbbing.

Blake's abs were smooth and firm. I licked and kissed them. He pushed my head down more. There was only one place to go. I felt the bulge in his jeans and it flexed.

Something came over me. I ripped my way through his belt, unbutton his jeans, and pulled down his zipper. Blake lifted his hips so I could pull his pants down. He pushed me back and climbed into the backseat of his car. I followed.

I ran my hand over Blake's boxers and then pulled them down too. I leaned down and pulled Blake into my mouth. I almost immediately choked and had to pull off.

"You can't take it all, so don't try," Blake said. "Take your time. I want it to last."

I nodded and went down on Blake again.

"Yeah, that's it. You're a natural."

I felt like instinct had taken over. I had never given head before, but with minimal instruction from Blake I knew exactly what to do. My body reacted as if it had been waiting for this moment. Nothing mattered to me right then, but making Blake moan. I couldn't believe Blake and I were sharing such an intimate and personal experience.

Blake pushed me off.

"Take off your clothes."

I looked around, but the parking lot was deserted. I pulled off my shirt, then the rest of my clothing. I was completely naked in the back of Blake's car.

"Hand me that tube between the front seats."

I did as he asked and grew increasingly nervous. Blake wanted to go all the way!

"Uh, I'm not sure I'm ready," I said.

"Leave everything to me. I'm an expert at breaking in virgins. I won't hurt you. I promise."

Blake looked so incredibly hot and I was so aroused I nodded my head.

"Lay on your back."

I did as Blake said. I felt so vulnerable as he pulled my legs up. My breath came faster and my heart pounded.

"It's going to hurt a little at first, but the pain will quickly go away. I'll take it slow."

I just nodded.

Blake pushed and I cried out in pain. If he hadn't held me down by placing his hands on my shoulders I would've jumped up off the seat. My ass was on fire.

"Easy, easy. The pain will stop once I'm all...the...way...in."

Oddly enough, the pain eased greatly. Blake held perfectly still. He was buried inside me.

"The more you do it, the less it hurts. Mostly, it's just pure pleasure."

I tried to get my breath under control, but I was just plain scared. Blake pulled out most of the way and the slid back in. It hurt, but less. Pleasure began to overwhelm the pain.

"You like it?" Blake asked.

"Mmm, yes!"

Blake looked magnificent above me as his muscles tensed and flexed. I had never experienced anything so intense or so incredible in my life. There was still some pain, but it got so mixed up with pleasure that it became a part of the pleasure. I was in Heaven. I began to moan and groan as Blake thrust.

Then, just like that, Heaven turned to Hell. I looked over Blake's shoulder and saw the last thing I expected or wanted to see.

"Justin!"

"I'm Blake."

"No, my brother!"

Blake's head whipped around and he spotted my brother, who was already turning and racing away. Blake climbed off me and was out the car in a flash. I couldn't believe it. He chased Justin across the parking lot while he was completely naked!

Justin had a good head start and he was wearing shoes. Blake soon gave up the pursuit and returned to the car. I was already pulling on my clothes. Tears streamed from my eyes.

"What the hell was he doing? Is your brother some kind of pervert? Did you know he was going to watch?"

"Of course I didn't know! I didn't know we were... I've got to talk to him before he tells my dad!"

I was crying and shaking. That convinced Blake this wasn't some kind of set up, although how it could have been was beyond me.

"Dude, calm down!"

"You don't understand! I've got to stop him!"

I started to climb out of the car. Blake grabbed the back of my shirt and jerked me back in so hard I feared he was going to attack me.

"I'll drive you. Just tell me where to go."

I gave Blake directions to my house. I'd start there. My best bet was probably to wait for Justin outside. Maybe I could talk him or bribe him into keeping quiet. It didn't take us long to reach the house.

"Thanks," I said.

"I hope everything works out. Let's hook up again sometime. I want to finish what I started." Blake grinned. He was so sexy!

"I hope we can," I said.

I hurried out of the car. I didn't see Justin anywhere nearby. Maybe he hadn't even gone straight home.

I walked up the steps and opened the front door. My face paled. There was Justin, talking to my dad. They both turned and looked at me. I had never seen my dad so angry before. I almost turned and bolted as he came toward me. I thought he was going to belt me. He grabbed the front of my shirt, jerked me across the room, and shoved me onto the couch.

"How could you..."

My father was so angry he couldn't even speak. His face was red and he was shaking. Justin was staring at him with an open mouth and wide eyes.

"Watch your blood pressure, dear."

Mom's lips were thinned, but she wasn't so much angry as shocked and disappointed.

Tears streamed from my eyes. I sat there on the couch and sobbed while Dad got himself under control.

"Is what your brother told us true? Were you... were you being a girl for another boy?"

I nodded as tears streamed from my eyes. I was too frightened and shaken to think of lying.

"I told you he's a faggot," Justin said.

Dad turned on my brother.

"You will not use that word in this house!"

"Yes, sir."

"We did not raise you to act in this immoral and reprehensible manner!"

I wasn't even sure of what Dad said after that. It all kind of impacted on my brain. Only certain words and phrases made it through: sin, unnatural act, Sodom and Gomorrah, Hell, perverted, and more. He kept going until he was exhausted.

"You will never see that boy again. You will never repeat what you have done. We're all going to pray for you and help you to turn from your sinful ways."

My mom sat on the couch with me and took my hands in hers.

"I don't know what has led you down this sinful path, but you must turn back, Scotty. Homosexuals burn in Hell. You can't choose that lifestyle. You know better than this. We've taught you better and so has the church."

Mom was so worried about me there were tears in her eyes. I hated that she was disappointed in me. I hated that I'd made her cry.

"You have to fight the sick and disgusting desires the Devil put into you, Scotty. You have to fight as hard as you can."

Mom and Dad quoted a lot of Bible versus at me and they just kept talking and talking. It went on and on until I thought it would never end.

Dad reached out toward me. I flinched slightly, although my father had never struck me. He took my hand, pulled me to my feet, reached out for mom, and then motioned for Justin to join us. We formed a circle, holding hands.

"Dear God, please help Scotty overcome the unnatural and perverted lust that caused him to sin against you. Please help him to fight his deviant desires and please help us to help him. Amen."

My mom smiled at me briefly. My face felt hot. I was mortified.

"I'm going to make an appointment for you with the pastor tomorrow. We're going to take care of this before it can get a hold on you. I think you need to go to your room and think about this," Dad said.

I got up and walked away. Justin mouthed "faggot" to me while Mom and Dad weren't looking.

I sat down on my bed and stared at the floor. I could not believe this was happening to me. I had never done anything with another guy before. My very first time and I got caught! Maybe it was a sign. Maybe I wasn't supposed to be doing what I'd done. I hadn't planned for things to go so far, but Blake was so hot I just couldn't say no.

I was really afraid Dad was going to hit me at first. I had never seen him so angry before. I think it was worse when he calmed down. My parents were so disappointed in me. I never wanted to disappoint them. I wanted them to be proud of me. They sure weren't proud now.

Justin came in room and looked at me with disgust and glee. It was an unpleasant combination.

"You're gonna go to Hell for being a faggot."

"Just shut up, Justin. This is your fault. Why did you have to run and tell Mom and Dad?"

"No, it's your fault for choosing to be a faggot. Don't blame this on me. I told Mom and Dad to stop you. I don't want a faggot for a brother. You'd better change and you'd better do it quick or you're going to Hell for sure."

"Shut the fuck up!"

"You shut up, faggot!"

"Boys!"

Justin and I looked toward the door.

"I had better never hear those words coming from your mouths again," Dad said. His tone was angry and stern.

"Yes, sir," we both said.

"Justin, you need to show your brother compassion. We have to forgive him for what he's done and help him to turn from the path of depravity. We have to save him."

"Yes, sir."

As soon as Dad was gone, Justin turned to me and said "faggot" under this breath.

I lay down on my bed and turned my back to Justin. Tears flowed from my eyes. I hurt so bad inside I just wanted to die. What was I going to do now?

I tried to calm myself down, but I kept getting more and more upset. I couldn't believe my brother had seen me with Blake and I couldn't believe he'd told our parents about it. My parents knew I'd let a boy fuck me. How could I even face them now? What if word got out? What if everyone started calling me faggot and all those other names?

I tried not to, but I thought of Blake. His naked body was etched in my mind. Images of what we had done together played out in my head even as I tried to stop them. I was kind of sore from what he'd done to me. It was so hot and it felt so good! No. I couldn't think about that. I couldn't be with Blake again. I couldn't let myself be gay.

The images in my mind roiled over each other; Dad yelling at me; Mom crying; Blake's muscular body above me; Justin calling me a faggot. The images just kept coming and coming no matter how I tried to think of something else.

I didn't know if I was allowed to leave the house or not, but I had to get out. I climbed out of bed and stood. Justin looked at me, but didn't say anything. I didn't see my parents as I made my way out of the house. I was glad. I needed to think. No, I needed to stop thinking.

I'd always wondered what sex would be like. I knew it was supposed to be incredible, but I'd never guessed just how incredible. When I'd been with Blake it was the most intensely pleasurable experience of my life. Blake was so hot. His body was magnificent and when he took my virginity... even the pain was pleasure. I wanted it again so bad I couldn't stand it, but I couldn't have that life. I had to choose between my family and being gay, but I didn't think I could choose not to be gay. What was I going to do?

I began to freak out. I kept thinking about being kicked out on the street. I kept seeing Mom and Dad telling me they didn't love me. If I couldn't live at home I couldn't finish school. I pictured myself in dark alleys doing nasty things for cash. I'd have to sleep in doorways and I'd freeze in winter. All the things I wanted to do with my life were gone. It was like one event swept everything away and I didn't have anything to live for anymore. There was no way out. I couldn't stop being me. I couldn't stop wanting Blake. My family would never accept me. They'd hate me for choosing to be gay. They'd turn their backs on me and tell me they didn't love me. I'd have no one and no one would care about me. I was better off dead.

I was crying so hard I could barely see where I was going. Maybe I'd get lucky and step in front of a car and all the pain would disappear. Maybe I could jump in front of a car, or better yet a truck—yeah, a big truck. That would be quicker. Maybe it would be so quick it wouldn't hurt.

I didn't think I had the courage to step in front of a truck, but there were other ways to die... No. I couldn't do that to my friends. I couldn't. I did have friends. I had Dorian, Marc, and all the others. I couldn't hurt them like that. I couldn't.

I had to pull myself together. I had to get my thoughts away from killing myself. I couldn't kill myself and yet I feared I might. I thought about my friends. I pictured their faces in my mind. I smiled for a moment when I remembered playing capture the flag at Dane's place. I was happy then and there would surely be such times again even though at the moment I felt I'd never be happy again. I tried to hold onto the images of my friends so I wouldn't do anything crazy.

The few people I was passing either looked at me like I was a freak or looked worried. I fought to calm myself down. Crying my eyes out only served to make me look like a nut case.

I was nearing the park, so I found a remote bench and sat down. I slowly became less hysterical. I sat there starting into nothingness for several minutes. I looked at my watch. It was then I remembered I was supposed to begin a shift at Ofarim's soon. Why should I care? Nothing mattered. Then again, I didn't particularly want to wander around depressed the rest of the day. I stood up and headed for Ofarim's, even as I began sobbing once more.

Dorian

"Dorian, phone," Mom called out.

I hurried into the living room. Perhaps it was Marc. Maybe he wanted to pick up where we'd left off the night before. I grinned. I grabbed the phone.

"Yeah?" I said.

"Dorian, can you come to Ofarim's?" Shawn asked.

"Um, yeah..."

"Scotty is... I don't know. He's messed up. Agnes asked me to stay and cover for him. He showed up for work, but he's just sitting in a booth staring at the table and I can't get him to talk. He's been crying..."

"Messed up? Like beat up or...?"

"No. I think he's okay, physically, but he's a mess. I'm the only one here besides Agnes, so..."

"I'll be right there," I said and hung up.

"Mom! I need a ride. Right now!" I called out.

Mom came out of the kitchen with a question in her eyes.

"Can you take me to Ofarim's right now? Scotty, the friend I told you about, is really upset. Something bad has happened."

Mom nodded and went for her keys. A minute later we were in the car. Five minutes later and we pulled up in front of Ofarim's.

"Thanks, Mom!" I said and then kissed her on the cheek. She smiled at me.

The bells on the door jingled as I entered Ofarim's. Shawn released a sigh of relief when he spotted me. Agnes, the owner, looked relieved too. Scotty was sitting in a booth, staring at nothing while tears flowed down his cheeks. His eyes were red and puffy. He looked just awful.

"Hey, Scotty."

I scooted right in beside him and hugged him to me. His lower lip trembled and he began to sob. I hugged him tighter.

"It's going to be okay, Scotty. I don't know what's happened, but I'm here and you've got friends who will help you."

Scotty shuddered and sobbed some more. I sat there and held him close with one arm wrapped around his shoulder. I reached out with my other hand. Scotty just kept staring at nothing, but he took my hand and held it.

I tried not to imagine all the horrible things that might have happened. Scotty would tell me when he was ready. He looked up as if he didn't know where he was, but then recognized Ofarim's.

"I came to work," he said.

Scotty was freaking me out. He didn't seem at all himself. I wondered if he was on drugs or if he'd been drinking.

"Uh, yeah, but Shawn is here. It's okay. You want to go somewhere more private and talk?" I asked.

Scotty looked at me for the first time. His eyes were red and his face puffy. He nodded. We climbed out of the booth. I looked toward Shawn and Agnes and nodded. Shawn mouthed "thanks."

We walked out into a gorgeous spring day. The daffodils were coming up in the park across the street and everything was becoming green. It was a day to be happy and enjoy life and I was determined I was going to make Scotty happy before the day was over.

We walked in silence at first. Scotty was reluctant to speak, but I knew I had to get him talking to get the pain out of him.

"Have you been drinking or..."

Scotty shook his head.

"No, but I feel like starting to drink, right now."

"So, what happened?"

"I got caught," Scotty said quietly. "My brother caught me with another boy, with Blake York."

"Damn. He's way hot!"

I looked at Scotty. He was staring at the sidewalk as we walked.

"Sorry. I got sidetracked. So, your brother caught the two of you together?"

"I was so stupid. Blake and I hooked up in the VHS parking lot. I don't know what Justin was doing there, but he walked up when Blake and I were in the backseat. Blake was... uh... on top."

"Shit. So Justin saw you?"

"Yeah. Blake got out of the car and ran after Justin, but he couldn't catch him."

"He got out of the car naked or..."

"Naked."

I would have paid to see that! I looked at Scotty and saw the anguished look on his face. It helped me to focus.

"So, then what happened?"

"Blake drove me home. I wanted to get to Justin before he told anyone, but when I walked in there he was. He'd already told our parents."

I walked along by Scotty's side. I didn't pressure him. I just let him talk at his own speed.

"Dad looked at me like he didn't even know me. He was so angry and he looked... hurt."

"Did he... hit you?"

"No. I thought he was going to, but he didn't. He just started in on me. It's all kind of blur, but he kept telling me he couldn't believe what I'd just done. Then he started quoting the Bible, I think."

"It was so humiliating. My brother called me a faggot. Dad told him he wasn't to use that word, but Justin mouthed it to me every chance he got. Mom and Dad started in on me, talking about what I'd done was a sin and an abomination and that if I didn't repent and give up my unnatural ways that I was going to Hell."

Scotty began sobbing all over again. I couldn't even imagine how horrible that must have been for him.

"What if they're right?" Scotty asked.

"About going to Hell?"

He nodded.

"That's complete and utter bullshit," I said. "I don't believe in Hell. No one is bad enough to be punished forever. Even if

71

there is a Hell, it would take a mean and nasty god to send someone there for something he has no control over."

"No one made me blow Blake and no one made me... you know."

"No, but the universe made you gay."

"My parents and my church say being gay is a choice."

"They don't know what they are talking about. It's not a choice. Saying that you decided to like boys is like saying you decided to be white instead of black. There is no choice involved. You are stuck with what you get, like it or not."

"Right now, I don't like it."

"Listen. I won't pretend I know what it's like for you. My parents have always been cool with what I am. I do know how rough it sometimes is to be gay. Verona is a very accepting place, but I still get called fag and homo and a lot of other names and it hurts. Guys trip me or shoulder me and sometimes even threaten to beat me up. Back in my old school I did get beat up a few times—just because I was gay. So, I know it's rough being gay, but you know something? I am gay and I like it. I wouldn't change if I could."

Scotty looked at me.

"You mean that, don't you?"

"I wouldn't say it if I didn't mean it. I'll never lie to you, Scotty, or say something I don't mean just to make you feel good. I know this is hard for you, but remember that you aren't the problem. Being gay isn't the problem. People who don't understand and people who are prejudiced and hateful are the problem."

"It would just be so much easier if I wasn't gay."

"It likely would be, but I'm sure we don't have a monopoly on problems. Everyone has problems and most people aren't gay."

"It still sucks."

"Yeah, it does, but only because of the way other people treat us. There are plenty of good things about it too. In your case, there's Blake York. Marc used to hook up with him before we started dating and he's told me stories. All I can say is, Damn boy!"

72

"He is really, really hot."

"There are a lot of other good things about being gay too. I couldn't be me if I wasn't gay and I like being me!" I said.

"I'm not sure I like being me. I did, but now I just feel like I'm such a disappointment. My parents... I'm starting to remember more of it now... they just kept at me and at me with Bible verses and telling me how disappointed they were in me. I was so humiliated and I couldn't even defend myself. They started in with this "hate the sin, but love the sinner" stuff. Justin was standing there watching just eating it up. His eyes gleamed with delight. Seeing me humiliated was an early Christmas present for him. Maybe they are right. Maybe it is a sin."

"It's not a sin."

"How do you know? Mom and Dad were quoting the Bible..."

"People like your parents twist the Bible to make it say what they want."

"I don't know. I'm not religious like the rest of my family, but... why did God make me gay and then cause religious people to hate me for it? Why does he do that to anyone?"

"I'm not so sure about the whole God thing. I believe there's a god or some god-like force moving things, but I don't think anyone really knows anything about it. Maybe God did make us gay or maybe it just happened, but however it happened, it was meant to be. God doesn't make people hate other people. They do that all on their own. If there is a god I think he or she would want us to take care of each other, not hate each other. Don't listen to all the crap your family is shooting at you. They aren't even following their own beliefs. They aren't Christians, they're anti-Christians."

"It's just hard when everyone around me is telling me I'm wrong."

"I'm not telling you that you're wrong and none of your friends will either. I think your family cares about you in their own messed up way, but they are the ones who are wrong."

We walked along in silence for a while. When we reached VHS we cut around the back and walked out to the soccer fields. We came to the big boulder with a plaque and stopped. We stood there and each of us silently read it.

**THIS FIELD IS DEDICATED
TO THE MEMORY OF
MARK BAILEY AND TAYLOR POTTER.
THEY DIED HERE ALL TOO EARLY
BECAUSE OF HATRED AND INTOLERANCE.
MAY THE FUTURE LEARN FROM WHAT HAPPENED
AND NOT LET IT HAPPEN AGAIN.**

"They were friends of Brandon you know. They were friends of most of our friends," I said.

"Yeah. I know."

"It wasn't being gay that made their lives so hard. It wasn't being gay that killed them. It was the way so many people abused them. Mark and Taylor are the reason things are a lot better for gays here. When they killed themselves a lot of people realized how horrible they had been. They realized that these boys didn't kill themselves. They were killed by all the hatred and abuse hurled at them. This boulder wouldn't be here if a lot of people hadn't realized they were wrong. It wouldn't be here if there weren't people who loved Mark and Taylor. Your parents and everyone like them are wrong about you, Scotty. There is nothing wrong with what you are. The problem rests with them."

We stood there in silence for a few moments and then walked across the soccer fields where Mark and Taylor once played. Now they were gone, dead, because of people like Scotty's parents. I was determined not to let Scotty's family destroy him.

"I have to talk to our pastor tomorrow," Scotty said after a few more moments of silence.

"What's your plan?"

"What do you mean?"

"Are you going to stand your ground or pretend to go along with what he says?"

"I can't stand my ground, Dorian. I know you probably think I'm a coward, but my family is very religious. The church is their life. My brother isn't into it so much, but my parents sure are. How can I sit there and say what they believe is wrong? If I stand up for myself to my pastor that's exactly what I'll be doing."

"I don't think you're a coward, Scotty."

"I wish I was as strong as you."

"As me? Most people think I'm a wussy."

"No one who is fearlessly himself like you are is a wussy."

"I wouldn't say fearlessly. I get scared sometimes. I was scared a lot at my old school, but I was determined to be me and not hide."

"That's what I mean. I've been hiding all my life. You have the guts to be yourself. I don't."

"Well, I don't have parents with a warped religious view."

"I guess that does make a difference."

"It makes a big difference. I like to think I'd still be myself if I had parents like yours, but the truth is I might be hiding too. I can't say for sure. Either way, I do not think you're a coward. You have to protect yourself."

"What if my parents are right? What if it is a sin?"

"They aren't. Think about it. They can't be. God is supposed to love everyone, right?"

"Yeah."

"You didn't choose to be gay?"

"I don't think so."

"Think about it. Did you decide to be gay?"

"No, I didn't decide. It's just... there."

"So, if God loves everyone and you have no choice but to be gay, how could being gay be a sin? Would God screw you over by making something you have no control over a sin?"

"No."

"So there you are."

"I could choose not to act on it."

"Yes, you could, but then you wouldn't be yourself, would you? Sex is a biological need so it's hard to deny. You could force yourself to have sex with girls or never have sex at all, but do you think you would be happy?"

Scotty shook his head.

"It seems to me that if God exists he or she loves everyone and wants them to be happy."

"Makes sense."

"I'm guessing your parents would not react well if you stood up to your pastor?"

"They would be sure I was going straight to Hell. They might kick me out. I don't know. I'm afraid they would. All I know is that things would be very unpleasant for me."

"Well, I think you're doing the best you can then. I can be out because I have parents who support me, but your family doesn't support you. Now isn't the time for you to be out. You can be out when you are no longer dependent on your parents."

"The problem is I am out. Letting Blake do me in his sweet car took care of that."

"True."

"I just don't know if I can get through all this, Dorian. You don't know what it's like at my house. I was only in the living room with my parents going off on me for maybe twenty minutes, but it felt like an eternity. My dad prayed for me, but in his prayer Dad asked God to help me overcome my unnatural and perverted lust. My parents are always saying they don't judge, but that's exactly what they did. They judged me."

"It's called hypocrisy."

"It's so messed up. My whole family acts like I went out and shot up a grade school."

"Don't forget the most important point. There is nothing to forgive because you did nothing wrong. They are the ones who should be seeking your forgiveness and perhaps God's forgiveness as well."

"I think they believe they're doing the right thing. They really believe I've chosen to do something horrible."

"I think that's the problem with religion. People get lost in all the writings and the preaching and forget to just listen to their heart. They forget to be kind and understanding."

"I wish my parents believed like you, Dorian."

We slipped into silence again. Scotty wasn't sobbing anymore, but he looked so very sad. I wished I could make everything okay for him, but he had some rough times ahead.

We left the soccer fields and walked onto the paths that led through the woods. The whole forest was surging with green life.

"Thanks, Dorian. Talking about this makes me feel better, even if it doesn't solve anything."

"I don't think there is an easy solution. You've just got to hang in there and keep going. The important thing to remember is that you have friends who will help you through this. You aren't alone. If things get really bad you can stay with me, or Marc, or with the Selby's. You have lots of friends to talk to about everything that's bothering you. You aren't alone, Scotty."

"That's why I didn't do it," Scotty said fearfully.

"Do what?" I asked, although I feared I knew the answer.

"I thought about killing myself. I hurt so bad inside and everything seemed so hopeless that it felt like killing myself was the only way out. The only reason I didn't do it was because I knew I had friends who would help me. I guess that's why I showed up at Ofarim's, even though I was in no shape to work. I think a part of me knew Shawn would help me."

"I'm glad you didn't kill yourself, Scotty. There are a lot of people who care about you. I care about you. If you killed yourself... I can't even describe how that would tear me up and I wouldn't be the only one. I wasn't around when Mark and Taylor killed themselves, but Shawn told me it almost destroyed Brandon. He's still messed up about it."

"I was here," Scotty said quietly. "I guess there was more than one reason I didn't do it. I didn't want to hurt anyone and, even while I was completely losing it, I thought about hanging out at Dane's. I had so much fun and I felt so at ease. I could just be me and it felt good. I held onto that. I wanted to feel that again so I held onto those memories hoping that I could someday feel that way again."

"You will, Scotty. We're your friends and that isn't going to change. I know I can speak for all the others in this. We will always be here for you and we'll help you in any way we can. There will be more good times, Scotty. I know it's hard to see that now, but there will be."

77

"I feel like my whole life is over," Scotty said. He began to sob again.

"It's not. Your life is just beginning. It isn't over because you aren't going to give up. You aren't going to give in. We won't let you."

"Thanks," Scotty said, wiping his eyes. "I'm sorry for crying. It's just that I feel so bad."

"Don't apologize. You should cry. Crying makes you feel better and there's nothing wrong with it. Everyone cries."

"I don't know what I'm going to do, Dorian. I don't want to go home, but I have to."

"You can stay with my family, Scotty."

"No. That would only stir up more trouble. If things get really, really bad, then yeah, I may come running to your door, but for now at least, I have to go home."

"If you do come running to my door, you know that door will be opened and you'll be welcome inside."

"Thanks, Dorian."

"You know, you said earlier that you didn't have courage, but you do. If you didn't, you'd run away."

"I did run away."

"You ran out of the house. You didn't run away."

"I don't want to go to church tomorrow and I sure don't want to talk to the pastor. I don't want to deal with my parents. I don't want them looking at me like I'm a criminal. My life sucks."

"Life sucks sometimes and this is one of those times, but it will get better. This is the worst of it, or at least nearly the worst. Things will get better, Scotty. It may not happen soon. Maybe things will be rough until you start college. I don't know when things will get better, but they will. Until then, you've got me. You've got Brandon and Jon and Shawn and Tristan and all the others. You can come and cry on my shoulder anytime. I'll always be here when you need to talk or when you just need someone to be with. It doesn't matter what time of the day or night, call me and I'll come."

"What did I do to deserve such a good friend? We didn't even know each other very well before last fall."

"We know each other now. We're friends and friends are there for each other, no matter what."

"Thanks, Dorian."

I pulled Scotty to me and hugged him tight. He held on and hugged me back. We just stood there in the forest, hugging each other.

Scotty and I walked the paths and talked. I even got him to laugh once while we were talking about Brandon and Jon and how they go off on each other. I talked about how wonderful it was to have a boyfriend and how someday Scotty would have a boyfriend too. Scotty told me about sex with Blake and it made me want to run straight to Marc and get it on. We talked about the play and acting and a whole lot of other things.

When Scotty was ready, I walked him back home. We stopped at the end of his block and Scotty looked up the street to his house. He took a deep breath and let it out.

"You can do this, Scotty. Remember, you aren't alone. We're all here for you and we aren't going anywhere."

Scotty smiled at me for a moment and then his face became sat in grim determination.

"Thanks, Dorian. I'll see you at school on Monday?"

"You know it and if you need me before then I'm only a phone call away. I mean it. Any time of the day or night."

"Thank you."

Scotty turned, squared his shoulders, and walked toward home. I stood there and watched him until he turned and walked inside. I remained there a few moments more, just in case, but Scotty was stronger than he thought he was. He could get through this and we were all going to help him.

Scotty

Supper on Saturday night was closer to normal than I expected. Mom called me down about six and I joined the rest of the family at the dining room table. I expected the prayer to be focused on me, but instead it was a standard prayer of thanks for our food.

Justin was more than usually polite to me, which meant Mom or Dad had talked with him. I could tell it was fake politeness. Justin and I had always gotten along fairly well, but we weren't especially close and we didn't go out of our way to be nice to each other. Justin wasn't known for kindness where I was concerned. He wasn't outright mean, but he certainly wasn't my best pal. Now that he knew I was gay he'd gone cold. I could read distaste and maybe even a little hatred in his eyes. Hatred might be too strong a word for it, but my brother didn't like me anymore.

I tried to do some homework before bed, but it's hard to concentrate when an unpleasant event is just ahead. I wished I could skip over Sunday completely, but that wasn't an option. I couldn't even keep my mind on the Eleanor Roosevelt book I was reading.

Justin came into the room a little before eleven and began undressing like always. I glanced up as he pulled his shirt off.

"Don't look at me and don't be coming over to my bed in the night while I'm sleeping."

I shot Justin a look that told him I thought he was an idiot.

"Don't flatter yourself."

"I heard Mom and Dad talking. If you don't shape up they might send you away."

"Yeah, right," I said, using every ounce of acting ability I had to hide my fear.

What if they did send me away to one of those treatment places? Brendan had been sent to one, but he'd escaped. I hadn't heard many details, but I knew such places were downright evil.

"It's up to you. If you want to stop being a pervert you can stay here, although I wouldn't mind you going. I'd have a room to myself."

"Thanks for your concern. Now shut up and go to sleep."

Justin stripped down to his boxers and climbed into bed.

"Goodnight, faggot."

"Dad told you not to use that word."

"It's what you are. I saw what you were doing. It's disgusting."

"Shut up, Justin, or I'll smother you in your sleep. I have nothing to lose now."

I put just enough menace into my voice to make Justin wonder. He turned away from me and left me alone.

I prepared for bed soon after, but I couldn't sleep. I just lay there and thought about what was going to happen the next day. I dreaded Sunday as I never had before. I didn't know if I could make it though the day. I was going to be surrounded by prejudiced bigots who claimed the moral high ground even while they wallowed in immorality.

I was so glad I'd talked to Dorian. He helped me understand things better. I didn't feel perverted or evil. When I was with Blake I felt like I was doing what I was supposed to be doing. I know there's a lot more to life than sex. I'd only had sex once in seventeen years so there had to be more. Sex with Blake just felt right. It was an intimate, shared experience. It felt natural.

Maybe I shouldn't have hooked up with someone I didn't care about. I might have done wrong there, but was sex outside of a relationship really a bad thing? My church preached that any sex outside of marriage was a sin, but that was an old-fashioned idea that was pretty much ignored even in the old days. I bet my brother wouldn't hesitate to do a girl if he got the chance. When I was with Blake we were satisfying a mutual, physical need. That was a relationship in itself. I needed what we'd done. I'd needed it for a long time. Blake pressured me into going further than I'd planned and I'd given in, but even that was okay. In hindsight I should have made him wear a condom. If Blake had some sexually transmitted disease I'd end up with it too. Great, that's just what I needed; something else to worry about.

I thought about what Blake and I had done together. It had felt soo good. I wondered what it would have been like to finish. Next time, I'd find out and next time I'd be smart enough to make

Blake wear a condom. If he protested I'd just tell him he had to wear one or he couldn't do me.

I wondered if there would be a next time. My parents knew I was gay so now I'd be watched extra close. I'd find a way. It might take a long time for an opportunity to present itself, but I'd waited seventeen years for my first time so surely I could be patient. I knew Blake now, too. That was a huge advantage. I was willing to bet he'd come to Ofarim's looking for me. He'd want some more. When he came, we'd find a way.

I drifted off and was untroubled by dreams, which surprised me. I feared I'd have nightmares about church or being sent away to be tortured.

My sleep was untroubled, but the moment I opened my eyes the next morning I was aware of what lie ahead. I did not want to get out of bed, but I knew I had no choice. As I showered and dressed in my Sunday clothes I tried not to think about what was going to happen later.

I ate my scrambled eggs, toast, and bacon without giving any outward sign I wanted to bolt for the door and just keep on running. I drank my juice, concentrating on the tangy orange flavor. I tried to lose myself as completely as possible in all the little details of breakfast, from the taste of the pepper on my eggs to the sweetness of the blackberry jam I spread on my toast. I just hoped I could get through the service without throwing up.

I wondered if condemned men walking toward the gallows felt as I did as I rode with my family to church. I grew more edgy and fearful as we walked up the steps and into the church. I felt like a vampire who had just been found out by the villagers. I was just waiting for them to pull stakes from their shirts and pounce on me.

Devon Devlin glared at me from the pew where he sat with his parents. His expression was one of hatred. He knew. I wasn't sure how, but he knew. I wondered how many others in the church knew I was a homo. The sense of being trapped by my enemies increased. I began to breathe a little harder and felt panicky. Then, I heard Dorian's voice in my head telling me that my accusers were the ones who were wrong, that those who called me an abomination were the ones committing the sin. I calmed down a little, but being in the right might not help me. All the people who were tortured and killed for being witches were innocent, but they'd still died in agony. Being right didn't mean I was safe.

You have friends who care about you. We're here for you. You are not alone.

Dorian's voice spoke out more clearly in my mind. I smiled. I did have friends. They understood me. They cared about me. My biological family wasn't there to support me, but I had another family, one that truly understood and cared.

The service began with a hymn. That wasn't so bad, but then the pastor began his sermon. Sodom and Gomorrah. What a surprise. The pastor kept looking at me as he spoke and I could feel my family gazing at me too. Devon kept looking over at me with a disgusted look on his face.

Next, the pastor moved on to a talk about helping those who had stumbled. He spoke of vigilance against sin. He said we all have to keep an eye on each other and do whatever was necessary to bring sinful acts to the attention of the congregation to save the soul of the sinner. I grew increasingly uncomfortable as the pastor announced that a member of the congregation had recently been caught performing an immoral act. I looked over at my brother. His chest was puffed out. He was so pleased with himself. I wanted to punch him in the face.

My heart beat faster and my breath quicken its pace as the pastor told the congregation that one among us needed watching over for his own sake. My face turned pale as he asked me to stand up.

I could not believe this was happening. Everyone was looking at me. The sense of panic I'd felt before increased a hundred-fold. I wanted nothing more than to bolt from the church.

The pastor didn't spell out what I'd done, but he said everyone had to watch over me and help me to return to the path of righteousness. I knew what that meant. All the busybodies of the church would be spying on me. I wouldn't be able to go anywhere without someone watching. I looked toward Devon. He was grinning at me with a wicked gleam in his eyes.

I could feel judgmental eyes boring into me from every direction. I could hear my family stirring uncomfortably, but everyone was staring at me. I despised the expressions on the faces around me; self-satisfied smirks, holier-than-thou haughtiness, and everywhere hypocritical, judgmental stares. The congregation loved nothing better than one of their own to fall. They were just waiting to feed upon the carcass. Well, I wasn't one of them. I never had been. Even if I had never suspected before what a wicked lot they were I would have known it without a doubt as I stood there with them all staring at me. I wanted to shout at them and tell them what hypocrites they were, but I didn't dare.

I was allowed to sit and more preaching followed. Some of it was about the terrors of Hell. Some was about the importance of forgiveness. All of it was aimed at me. It was "for my benefit," but the sermon's real purpose was singling me out and allowing everyone to talk about me. Dorian was right. The members of my church were Anti-Christians.

When the service was over all kinds of people rushed up to my parents outside, saying a bunch of crap about how they admired their courage and what good Christians they were for taking the difficult path and not just ignoring my immoral behavior. What they were really saying was, "Thanks for giving us someone to judge and to trash while we pretend we're not prejudiced, immoral assholes."

Justin looked uncomfortable as Devon neared. After shooting me a look of disgust, Devon approached my brother and commiserated with him on his misfortune. I knew exactly what Devon meant. He was sorry for my brother because Justin had a faggot in the family.

As everyone left, including my parents, I was dragged into the pastor's private office. I looked around nervously, half-fearing that he might try to molest me. I knew a lot of that went on in some churches. I told myself I was being ridiculous. Maybe a lot of molesting did go on, but it didn't happen everywhere and probably wouldn't here. I'd know one way or another soon.

"You're a very luck boy," my pastor said.

"Lucky?"

"To have a family that cares about you so much. Your brother could have taken the easy path and kept what he saw to himself, but instead he thought of your welfare and told your parents so you could get the help you need."

Yeah, right. Justin was thinking about my welfare and not the chance to trash me and make himself look better.

"I don't think I would have agreed with you yesterday, but I've had time to think and you are right," I said. I was an actor. I could lie just as well as anyone else in my church.

"That is a refreshing attitude. Most boys in your position get defensive."

"Well... I'm here to talk about... what happened, right?"

"You're here to talk about how to resist your unnatural urges, get yourself back on track, and walk in the ways of the Lord."

"Exactly, but... when... what happened happened... it felt wrong. I wanted to do it at first, but then I didn't. It felt unnatural like you said. I wanted to stop, but I was afraid."

"Afraid of what?"

"That the boy who had lured me into temptation might hurt me. I don't know how much my parents told you, but I didn't want to do what we were doing. I'll admit I was curious and wanted to explore, but he... he took things way too far. I resisted, but he was a lot stronger than me."

"Are you saying you were forced?"

"Not exactly. I'm not trying to lay the blame for what I did on someone else. It's just that certain things happened that I didn't want to happen. I was too big of a coward to stand up for myself and try to make him stop."

"I think anyone would be frightened in such circumstances. You fell into the hands of a predator. Such vile people are in league with Satan. Don't be too hard on yourself. Satan has many ways to come at you."

"When my brother found us I was angry because I felt so humiliated and yet he saved me. The other boy stopped when Justin saw what he was doing to me."

"You're very lucky to have such a fine, courageous brother."

"Yes, sir."

I wondered if I'd make it out of that office without choking on my own insincerity.

"I see that Satan does not have as strong a hold on you as I feared. Make no mistake, though, Scotty, you are still in great danger. He will tempt you again."

"I understand."

"One thing that will help is to think about your family and the lengths they are going to in order to help you. Also, stop and think, what would Jesus do?"

Call you a hypocrite and toss you out of your own church? I managed to think without cracking a smile.

"If you begin thinking unnatural thoughts, cold showers will help, as will reading the Bible. When tempted, think about how your family will feel if you give into temptation.

"I've made a list of passages for you to read. I want you to study them," said the pastor as he pushed a list toward me. I took it and held it as if it was a lifeline.

The pastor then prayed for me as I sat there. I didn't agree with the things he was telling me and I thought he was a hypocrite, but he wasn't all bad either. I think that in his own twisted way he did care. I wondered how he'd become so warped. I wondered how he'd lost his way. I wondered if he'd ever realize he was the one who truly needed help. I went into his office disgusted by him, but I found myself feeling sorry for him.

"I must say I am very pleased that you're so willing to cooperate. I was expecting a great battle with Satan, but his hold on you is weak. You are still in danger, but I have high hopes for you."

"Thank you, sir."

That was it. The ordeal was over. I felt like a big old hypocrite myself for saying so many things I didn't believe, but if I said what I really thought I'd either be out on the street or in one of those horrible institutions where they tried to "fix" gay kids. I'd lied for sure, but it was for self-preservation.

I walked home feeling a good deal better. Maybe I could just lay low and get through the rest of high school. It wouldn't be easy and I wouldn't be able to live the life I wanted, but at least I'd have a home and not have to worry about being tortured in the name of curing me. I wasn't happy. My life sucked. The rest of my high school years would be an ordeal, but I did have friends and I had the play. I was going to have to hold onto the good things if I was going to survive. I wouldn't allow myself to become a suicide statistic. I wouldn't hurt my friends by killing myself. I was going to get through this somehow. Once I went away to college, I could begin to become myself. Until then, I'd just have to hide.

My dad nodded at me when I entered the house. When I went into the kitchen Mom hugged me. I knew then the pastor had called and given his report. I felt like a fake accepting a hug from Mom for something I didn't do, but didn't I deserve a hug anyway? She should have been hugging me and apologizing for all I'd been put through since Justin opened his big mouth and ratted me out. I forced my anger down for the moment. Suppressing it wasn't good, but now was not the time. I'd get it out later. Maybe I could attack a punching bag in the gym at school tomorrow. It wouldn't be as satisfying as punching Justin in the face, but it would have to do. I smiled at the mental image of decking Justin. Mom mussed my hair.

"See, it's going to be okay."

I nodded and headed for my room.

"So, the pastor and Mom and Dad bought your act, huh?" Justin said.

"What act?"

"Oh please. Don't act like you aren't going to go out and do the same thing all over again. You're a homo and you're going to stay a homo."

"I thought you said I chose to be gay. If I did, then I can choose to not be gay, right?"

"Oh, you chose it or someone made you gay, but you're not going to choose not to be gay. You like it too much."

"What does that mean?"

"I heard you moaning when that guy was doing you."

"How long did you watch? You're a pervert, you know that?"

"You're the pervert! I didn't watch long. Who would want to see that?"

"Apparently you."

Justin was getting angry and frustrated. I loved it.

"I'm not the pervert! You are! You're a faggot!"

"Say it a little louder and maybe Dad will hear you."

Justin fearfully jerked his head in the direction of the open door, but there was no sign of either of our parents coming our way.

"You have them fooled, but not me. Devon came and talked to me after church. Do you know how embarrassing that was? He knows I have a homo for a brother. He said that no matter what you say you won't change. He said we'd have to watch you."

"Devon is just a busybody that likes to get into other people's business and he hates gays."

"Ha! So you admit what you are!"

I knew I'd slipped up.

"I didn't say I was gay, but Devon thinks I am, so he hates me."

"Well, he said he was going to talk to the other kids from church who go to VHS and they're all going to watch you."

"I bet you'll be glad to help them, won't you?"

"Believe it or not, Scotty, I'm doing it for you."

"Bull."

Justin looked just enough hurt that I wondered if maybe he really did think he was looking out for me. Either way, he was certainly enjoying my predicament.

"Just mind your own business," I said.

The atmosphere in our shared bedroom was a lot cooler after that. Did Justin really think he was helping me by spying on me? Did my parents really think they were being there for me as parents should? I'd just been through a horrible ordeal, courtesy of my family, and yet I felt that in their own twisted way they thought they were doing the right thing. Things might have been easier if could just hate them, but I didn't hate them and they didn't hate me. Man, my life was a warped mess.

Dorian

I didn't have to tell the guys about Scotty's troubles. When I walked into school on Monday morning it was obvious that everyone knew Scotty was a homo. The rumor mill was working overtime. I spotted Scotty at his locker. He looked like he wanted to crawl inside. I poked Marc in the shoulder and nodded toward Scotty. We walked toward him.

Scotty stiffened at the sound of our approach, but relaxed when he turned around and spotted us. He looked horrible. There were dark patches under his eyes. His face was puffy and his eyes red.

"Everyone is looking at me," Scotty said. "They *know*. I thought maybe I was going to be okay after yesterday, but this is so hard."

Devon spotted Scotty. He shook his head in disgust. I moved in front of Scotty. He didn't need any of Devon's crap. Devon suddenly looked uncomfortable and angled away. I was all ready to congratulate myself on scaring him away when I heard Brandon's voice behind me. It figured. I wasn't exactly a frightening presence.

"We've got your back, Scotty," Brandon said.

I turned. Jon was standing beside Brandon. I loved those guys! They weren't gay, but they were always looking out for anyone who was getting picked on.

"I don't know if I can do this," Scotty said. "Everyone is talking about me. I know what they're all thinking."

"Wow, don't we think we're the center of universe?" Jon teased. "Listen, a lot of people are going to be talking about you until the next juicy bit of gossip comes along, but they aren't all talking about you, not even close. You just think they are."

"It's still bad enough."

"That's where your friends come in," Marc said. "We know what it's like. Most of us have been victims of the rumor mill. Look at the bright side. You can sit with us at lunch now."

Scotty shook his head.

"I can't. My brother might see me. He'll tell Mom and Dad. The kids from my church are going to spy on me to see if I do anything gay."

"Why don't Marc and I walk you to class?" I suggested. "Since you are still in the play we'll just talk about the upcoming performance if your brother or any other unfriendlies gets near."

Scotty nodded. I felt so sorry for him. He was so frightened.

"Later, Scotty," Brandon and Jon said.

"So... I guess things have not been going so well," I said.

"Church was a nightmare. The sermon was on Sodom and Gomorrah and the evils of homosexuality."

"Seriously?" Marc asked.

Scotty nodded.

"I'm sure my parents put the pastor up to it. It was horrible. He kept looking at me during the sermon. Justin kept looking at me too and grinning. I wanted to punch him in the mouth.

"I had to sit through an hour and a half of serious homo bashing and as if that wasn't enough the pastor made me stand up and asked everyone to help me resist temptation."

"Dude, I'm so sorry," Marc said.

"After church, I had to meet with the pastor. That didn't go too bad since I pretended to agree with what he said. The worst part was having to lie and not being able to defend myself.

"Attending church was so embarrassing and humiliating and it's never going to change. Now that I'm pretending that I agree with them, my parents aren't too bad, but Justin is a prick. I feel like a total fake around my parents. I'm pretending to be this whole other person. I hate it. I hate being forced to lie. I hate not being able to be myself in my own home! Now, everyone at school knows about me. Everywhere I go I feel like I'm under a microscope."

"The situation will be better in drama class and play practice," I said.

"Yeah, but even there everyone will know I'm a homo."

"You'll get used to that," Marc said. "Being out at VHS isn't so bad. Sure, a lot of people are talking about you now, but only because they didn't know you were gay. You're news now, but in a couple of days you won't be. No one talks about Dorian or me."

"Unless we do something homo-spectacular!" I said.

Scotty grinned for just a moment.

"I don't like them knowing about me and about what I did."

"You aren't the first guy to give head," Marc said. "There are several gay boys in VHS and don't forget a lot of the girls we are walking past right now have given head too. I did just yesterday and so did Dorian."

I grinned and lost myself for a few moments in pleasant memories.

"Mmm, yeah. What my incredibly cute and sexy boyfriend is trying to say is that you aren't alone. Being out is the hardest at the very beginning, but it gets much easier."

"I did more than give head. Blake and I went all the way," Scotty said.

"You aren't the first guy to do that either," I said, and then giggled. Scotty smiled for a moment, but only for a moment.

"It's almost a relief in a way," Scotty said. "I don't feel like I have this huge secret anymore."

"You can start to be yourself now," Marc said.

"Maybe a little in drama class and during play practice, but not at home, not at church, and not around anyone who goes to my church. I know Devon has put the kids who go to my church up to spying on me."

"It would be nice if Devon would mind his own business for once," Marc said.

"You can forget that. He will be watching me every chance he gets. I've got to watch my step. My parents aren't stupid. I've been telling them what they want to hear and acting as if I regret what happened with Blake, but they'll catch on to the fact it's all an act if I'm not careful. If that happens... I don't even want to think about it. Here's my class. Thanks for walking with me, guys."

Scotty took a deep breath and then walked through the doorway. He was in for a rough day.

"How long do you think he can keep up his act?" I asked.

"I don't know, but even if he can keep it up he'll crack under the pressure sooner or later. Just think about it. He can't be himself. He has to keep his guard up all the time. He has to not only completely hide an important part of himself, but also pretend to completely reject that whole way of life. He has to act against his own nature. Think about what that would be like. How can he possibly be happy? How can he feel good about himself?"

"He shouldn't have to pretend to be something he's not."

"No. He shouldn't, but he doesn't have much of a choice."

"I wish there was more we could do to help him," I said.

"Maybe the guys can help us figure something out at lunch. One thing we can do is keeping doing what we've been doing— remind him that he has friends who care and that he isn't alone."

"Yeah. He is alone at church, though. Can you image what it would be like to sit there and have a sermon preached *at* you while everyone around you is nodding their heads in agreement?"

"I think that would make anyone want to crawl under a pew and hide."

"He's alone at home too," I said. "I don't know if I could handle that."

We didn't have time for more talk. Marc gave me a quick peck on the lips and then we went to our separate classes.

I thought on the problem all through morning classes, but didn't come up with any solutions. I wished Scotty would sit with us at lunch. We could protect him from all the whispers and stares if he was at our table.

I was hungry by the time lunch rolled around. The baked ham and scalloped potatoes smelled great, as did the biscuit. I was hungry enough that even the green beans smelled good.

Marc and I walked through the line together and joined those who were already seated. The only members of the gang missing were Brandon and Jon and they soon appeared—with Scotty walking between them!

Brandon and Jon didn't take their usual places. They both sat on the same side of the table. Scotty looked about uncomfortably as he sat down between them.

"Scotty, I'm so glad you're sitting with us," I said with a grin.

"Brandon and Jon convinced me."

"Yeah, we told him he could sit between us. We're kind of a homo-buffer," Jon said.

Shawn stuck out his tongue at Jon.

"We also had a little talk with Justin," Brandon said, cracking his knuckles.

"A talk?" Dane asked. "You guys didn't beat him up, did you?"

"No. We just threatened to beat him up if he told his parents Scotty is sitting with us," Brandon said.

"Are you sure he won't tell?" Scotty asked.

"He's not going to tell," Jon said.

"He won't say a word," Tim said, then laughed. "Brandon and Jon can scare the crap out of anyone when they're in bad-ass mode. They make Devon cry."

"Like that's difficult," Brandon said, "but Tim is right. We are quite the intimidating pair."

I laughed.

"What about Devon?" Scotty asked.

"Devon is under control," Brandon said.

"I still don't know if this is a good idea. Kids from my church will see me."

"They will see you sitting with us," Brandon said. "This little part of the table is hetero territory."

"I don't know. Sitting here makes me feel uncomfortable. Maybe I'm being paranoid, but what if word gets back to my parents that I'm sitting with the gay boys."

"First of all, Jon and I are not gay," Brandon said.

"And we're not all boys!" Casey added.

"True, although confusing Casey for a boy is an easy mistake to make," Brandon said.

"Don't make me kick your butt, Brandon Hanson."

"Oh, I think we're seeing a little latent heterosexuality here." Brandon turned to Scotty. "She secretly wants me."

95

"Keep fantasizing!" Casey said.

"Second, you aren't sitting with the gay boys. You are sitting with your fellow cast members. There's Dorian, drama-queen extraordinaire, as well at three other cast members of, well, shall we say... varying talents."

"Don't you love how he manages to insult us even while he's being helpful?" Dane asked.

"It's one of my talents," Brandon said. "My point is that, although this is the homo table, it's also the drama table and not everyone who sits here is gay. You are sitting here to be with your cast mates as well as Jon, and me."

"I don't know how much that will help," Scotty said. "I still think this is a bad idea."

"Your brother will back you up," Brandon said.

"Unless he wants his face rearranged and when we spoke to him I got the feeling that is not what he wanted," Jon said.

"Ah, acceptance through violence," Shawn said.

"Crude, but effective," Brandon said.

Scotty was uneasy so we surrounded him with conversation about the play and any and everything else we could think of to talk about. It wasn't hard. Our table was usually filled with conversation. I noticed Brandon and Jon didn't cut each other down with homo-innuendo like they often did, but they still managed to keep all of us, and most importantly Scotty, entertained.

When lunch ended, Brandon and Jon walked with Scotty to dump his tray. It furthered the illusion that Scotty was with them instead of the gay boys. It also provided Scotty with two bodyguards. I didn't think anyone would jump Scotty, but sometimes words can hurt as much as fists.

I spotted Scotty once between classes while I was walking with Marc, but couldn't get at him across the crowded hallway.

"He looks nervous and tired," Marc said, following my gaze.

"I wish he could have supportive parents like mine. This is entirely his parent's fault! Why can't they just accept him? Don't they realize how horrible they are being to him? How can they be cruel enough to have their pastor preach a sermon directly attacking Scotty?!"

96

"They mean well, even Scotty said so."

"Yeah, but it's all so screwed up! Scotty's parents, his brother, his pastor, his church... they should all be supporting him. They should all be part of the solution. Instead, they're the problem!"

"I don't think they know they are being cruel or if they know they think it's for Scotty's own good."

"I've got a good mind to give them all a piece of my mind! I should march up to his parents and let them have it, then to go his church, stand up, and let them all have it!"

Marc began laughing.

"What?"

"I was picturing you doing just that."

"I guess it wouldn't help, but it would feel so good."

"I'm sure it would feel good, but it would probably make the situation much worse."

"It's still a good fantasy."

"I have some better ones."

"Yeah?"

"I have one that involves you, me, and the boys' locker room."

"You're just trying to distract me," I said.

"Is it working?"

"Yes, tell me more..."

***

"What are you smiling about?" Marc asked as we entered the auditorium for our last period drama class.

"Look at Trent," I said, then began acting as if I was narrating a nature documentary. "Notice how the straight male draws his mate closer when he suddenly finds himself surrounded by gays. This particular hetero, while generally accepting, has just been agitated by the discovery that yet another of the males around him bats for the other team."

97

"Not bad," Marc said. "Maybe you can be a narrator as well as an actor."

"I think he's freaking out because he's found out Scotty is gay. He probably feels more outnumbered than ever."

"There are a lot of gays involved with theatre."

"There are only five gay guys involved with this play. Most of the cast is straight. Of course, the heteros desperately need us to make the play fabulous!"

Trent noticed us watching him and grew a little more uncomfortable. I waved, winked, and blew him a kiss.

"You really should stop tormenting him," Marc said.

"He knows I'm just playing with him. I do have a boyfriend and his girlfriend is one of my best girl friends. Besides, it's too much fun to stop."

Marc and I joined the others milling in the front of the auditorium.

"Hi, Tess," I said, stepping in beside Trent. I slipped my arm over his shoulder and he just as quickly slipped away. I grinned and Marc punched me lightly in the shoulder.

Scotty joined us, so I put my arm around his shoulder. He didn't pull away. He would have anywhere else, but the auditorium was our world.

"I should have known you were gay, Scotty. All the really pretty boys are," Tess said.

Trent shifted from one foot to the other and scowled. I grinned. He was jealous!

"It is true isn't it?" Tess asked.

"This can't go beyond us, but yeah. I am gay, but most of the rumors flying around about me aren't true."

Marc opened his mouth, but then closed it. I could tell he was about to tease Scotty, but then decided he'd better not. Scotty was blushing. Saying he was gay out loud wasn't easy for him, even in such an accepting group.

"I never believe most of the rumors, unless they're about Marc and Dorian." Tess winked at us.

"Oh, the rumors about us are always true," Marc said.

"So you did do the entire soccer team last season then?" Tess asked and then giggled.

"Oh yeah. Your boyfriend was the first in line."

"Hey!" Trent yelled.

"I'm just kidding," Marc said. "You know I am."

"Yeah, but..."

"Okay, Trent wasn't the first in line, but he did keep coming back for more."

"Dude! Stop! This is how rumors get started."

"Leave Trent alone, Marc. Besides, he's my toy," I said.

Trent was turning red.

"Okay. Okay. Sorry, Trent. We all know you're a hetero stud and I, for one, admire your courage in joining the cast when you knew it would make others question your sexual orientation," Marc said.

I pinched Marc's butt and he jumped. I wasn't the "punch in the shoulder" type.

"What have you heard?" Trent asked.

"Don't be so insecure," Tess said. "Everyone knows you're my boyfriend."

Tess leaned toward Trent and he gave her a lingering kiss.

"Eww, what a disgusting heterosexual display," Dane said as he and Tim joined us.

"It does seem only fair, after all the homo displays Tim and you put on," Marc pointed out.

"You mean like this?" Dane said and then kissed Tim deeply.

Mrs. Cook cleared her throat as she stepped to the front of the auditorium. The two couples quickly pulled apart and we all took our seats. Mrs. Cook was cool and not a big stickler on rules, but we could only go so far. Besides, everyone loved Mrs. Cook. I don't think she ever had trouble with a class. Everyone wanted to please her.

We worked first on the last scene, where Willy Wonka gives his chocolate factory to Charlie. Scotty was brilliant. He really lost himself in his part. I couldn't tell he had any problems as I stood on the stage with him. I wondered for a moment if that wasn't one reason so many gays were involved with theatre. The stage offered the opportunity to become someone else and forget about your troubles. Maybe that was one of the reasons I loved it so, but mostly I just loved to show off!

Marc did the same scene with me next. He was Scotty's understudy and since Charlie was a major role Marc had to have the part down, just in case. Mrs. Cook worked with Charlie and his grandparents while Marc and I ran through our scene. Marc was an excellent actor. I hoped that someday he'd get a role and we could act on stage together, but I guess that wasn't likely. This was our senior year and my last high school play. I seriously doubted Marc would take a drama class in college. Maybe we'd never appear in front of an audience together, but we did have an occasional practice together and that was enough.

Class was over before we knew it and those of us returning for play practice took a short break while the others went home. Trent disappeared with Tess; probably fearful we'd tease him some more. Tim and Dane disappeared too, no doubt to make out. Scotty joined Marc and me. He seemed happier than he had all day.

Scotty stiffened and I didn't know why. I looked at him with a question in my eyes.

"Those kids go to my church," he said.

I followed my gaze to a girl and two boys who were looking at us as they headed for the back doors.

"You'll get the lines down, Scotty. You know you will," Marc said loudly enough the spies could hear.

I felt like marching over and telling the trio to mind their own business, but Marc's approach was better. In moments the busybodies exited the back doors and were gone. Scotty relaxed immediately.

It was soon back to practice. I returned to being Willy Wonka and Scotty once again became Charlie. For the next two hours I saw Scotty as he should be; relaxed and happy. He even laughed. I wished the rest of his life could be like the few precious hours he spent inside the auditorium each day.

***

Scotty sat with us each day at lunch, always between Brandon and Jon. He grew more at ease and even laughed when Brandon and Jon went off on each other. He stiffened and grew silent at times when a kid who attended his church was near. Justin walked by once and shot his brother a disapproving look, but Brandon glared at him and Justin scurried off.

It was in drama and during play practices that Scotty truly came alive. It was then that we all got a glimpse of the life Scotty could live. For that short space of time all the weight was lifted off his shoulders and he was truly happy. Between his drama activities and eating lunch with us Scotty's life had improved. I began to hope that everything might work out for him after all.

Scotty

I knew I was in trouble as soon as I walked in the door. Dad scowled at me. He pointed to the spot next to him on the couch.

"Sit."

I did as I was told and looked at him questioningly.

"It has come to my attention that you have been hanging out with a group of boys at school who participate in immoral acts."

"Huh?"

"You have been hanging out with homosexuals."

"I don't understand."

"Aren't several of the boys you sit with at lunch homosexual?"

"Oh, that! I sit with Brandon and Jon. They are really cool and they aren't homosexual. They're both on the soccer team."

"Who else sits there?"

"There are four guys who are in the play with me."

"I've been told they are homosexuals."

"They might be. I don't know. All I discuss with them is play related stuff. I've heard rumors about then, but I don't know if the rumors are true or not. I'm careful. I always sit between Brandon and Jon, just to be safe."

I was beginning to sweat. I wasn't sure Dad was buying it.

"Your mother and I are very concerned about the company you keep and I'm concerned about your participation in the play. I think there are far too many homosexuals involved."

"There might be one or two in the cast, but I'm sure most of them are straight. Trent Blackwell is in the cast and so is his girlfriend, Tess."

"Your mother and I disagree on this, but I don't think you should continue to participate in the play."

"I have a lead role. I can't quit so close to the performances. A lot of people have put in a lot of work. I would be letting them all down. I made a commitment. You told me it's important to keep my word."

"Perhaps, but you are fighting a difficult fight and I don't want you near temptation."

"The world is filled with temptation. I can't avoid it all. If I walk out of the play now I might fail my drama class and that will blow my G.P.A. I'm up for some scholarships and if my grades go down I won't stand a chance."

"I don't want you sitting with those boys at lunch."

"Dad, please!"

"That's final. You will not sit with those boys. If your friends, Brandon and Jon, want to sit elsewhere with you, that's fine, but I do not want you near those perverts."

I had to fight to keep from crying. Little by little my entire life was being taken away from me. Now, I couldn't sit with my friends. Lunch was one of the few times during the day I didn't feel alone.

"What about the play?" I asked.

"I'm not happy about your participation in the play, but you have made a commitment. You can continue. I want you to stay away from those who might lead you astray. You are to have nothing to do with them outside of play practice. If I find out you are hanging out with any of them, for any reason, I will pull you out of the play."

I knew better than to argue.

"Yes, sir."

"You've been doing a good job, Scotty. I know I'm being hard on you, but it's for your own good. I want you to see the pastor after church every Sunday and I want you to come straight home after play practice."

"I can't go out at all? I can't go to Ofarim's or..."

"Not until I'm convinced that you're strong enough to fight temptation. You can go to Ofarim's only to work."

"You said I'm doing a good job."

"You are and I'm proud of you, but Satan will use every trick he has to trip you up."

"Dad, please."

"No. I've made my decision. I'm not doing this to punish you. I'm doing it to help you. You do understand that, right?"

"Yes," I said.

In his own messed up way of thinking Dad did think he was helping me. I wanted to shout at him; *I'm gay! Quit trying to change me and quit trying to ruin my life!* I couldn't do it. Nothing would change and I'd lose the play too.

"Good boy."

Dad patted me on the leg. I got up and walked to my room, trying not to cry. When I arrived, Justin was reading a magazine on his bed. I just stared at him.

"Did you tell him?" I asked.

"I didn't. I really didn't. I don't know how he found out."

Justin seemed sincere. He was also afraid. He was probably scared that Brandon and Jon would make good on their promise and beat the crap out of him.

I lay down on my bed and faced away from Justin. Tears ran down my cheeks, but I kept as quiet as I could. I didn't want my brother to know I was crying. I wished I could go for a walk, but I wasn't allowed outside now. My dad feared I might run into a gay boy and be tempted to do it with him.

I didn't have much left now. I couldn't sit with my friends at lunch. I had to come straight home after school. That meant there would be no chance of spending time with the guys like I did the evening we played capture the flag. All I had left was the play. What would I have when the last performance was over? Nothing. No friends. No fun. Nothing. My life just kept getting worse and worse. I wasn't so sure I was going to make it after all.

Dorian

My hope that Scotty was going to be okay was short-lived. When I spotted Scotty at school on Monday morning he was downcast and had obviously been crying. Marc and I started to move toward him but he shook his head, fearfully looked around, and disappeared into the crowd. Marc and I looked at each other, both of us wondering what was up.

I spotted Scotty twice between classes that morning and both times he avoided me. When lunch rolled around Scotty was conspicuous by his absence. I saw him come out of the line with his tray, look towards our table, and then dart off in the opposite direction.

"Does anyone know what's up with Scotty?" I asked.

"I was hoping you'd know. He won't talk to me," Dane said.

"Every time he spots me he runs," Casper said.

"I'll try to find out what's going on when I get to drama class. I have a bad feeling about this," I said.

Scotty was edgy as I approached him in the auditorium before class started. His eyes darted around as if he was looking for someone.

"Hey," I said.

"Hey."

It was the first word he's spoken to me all day.

"What's wrong?" I asked.

"I can't be seen with you guys anymore," Scotty said, looking at Marc and me. His lower lip trembled slightly.

"Why not?"

"If I'm seen with any of you I can't do the play. Dad will make me quit. They're all watching me."

"Who?"

"Everyone who goes to my church."

"What happened?" Marc asked.

Scotty started to answer, but then began to cry. I looked toward Marc.

"Tell Mrs. Cook that Scotty and I have to discuss something important and we'll be back soon."

Marc nodded. I led Scotty up onto the stage and then backstage. I took him into a dressing room/storage area where we could talk alone. As soon as I closed the door Scotty lost it. He cried his eyes out. I hook him in my arms and held him. I was so upset I cried too.

"What happened?" I asked when he quieted down.

"Someone told my parents I'd been hanging out with you and eating lunch with you guys."

"Your brother?"

"No. He said he didn't do it and I think he was telling the truth. He's way too scared of Brandon and Jon. It was someone from my church. I'm almost sure of it. They are all so nosey and a lot of kids from my church go to VHS. I should never have started sitting with you guys at lunch! It was stupid, stupid, stupid!"

"So your dad will make you quit the play if he sees you with any of us?"

"He said I should not be hanging out with perverts. I lied and told him I only spent time with you guys because we were discussing the play, but that didn't change his mind. He almost made me quit the play, period. He said it's dangerous for me to be around you. He thinks you'll try to lead me astray. I pointed out that I was sitting with Brandon and Jon and that they have girlfriends, but he's still suspicious."

"Why can't people mind their own business?"

"I go to the church of busybodies. They don't know what "mind your own business" means. Mom doesn't think I should quit the play and I hinted that quitting would wreck my G.P.A., but the real reason I'm being allowed to stay in is the act I've been putting on."

"Then why is your dad still threatening to make you quit?"

"He's afraid you guys will try to recruit me. He came close to forcing me to quit. I could see it in his eyes. I agreed not to have anything to do with any of you outside of class. I also had to promise to meet with our pastor after church *every* Sunday. I have to come straight home from play practice from now on. The only places I can go are school and work."

"I can't believe I'm hearing any of this," I said.

"I'm sorry, Dorian, but what could I do? I know I should stand up to my parents and everyone else, but I can't! I don't want them to kick me out. I don't want them to stop loving me. I know I'm weak but..." Scotty's sobs drowned out his voice.

"No. No. I don't mean I'm disappointed in *you*. I mean I can't believe your dad is being so horrible or so stupid."

"He's not the only one. Church was horrendous last Sunday. The pastor did a whole sermon centered around the evils of homosexuality and warned everyone that homosexuals were out to recruit their children. Word has gotten around about what I did. Everyone was looking at me. I wanted to bolt out of the church, but I knew I had to sit there and take it."

"I'm so sorry, Scotty."

"I can't hang out with you guys anymore. I really liked being with you guys. I felt like I was surrounded by friends who understood me and cared about me, but I can't be with you anymore."

"We do understand and we do care."

"Then you've got to stay away from me. Don't try to talk to me. Don't approach me. If I get spotted with one of you guys just once it's all over."

"Scotty..."

"Please, Dorian! I'm begging you! I can talk to you in drama class and during play practice, but that's it. The second practice ends you can't talk to me. I can't be near you. Please tell all the others that if they want to help me they have to stay away from me."

Scotty sobbed even more. I held him tight and hugged him. It was a good long while before he stopped crying. When he did, he pulled back and wiped his eyes with the back of his hand.

"Please, Dorian. Tell the guys to stay away from me."

I nodded through my own tears as Scotty left the dressing room. I was stunned. What was being done to Scotty was beyond horrible.

When I stepped out of backstage area, I could hear Mrs. Cook giving one of her pep talks. The words flowed over me. All I could think about was Scotty.

As soon as Mrs. Cook spotted me she wrapped up her talk. We ran through the contract-signing scene, which had some tricky legalese for me to reel off. While Scotty played the scene there was no trace of sadness upon his face and no sign of the pain he was experiencing. While we were practicing, he wasn't Scotty anymore. He was Charlie. For a few minutes at least Scotty could be happy.

During the break between class and play practice I gathered Marc, Tim, and Dane. We walked outside and sat on a bench away from the end-of-the-school-day mass exodus.

"What did you find out?" Dane asked.

"It's bad," I said and then proceeded to tell the others what Scotty had told me.

"This is bullshit!" Tim said. "I'm not letting some holier-than-thou, Bible-thumping, judgmental, control freaks tell me what I can do! I say we go ahead and hang out with Scotty anyway."

"If we do that Scotty's dad will force him to quit the play. It's all he's got left, Tim. You saw him on the stage during class. He was happy. He loves acting. We can't do anything to jeopardize that," I said.

"He's right, Tim. It pisses me off too, but we've got to think of Scotty," Dane said.

"So, we're just going to do nothing?" Tim asked.

"No," Marc said. "We're going to do something all right. We just have to figure out what to do."

"Strategy meeting!" Dane said.

"I was thinking more council of war, but yeah," Marc said.

I grinned. I knew none of my friends would abandon Scotty.

"How about my place after practice? We're usually done by six so...six-thirty?" Marc said.

Everyone nodded.

"We need to get the word out," Marc said.

"I'll catch Shawn before he leaves. I don't think he's working tonight," Tim said. "He can tell the rest of the gang. Maybe we can catch a few of the others before they leave school too."

Tim and Dane took off.

"We've got to help Scotty," I said. "He was bawling on my shoulder in the dressing room, Marc. His parents and his church are trying to isolate him. They're trying to beat him down and change him."

"They're fools for thinking they can change him and isolating him can only end in tragedy. We will help him, Dorian. I don't know how, but we will."

I nodded. Tears streamed down my cheeks. Marc hugged me. I felt so safe in his arms. I wished Scotty could have what I had. He needed someone to hold him and make him feel safe.

Scotty and I were on stage during most of practice. I was so glad he had a lead role. It put him in the thick of things for nearly every minute of practice. He could lose himself in the role of Charlie and hopefully take a little bit of that magic with him when he departed.

I wondered what would happen when the play was over. What would Scotty have then? We had to help him. We had to make things better for him and soon.

After practice, Marc, Tim, Dane, and I all headed for Marc's old Camaro. I watched Scotty walk off alone. My heart ached for him.

We stopped off at the grocery where Marc bought soft drinks, a bag of chocolate chips, and the makings for cookies. As soon as we finished shopping we headed for Marc's loft.

"Show the guys to the loft," Marc said to me as we got out of the car. "I'm going to warn Mom and Dad that I'm having a lot of friends over."

"So, you've been here before?" Dane asked, as if he didn't know.

I wiggled my eyebrows and grinned.

I took the guys into the barn behind Marc's parent's house, past his dad's small collection of vintage cars and up the stairs into the loft.

"This is sweet!" Tim said as I turned on the lights.

The old barn loft had been turned into an apartment, complete with a small kitchen off to the side. The part I liked best was the huge windows at the back that looked out over the fields.

"This is cool," Dane said. "Marc lives in town, but the country starts right behind his barn!"

"I like the old barn stuff that is still here, like the cool pulley way overhead," Tim said. "This is as big as your room, Dane."

Dane's bedroom had once been a classroom in the old Verona school. The poor boy went home from school only to be at school again!

"So, what do you guys think?" Marc asked as he climbed the stairs.

"It's awesome!" Tim said.

Marc smiled.

"The others will probably show up soon. Let's make some cookies!"

I don't think Marc did much cooking, but he did have a big mixing bowl, two cookie sheets, and everything we needed to make cookies, except eggs, which he ran and got from his mom. We followed the directions on the package of chocolate chips and soon had cookies baking in the oven.

Tristan and Shawn arrived and were soon followed by Brandon and Jon. Casey wandered in just in time for the first batch of cookies to come out of the oven. Ethan, Nathan, and Casper showed up just after the first batch of cookies had been devoured, but we already had more baking.

Marc gave those who hadn't seen it a tour of his loft. The tour didn't take long because it was all one big room, except for the bathroom. The loft was furnished with cast-off couches, tables, and chairs, but it looked great. My boyfriend had wonderful taste.

"You are truly, truly obsessed with Dorian, Marc," Brandon said.

"Why do you say that?"

"Come on! You have a life-sized painting of him on your wall!"

I laughed. It was true. Tristan had painted a life-sized portrait of me as a prop for *The Picture of Dorian Gray* and had given it to Marc when the play was over.

"Hey, that's a Tristan Graham Cole original. It will be worth a fortune someday," Marc said.

Tristan grinned.

"Yeah. Yeah. Try to make excuses to cover up your obsession," Brandon said.

Marc just smiled, then leaned over and kissed me.

"Don't get started you two or we won't get anything done," Jon said.

Everyone settled in with a drink and some cookies. I stood up and told everyone what Scotty had told me and I told them how very wretched he felt, although they could have guessed that without me telling.

Everyone was pissed off, to put it mildly.

"I am so sick of religious, judgmental assholes!" Brandon said.

"Just remember that not everyone who goes to church is a bad person and not all churches are like that," Casey said. "I think Scotty's church is in the minority."

"I don't know about that," Shawn said. "All I ever hear from anyone who is religious is a bunch of anti-gay crap. It makes me want to burn down a church."

"I go to church and my church isn't like that at all. I'm religious," Casey said.

"Sorry, I just get so mad!" Shawn said.

"Church's like Scotty's do give the rest a bad name," Casey said.

"We need to concentrate on Scotty's problem instead of sitting here church-bashing," Tristan said.

"True, as fun as it is," Jon said.

"We could do what we damn well please and act as if nothing has changed," Brandon said.

"That's not what Scotty wants," I said.

"We can't exactly kidnap him and force him to sit with us," Nathan said.

"If we don't keep our distance his parents will make him quit the play. We cannot let that happen," I said. "Marc, Tim, Dane, and I have all seen Scotty when he's up on the stage. He's happy then. It's the only time he is happy. We can't do anything that would cause him to lose that."

"What happens when the play is performed and it's all over?" Tristan asked.

"Scotty will still have drama class until the end of the school year. After that..." I said.

We all sat in silence for a few moments.

"We have to find a way to help him," I said. "Scotty is a mess right now and it's only going to get worse. When the play is over and the school year ends I'm really afraid that he's going to feel like he has nothing to live for. I don't like to say this, but if we don't do something I'm afraid he might get so depressed he'll kill himself."

Brandon's eyes were watery. Jon put his arm around Brandon's shoulder and squeezed.

"I'm not losing another friend like that," Ethan said. "The bastards are not going to drive another one of my friends to kill himself."

"I say we strike back at these bastards," Brandon said. "If they're going to make Scotty's life difficult we'll make theirs difficult."

"We can't attack a church," Tristan said.

"I'm not talking about burning their church down or any kind of vandalism. That would make us the bad guys too. I don't think these people are evil, they're just stupid and misguided."

"They're assholes," Tim said.

"That too," Brandon said. "We just need to create some... annoyances that can't be traced back to us."

"Such as?" Casper asked.

"I have one in mind but I want to keep it a secret until I pull it off. I think we mostly need to concentrate not on the church but on the individuals who are spying on Scotty. They are the busybodies who are sticking their noses in where they don't belong."

"Yes, I'm sure not everyone in that church is out to get Scotty," Casey said.

"I've seen a couple of guys watching Scotty," Casper said.

"I've noticed one or two as well," Shawn said.

"We just need to make their lives difficult," Ethan said. "I'm afraid I can't do much since I'm not in school anymore, but the rest of you can. I do think we need to be careful and not go too far."

"I guess beating the crap out of them is out," Marc said.

"Yes, I'm afraid so," Ethan said. "So is vandalizing their cars."

"Sure, take all the fun out of it," Jon said.

"Like you'd vandalize someone's car anyway," Casey said.

"Shh! You'll ruin my bad-ass image," Jon said.

"You have one?" Casey asked.

Jon growled.

"We can't vandalize cars, but what if perhaps... a banana was to get stuck in an exhaust pipe? I hear cars don't run well with a banana in the tailpipe, haven't you, Jon?" Brandon asked.

"I think I have heard that. It's also very hard to clean Vaseline off of a windshield."

"It can be hard to open a locker when the combination has been changed," Nathan said.

"Yeah, but how can we do that?"

"Well, I am an office assistant. I know where the list of combinations is kept and I know how to change a combination."

More ideas were floated and I laughed at times. My friends were inventive.

"Is any of this going to help Scotty much?" I wondered out loud.

"Maybe we can make it difficult enough on the spies they will give it up," Shawn said. "We can keep hitting them until they take the hint. If they stop spying we don't have to avoid Scotty. We can keep things on the Q T if Scotty's every move isn't being watched."

"What about Scotty's brother?" Marc asked.

"Leave him to us," Jon said, smacking his fist into his palm.

Casey crossed her arms and stared at Jon.

"We aren't going to beat him up. We're just going to make him think we'll beat him up. We intimidated him into keeping his mouth shut before. We'll just give him a reminder."

"What if he calls your bluff?" Nathan asked.

"Then we'll beat him up," Brandon said.

I wouldn't want to be Brandon or Jon's enemy.

"Just don't go too far," Casey said.

"Yes, mother," Brandon said. Casey stared at him. "Okay! Okay! We get it. We don't want to become as bad as the people we're fighting against."

"I don't think this is the solution we're seeking, but it is a start," Tristan said.

"Yeah, if we can eliminate the spies we can interact with Scotty and maybe even secretly include him in some get-togethers again," Nathan said.

"If we can do that he won't feel so alone," Dane said.

"If we have access to Scotty we can talk to him and hopefully come up with something that will *really* help," Tristan said.

"Can't we try to include him now? On the Q T?" Tim asked.

Tristan shook his head.

"Too risky. He's being watched too closely."

"And he has to go straight home after practice," I said.

"So we kill... I mean harass the busybody spies until they give it up," Brandon said.

I wasn't convinced, but at least it was better than doing nothing.

"We'll all keep thinking on it and try to come up with something better," Marc said. "We aren't going to give up or forget about Scotty. I know this won't make all his problems go away, but if we succeed it will help. Anything we can do to let Scotty know he has friends will make life easier on him."

"We should watch Scotty too," Ethan said. "If he shows any signs of becoming suicidal we'll have to do something drastic."

Our plans, such as they were, were set. We'd attack the spies and keep an eye on Scotty ourselves. I thought of my own little idea too. I couldn't talk freely with Scotty, but there was nothing stopping me from slipping a note into his locker from time to time when no one was looking. There would be opportunities to speak with him in drama class and during practices as well.

We hadn't come up with a brilliant solution, but at least we were doing something. Maybe at least our efforts would show Scotty that a lot of people cared about him and liked him just as he was.

We sat and talked and ate cookies for another hour, and then everyone departed. Soon, it was just Marc and me. We began to make out on the couch. That got us all worked up, of course, so we stripped each other naked and moved to Marc's bed. We spent the next hour kissing and groping and making each other moan. After we finished we lay in each other's arms. I know both of us wished that someday Scotty could know such contentment and love.

***

There is nothing like looking for clues, and once I started looking I began to notice a few guys who were just a little too interested in Scotty. Marc pointed out a few faces as we walked the halls of VHS and I slowly committed them to memory. Once I took note of those spying on Scotty I began to see them everywhere. I had thought Scotty was paranoid, but I quickly realized members of his church really *were* stalking him. Church! Ha! It was more like a cult! I was trying hard to remember that Scotty's church was a bad example and not like most churches at all.

The busybodies found their task increasingly difficult as the homos and their allies began to strike back. I grinned when I noticed three different spies fighting with their lockers trying to get them open. I knew that Nathan had struck. Over the coming days, Nathan enlisted allies among the student office assistants. Every time one of the spies obtained a new combination it only worked a short time before Nathan or one of his allies changed it again. The spies found it difficult to watch Scotty when most of their time between classes was spent trying to figure out why their lockers had turned against them.

Marc and I spotted one of the busybodies trailing Scotty between third and fourth period. We cut him off by pretending to argue. Whichever way the busybody tried to move, one of us pushed the other in his way. Scotty was long gone before our target escaped.

During third period I wrote Scotty the first of many encouraging notes that I slipped into his locker over the next few days. Now that I knew the identity of the spies I could easily watch for them and stuff my note into Scotty's locker without being seen by anyone who would cause trouble. My first note was short and to the point; "Don't let the bastards get you down. We've got your back. D."

There were mischievous smiles around our lunch table and we were just getting started. The goal was to help Scotty, but I don't think any of us realized helping him would be so much fun.

"I saw Devon cussing at his locker just before lunch. You wouldn't know anything about that, would you, Nathan?" Jon asked.

"Who me?"

"Good job!" Shawn said and gave Nathan a high-five.

"Who has something to report?" Brandon asked.

"Marc and I blocked one of the enemy by staging a fake argument," I said.

"I skipped second period and used up an entire jar of Vaseline," Dane said.

"We don't need to hear about your sex life, Dane," Jon said.

"I didn't use it like *that!* I put it on a few car windows."

"Oh!" Jon said, pretending stupidity.

"You are not funny, Jon," Dane said.

"Yes, he is," Brandon said. "Funny looking!"

The entire table groaned.

"Why don't we just have Brandon bore the enemy into unconsciousness," Nathan said.

"Maybe they'll jump off a cliff to avoid his pathetic jokes," Casper said.

"Don't make me come down there, Casper," Brandon threatened.

"What are you going to do, torment me with bad puns?"

"Hey, let's stick to tormenting the enemy," Brandon said.

"You're only saying that because you're losing the battle of wits with Casper," Jon said.

"Yeah, right! He's blond!"

"That only makes you more pathetic," Jon pointed out.

Brandon crossed his arms and glared at Jon with fake fury, but he couldn't maintain it. He began to laugh.

"Damn it!"

"One of the guys following Scotty mysteriously tripped as he passed me," Casper said innocently.

"Your foot didn't happen to get in his way, did it?" Tristan asked.

"I was having a little trouble walking just then."

Brandon started to open his mouth.

"Don't go there, Brandon," Casey warned.

"Come on! A gay boy saying he had trouble walking? You know what *that* means."

"Brendan is down at IU, otherwise you would be right," Casper said.

Shawn laughed.

"I can't believe you said that!"

I was surprised too. Casper wasn't known for talking about his sex life.

"Anyway... I helped pick up his books, but I kept dropping them. I was so clumsy."

"Nice," Tim said.

I grinned. We had made a start. The lives of the busybodies were becoming difficult and we were just beginning to warm up. If the enemy wanted to make Scotty's life hard they were going to pay the price. We wouldn't stop or give up.

I looked across the cafeteria. Scotty was sitting with Tess and Trent. I was glad he wasn't alone. He didn't look happy, but at least he had friends to sit with. I knew Tess would take care of him and no one from Scotty's church could claim that she or Trent was gay.

Seeing Scotty so down made all of us more determined to help him. We stepped up our sabotage activities. Everywhere I turned there was evidence of our work. I saw Devon kicking the tires of his car in frustration because it would not keep running. Over the course of the week I observed a few of the other busybodies having trouble with their cars too. I knew someone in our group was making good use of bananas.

The busybodies mysteriously tripped quite often and found their path blocked by clumsy homos. They continued to have horrible problems getting their lockers open and then their homework and books began to disappear only to be found in the oddest of places.

Devon fared the worst. The day after he received a banana in the tailpipe he walked out to his car to find it encased in plastic wrap. Another evildoer found his car completely filled with pink balloons.

Most of the annoyances were small, but they kept coming and coming. They began to wear on the enemy. Each of the evildoers looked about with increasing paranoia, wondering when the next prank would come. Us homos were the main suspects, of course, but nothing could be pinned on us. None of the things we did crossed over the line into vandalism or assault. We merely got in the way and pestered the enemy so continuously that their nerves began to fray.

Scotty

I dreaded another boring church service surrounded by judgmental hypocrites. I wondered if the sermon would be another barrage against gays or if the pastor would move on to another topic. Going to church might not have been so bad if we went to a real church. Casey had once told me her church was nothing like ours. She'd also said her grandparents attended church, were very religious, and yet treated her girlfriend like a member of the family. I was glad I knew Casey; otherwise I might well have thought that all churches were evil.

Devon scowled at me as I scooted into a pew with my family. That was one of his hobbies, shooting me nasty looks. I noticed a few kids who went to VHS giving me the evil eye too. I wondered how people could be like that. I didn't imagine being hateful could be much fun.

I saw mostly the same old faces. There were visitors from time to time. They were most likely relatives of parishioners or out-of-towners who felt they couldn't skip church even when they were away from home. I wondered if they went back to their church and told horror tales of what they had heard sitting in the pews here.

An elderly lady slowly made her way up the aisle with the help of a cane. She was dressed in black as if she was mourning, and even wore a hat with a veil. She looked at me as she passed. There was something oddly familiar about her, but I was quite sure I had not seen her in church before. She had probably been in Ofarim's. Everyone stopped in sooner or later.

The service began with a hymn. I liked singing, but hymns left much to be desired. We sang some of the same hymns week after week after week. It was almost as if people thought church had to be boring. I wondered if they sang any cool songs in Casey's church.

The hymn was completed and soon it was time for the sermon. I had to fight myself to keep from releasing a frustrated sigh when the pastor began talking about Sodom and Gomorrah *again*. He somehow managed to work in Sodom and Gomorrah every week. I bet no other preacher had ever found so many ways to beat a topic to death.

I began to grow drowsy as the pastor delivered his verbal sedative. I'd discovered that the best way to survive church was to zone out. I'd almost nodded off when Justin elbowed me. He wrinkled his nose and looked at me with disgust. I didn't know what he was on about until I smelled a foul odor, like rotten eggs or sulfur. I looked back at him with loathing. It just figured he'd try to blame something he did on me. The stench grew so bad I had to hold my nose.

That's when I noticed our whole section looking around with wrinkled noses. The pastor's voice faltered as the stench reached him. More and more of the congregation began to look uncomfortable. I held my hand over my mouth. The stench grew in intensity until I thought I was going to hurl. Some people began to get up and leave. The smell was so bad they couldn't stand it.

"I think we should…" the pastor began but the stench was too much for him. He waved it away and pointed to the exit.

A mass exodus ensued as everyone scrambled to get out. The crowd pushed me about as I struggled not to hurl. I had never smelled anything so nasty before. Once outside I gasped for breath and I wasn't alone.

The pastor stood up on a stump.

"I believe we may have a gas line or sewer line leak. We will dispense with the rest of the service. May God bless you and go with you."

Even as the pastor said the words he was fanning the air. The stench was flowing out the open doors.

Everyone moved quickly away from the church. I fought not to smile. It was the shortest church service ever and I, for one, was thrilled!

As Dad pushed us toward the parking lot the old woman in black caught my eye and winked. I looked at her with a question in my eyes, but she only smiled. She turned and slowly walked down the sidewalk using her cane for support.

Justin and I stripped out of our Sunday best as soon as we were back home. Justin grabbed a basketball and headed for the park. I was still under house arrest so I picked up my Eleanor Roosevelt biography, made myself comfortable on my bed, and began to read. With Justin out of the house my bedroom was a pleasant sanctuary.

I didn't have to start work until 1 p.m. so I spent the rest of the morning reading and napping. At noon I went down to the kitchen and made myself a peanut butter & blackberry jelly sandwich. I wished I could go out and run around town, but my parents feared I'd meet some dangerous homosexuals who would recruit me. I was so tired of suffering for their ignorance.

I left for work just a little before 1 p.m. I mostly liked working at Ofarim's, but now I wished I had more hours. Anything that got me away from home was welcome.

Waiting on tables was a tougher job than it looked. When I first started at Ofarim's my feet were aching at the end of the day. I was accustomed to being on my feet for long hours now, but I still went home tired.

Working at Ofarim's gave me a chance to see my friends. Everyone stopped in and many were regulars. Unfortunately, the likes of Devon and his buddies frequented Ofarim's too. There was good and bad in just about everything so I concentrated on the good. I considered that I worked at Ofarim's for free and that the money I was paid was compensation for all the unpleasant parts. Thinking of it that way made dealing with Devon and those like him more tolerable.

Business was steady. There were enough customers that I was kept busy and time passed quickly, but not so many I had to rush around like a crazy man. More customers meant more tips, but if there were too many it was just too much.

Around five Brandon and Jon came in. They ordered triple cheeseburgers, fries, chocolate milkshakes, and Cokes. They were laughing their butts off as I made their shakes. I thought maybe one of them had made some crack about me and I eyed them suspiciously when I brought their orders to their booths. Brandon looked at me and grinned.

"Did you enjoy church this morning?" he asked.

"Uh, no. I never do."

"It was a rather short service today, wasn't it?"

I gazed at Brandon curiously.

"You still don't get it, do you?" he asked. Brandon and Jon began a new round of laughing. Finally, Brandon winked at me.

"That was you!" I said much too loudly. I looked around, but none of the other customers paid much attention.

I dropped into the booth beside Brandon.

"You were that old lady?" I asked.

"He's not terribly bright, is he?" Jon asked Brandon.

"You caused that horrible smell!" I said.

"Hey! He finally caught on!" Brandon said to Jon and then looked back at me. "Stink bombs are my specialty and today's was especially powerful."

"Ha! It almost made me sick!"

"It sure cleared the place out," Brandon said. "You really should have been there Jon."

"No thanks. I don't get up early on Sunday for anything."

"You are my hero," I said.

"I'm just doing my part to strike back at the enemy. It was rather brilliant, wasn't it?"

"Uh oh... and so begins the self congratulations. This could go on for hours," Jon said.

I laughed.

"Dude, that was the best! I have never enjoyed church more."

"You are welcome," Brandon said.

The doorbell rang and an elderly couple entered so I had to get back to work. I patted Brandon on the back and laughed as I walked away from his booth. My day had just improved tenfold. With friends like Brandon I just might survive high school.

Dorian

I knew something was up when Marc and I got out of his Camaro in the VHS parking lot. There were little groups talking excitedly and laughing. I heard the words "stink bomb" and "best practical joke ever" before we even made it to the back doors.

By the time Marc and I reached our lockers we knew what had gone down. During Sunday services at Scotty's church a foul odor had engulfed the church, sending parishioners scurrying for the exits. The stench was so bad services were cancelled and no one could go back inside for hours. I knew Brandon was behind it even before I saw him grinning with satisfaction. I walked up to him between second and third periods.

"You did it, didn't you?" I asked quietly.

"Homemade stink bombs are the best," was Brandon's only response. He walked away still smiling.

I thought we'd all been rather clever, but Brandon was clearly the best. He'd taken out the entire congregation of Scotty's church. It was just too bad he couldn't break up their services every Sunday.

As the days passed and our barrage of harassment continued the busybodies began to give up one by one. The price was becoming too high for them. They couldn't quite figure out who was to blame for their misfortune, but they were smart enough to realize they were being targeted and why. As their numbers grew fewer I began to hope that we could make things better for Scotty, but as so often happens, just when there was real hope everything crashed into ruin.

On Wednesday, Scott was absent from last period drama. I'd seen him in the hallways earlier and spotted him at lunch, but he was nowhere to be found when last period rolled around. I asked Tess if she knew anything, but she only said that Scotty had seemed more depressed than ever at lunch. I had a bad feeling.

We didn't find out what had happened until the beginning of play practice. Mrs. Cook called Marc to the side and he came walking back toward me with a stunned look on his face.

"What is it?"

"I have to take over for Scotty. He's dropped out of drama class and the play."

"*What?*"

"I guess his dad made him quit after all."

"That's not fair! He hasn't been around any of us outside of drama class and play practice! We have to go look for him. Now!"

I motioned for Dane to join us.

"Scotty's quit the play. Go and find Brandon or any of the guys and tell them what's happened. We need to find him and quickly."

Dane took off without a second's hesitation, pausing only long enough to grab Tim. I hurried over to Mrs. Cook.

"Marc and I have to leave. I'm really worried about Scotty. He's... well, I don't have time to explain, but... I'm afraid he might kill himself... I..."

Tears welled up in my eyes. Mrs. Cook patted me on the shoulder and turned to look out into the auditorium.

"Play practice is cancelled for this afternoon everyone, but work on your lines. The performances are coming up quickly."

I grinned at Mrs. Cook and then Marc and I hurried out of the auditorium. The parking lot had mostly cleared out so we had no trouble escaping from school.

"Do you have any clue about where we should look?" Marc asked.

"Not really."

"Let's swing by my house first in case Scotty has called. We'll call out to the Selby's and see if he's contacted them. We might as well call all the others too since we don't know who Dane and Tim found. Most of the guys were probably already gone by the time we found out Scotty quit the play," Marc said.

"What if Scotty is home?"

"I don't think he will be, but I guess we can call there too. His parents will be nasty but who cares about them?"

I racked my brain to think of where Scotty might go when he was upset, but I didn't know him well enough. We would just have to look everywhere until we found him. I hoped I was wrong and that he wasn't suicidal, but at the very least he was going to need a friend.

Marc pulled into his drive and parked the Camaro near the barn.

"Let's check with Mom and see if there are any messages," Marc said.

We walked to the back door and went inside. There, our search for Scotty ended. He was sitting at the kitchen table with Mom, drinking hot cocoa. He looked distinctly unhappy and his eyes were puffy from crying. He was also quite a mess. He looked as if he'd fallen in the mud.

"Scotty!" I said too loudly.

He tried to grin, but he had tears in his eyes.

"We just found out your dad made you quit the play. We're all getting ready to search for you," Marc said.

I was so happy Scotty was safe. I had feared the worst.

"I'll call the guys and let them know Scotty is here," Marc said, and then turned to Scotty.

"Want to come out to the loft? We'll talk and figure things out."

Scotty nodded.

"Thank you, Mrs. Peralta, for everything," Scotty said.

"You are welcome here anytime," Marc's mom said and patted Scotty's shoulder.

"Come on," I said.

I wrapped my arm around Scotty's shoulder and led him outside and to the barn. Marc began making phone calls as soon as we reached the loft. I pulled Scotty into a hug. He lost it then and began sobbing. I couldn't help but cry too. Marc looked almost as if he might join us, but he maintained control as he made his calls.

After a few minutes, Marc turned to us.

"I reached everyone but Dane and Tim. I left a message with Dane's mom, but no one answered at Tim and Shawn's place. I'm going to go out and see if I can track them down. They may be walking home. In our rush I kind of forgot I usually give him a ride."

Marc came over and gave me a kiss.

"Love you," he said.

"I love you too."

Marc wrapped his arms around Scotty and hugged us both.

"We'll make it okay, Scotty."

Scotty nodded, but tears still flowed from his eyes. I just stood there and held him as Marc departed. It wasn't until several minutes later than his sobs quieted. I pulled him toward the loveseat and sat down with him, keeping my arm around his shoulder.

"I'm not going back to that house," Scotty said. "They hate me."

I wanted to tell Scotty his family didn't hate him, but they sure weren't nice to him and arguing would only make the situation worse.

"You have a lot of friends who care about you, Scotty. You know you can stay here and you have other places to stay too."

Scotty nodded.

"That's why I didn't... well, for just a moment I thought about killing myself again."

"Scotty..."

"I know, but it just hurts so bad!"

He began crying again, but didn't cry long.

"You can stay here and we'll figure things out."

"My parents will find me. This is probably the first place they'll look."

"Then you can stay at the Selby farm or Shawn and Tim's apartment."

"They'll still find me."

"Well, they may find you, but they aren't taking you anywhere. None of us will let them. We can talk to a lawyer. I don't know anything about it, but there is something called emancipation that will remove you from your parents' control."

"I don't know, Dorian..."

"Listen, I don't have the solution, but we will find a solution. We'll get the guys together and we will figure something out. Until them, we'll hide you."

"Even if you can hide me, my parents will find me at school. I can't just stop going to school."

"Yeah, there is that. Maybe you can miss a couple of days. We'll figure something out, Scotty. I won't let anyone hurt you and neither will the others."

Scotty nodded, but his eyes were filled with tears. I didn't have a clue about how to truly help him, but I was telling the truth. We would figure something out.

"My father got so nasty," Scotty said. "He actually showed up at school before last period and had me called out of class. He told me he'd pulled me out of drama and that I had to quit the play. He said he didn't want me around immoral abominations. I protested that I hadn't been hanging out with any gay guys, but he said you were in my drama class and the play and that was bad enough. I tried to argue but he told me to shut my mouth. He said that as long as I led an immoral life I didn't have the right to speak."

"What happened with him?" I said. "Why the change?"

"I think he's been talking to the pastor and some of the others at the church. They've convinced him that I'm only pretending to change. I don't know. Maybe I've been acting a little too cooperative. I've been telling my parents and the pastor what I think they want to hear. Maybe I should have resisted more to make it seem more realistic. It doesn't matter now. Dad is convinced I'm in serious danger of losing my soul. Who knows what he'll do?"

"Why are they so stupid?" I asked.

"Why doesn't matter. Nothing matters. I can't do anything I want now. I can't take drama. I can't be in the play. I can't talk to my friends. Not only do I have to come straight home from school, but now I have to read the Bible until I go to bed. Oh, and get this! When Dad came and jerked me out of class he took me to the principal's office. I had to sit in the outer office while Dad yelled at the principal for not having Bible classes!"

"Your dad is seriously messed up."

"I'm afraid he'll try to have me brainwashed. Who knows what the pastor has him believing. I thought things were going well with the pastor. He never gave any indication he didn't believe me. I'm scared to go to the church. They're all a bunch of freaks. It's not a church at all. It's some kind of cult. I'm afraid they'll start beating me to force me to 'repent' but fuck them. I don't have anything to repent for."

"Good for you," I said.

"I've had it! I've tried to make the best of the situation. I tried pretending I'm not gay, but nothing makes my parents or any of that church lot happy. I'm not going back home and I'm not going back to that evil, evil church."

I heard footsteps on the stairs. Marc's blond head popped into view.

"I found them. Nathan and Casper were with them. They thought we should get everyone together for a meeting. I suggested everyone come here. They'll start arriving soon."

"Um... I should clean up. I'm a mess," Scotty said.

"What happened anyway? How did you get so muddy?"

"I was crying and not watching where I was going. I fell in a ditch. It was so stupid."

"You can use my shower," Marc said. "I'll give you some of my clothes to wear."

"Thanks, Marc."

Scotty and I walked back to the bathroom where I pulled out a towel and washcloth for him. I knew where everything was. I'd showered at Marc's before, usually with him.

I left Scotty alone in the bathroom. Marc slipped in with a stack of clothes for him and then returned.

Fifteen minutes later Scotty came out of the bathroom, all clean and looking good in Marc's jeans and a VHS soccer jersey. We heard footsteps on the stairs and turned to see Dane, Tim, Nathan, and Casper enter the loft.

"We made some quick phone calls and everyone who can is coming. Shawn is working tonight so we didn't call him," Tim said.

130

Within half an hour Ethan, Tristan, Brandon, Jon, and Casey had joined us. Everyone patted Scotty on the back or gripped his shoulder. Tristan and Casey hugged him. Scotty was obviously still frightened and upset, but at least friends surrounded him. With Scotty's permission, I filled everyone in.

"Your dad and his church can go fuck themselves," Brandon said. "They aren't getting their hands on you."

Scotty actually smiled for a moment.

"No matter where I go they'll track me down," Scotty said. "If Dad finds me he can make me go home."

"If he shows up here he's going to have to go through us," Jon said, smacking his fist.

"We could keep moving you around," Nathan said. "You can stay here with Marc some, with us on the farm, at Dane's place. I'll talk to Uncle Jack and see what he can figure out about keeping your dad away. He has a lawyer friend."

"My parents will just grab me at school," Scotty said.

"So don't go," Jon said. "The police may come looking for you after a few days, but it is your parents, not you, who will be in trouble."

"Maybe..." Scotty said.

I looked over and noticed Ethan grinning. His smile was completely out of place.

"I know where we can hide you, Scotty. I know somewhere your dad will never find you and never even think to look," Ethan said.

Everyone turned to Ethan.

"Think about it for a moment," Ethan said.

"Aunt Anne's," Brandon said after a few moments. Several faces lit up.

"Who is Aunt Anne?" I asked. I did not have a clue.

"She is Mark's aunt," Brandon said. "Mark and Taylor escaped their parents by hiding out on her farm. She lives way down south by Bloomington.

"And Brendan is coming home for a visit this weekend!" Casper said. "He can take Scotty with him when he leaves!"

131

"If he's not too exhausted to drive when you're through with him," Brandon said.

"I'll let him get some sleep Saturday night." Casper grinned.

Everyone looked at Scotty next.

"What do you think?" Tristan asked.

"Well, how do you know Mark's aunt will take me in?"

"She will," Brandon said. "I know she will. I still have her number. She will be glad to help. I'm sure of it."

"Well, I can't stay here. My dad will find me. He was talking about sending me away for treatment."

"That settles it. We have to get you out of town," Casper said.

Casper looked truly frightened and I knew he was remembering what had happened to Brendan. I didn't know all the details, but I knew Brendan's parents had forced him to go to a clinic where they tried to torture him into being straight. That was probably why Brendan had nothing to do with his father.

"If she'll have me, I'll go," Scotty said. "I'm so scared."

Tears began to flow from Scotty's eyes. Tristan hugged him close.

"We'll hide you until you can escape with Brendan," I said.

"It will be like the underground railroad. We'll move you around at night," Brandon said.

"Yeah, Uncle Jack will be up for it," Ethan said confidently.

"My parents too," I said.

"And mine," Dane said.

"I'm sure Mom will be okay with it," Tristan said.

"I know Shawn will!" Tim said.

Scotty smiled.

"Thanks so much guys."

"That's settled then," I said. "Now, since we're all here... party at Marc's place!"

"We can order pizzas, but I only have $8," Marc said.

"I've got $5," Nathan said.

"I have $10," Tristan said.

"I bet $5 each will be enough," Ethan said. "We can get some Cokes and ice at the grocery."

We all chipped in. Ethan volunteered to go out for the pizza, Coke, and ice. Tristan volunteered to go with him.

"Are you sure you trust Tristan with your boyfriend?" Jon asked Nathan. "I hear Tristan is pretty wild."

"I'm only wild with Shawn," Tristan said with a grin. Tristan was so handsome. He even made glasses look sexy.

Marc called in our order to Parrot's Pizza and Ethan and Tristan took off.

"Just remember guys, no orgy! There are two straight boys in the room," Brandon said.

"Quit dreaming, Brandon," Nathan said.

"I bet that's his big fantasy," Casper said.

"Yeah, right! Like I fantasize about you guys. I have a girlfriend you know."

"I've noticed you spend more time with us than her," Marc said.

"Well, you guys are fun. Dorian alone is always good for a laugh."

"Me?"

"You're excited about *everything*." Brandon pretended to flip his hair back, as I did sometimes, and ran to Casey who was wearing earrings. "Oh! Sparkly!"

I couldn't help but laugh. Brandon did a good imitation of me. Shiny objects easily distracted me. I could also completely lose myself in beautiful flowers, paintings, and... I guess a lot of things.

"I still think you're a little too interested in the gay boys, Brandon," Casey said.

"Hey! I already pointed out I have a girlfriend."

"I bet she's just a cover," Casper teased. "I almost never see you with her."

"That's because girls are only good for one thing."

"Brandon Hanson, you did not just say that!" Casey said.

"Um, yeah I did! She loves it too. She can't get enough of me!"

"That's only because you don't have enough to satisfy her," Casey said.

Brandon looked confused for a moment.

"Hey! I have more than enough! I'll show you!"

Brandon began to unzip his pants.

"No!" Casey said.

Brandon laughed and zipped his pants back up. I wouldn't have minded a look. Marc said it was big. He'd seen it in the locker room and showers often enough. That was the one bad thing about not liking sports. I never got to check out the jocks in the showers.

"Maybe we should let Brandon take his clothes off. It would be like having a male stripper and we won't have to pay him," Nathan said.

"Yeah, but aren't strippers usually good looking?" Jon asked.

"Hey, just look at this face," Brandon said, pointing to himself.

"Yeah, like I said... aren't strippers usually good looking?"

"I'm good looking *and* I have a hot bod. Check this out!"

Brandon stripped off his shirt and flexed. He did have a hot bod. He had defined abs and everything. Brandon began dancing and twirling his shirt over his head.

"This is my worst nightmare come true," Casey said.

"Woo! Take it all off!" I shouted.

"Don't encourage him or he will," Jon said.

Brandon laughed and then slipped his shirt back on. The sight of Brandon shirtless had gotten me worked up. I suddenly wished Marc and I were alone, but that would have to wait. I looked over at Scotty. He was laughing at Brandon's antics. I smiled. It was good to see him laugh, even for a few moments.

Marc had cards so some of the guys played bullshit. Brandon suggested strip poker, but Jon and Casey shouted out that it was a bad idea because no one wanted to see Brandon naked. That wasn't true. *I* wanted to see him naked! I couldn't count on him losing, though, and I could just picture myself having to expose more and more of my slim body. I wasn't accustomed to being naked around anyone but Marc.

Some of the guys played cards. Some just talked. I helped Marc get out glasses and plates. He had his own little kitchen so he was much better prepared to host an impromptu party than the rest of us.

Casper and Nathan pulled Scotty into a card game. Scotty was nervous and frightened, but at least he could lose himself for a few moments in playing cards and talking with his friends. That was my goal when I had shouted out "Party at Marc's place!" Scotty needed time with his friends. He needed to see that life was worth living. Besides, a party was always good.

Ethan and Tristan returned in about half an hour with drinks, ice, and hot pizzas. As I stood there eating pizza and looking around at my friends I realized how very lucky I was. I had friends back at my old school and I was more or less happy, but I didn't have friends like these. The way everyone came together to help Scotty said a lot about them. These guys were incredible!

The gang had pulled me in quickly when I was new too. There were cliques at school that wouldn't let anyone new in, but the gay boys weren't one of them. I was different from the other out gay boys and I knew it. Most of the out gay boys at VHS were jocks. My boyfriend was a soccer player. Shawn and Tim played football and so had Casper's boyfriend when he was in high school. Ethan had been a wrestler. Nathan and Casper weren't athletes, but they were kind of buff from all the farm work. Dane wasn't on a team, but I thought of him as athletic. Tristan was artistic and intellectual, but he still wasn't like me. I was the only gay boy who was feminine and fit the stereotype most people had of gay boys. I was different and still the others had included me and tried to make me feel comfortable. I was one lucky boy!

I was afraid Scotty's parents might show up and try to kidnap him. They had to know he wasn't coming home by now. His parents also knew Scotty was, or rather had been, in the play with Marc, Tim, Dane, and me. That meant that Marc's place was one of the four most likely locations for them to look. Of course, they'd have to find out where Marc lived, but I doubted that would be difficult. If they did show up Scotty was well guarded. They wouldn't get past any of us. I wasn't tough, but they'd only take him away over my dead or at least unconscious body. A lot of people might think I'm girly, but I could be fierce! Rowr!

"You look ready to pounce on someone," Marc said with a grin when he came over and stood beside me.

"I was just thinking of what I'd do if Scotty's parents tried to nab him."

"I bet you'd scare the crap out of them."

"As I was just thinking to myself that I'm not tough, but I can be fierce."

"Oh, you're tough, just not in the surviving-a-grueling-soccer-practice way."

Marc laughed.

"What?"

"I was just picturing what would happen if Scotty's parents did show up. They would find they had walked into the dragon's lair."

"We need to protect him. What if they did manage to grab him?"

"They won't and even if they did we would grab him back."

"Do you think he's going to be okay?" I asked.

"I don't know, Dorian. Spiriting Scotty out of town is only a temporary solution. We can't hide him forever and he can't stay out of school for long. This is just buying us time until we can figure something out. I like that emancipation idea, but I have no idea how that works. Even if that idea will work it's going to be expensive to pay a lawyer."

"I'm sure everyone will help. I'll get a job if I have to!"

Marc grinned at me.

"What?"

"Did anyone ever tell you how special you are?"

"Yuck! Sweetness overdose!" Jon said. I wasn't aware anyone could hear us, but Jon was the closest.

I giggled then leaned in and kissed Marc on the lips.

"My eyes! My eyes!" Jon said, but then he smiled and ruined his pretend disgust.

Marc stuck his tongue out at Jon and then stuck it in my mouth. Mmm.

Shawn arrived near the end of our party, but there was still pizza left. He sat on a couch and talked with Tristan. They made a good, if unpredictable pair, the football player and the artist. Seeing them together gave me hope that Marc and I would work out. Marc and I showed every sign of staying together so far, but we'd hadn't been together long and we were very different. We were the soccer stud and the feminine boy.

I smiled at Marc. He loved me for *me*. I was comfortable with myself, but a lot of guys would not have been comfortable dating me. Marc wasn't, at first. He had even rejected me because his teammates teased him about his "girlfriend." He had decided that he liked me and cared enough about me to withstand the teasing. He'd even told off his teammates. I think overcoming that obstacle made us a stronger couple and made Marc a stronger person.

Tristan and Scotty walked over to us, as we were talking, and occasionally kissing.

"Scotty and I have decided it might be best if he stays with me for a while," Tristan said.

"I don't think my parents are as likely to track me down at his place as they would be here, or on the Selby farm, or even in Shawn and Tim's loft."

"You're probably right. It's only a couple of days until Brendan arrives on Saturday and he's going back in Sunday so maybe we won't even have to move you around," I said.

"That's what I'm thinking," Tristan said. "I don't think they'll suspect he's with me. If they do catch on we can move him to the next location."

Scotty leaned in and hugged me.

"Thank you so much, Dorian. I don't know what I would have done without you. This is all thanks to you."

"I think you're giving me too much credit. Anyone here would have done the same thing."

"Yeah!" Brandon said. "You're definitely giving Dorian too much credit! He's blond. There is no way he could have thought this all out on his own!"

I laughed as Casper, Nathan, and Marc all rushed and jumped on Brandon. They pummeled him with pillows until he begged for mercy.

"It's going to be okay, Scotty. While you're hiding out in Bloomington we'll find a way to make things better for you."

"You guys have saved my life," Scotty said.

I didn't know what to say to that, so I hugged him.

Our party began to break up. For the sake of paranoia, Brandon and Jon went out and checked the area to make certain Scotty's parents weren't lurking about. When they gave the all clear Shawn, Tristan, and Scotty departed together. In just a few minutes, Marc and I were alone. I helped Marc clean things up and put his loft back in order.

"At least we have a temporary solution," I said.

Marc smiled. He knew I couldn't stop thinking about Scotty.

"We've done more than that. Scotty knows we're all here for him and that we will be here no matter what. Sending him away to hide out is only a temporary solution, but time is on our side. In a little more than a year he'll be out of high school. He'll be eighteen before he graduates. His parents have no say in his life after he turns eighteen."

"Why can't they just accept him? We can hide him and protect him, but... I don't know what I would do if my parents didn't accept me, Marc. I'm sure my dad would have been thrilled if I turned out to be a jock like you, but I know he's okay with who and what I am. He loves me. Scotty doesn't have that. His parents aren't okay with who and what he is. How must that feel?"

Marc shrugged.

"His parents are messed up and they're dangerous, but I think they do love him. If only they didn't go to that screwed up church."

"It's more than the church. Anyone with common sense wouldn't belong to a church like that. They might attend one service, but they wouldn't come back for another. His parents must have some pretty deranged thinking of their own. Still, I can't help but think that there is hope for them. They aren't bad people. They mean well. They're just doing all the wrong things."

"Maybe a good knock on the head would help," Marc suggested.

"I don't think so! I wish we could help Scotty more. I wish we could make his parents understand. I wish we could make them see how horribly foolish they are and how much they are hurting him."

"I don't think there is any talking to people like them, Dorian. They have their beliefs and won't listen to any evidence to the contrary."

"I think their beliefs are stupid, maybe even evil if they cause them to be cruel to their own son."

"Well, don't tell them that!"

"Oh, I won't, but I've just never understood how people can turn their backs on others because of their religion; like that whole Abraham and Isaac story in the Bible. That's such a load of crap. Abraham was a horrible, horrible father for being willing to sacrifice his son and no good and kind god would appreciate such a thing."

"It's nothing more than a story someone made up," Marc said.

"Oh, it has to be made up, but it seems to me that if someone's religion causes them to be cruel that they should question their religion."

"Beliefs are a tricky thing," Marc said. "We will take care of Scotty. I know you won't stop worrying about him until we find a permanent solution."

I grinned. Marc was right.

Marc and I sat down on the couch. I was tired. I leaned my head against his shoulder and he held me close. We just sat there like that for the longest time. Finally, I leaned back and smiled at Marc.

"Drive me home?"

"For a kiss."

I leaned in and kissed Marc on the lips. He stood, took my hand, and pulled me up. He gave me a hug and then drove me home.

***

Brandon stopped Marc and me in the parking lot Thursday morning before school. He looked around to make sure no one was near and then told us that Aunt Anne was more than willing to have Scotty as a houseguest for however long he needed to stay. That was a relief, although Brandon had seemed to think there was no doubt she would say "yes."

Rumors were already starting up about Scotty. I didn't hear anything before school, but the rumor mill was at work by the end of second period. Scotty's parents had shown up looking for him and that firmly established that Scotty was a missing person. After the events of the past fall anyone going missing was big news. Three athletes had disappeared last autumn only to be found dead later. I shuddered. I didn't even want to think about the events of last fall.

Those of us who knew the truth feigned ignorance. The first rumor I heard was that his parents had joined a cult and Scotty had run away to escape having his head shaved. I liked that rumor so much I repeated it when anyone asked what I'd heard. It was the truth. I had heard the rumor. I just didn't tell anyone I knew it wasn't true. The rumor made no sense anyway. If Scotty's parents were going to force him to shave his head then wouldn't Justin have shown up at school with a shaved head? I hadn't spotted Scotty's little brother yet, but I was reasonably sure he still had all his hair.

I had learned long ago that rumors did not have to make sense. There were those who would believe them regardless of the facts. I was happy this rumor made Scotty's parents look like freaks. That's what they were in my book; dangerous freaks.

I was called the office in the middle of third period. I wasn't sure why until the principal asked if I knew anything about the whereabouts of Scotty Jackson. He said he was asking because Scotty and I had worked closely together during play practices, which made some sense, but I was willing to bet Scotty's parents had put him up to it. They probably thought I'd kidnapped their son. Of course, that wasn't so far from the truth. I told the principal the last time I'd seen Scotty in school was the day before, which was the truth. I just didn't tell him I'd been hanging out with Scotty last night.

140

Marc met me at my locker just before lunch, as usual.

"Did you get called into the office?" I asked.

"Yeah."

"Me too."

"Scotty's parents have probably told the cops they think we murdered him," Marc said.

"I wouldn't be surprised."

We walked down to the cafeteria and through the lunch line. It was taco day! There was also Spanish rice, refried beans, corn, fruit salad, and a chocolate chip cookie. Yes!

Marc and I joined the others.

"What are you grinning about?" Brandon asked.

"I love taco day!"

"Wow. What a surprise. Dorian is excited about something," Brandon said.

I stuck my tongue out at him.

"Save the tongue for Marc, homo," Brandon said.

"Great idea!"

I turned to Marc and gave him a lingering kiss.

"You just had to encourage him, didn't you?" Jon asked. "Those two are bad enough as it is."

"Hey, did anyone else get hauled into the office?" Marc asked.

"Did you and Dorian get caught doing it in the restroom again?" Brandon asked.

"We have my loft for doing it. We don't need the restroom."

"I was," Dane said.

"Me too," Tim said.

"You guys were doing it in the restroom?" Brandon asked.

"Well, yeah, but that's not why we were called in," Dane said. "We were questioned about the location of Scotty Jackson."

"I knew you homos were dangerous. You did unspeakable sexual things to him and then killed him to keep him quiet, didn't you?" Brandon said.

"Yeah, you've got us," Tim said. "Want to be next Brandon?"

"Of course he does!" Jon said.

"Speak for yourself."

No one listening in would have a clue that we knew where Scotty was located. I was quiet sure members of his church was spying on us. Devon passed by closely twice and I bet he was listening to every detail he could. I kind of missed tormenting the spies. Maybe we'd have to start up again.

Lunch with the guys was fun as always, but I kept thinking that Scotty should be there with us. His parents should have loved and accepted him instead of trying to change him. They should have supported him. He'd landed a lead role and they didn't even care! A good parent would have been proud. My parents were proud of me and landing a lead role wasn't a rarity for me at all! I appreciated my parents before I met Scotty, but I appreciated them even more after hearing about his horrible parents.

In the back of my mind, and often in the front, I was always trying to think of a way to make things okay for Scotty. I couldn't magically transform his family and make them loving and accepting, but there had to be something I could do! At least Scotty was safe at Tristan's house. Tristan's mom was kind. She would take good care of him and keep him safe.

I called Tristan's home after play practice and talked to Scotty. I interrupted his supper with Tristan and his mom so I didn't talk long. He seemed to be doing okay, but I could clearly hear the sadness in his voice. No one should be treated the way his family treated him. I wanted to march over to Scotty's house and give his parents and brother a piece of my mind, but I knew it wouldn't do any good. It also might make them suspicious. I wasn't about to endanger Scotty.

Friday was filled with wild tales about Scotty. There was a rumor that a body had been found in the Tippecanoe River and that it was thought to be Scotty. That would have scared me if he'd really been missing. There were rumors Scotty had been kidnapped and that he'd run away because he'd gotten a girl pregnant. There was just about any rumor one wanted to hear. It was a rumor buffet where one could pick what one liked best. My favorite was that his parents were under suspicion for murder and that the cops were searching their freezer for body parts.

Brendan was due to arrive on Friday after his classes. Everyone was staying away so Brendan and Casper could have some "quality" time, but we were all going over on Saturday afternoon to see him. The plan was to go after lunch but well before supper so Ardelene wouldn't feel the need to cook for us. Scotty was coming with Tristan and Shawn. So far his parents didn't have a clue that he was hiding out at Tristan's place.

I went over to Marc's Saturday morning for some quality time of our own. In other words we did it all morning! Often we were content to just hold each other, but sometimes we both needed intense sex. I was panting so hard I had to stop and catch my breath sometimes. Marc had greater endurance. I guess running up and down a soccer field was good training for sex. That's probably the only reason all those boys played soccer. Marc and I were totally exhausted when we did it the final time that morning. We actually had to take a nap. We wore ourselves out!

Marc made us toasted cheese sandwiches for lunch. I love a man who can cook. We rounded out our meal with Cokes and sour cream and onion potato chips. As we sat eating at his kitchen table I almost felt like we lived together. I wondered if we would someday. I sure hoped so! Maybe it wasn't likely we'd stick together since we were both so young. There were a lot of things that could pull us apart. I wasn't going to worry about it. Instead, I was determined to enjoy what we had right now. That's all that really mattered anyway. Now. Nothing in life is permanent. The trick was to enjoy everyone and everything while they are a part of your life. I sure enjoyed my time with Marc!

Marc drove me out to the Selby farm a little after one. There were already a few cars there and I could see some of the guys sitting at a picnic table under a huge oak tree. Others loitered nearby. I didn't know Brendan all that well, but most of the guys were close to him. I'd mostly heard stories. Brendan had been hot stuff at school. He was the quarterback of the football team and team captain! An out gay boy had been one of the most popular guys in school. Imagine that!

I had met Brendan before. He was very handsome with his light brown hair and sexy brown eyes and his body... all I can say is wow! Casper was one lucky boy.

Marc caught me checking out Brendan.

"Thinking of trading me in?"

"Nah, I figure you're good for 100,000... miles. Yeah, that's it... miles."

Marc laughed.

"I think I know what you *really* mean. Hmm, 100,000? I'm going to need a lot of naps."

Brandon rolled his eyes at us.

"You're just jealous, Brandon, because you don't get it as often as we do," Marc teased.

"True, but I don't want what you get."

"Try it, you might like it," Marc said.

"Hey, it's not cool to proposition me right in front of your boyfriend," Brandon said.

"It is kind of a shame that Brandon isn't at least bi," I said to Marc, pretending Brandon wasn't standing near.

"I guess, but there are much hotter straight boys around, like Jon," Marc said.

"Yeah, he is hotter."

"*What?*" Brandon said loudly. "No way is Jon hotter than me! I should beat you both."

"Oh yeah! Get rough with me stud," I said, then giggled.

"There is just no winning with gay boys. I'm going to go hang out with Brendan."

Brandon left us. Marc draped his arm over my shoulder.

"It is too bad Brandon isn't bi, but then it doesn't matter because I have you," Marc said. He leaned in and kissed me.

"Yeah, but I don't have Brandon's muscles and I don't play soccer."

"You are beyond sexy, baby. I love your slim, defined body and I like the games we play together much better than soccer."

We looked into each other's eyes and then kissed more deeply.

"Come and see our new chickens!"

Marc and I broke our kiss. Dave, Nathan's twelve-year-old brother, smiled at us eagerly. He took our hands and led us toward the barn.

Dave was a smaller version of Nathan. He had the same features, the same blond hair, and the same blue eyes. He looked younger then twelve, but then Nathan looked younger than his years too.

I had already been introduced to Henrietta, Dave's favorite chicken, but he showed us a lot of others.

"The little white fluffy chickens are silkies," Dave said.

"They look so soft," I said.

"They are. Want to pet one?"

Before I could answer, Dave picked one up. It was completely unafraid. I wished I could say the same. I reached out carefully, afraid the little chicken would peck me, but it just turned its head to the side and closed its eyes, clearly enjoying itself as I stroked it.

"Those are guineas," Dave said, pointing out odd little chickens with red beaks and small white polka dots all over their dark feathers. "We mostly keep the guineas because they eat ticks."

"Then I like guineas because I hate ticks," I said. "I got one on me once."

"Just once? We check for them whenever we've been in the woods or the tall grass. The tiny deer ticks are the worst. They are so small they are very hard to see," Dave said.

I looked about fearfully, but I was being silly. Ticks wouldn't be in a barn, especially one where tick-eating guineas lived. I'd think twice before I entered the woods again.

"I always thought chickens all looked alike, but I guess was wrong," I said, trying to forget about ticks.

"Oh, there are all kinds."

Dave picked up Henrietta and then let me hold her. I didn't really want to hold her, but I also didn't want to admit I was afraid of her. I still remembered the "chicken-incident" that took place at a bon fire here on the Selby farm. A chicken came up behind me and pecked me. I had no idea what it was. I just felt something bite me and then saw something I thought was furry. I screamed and ran. The guys thought it was hilarious and I felt like an idiot.

Henrietta made little clucking sounds as I held her. She gave no indication she wanted to peck me. She seemed very happy in my arms.

"She likes you," Dave said.

I smiled. I liked her too. She wasn't scary at all.

"You live in a barn. Maybe you could have chickens, Marc," I teased.

"Yeah, right. Dad would kill me the first time a chicken climbed on one of his cars. My loft isn't exactly suitable for chickens. I kind of wish I could have chickens. They're cool."

"I have them all named," Dave said. "You know Henrietta. That's Sayward. That's Portius. That's Jary, Achsa, and that's Sulie."

"Where did you get those names?" Marc asked.

"I watched a miniseries on TV called *The Awakening Land*. It's based on some books by Conrad Richter called *The Trees*, *The Fields*, and *The Town*. I've been reading the books. I'm just half-way through *The Fields*. It's all about pioneers in the 1790s and early 1800s. I named all the new chickens after characters."

"I've never heard names like those before," I said.

"Uncle Jack said one of his ancestors was named Portius, but I've never heard that one before either," Dave said.

I loved the smell of the hay and I liked the chickens. I wasn't so sure about the horses, but they were separated from the part of the barn we were in. They were so big! I was glad Marc wasn't a horse rider because I would have been scared to death to climb up on one of those huge things.

When we walked back outside Scotty and Brendan were talking. Brendan had his hand on Scotty's shoulder. I knew Brendan would look after Scotty. He'd probably check in on him at Aunt Anne's farm after he dropped him off.

It was funny how everyone called the lady Scotty was going to stay with Aunt Anne, when she wasn't an actual aunt to any of us. I guess it was the same as Uncle Jack. He was only Ethan's uncle, but he was Uncle Jack to everyone. I guess it made sense. He acted as an uncle to everyone, maybe even a dad. Family didn't have to be based on biology. I hadn't given kids much thought, but if I someday adopted one he'd be my son just as if I'd made him the old fashioned way.

"I wondered where you two wandered off to," Dane said as we rejoined the group. "If I hadn't seen you coming out of the barn with Dave I would have been sure you were getting it on."

"We aren't like you and Tim," Marc said. "We don't do it all the time. We haven't done it for... two whole hours!"

"Wow, you are so deprived."

"Did someone say Marc is depraved?" Jon asked.

"No. Deprived." I said.

"I found that doubtful. I think it's more likely you're depraved."

"Like you aren't," Marc said.

"I didn't say it was a bad thing."

It was warm out, but Ethan decided we needed a bonfire. Marc went off to help him gather brush, along with Brendan, Brandon, and Jon. I offered, but I was glad when they said they had more than enough to handle the job. I didn't want to make my hands all rough and I didn't want to get dirty.

There was soon a merry blaze burning away a safe distance from the barn. Ethan and Nathan whittled roasting sticks. No one was hungry, but once the fire calmed down we roasted marshmallows. We rolled a couple of logs up near the fire and Ethan brought out some bales of straw for seats. Marc and I sat close together on one of the bales while he watched Casper turn a marshmallow into a torch.

"You'd better watch your back, Dorian. There might be vicious chickens about," Shawn said.

"Is anyone *ever* going to forget that?" I asked.

"Forget you squealing like a girl because a chicken pecked you. I'd say... NO!" Brandon said and laughed.

"What's this about a ferocious chicken?" Scotty asked.

I had to endure Brandon's gleeful retelling of the tale. At least he didn't embellish, but then it was hardly necessary.

"I was just in the barn with the chickens," I said.

"He petted one and he held Henrietta," Dave said.

147

"That's only because you were there to protect him, Dave," Jon said.

I stuck out my tongue at Jon.

Mercifully, I didn't have to endure much more chicken talk, although Nathan suggested we turn the story of my encounter with the ferocious chicken into an epic tale like *The Iliad* or *Beowulf*. Tristan said it would never sell.

Scotty had a good time. I wished he could be emancipated from his parents and live on the Selby farm. Maybe my parents could adopt him and I could have a brother! That would be asking a lot. I'd tried and tried to think of ways to help Scotty, but I wasn't having much luck. I was trying not to think about it for a while so that maybe an idea would just come to me.

We talked and laughed and roasted marshmallows. Brandon and Jon got into an insult war, but when didn't they? They made Scotty laugh and he needed to laugh. He needed to see that life could be good.

Scotty

"What do you think?" Tristan asked as we walked into the kitchen where his mom was preparing lunch.

"Oh. That's wonderful, Tristan!"

She took the drawing and held it up near my face for comparison.

"You've captured Scotty perfectly. You're so handsome when you smile, Scotty. You should smile more often."

I smiled just then for a moment.

"I had to keep bribing him with your oatmeal cookies to get him to smile," Tristan said.

"They are sooo good!" I said.

"I hope you didn't eat too many. Lunch is almost ready. I'm making lasagna with cooked apples and garlic toast."

"Those are my favorites!"

"Tristan told me."

"You've been so nice to me. I... I don't know how to thank you."

"You can thank me by smiling more."

I grinned and nodded. I hadn't had much to smile about in recent days and yet I did have a few reasons to be happy. My life was a mess, but I almost couldn't believe how my friends had banded together to help me. Mrs. Cole even took me in, gave me a place to sleep, and fed me. She barely knew me and yet she'd done so much for me.

Tristan and I went back into the room I'd been sharing with him. It was time to pack up the last of my things. Brendan was due to arrive at one. I'd be leaving with him for Bloomington where my parents would never find me.

Tristan made a much better roommate than my brother. He was actually nice to me and he was fascinating. I could see why Shawn was so into him. Tristan knew a lot about art and had made it interesting. I had sat and talked to him while he did a watercolor of the view from his bedroom window. I was fascinated to watch as he turned brushstrokes into a beautiful painting of the view outside. It was a form of magic as far as I was concerned.

I looked around the room. I hadn't been there long, but I was going to miss it. I was going to miss Tristan too. I wished I could exchange him for my brother.

"I have a couple of presents for you," Tristan said.

"I should be giving you presents for letting me stay with you."

"I've enjoyed it. I've always wanted a brother and with you here these past couple of days it's almost been like having one."

"I'd give you mine, but you wouldn't want him."

Tristan laughed.

"Here, this is for you."

Tristan handed me the small painting I'd just been thinking about it. He'd framed and matted it.

"Thank you!"

"You're welcome. I also bought you this. I thought you might want something to read."

Tristan handed me a book. I read the title; *The Poems of Robert Frost*.

"Give it a try. I know poems probably aren't your thing, but since you're going to the countryside I thought you might like it. He wrote a lot about woods and country lanes."

"Thanks, Tristan."

I reached out and hugged Tristan. It felt so good to be able to hug one of my friends without being judged. No one in my family was a hugger. On the rare occasions we hugged it was stiff and formal. Tristan took me in his arms and held me close. When he hugged me I could feel love.

I put the book into my overstuffed backpack. I didn't dare go home, but the guys had gathered up some clothes for me. I didn't know what I'd do without my friends.

"We won't forget about you while you're gone," Tristan said. "We will all be working on a way to make things better for you. If worst comes to worst you'll just have to hide out on Aunt Anne's farm until you're eighteen."

"I hope I don't have to do that, but it would definitely be better than the life I'd have here."

"Just remember you have friends. I promise I'll write. I already have the address. I'll write you first thing and I know the other guys are planning to write you too."

I nodded. Sadness tugged at my heart. I didn't want to leave my friends, but it wasn't safe for me in Verona anymore.

"Lunch is almost ready, boys! Come and set the table."

Tristan and I walked to the kitchen. I loved the Cole's kitchen. It was much more comfortable and cheerful than the formal dining room at my parent's house. Mrs. Cole had decorated it with a 1950s theme. Every time I walked in I felt like I'd stepped onto the set of *I Love Lucy*. Even the stove was vintage.

I pulled the plates out of the cabinet while Tristan grabbed the glasses and silverware. The plates were from the '50s, too. Mrs. Cole said they were Fiestaware. I set a yellow one at my place. Tristan's was cobalt blue and Mrs. Cole's was green.

The lasagna was sitting on the counter cooling and the scent made my stomach rumble with hunger. Tristan's mom opened the oven door and the scent of garlic bread flooded the kitchen too. I couldn't wait to eat!

I didn't have to wait long. As soon as the garlic bread was toasted all was ready.

Tristan's mom poured us all iced tea and we each helped ourselves to the rest. Cheese strung out from the pan as I scooped up a big piece of lasagna and put it on my plate. The cooked apples smelled wonderful.

I sat back down and tried the lasagna. It was gooey, cheesy, and tasted heavenly. The garlic toast was toasted just the way I liked it; it was still soft on the top. The apples tasted almost like a dessert.

"I love these apples. I've never tasted apples like these before," I said.

"We get them from the Selby farm. Tristan and I went and picked a couple of bushels last fall."

"I love them. Everything is so good."

"Thank you."

We talked while we ate, mostly about small Verona events like the Community Bake Sale and the weekly Farmer's Market. There was always so much going on in Verona. I wished I didn't have to leave, but I didn't even want to think about what would happen if I stayed. My biggest fear is that my parents would send me away to a clinic or church camp for "treatment." That was not going to happen because I wasn't sticking around to let it happen.

I ate and ate. By the time I finished I was completely stuffed. I looked at the clock. It was nearly one, which was when Brendan was supposed to pick me up.

Tristan and I put the dishes in the dishwasher while his mom put away the leftovers. I was sorry I wouldn't be around to eat them, but at the moment I couldn't even think of eating!

By the time we were finished, there was a knock at the door. Tristan went to answer it and I went into his room to grab my backpack and the little painting Tristan had given me. When I came back out, Brendan was standing in the living room looking very fit and handsome in jeans and an IU Football tee shirt.

"Ready?" Brendan asked.

I nodded.

Tristan gave me a big hug and even kissed me on the cheek.

"Thanks again for everything," I said.

"Any time."

Mrs. Cole came out of the kitchen carrying two large paper sacks. She handed one to Brendan and one to me.

"They're oatmeal cookies," she said.

"Thanks," Brendan said.

"Yeah, thanks! I love your cookies! Thank you for letting me stay and for all the wonderful food. You are a great cook!"

"You are welcome and you're welcome to come back any time."

Tristan's mom hugged me. I hugged her back. I wished my mom would hug me like that. When I pulled back my eyes were a little moist, but I smiled.

I followed Brendan out to his car, a silver and maroon Cutlass Supreme with cool spoke-hubcaps. In moments we were on our way.

"Brandon gave me directions to Aunt Anne's farm. It's just outside of Bloomington. I thought you might like to camp out in my dorm room tonight. I can show you around IU today and then take you out to the farm before my first class."

"That would be really cool. You like IU?"

"I love it. It's way better than high school. I miss the guys, and most of all Casper, but I love the freedom of college. I like being able to do my own thing and make my own plans. The professors don't hover over your shoulder to make sure you get your work done. They just assign it, give a due date, and that's it."

"Is IU more accepting than VHS?"

"You mean because I'm gay? Yes. It's not perfect, but it's better than VHS. Everyone is more mature about it. It's part of the freedom I mentioned. College is different. No one is stuck in a rut. No one is expected to act a certain way or be a certain thing. There are some expectations. Like... since I'm a football player people have preconceived notions about what I'm going to be like, but they don't expect me to stick to that."

"Do a lot of people know you're gay?"

"Quite a few. It's not a secret. Of course, IU is a big school. Most people there don't know me at all. Since I play football I'm more visible than a lot of students, but most still don't know my name or that I'm gay. The cool thing is that most wouldn't care if they did know."

"You have a roommate?"

"Yeah, Jeff."

"Does he know?"

"Yeah. He's cool with it. He's bisexual. He's always taunting me and telling me he knows I want him bad. You'll like Jeff. He has a very in-your-face personality. Be warned, he will call you on your crap. He keeps me on my toes. Oh, I only have a small bunk. I hope you won't mind sleeping with me. It will be a little cramped."

"I won't mind. The question is; will Casper mind?"

"Nah. He trusts me. He already knows I was planning on you spending the night. He completely drained me of all sexual desire anyway. I don't think I'll be horny for days."

Brendan grinned. I pictured just how Casper might have drained away Brendan's sexual desire, but then stopped myself because I was getting aroused. I had to control myself if I was going to be sleeping next to Brendan. He was a stud!

"You'll like IU and Bloomington. The stadium is huge! If you're still staying with Aunt Anne in the fall I'll get you some tickets to a game. I'll introduce you to the quarterback. He's gay too."

"Really?"

"Yeah. We hang out a lot. We mostly talk football but if you go out with us sometime we'll try to talk about something else."

"I like football. I just don't play it. It must be scary. Some of those guys are huge."

"Yeah, there are linebackers who outweigh me by a hundred pounds. It hurts when one of those guys plows into me, even with all the padding. I try not to get hit!"

"Good plan."

"Casper is coming to IU when he finishes high school. After I graduate, I'm going to stay in Bloomington until he finishes school. After that, we'll decide where we want to go."

"You think you two will still be together?"

"I hope so and I think we will be. If something does break us up I'm sure we'll remain friends. We've been through too much to just forget about each other."

We grew silent for a few moments and I looked out the window. The flat plains of northern Indiana stretched out for as far as the eye could see. Later, they would mostly be covered with tall corn, but this early in the spring farmers were only beginning to prepare the ground for planting.

"From what I hear, Aunt Anne is really nice," Brendan said. "I've never met her, but Brandon has and he had only good things to stay."

"Everyone says she is wonderful, but I'm still a little nervous. I'm going to live with her and we don't even know each other."

"I bet the two of you will get along great. I'll keep in touch with you while you're there. I'll come and get you now and then so we can hang out."

"How about hooking me up with a college boy?"

"That might be arranged."

"Nice. I was kind of kidding when I said that, but... not really."

"I understand. I know what it's like. Guys our age need sex bad."

"Yeah. How do you manage without Casper? You only get to see him once every few weeks, right?"

"It varies. I have been home a couple of weekends in a row, but it's usually a lot longer between visits. School and football keep me busy. Right now, there is no football so I have more free time. In the fall it's almost impossible to get away. It's rough without Casper. I'll be honest. I jerk off a lot." Brendan laughed.

"Me too."

"When I'm with Casper the sex is intense. We go at it over and over again. It's more grueling than a football practice, but way more fun!"

"I'm sure."

Brendan and I talked all the way to Bloomington. Brendan was very friendly and just plain nice. He could easily have been a stuck up prick instead. He was extremely handsome and had an incredibly hot body. I wouldn't have minded a shirtless Brendan poster for my wall! Maybe someday I'd have a dorm room or apartment where I could hang shirtless posters of guys if I wanted.

When we reached Bloomington, Brendan drove by the stadium where he played football. He was right. It was huge! Next, we drove by Assembly Hall where all the basketball games were played. I saw a big dorm on the corner across the street and figured that must be where Brendan lived. I was wrong. He turned the corner and drove on past. We passed another dorm and then another. I don't know what made me think a big school like IU had only one dorm! I guess I wasn't thinking.

We drove past a huge library, classroom buildings, and more dorms. Brendan finally pulled into a parking lot near yet another big dorm and parked.

"Welcome to Forest Quad," he said.

I grabbed my backpack since I was spending the night and followed Brendan as he carried a box and a huge laundry bag toward the dorm.

Forest Quad was big inside and I lost track of where we were going quickly. Brendan unlocked room 514 and we went inside. The room was very small.

"I've never seen beds like these before. They're like bunk beds, but there's no bottom bunk," I said.

"They're called lofts. It's a way of creating space in a small room."

I could see what Brendan meant. He had a small refrigerator under his bed as well as a bookshelf stuffed with books, notebooks, and all kinds of other stuff. On the top of the bookshelf rested a stereo.

"Wow, this is barely enough room for one person," I said.

"Yeah, it's cramped, but I only sleep and study here. I'm out most of the time. I even do a lot of my studying in Dunn's Woods or one of the lounges in the IMU.

"The IMU?"

"Indiana Memorial Union. It's the student union and it's the largest in the world."

"Wow."

I looked at Brendan's bunk. I didn't know how I was going to survive sleeping with him. We would be pressed up against each other. I was going to have to face away from him for sure or he'd know how much his hunky body turned me on. I wasn't about to try anything with him. There was no way I'd do that to Casper. Even if I had no conscience I was sure putting a move on Brendan would only make him mad. He obviously cared about Casper very much.

I hoped Brendan didn't sleep shirtless. Then again...

I heard a key in the lock and moments later the door opened. A handsome boy with glasses entered.

"You're back already? I was hoping you'd decide to skip classes and stay a few days longer. I love having a room to myself," the boy said.

"Don't let him fool you. I'm sure he cries himself to sleep at night when I'm not here," Brendan said.

"As if!"

"Jeff, this is my friend Scotty."

"I won't hold that against you," Jeff said.

"He will be spending the night."

Jeff raised an eyebrow.

"Don't even think it."

"What? What was I thinking?"

"Something crude. Scotty is just a friend."

"Ah. I thought maybe Casper wised up and dumped your sorry ass."

"You see what I have to live with?" Brendan asked me.

"At least he's hot," I said, and then turned red when I realized I'd said it out loud.

"Now here is someone with good taste!" Jeff said.

"Obviously not if he thinks you're hot."

"You can never keep your eyes off me, Brendan." Jeff turned to me. "If Brendan wasn't so loyal to his boyfriend he would be all over me. He practically drools every time he looks in my direction."

"Jeff has trouble separating fantasy from reality."

"The reality is that I am Brendan's fantasy."

"Let's walk around campus. A little Jeff goes a very long way," Brendan said.

"That means he's losing control and won't be able to keep his hands off me if he doesn't leave now," Jeff said. "It's nice meeting you, Scotty. If Brendan tries to violate you tonight you can crawl into bed with me, but I won't promise not to violate you too."

"I might like that," I said, then grinned.

Brendan led me out into the hall. I could feel my face growing red.

"I can't believe I just said that."

Brendan laughed.

"I also can't believe I was that bold."

"Think of it as a taste of what college life will be like," Brendan said.

"I want to start right now!"

"You might want to finish high school first."

"I just hope I can."

Brendan looked at me. He could detect the sadness in my voice. I'd been fine a moment before, but all of a sudden I felt dejected and alone.

"You'll finish high school, Scotty. If you can't return to Verona, you'll finish somewhere else or you can get your G.E.D. Don't forget you have friends. We will do a lot more for you than just hide you from your parents."

"You barely know me."

"I know you well enough and gay boys have to stick together. I would never have escaped from the Cloverdale Center without help. If Uncle Jack hadn't taken Casper and me in I don't know what we would have done. Others have been there for me time and again and most often they have nothing to gain. As far as I'm concerned, that's what life is all about—helping others. Nothing much matters if you can't be there to help someone when they need you."

"You know, I've attended church most of my life, but you seem more religious than any of the people in my church. Perhaps religious isn't the right word, but you just seem... I guess what I'm trying to say is that you act the way people who go to church should act."

"I just think that if someone needs help, you should help them if you can. If we all did that there would be a lot fewer problems in the world."

We walked out into the afternoon sunlight. There were college kids everywhere—walking, running, and just hanging out. Brendan led me across campus, pointing out places like the Read dorm and the Simon Music Library. We passed large classroom buildings and lots and lots of sexy college boys.

There were trees everywhere. The campus was like one big park. It was a truly beautiful place.

"This is one of my favorite places on campus," Brendan said as we neared what looked like a forest. "This is Dunn's Woods."

We followed one of the many brick paths that led into and through Dunn's Woods. Soon, we were surrounded by trees, some just saplings, but most enormous. Chipmunks scampered about and squirrels nosed through the carpet of leaves only feet away. They seemed completely undisturbed by our presence.

"This is incredible," I said when we'd walked into the woods. "There are buildings all around us, but I can't see them. I feel like I'm in a forest, far from civilization."

"That's one reason I love this place. The entire campus has a park-like feel. It was designed that way on purpose. There are direct paths from one building to another for those who are in a hurry, but there are scenic routes everywhere with trees, flowers, and even streams. Most of that is thanks to Herman Wells. He was the president of IU for years and he's the chancellor now. I met him right here in Dunn's Woods. I was sitting on a bench gazing at the trees and this older guy came and joined me. We started talking and I finally realized who he was. He was so easy to talk to and so friendly. It might seem odd, but meeting him made me feel welcome at IU."

"That's really cool."

"Yeah. You know what you were saying about feeling like you're away from civilization? Well, civilization is much closer than you think. Check this out."

We walked out of Dunn's Woods and there was downtown Bloomington.

"This is Kirkwood Avenue. It's one of the main business areas of Bloomington."

I couldn't believe it. We were in a woods one minute and the next there were cars, buses, restaurants, and shops everywhere.

"It's almost like magic," I said.

"Almost."

We didn't head into town, but instead walked north, staying on campus. Soon, we turned back the direction we'd come, only we were on a winding path with a stream to our right and a large open, grassy area on our left. Shirtless college boys played Frisbee while others tanned on beach towels. There were girls there too, but I was way too busy checking out the boys. Brendan noticed and smiled.

"This is Dunn Meadow. It's a hang out place and there are a lot of events like concerts held here."

"I love the scenery," I said.

"Yeah, the scenery is nice. The sexy boys almost drove me out of my mind when I first arrived."

"I bet."

An enormous building loomed on our right, just on the other side of the stream.

"That is the Indiana Memorial Union."

"That whole thing is the student union? No way!"

"I told you it was the largest in the world. The Biddle Hotel is inside. Restaurants, lounges, meeting rooms, and the IU Bookstore are all inside too."

The path let up onto the sidewalk that ran beside the street. A campus bus pulled up just as we arrived and bunches of college kids got on and off. Suddenly hot college boys who were making their way to various points on campus surrounded us.

"Yo! Brewer! You planning on becoming the quarterback next year?" asked an incredibly sexy boy with dark red hair. He wore a tank top and his arms bulged with muscle. I wanted to reach out and touch his bicep.

"Not a chance, but I'm coming back to play again for sure."

"Awesome! I can't believe some of those plays you made, man."

"Thanks."

"Later."

"Who was that?" I asked when the boy had gone.

"I have no idea."

"Do a lot of people come up to you like that?"

"Not a lot. I'm recognized more during football season. Gabrial, the quarterback, is the one who gets noticed. When I'm with him, people stop us all the time to talk."

160

"If I go to school here I'm sure I'll blend in because I won't be playing football."

"There are times when I wish I blended in more, especially when I'm with Gabrial."

We walked past Ernie Pyle Hall. It was a fairly large building, but was dwarfed by the IMU behind it. We crossed the street and walked by huge building called the HPER that Brendan said had a gym, a pool, and lots of classrooms. As we headed north there was a big grassy area with soccer goals. A bunch of guys were playing soccer and most of them were shirtless. College was so much better than high school!

"I'm coming to school here. I may have to get a job and save up money after high school before I can come, but I'm coming."

"Just because of the shirtless guys?"

"They're so hot! They aren't the only reason. I love the campus and everyone is so cool here. I know a lot of the Verona boys will be here as well."

"It is a great school."

We walked through the Arboretum, which had more grass than trees, but was still beautiful. Brendan pointed out the main library and yet more classroom buildings across the street from it. The campus was huge!

We turned south. Brendan pointed out the IU Auditorium, the Lily Library, and the IU Art Museum. We ended up back at the IMU.

We entered the Indiana Memorial Union through one of those cool rotating circular doors and stepped into the lobby of the Biddle Hotel. Brendan took me up the stairs to the left and we walked up to the next level.

"This is one of the lounges, but I prefer the one on the next level up because it has a fireplace."

We turned and walked down a long hallway. Original works of art by T.C. Steele and other artists were displayed on the walls.

"Tristan would love this place," I said.

"Yeah. I believe Tristan is thinking about coming here for art school."

"Cool."

Brendan pointed out the IU Bookstore straight ahead and then called my attention to a little shop on the right.

"That is one of my favorite spots on campus. It's called Sugar & Spice. It was incredible cupcakes and the most enormous drinks you've ever seen."

We turn a corner and then another and walked down a long hallway.

"This is the commons. There are lots of little restaurants. It's like the food court of a mall. My favorite place is just ahead. You hungry?"

"Yeah."

"Good. I'm buying."

We stepped through a pair of doorways and there was a Burger King.

"How cool is this?" Brendan asked. "There is a Burger King right in the IMU."

I laughed. Of all the things IU had to offer, Brendan was excited about the Burger King.

We both ordered Whopper value meals and then found a seat in the large dining area.

"This place can get really crowded around meal times through the week, but it's quiet since it's Sunday. Campus can be kind of deserted on weekends, unless there is a game."

"I bet campus does get busy."

"Oh yeah. IU is a little bigger than VHS." Brendan grinned.

My Whopper and fries were great. I think the atmosphere made the food taste better. There weren't a lot of others around, but like everywhere else at IU there were cute college boys. I wanted them all!

"This has been really great, Brendan. Thank you so much."

"It's only a Whopper," Brendan teased.

"The Whopper is great, but I mean everything. I haven't even been thinking about my parents and all the trouble I'm in."

"That's the idea, but I did want to show you IU and Bloomington too. Casper thinks highly of you, so I thought I'd encourage you to come to school here."

"I think you're getting kickbacks from IU."

"I wish!"

We both laughed.

"Everything is going to be okay, Scotty. I know things are rough now, but the guys are working on a plan. They will come up with something. Keep in mind that your problem is temporary. When you're eighteen, you'll be free."

"Yeah, but I wish my family could understand."

"Maybe they'll come around. My mom did. She wasn't as upset when she found out about me as your parents are about you, but she was upset. She's fine with it now and she loves Casper, but acceptance didn't come easy for her. I hope your family will come around. My dad and I haven't spoken since Casper and I visited my old hometown. He did some nasty things then, so bad that Mom left him. My dad has been hateful and even abusive, but it still hurts knowing that he doesn't love me. Despite everything he's still my dad."

"The screwed up thing is I think my family does love me. They just don't love me more than their church or their brand of religion," I said.

"You're actually better off than I was when things were bad for me. Maybe things will be okay between you and your family in the future. I don't think things will ever be right between my father and me. I'm just glad Mom came around. That means so much to me."

I nodded.

"Thanks, Brendan. Talking to you helps."

"Talking does help. Casper and I talk to each other a lot about our problems—everything from huge stuff about our parents to little things."

"What about Casper's family?"

"His mom died when he was young. His older brother killed their father."

"Really?"

"Yes. Jason tried to kill Casper, but their dad stopped him. He gave up his life to save Casper."

"That's heroic."

"Well, Casper's dad wasn't much of a father. He was abusive, but he was heroic in the end. Casper's parents are gone and they aren't ever coming back. His brother is who-knows-where? You aren't the only one with family troubles. I'm not trying to downplay your problems, but I just want you to know you aren't alone."

"It is easy to think that everyone else has it made."

"Yeah, but they don't. Think about it. Both of Ethan's parents are dead. Nathan and Dave's parents care so little about them that they made no objection when Uncle Jack wanted legal custody. Tristan lost his dad just a couple of years ago. Shawn and Tim don't have much to do with their dad and they have no idea if their mom is dead or alive. Dorian, Marc, and Dane are the only ones who have parents that are truly accepting."

"Wow."

"Yeah. I'm sure that doesn't make what you're facing any easier, but everyone has troubles."

Brendan tore a piece off the paper placemat and wrote something down on it.

"This is the number for the payphone that is closest to my dorm room. Call it anytime you want to talk. Just tell whomever answers you want to talk to me and they'll knock on my door. If I'm not around you can leave a message and I'll call you back. Brandon already gave me Aunt Anne's number."

"Thanks." I took the number and stuffed it in my pocket.

Brendan and I finished our burgers and fries. We dumped our trash, but took our drinks with us. We walked the short distance to Sugar & Spice where Brendan bought us both a chocolate cupcake. They were big and delicious!

Brendan took me up to the next level and showed me his favorite lounge, the South Lounge. There was a cool sitting area by a fireplace. Brendan told me the fire was gas and never went out. It looked like a cozy place to sit and I could imagine sitting there with a book studying. There was a good-looking college boy sleeping on one of the loveseats by the fire. I felt the urge to lean over and kiss him on the lips, but I resisted. There were two others asleep in different parts of the lounge. I guess it was a good napping area.

We wandered around the IMU then went back outside. My eyes widened a little when I saw two girls holding hands, but then I figured I was reading too much into it because girls sometimes did that. Right as that thought passed through my mind one of them leaned over and kissed the other on the mouth! I managed to hide my reaction until they had passed and were out of earshot.

"Do you see that a lot?" I asked.

"No. I've never seen two girls kissing on campus before. I've seen a few I'm sure are couples."

"Wow."

We walked back to Brendan's dorm. Jeff was listening to music on his headphones, but pulled them off when we entered.

"Hey, want to go out for pizza later?" Brendan asked. "I thought I might ask Jen and Janet. We can take Scotty to Mother Bear's."

"Sure. I wouldn't mind to see Janet again," Jeff said.

"Jeff has a thing for Janet," Brendan told me.

"No. Janet has a thing for me. I just like her."

"Sure you do."

"Shut up, homo."

"Ah, don't get upset, Jeff. I know you have a crush on her," Brendan said, patting Jeff's back.

"He'll use any excuse to touch me. Who knows what he does to me while I'm sleeping?" Jeff said to me.

"You wish," Brendan said. "I'll be right back."

Brendan left, presumably to call the girls he mentioned, leaving Jeff and I alone.

"So, how do you know Brendan?"

"I go to his old high school. I'm a friend of his boyfriend. How do you like him for a roommate?"

"He's actually kind of cool, but I'll kill you if you tell him I said that. We stay out of each other's way and I don't have to worry about him stealing my shit. He also gets lost if I'm going to have someone over."

"Yeah? You hook up a lot?"

"Not much. I was hooking up with this one girl quite a bit, but that's over. She was getting kind of clingy. I hate that. I'm more in the mood for guys here lately anyway."

"Brendan said you were bi."

"Yeah. I'm not too fond of labels. I'm just into what I'm into at the time, you know? Sometimes I want a girl and sometimes I want a guy."

"Ever have both at once?"

"Yes."

"Nice."

"So, are you gay, bi, straight?" Jeff asked.

"Gay."

"I figured, especially after you said I was hot."

"I can't believe I was that bold."

"Well. You're right. I am hot."

Jeff grinned. He didn't smile much, but he was especially good looking when he did. I began to wonder what he'd look like naked.

"Doesn't rooming with Brendan drive you crazy? I mean, he's sooo hot."

"You're hot for him, aren't you?" Jeff asked, grinning evilly.

"Well, kinda. I mean. I think he's extremely hot, but he has a boyfriend and I wouldn't think of trying anything, even if I had the nerve."

"Yeah, it would be a waste of time. He's totally devoted to Casper. I actually respect him for that a lot, but don't tell him that either!"

"I promise not to breathe a word. Would you make a move on Brendan if he wasn't taken?"

"No. Things could get weird since he's my roommate. I think it's best for roommates just to be friends. Anything more is trouble."

"Yeah. I guess."

"Besides. I would never give him the pleasure of knowing that I think he's hot."

"I like you."

"What's not to like?"

Brendan came back just then.

"I can make you a list if you want, Jeff," Brendan said.

"Why don't you go hang out in a bathroom and try to pick someone up? That's your usual Sunday evening activity, isn't it?" Jeff asked.

"No, that's how you pick up guys. I have a boyfriend."

"I think Brendan pays him," Jeff said to me.

"No, that's how *you* get girls," Brendan said.

"You guys remind me of Brandon and Jon," I said.

"Don't make me hurt you, Scotty," Brendan said.

"Hey, you know they're cool. They just bicker and exchange insults all the time."

"Yeah, they're cool, but don't tell them I said that."

Jeff and I exchanged a look.

"What?" Brendan asked.

"Nothing," Jeff and I said at the same time.

"I think you two are plotting."

"Us?" Jeff said, putting his hand over his heart. "He's your friend and you know how innocent I am."

"Innocent my ass."

Jeff started to open his mouth, but Brendan held up his hand.

"Do not go there. I don't know what you were about to say, but I'm sure it wasn't nice."

"Aren't I always nice?"

Brendan rolled his eyes.

"The girls said they would meet us at Mother Bear's at 8:30. Is that cool?"

"Yeah," Jeff said.

"I'm going to show Scotty around Bloomington for a while, but we'll be back in time to walk over to Mother Bear's."

167

"Yeah, yeah, whatever—just so you go."

"I love you too, Jeff."

Jeff flipped Brendan off.

"I think you have a cool roommate," I said as we left.

"Yeah. He can be annoying at times, but anyone can be annoying when you're sharing such a small living space. I don't know what I'd do with a roommate I hated."

"So, what is this Mother Bear's place?"

"It has some of the best pizza in Bloomington. It's located just down the block, across the street. I'll point it out as we drive past."

"It must be nice to have a restaurant in walking distance."

"Yeah. There are a few within walking distance and it's great since I can't keep my car in the Forest parking lot. Freshmen have to park off-campus or by the stadium. I'm not supposed to have my car parked here now, but I'm hoping they won't check since it's Sunday."

We climbed in the Cutlass and Brendan began driving.

"That is Mother Bear's," he said as we passed. It was a small restaurant with a dark front. The bottom half of the wall was stone. It didn't look like anything special, but then it was the food and not the exterior that was important.

We passed one campus building after another as we drove down 3rd Street: the Simon Music Library, Jordan Hall, Swain East and West, the Maurer School of Law, and lots more that went by too quickly for me to read the signs. On the left side of the street were sorority houses and yet more campus buildings.

Brendan took a right on Indiana Avenue. He pointed to the right as we stopped at the first stop sign.

"Dunn's Woods is right behind those buildings. You can see some of the trees from here."

I still couldn't believe a forest was located right on campus and so very near the business district of Bloomington. On the left side of Indiana Avenue was one restaurant after another.

Brendan took a left on Kirkwood and pointed out significant points of interest as we slowly drove down the street: Kilroy's Bar,

Nick's English Hut, the public library, and more. There was so much to see it was all kind of blur.

Next, Brendan drove around the town square. There was a huge courthouse in the center. Across from the courthouse, on all four sides, were restaurants and shops: Opie Taylors, Grazie, Scholar's Inn Bakehouse, two bookstores, the Trojan Horse, and more.

I got kind of lost as Brendan kept driving and pointing things out. He talked about college life and how I was going to love it. His enthusiasm was contagious and I began to feel as if I actually had a future. Only a few days before I'd hurried to Marc's house because I was afraid of what I might do if I didn't. Everything seemed so hopeless then. What a difference a few days could make. I grew frightened thinking about what could have happened. What if I had killed myself? I would have died in despair and that would have been the end of it. I pushed the fear from my mind. I'd made the right choice. Instead of killing myself I sought out help and now I was riding around Bloomington with an incredibly sexy college boy. What's more, I was beginning to make plans to attend IU. I now knew I had something to live for.

I still had problems, big problems, but I wasn't going to give up. There were just too many things I wanted to experience, too many places I wanted to see, and too many hot guys I wanted to touch! Feeling hopeful when my life sucked ass made me feel even more hopeful. If I could feel this way when my life was in the toilet how might I feel when things were going well?

We drove all over town and arrived back at Forest Quad after eight. We walked up to Brendan's dorm room, but Jeff wasn't there so we headed back downstairs and down and across the street to our destination. I was hungry by then, so I couldn't wait to eat.

The scent of pizza wafted toward me even as we opened the door of Mother Bear's. The interior was slightly dark, but the restaurant was much bigger than it looked on the outside. We searched through the high-backed, wooden booths, but couldn't find Jeff or the girls.

"Brendan."

We turned. An attractive girl with light brown hair was headed our way.

"Janet couldn't make it. She has a major project due tomorrow and she's scrambling to finish. I promised to take her some pizza."

"Jen, this is my friend Scotty from back home. I've been showing him around."

"Hey, Scotty. What has Brendan told you about me?"

"Actually, nothing."

"Oh I'm hurt," Jen said.

"I thought it would be best if he just experienced you."

Jeff arrived as we stood there talking and we sat down in a booth, with Brendan and Jen on one side and Jeff and me on the other. The table, the backs of the booth, and part of the wall next to me were covered with signatures and graffiti. I spotted signatures dating back to the 1970s.

Jeff had changed into a hunter green polo. He was wearing a gold chain and he looked really sexy. I didn't know what cologne he was wearing, but I loved it. I was glad I was sitting beside him. I wondered if he'd go for a high school boy.

"How about pepperoni and pineapple with barbeque sauce?" Brendan suggested.

"You always want that," Jeff said.

"So, what do you want?" Brendan asked.

Jeff browsed the menu.

"I'm thinking pepperoni with pineapple, onion, and barbeque sauce."

"Yeah, that's a big difference," Brendan said. "What about you two?"

"Sounds good to me," I said.

"I'm easy," Jen said, then paused. "Don't say it."

"Don't give such good openings," Jeff warned.

When the waiter came he was a sexy college boy with blond hair and green eyes. I tried not to be obvious about checking him out. He was so cute! We placed our drink orders and Jeff ordered our pizza.

"I think you have a little drool there," Jeff teased when the blond boy was gone.

"Wow," I said, since I'd obviously been caught.

Jen laughed.

"He is sexy," she said.

"I bet he's gay," Jeff said.

"Well, I hope not," Jen said. "There have to be some hot guys who are straight around here."

"Forget that," Jeff said. "Straight guys are ugly. If you want hot, go for a bi boy like me."

Brendan started to open his mouth.

"Shut it," Jeff warned.

"So, are you planning to come to IU?" Jen asked me.

"Yeah, I am. I hadn't given it a lot of thought before Brendan showed me around, but I really like it here."

"Brendan is always trying to increase the gay population. I think he has plans for a homo takeover," Jeff said.

"I knew you were too cute to be straight," Jen said.

"Um... sorry?" I said.

"It's okay. I like hanging out with gay boys. I know they don't have an ulterior motive."

"Brendan always has an ulterior motive. He'll probably try to stick you with the bill," Jeff said.

"I'm paying tonight," Brendan said.

"Why didn't you say so before we ordered? We could have loaded the pizza," Jeff said.

"That's why!"

"This is really cool," I said. "Do you all hang out a lot?"

"We don't have a lot of time to get together, but we hang out sometimes. I try not to spend too much time with Jeff outside of our room."

"As a personal favor to me," Jeff said. "No one can stand Brendan for long."

Brendan stuck out his tongue.

"Brendan, I've told you before. I do not want to French kiss you."

"Me thinks thou doth protest too much," Brendan retorted.

"Shut up, Shakespeare."

I looked at Jeff. I wanted to French kiss him. I felt myself growing warmer as I sat there next to him. Jen looked across the table at me and smiled. I think she was onto me.

Our drinks arrived and we talked and laughed. I was a bit lost some of the time since I didn't go to IU, but they mostly stopped and explained if I looked confused. Our pizza was there in a very short time, or perhaps it only seemed like a short time since I was having so much fun.

"This is delicious," I said.

"Yeah, except for the onions," Brendan said.

"Ha! The onions make this pizza!" Jeff said.

Jen rolled her eyes.

"They're just a little competitive," Jen said.

I wished I didn't have to have to go to Aunt Anne's farm. I wanted to stay right where I was, room with Brendan and Jeff, and attend IU. I knew I couldn't, but that didn't stop me from wishing it.

I kept looking at Jeff as we ate. I don't know if it was because I was away from home where I didn't have to pretend or if it was because he was an unattached bi boy, but I found him *very* attractive. Jeff looked at me now and then and I got the feeling he found me attractive too. Being near him made me breathe a little faster.

We actually ate an entire large pizza, except for a couple of slices Jen saved for her friend, but then there were four of us. We sat and talked and laughed long after our pizza was finished. I had to go to the restroom before we left because I'd drunk so much Coke.

Jen gave me a hug out in front of Mother's Bears just before we parted. She was really sweet, but I sensed she was not one to mess with either. I would not want to be on her bad side.

Brendan, Jeff, and I walked back to Forest Quad. Jeff and I walked so close we were touching part of the time. I really, really wanted to kiss him, but I wasn't brave enough. When we got back to the room, Brendan said he needed a shower.

"Yeah, I didn't want to say anything in front of Jen, but you reek," Jeff said.

"Yeah, right."

I couldn't keep from looking as Brendan stripped. He had a beautifully proportioned and well-muscled chest that was completely smooth. I became seriously aroused when he pulled off his jeans. Thankfully... or not... he turned away when he stripped off his boxers and wrapped a town around his waist. Brendan had the hottest ass! I don't know what I would have done if I'd seen the front view.

"I'll be back in a few."

"Yeah, yeah. Like we care," Jeff said.

Brendan departed and Jeff and I were alone. We stood there gazing at each other for a moment, then Jeff crossed the distance between us, pulled me close, and kissed me.

I immediately responded and we made out right there in the dorm room. I had never kissed another boy before. Blake wasn't into kissing. He just wanted to get right to sex. Jeff was more erotic and sensual. His lips were soft and his tongue silky. I ran my hands all over his back and down onto his butt as we made out. Jeff felt my chest through my shirt and his hands wandered down my torso until he reached my belt. He didn't go any further but if he had he would've known I was totally hot for him.

We were so into making out we didn't even notice when Brendan returned. He cleared his throat.

"Really, Jeff, do you have to put the moves on every guy who comes in our room?"

I could feel my face turning red, but Brendan was smiling.

"Only those I can't resist," Jeff said. Hearing him say that made me feel so very attractive.

"Don't let me stop you," Brendan said.

I looked at Brendan, feeling self-conscious.

"It's okay," he said.

Jeff and I kissed more softly as Brendan dressed. Brendan didn't say another word, but he left the dorm room. Jeff tugged at my shirt. Soon, we were both shirtless and making out like mad.

Our hands began to roam and more clothing came off. Jeff was so sexy. His every touch set me on fire with desperate sexual need.

We stripped naked and climbed into Jeff's bunk. He lay on top of me; kissing, rubbing, and feeling. He grabbed my wrists and held them above my head while he kissed me. Something about being held down made me more fiercely aroused than ever.

We went at it for an hour. We were all over each other. We didn't do everything, but we did plenty. We ended with some sixty-nine and managed to both climax at once.

When we were finished, I stayed in Jeff's bed. He pulled the cover up over us and spooned me. I think I liked lying there with him after sex even more than the sex, but that might just be because Jeff had drained all sexual need from my body.

I'm not sure when I fell asleep, but I awakened sometime in the middle of night or very early morning. Jeff was still spooned against me and I could see Brendan lying asleep in his bunk only a few feet away. I guess I didn't have to worry about controlling myself while sleeping with Brendan. Who would have guessed I'd end up sleeping with his roommate?

I was slightly embarrassed the next morning as I climbed naked out of Jeff's bed, but Brendan didn't say a word about me having sex with his roommate. He just loaned me a towel and washcloth and his shower supplies and gave me directions to the showers.

The showers were at the far end of a restroom. I passed two college boys coming out as I was going in. Both were wearing only towels. One wasn't that great looking, but the other one had nice abs and a hot chest.

I hung my towel on a hook and took a shower stall. I wished VHS had shower stalls with curtains instead of a big communal shower area. I didn't have to take P.E. anymore, but I always hated the showers after gym. Sure, I could check out some hot guys, but I wasn't all the comfortable letting other guys see me naked. I would have been so much more comfortable in a shower room like the one on the 5th floor of Forest Quad.

The night before was like a dream. That's what life was supposed to be like. Here, I could go out with anyone I wanted. If I found someone attractive, I could try for him. If the feeling was mutual, we could do what Jeff and I had done. The further I got away from my family and their archaic ideas the more ridiculous those ideas seemed. Why did I have to suffer because of the stupidity of others? That's what their objections to homosexual were; pure stupidity.

I luxuriated in the hot shower, then stepped out, grabbed my towel, and dried off. A cute boy entered as I was wrapping my towel around my waist and I caught him checking out my stuff. He grinned and I smiled back. Oh how I wished I did not have to leave!

I returned to the dorm room and dressed. Jeff was still sleeping, but stirred as Brendan and I prepared to depart. Brendan had a class later so he had to get me to Aunt Anne's farm in time to get back.

Jeff slipped out of his bunk and pulled on his shorts as I made sure I had all my stuff. His hair was messy and he looked sleepy, but he was so sexy. He walked over to me and gave me a hug.

"I hope you'll come visit again soon," he said.

"Me too."

Jeff smiled at me and mussed my hair.

Brendan and I left the room and were soon on our way. We drove downtown and Brendan took me to the Scholar's Inn Bakehouse for breakfast. It was one of the places he'd pointed out the evening before. We ordered, got our drinks, and then took one of the little tables outside. I loved sitting and watching people as they walked by.

I looked up when someone called Brendan's name. It was the waiter with our orders. I'd ordered a three cheese omelet and Brendan got something called a Sriracha scramble. Both our orders came with home fries and the most incredible toast. We sat and ate and watched passersby. I loved it!

After breakfast, Brendan consulted his directions and we were on our way again.

"You didn't mind me sleeping with your roommate, did you?" I asked when I got brave enough.

"I think you did more than sleep." Brendan grinned.

"Yeah, that's what I meant." I could feel my face growing red.

"It's fine, Scotty. In fact, it's better than fine. I'm glad you two liked each other that much."

"He's really sexy."

"Well, Jeff is attractive, but *I'd* never sleep with him."

I could tell by the tone of Brendan's voice that he was teasing me.

"That's because you have a boyfriend."

"There is that."

"I feel kind of like a slut. I just met Jeff and we hooked up."

"How many guys have you been with if you don't mind me asking?"

"Two."

"I think you're going to have to work a lot harder to earn the slut label."

"How many guys have you been with?" I asked. Fair was fair.

"One."

"Really? You've never had sex with any guy but Casper?"

"No. I never had the opportunity before I met Casper and after I met him I didn't want anyone else."

I looked at Brendan skeptically.

"Well, okay. There are other guys I've wanted, but I'm in love with Casper so I don't act on those desires."

"Wow. I figured you'd been with lots of guys."

"Had me pegged for a slut, huh?"

"No, it's just that you're so incredibly attractive I figured you had lots of opportunities."

"I've had some, but I belong to Casper."

"It's really cool that the two of you mean so much to each other."

"Yeah. If you're very lucky you'll find someone like Casper."

"I don't know if I'll be that lucky, but just hooking up is great!"

Brendan laughed.

"I'm sure it doesn't suck."

"Oh, but it does!" I said and then laughed too.

"You know what I mean."

"Yeah."

"You have my number, right?" Brendan asked.

"Got it."

"Good.   Call any time you want. I'm out of the room a lot, but if you leave a message I'll call you back as soon as I can. You can always talk to Jeff, too."

"Maybe he'll want to come out and do it in the barn loft."

"You're dangerous now that you're away from Verona."

"I feel free!"

"You seem much happier too."

"I am.   I'm scared of what is going to happen and what's going to become of me. I'm scared about a lot of things. You've reminded me that my problems are only temporary. I had so much fun yesterday, even before sleeping with Jeff, that I began to feel a lot better. I was thinking to myself yesterday that if I can have that much fun while my life is a mess then maybe I can get through this."

"You can. I don't know what's going to happen, but you can get through it. We will all help you."

"That help has made all the difference," I said.

We didn't talk a lot for the rest of the trip, but then the trip from Bloomington to the farm was all of ten minutes.

Aunt Anne's farm reminded me of the Selby farm, but then I guess all farms are kind of similar. There was a two-story, white clapboard farmhouse, a big barn, and some out buildings. There were fields, of course, and the whole place was quite beautiful. Brendan parked the car out front. I gathered up my stuff and we headed for the nearest door.

We didn't get there before the door opened and Aunt Anne stepped out. I had expected her to be older, but she couldn't have been more than forty. She was somewhat short and thin with brown hair and kind eyes. She was ordinary, but nice looking.

"Scotty, I'm so glad to meet you. Brandon has told me a lot about you."

Aunt Anne hugged me, then held me by the shoulders and looked me over.

"My, you're such a handsome young man."

I blushed.

"Uh, thanks."

"I'm Brendan."

Aunt Anne gave Brendan a hug too, then peered at him.

"You look familiar... Oh yes, I've seen your picture in the paper. You play football for IU, don't you?"

"Yes, ma'am."

"I knew I had seen you somewhere. I don't go to the games. There are too many people! I do keep up with the *Bloomington Herald* and I listen to games on the radio. I hope you'll be playing this fall."

"Oh, I'll be playing. This is just my freshman year."

"Wonderful! Both of you come in and I'll show you to your room, Scotty."

"I have to head back for class," Brendan said.

"That's a pity, but I understand. You come and visit any time you want."

"Thank you," Brendan said. "I will. It was nice to meet you." Brendan turned to me. "Call if you need anything or just want to talk."

"Thanks, Brendan."

Brendan hugged me. I hugged him back. I was sure Casper wouldn't mind.

Brendan climbed back in his Cutlass and then it was just Aunt Anne and me.

"Come on. Let's go inside. I was just making some hot tea."

I smiled and followed Aunt Anne into the farmhouse.

Dorian

Casper called late Sunday afternoon to tell me that Scotty had departed with Brendan. There was now no way his parents could track him down. I was relieved he was safe, but I was still worried. I wasn't sure how to help Scotty. I only knew that I had to come up with something. Scotty couldn't hide out on Aunt Anne's farm forever. I guess he could hide out until he was eighteen, but that was a long time to put his life on hold.

Rumors about Scotty multiplied at school. The cops were searching for him. The *Verona Citizen* featured a story about his disappearance. According to the paper the authorities did not suspect foul play, but Scotty's parents weren't so sure. In the interview they gave the paper they stated that, "Scotty had been hanging around an undesirable element that was seeking to lead him astray. We think it highly likely that these individuals did something to Scotty when they discovered his family and church would not allow him to be corrupted."

I felt guilty that the cops were wasting their time looking for someone who didn't want to be found. I felt guilty about all the people who were worried about Scotty. I don't mean his parents. They deserved to worry. I hoped they were horribly upset. Maybe they'd be more accepting if they worried enough. I seriously wondered if they were concerned at all, but they almost had to be. They had been hurting Scotty, but they weren't exactly bad parents. Whether or not Scotty's parents were concerned about him, lots of others were worried about him. More than once I heard Mrs. Cook say, "that poor boy" and I knew she was talking about Scotty. I was sorry for upsetting kind people like Mrs. Cook, but there was no alternative. If we hadn't spirited Scotty out of Verona I feared he would have killed himself or his parents would have sent him away to one of those horrible treatment centers.

Brandon began referring to us gay boys, and especially Marc, Tim, Dane, and me as the "undesirable element." I kept expecting the cops to show up and question us. I'm sure Scotty's parents had accused us of killing him and probably of doing unspeakable things to him before we murdered him. I guess the cops were a lot smarter than that. Maybe they realized Scotty's parents were religious fanatics. People like that were crazy.

One good thing about Scotty hiding out was that Marc took over the role of Charlie in *Willy Wonka and the Chocolate Factory*. Having Marc on the stage was a dream come true for me. I wanted him to realize the talent he possessed. I knew he had no desire to become an actor, but I could never get him to recognize his talent. Besides, it was fun acting with my boyfriend on the stage! I loved acting and I loved sharing one of the most important parts of my life with Marc.

Marc's enthusiasm did not match my own. I could tell he was putting on more than one performance. He was playing the part of Charlie *and* the role of an actor who was confident and eager to perform upon the stage. He could fool the others, but not his boyfriend. I knew him too well. I could feel the tension when I held him and read the fear in his eyes. As the date of the first performance grew nearer Marc became increasingly anxious.

Near the end of practice on Wednesday we ran through the boat scene. The guys who were working on the sets had created a beautiful boat that moved on rollers. Of course, it was only beautiful on the side that faced the audience, but there were red velvet cushions and it wasn't hard to pretend it was a real boat. The lighting really sold the scene. The stage was completely dark except for rapidly flashing lights in shifting colors. I was proud of the eerie tone of my voice as I sang "There is no way or knowing, which direction we are going..." More than one of the cast said my voice and my eyes freaked them out during that scene which delighted me to no end. I noticed Marc was very pale when we finished the scene and I knew it wasn't because I was freaking him out. He was getting stressed out about having to perform in front of hundreds of people.

The April sunshine was cheerful as we stepped out the back doors of VHS, but Marc wasn't enjoying the weather. He smiled at me, but he couldn't fool me the way he could everyone else and he knew it. I took his hand and led him toward the football field.

"There are no sexy players to watch," Marc said as we neared the empty field.

"I have all the sexy I need right here with me."

We walked the remaining distance in silence and I sat with my boyfriend on the player's bench at the edge of the field. The field was emerald green and the just-mowed-grass scent filled the air. I took Marc's hand and held it.

"You're going to do just fine, you know that. Don't you?"

"I'm not so sure, Dorian. I'm not ready for this. I could handle a small role, but a lead role... How do you do it? How do you take the pressure? I watched you during every performance of *The Picture of Dorian Gray*. Everyone was watching you, but it was as if you didn't even know the audience was there. Even when one of the other actors messed up you just kept on going as if everything was exactly as it was supposed to be. You really were Dorian Gray."

"That's just it, Marc. When I'm up on the stage I am whatever character I'm playing. I was Dorian Gray when you watched me, just as I'm Willy Wonka in the play now. I'm not Dorian pretending to be Willy Wonka, I *am* Willy Wonka. You can be Charlie the same way. I've seen you do it. I've seen you lose yourself in the part. You can do it, Marc, I know you can."

"I'm not so sure about that."

"Listen. You have the lines down. You never miss an entrance or a mark. You have it all down, Marc, and you're talented. You're just worried about the audience."

"Yeah, hundreds of people, most of whom know me, staring at me and watching my every move."

"People watch when you play soccer."

"Yeah, but I'm just one member of a team."

"It's exactly the same in a play. You're a member of a team."

"I never thought of it like that."

"The audience won't be watching just you. They'll be watching everyone on the stage. They'll be looking at the scenery, listening to the music, and noticing the lighting. The audience will focus on you some of the time, just as they do when you're playing soccer. When you've got the ball, especially when you're making one of those great plays of yours, they're watching you. It will be the same when you're Charlie. The audience will focus on you some of the time, but not all the time."

"It's a big role, Dorian. I'm not you. I haven't done this before. I'm going to be so nervous."

"I get nervous too but it goes away when I start performing. There are some very famous actors who get nervous before they step onto the stage. Some of them get so nervous they hurl before a performance, and they're professionals."

"I don't know if that makes me feel better or not," Marc said with a grin.

"I know you feel like everyone will be watching just you, but it won't be that way at all. You are playing a lead role, but so I am. I'll be with you on the stage most of the time, looking fabulous in my purple suit. You know everyone's eyes will be glued to me much of the time."

"You'd better be glad Brandon isn't here. He'd go off on you for what you just said. He'd tease you for days about being conceited."

I laughed.

"True, but luckily he's not here. The audience will be watching all of us. You know Tess will mesmerize them when she sings *I Want it Now*. You've heard her during practice. She's fabulous!"

"Yeah."

"Others have their moments, too. With the stage lights and spotlights you won't even be able to see the audience very well. You'll probably forget they are there."

"What about when I mess up?"

"Not when, if. If you mess up, just go on as if that's the way it was supposed to be. Everyone else will carry on too. The cast is a team just like your soccer team, only we don't get naked in the locker room and showers after practice."

"It would be more fun if we did. What if I do something really stupid and the audience laughs?"

"Then go with it. Whatever happens becomes a part of the play. Sometimes, the screw-ups are the best parts. This isn't Broadway, Marc. This is a high school play."

Marc nodded.

"You probably think I'm pretty silly for getting scared about this," Marc said.

"No. Everyone gets scared. I'd be scared if I tried to play in a real soccer game. It's what you do about being scared that matters. I know that you'll go on even though you're scared. You won't let fear stop you. I also know that once you get started you'll have fun, just as you do during practice."

Marc hugged me.

"Thanks, Dorian. I love you."

"I love you too."

I gave Marc a lingering kiss, then we sat there and held hands while we breathed in the fresh air and enjoyed the sun on our faces.

"Here I am worrying about stage fright when Scotty has *real* problems," Marc said. "I feel foolish."

"You aren't being foolish."

"Still, my problems are nothing compared to his. My problems aren't even problems. They're more like... difficulties or minor inconveniences."

"It's so frustrating that I can't think of a way to help him," I said.

"You've helped him a lot already."

"I haven't helped him enough. I want him to have what I have. I want him to have a family who loves and accepts him. I want him to have a cute and sexy boyfriend who is good and kind."

"Dorian, you can't expect to work miracles."

"I know, but... I just want things to be better for him. I want Scotty to be able to live his life like I do mine. I want him to be happy."

Marc pulled me to my feet, hugged me, and kissed me. He took my hand and we began walking toward the soccer fields.

"We will think of something, Dorian. We'll probably think of something when we least expect it. I don't think we can make all Scotty's problems go away, but we will make his life better. I know you won't stop until you do. You are as stubborn as an ox."

I laughed.

"Are oxen stubborn?"

"I suppose so. I've never been around one. They must be or that saying wouldn't exist."

"I don't know about that. Dave says chickens can be really brave."

When we neared the soccer fields, Marc stopped at the big boulder that was a memorial to the two dead soccer players. I put my arm around his waist as he gazed at it.

"I bet Mark and Taylor's parents would give anything to have them back," Marc said. "I bet they'd treat them differently if they had it all to do over again. Mark and Taylor are like Romeo & Juliet. Remember the end of that play? I don't know what character it was, but after Romeo & Juliet killed themselves he looked at their families and said, "All are punished.""

"It was the Prince; *Where be these enemies? Capulet! Montague! See, what a scourge is laid upon your hate! That heaven finds means to kill your joy with love! And I, for winking at your discords too, have lost a brace of kinsmen. All are punish'd.*"

"Don't tell me. You've played Romeo, haven't you?"

I smiled. "As a summer theatre production, yes, but I remember that having read it."

"Maybe Scotty's parents will wise up after a while. They have to be feeling something. Surely, they're worried about him," Marc said.

"Maybe we should get Taylor's parents to talk to them."

"That's not a bad idea. They know the pain of losing a son. Maybe they could get through to Scotty's parents."

"Maybe, but... I have a feeling that words won't penetrate their skulls. I fear they'll only learn their lesson if Scotty kills himself and then it won't matter."

I held perfectly still for several moments as I stared at the boulder. Marc watched me intently.

"That's it!" I said, turning to look at Marc.

"What's it? We get Taylor's parents to..."

"No. We kill Scotty! His parents can't learn their lesson until he's dead so we'll kill him!"

"Um... there are a couple of problems with that solution, Dorian. If he's dead, it won't matter that his parents have learned their lesson. Then, there's the part about murdering one of our friends."

"I don't mean *really* kill him. We fake his death. We make everyone believe he's dead!"

"Uh... won't we need a body for that? Even if we could come up with one, which we can't without robbing a grave or murdering someone, everyone would know it's not Scotty. It's not like we can pick up a Scotty-lookalike-corpse at the mall."

"We can figure that part out later. We can do this. I know we can! We'll kill Scotty. His parents will learn their lesson, hopefully, and then we'll bring him back."

"I don't know, Dorian. The names Lucy and Ethel are coming to mind."

"All of us together can do this, Marc. If Scotty's parents really think he's dead they are bound to see things differently. Maybe it won't make everything perfect, but it's got to make things better for Scotty at home."

My boyfriend let out a loud breath and grinned at me.

"You're going to do this with or without help, aren't you?" he asked.

"You know I am!"

"Then I'm in."

"Thanks!" I said. I hugged Marc and kissed him.

"Thanks, guys!" I said and hugged and kissed the boulder.

"Come on! We have a lot to do! I can't wait to kill Scotty!"

***

"That's your brilliant idea? You want to *kill* Scotty? Need I point out the flaw in this plan?" Shawn asked.

Everyone was staring at me as if I was insane, except Marc. Shawn, Tristan, Brandon, Jon, Casey, Tim, Dane, Ethan, Nathan, and Casper were sitting all over Shawn and Tim's living room and kitchen. It was the one place we could meet without the risk of being overheard by anyone, including parents.

"The stress has finally gotten to him. Dorian has lost it," Brandon said.

"I don't mean *really* kill him. I mean fake his death," I said.

185

"How will that help him?" Dane said.

"It will hit his parents and maybe even some members of his church hard. If they think he's dead maybe they'll be sorry for what they've done to him. Maybe it will be a wakeup call."

"I don't know..." Dane said, shaking his head.

Casey, Casper, and some others looked doubtful.

"Wait, I think Dorian may have something here," Brandon said. "Mark's dad was a complete asshole. He outed Mark to our coach who in turn outed Mark to our team. He bullied Mark and for all I know he may have beaten him. After Mark killed himself, his dad was so remorseful he killed himself with the very same gun Mark used."

Brandon looked at me.

"That's where I got the idea," I said. "Marc and I were walking out by the soccer field. We were looking at that boulder with the plaque on it about Mark and Taylor. It made me think about how their parents would probably do anything to have them back."

"So, you want to create the same situation with Scotty's parents, only he won't really be dead?" Nathan said.

"Exactly. We make them think he's dead. We make everyone think he's dead. We make them sorry for what they've done. We make them think about it."

"I think your basic idea is sound, Dorian, how can we pull that off? We will need a body for one thing," Tristan said.

Dane suddenly looked uncomfortable.

"No, we won't," I said. "I've been thinking. We need to fake his death, but there's no way we can get a body. Even if we could it would be obvious it wasn't Scotty unless it was horribly burned and maybe that wouldn't even work. There was a rumor at school about Scotty drowning in the Tippecanoe River. What if an anonymous source came forth and reported they saw Scotty swim into the river, go under, and not come back up again?"

"Not bad, but is that enough?" Shawn said.

"Probably not, but what will be enough if Scotty's clothes are found caught in the brush by the river bank."

"But... he didn't drown himself, so his clothes can't be..." Tim said.

I grinned.

"How did you get some of Scotty's clothing?" Tristan asked. He caught on fast.

"Marc and I spent some time thinking about the details yesterday evening. We knew we'd need more than rumors and that maybe even an anonymous tip wouldn't do the trick. That's when Marc remembered Scotty had taken a shower at his place and borrowed clean clothes. Scotty's clothes were still in the hamper. We drove out to the Tippecanoe last evening and planted the clothes where they'll be found."

"You were pretty sure of yourselves," Jon said.

"Well, we need your help, but we'd already decided we would try it on our own if the rest of you wouldn't go for it. We wanted to let you know what we were doing at the very least. This will upset a lot of people who don't deserve to be upset, but if it will help Scotty..."

"They'll understand," Brandon said. "I would."

"We've got to be very careful that this cannot be traced back to us," Tristan said. "I don't know, but we could be breaking some laws. I don't see how this can be legal."

"No one will ever know we did it, except maybe Scotty. We'll have to decide whether or not to tell him, but we can't tell anyone who is not in this room right now."

"How about Brendan?" Casper asked.

"It's safe to tell Brendan if you do it when you are absolutely sure no one can overhear," Ethan said.

"Okay, only Brendan and those in this room can know. Agreed?" I asked.

Everyone nodded. I smiled.

"You're really quite devious," Brandon said. "Perhaps there is hope for you yet, Dorian."

"Thank you. We all have to play our parts. Think about it beforehand when the news breaks, act as you would if you had just learned that Scotty is dead. Don't overdo it, but make it real. If we all act unconcerned someone might get suspicious."

"What if Scotty's parents try to pin his death on us?" Tim asked.

"No body. No murder," Ethan said.

"Hmm, Ethan seems to know a bit too much about murder," Jon said.

"You'll never know," Ethan said mysteriously. "Or maybe you'd like to go for a walk in the woods with me, Jon… somewhere no one can hear you scream."

"When did Ethan become scary?" Jon asked.

"Oh, he's always been scary. You just never noticed," Brandon said.

"What else do we need to do?" Shawn asked.

"Nothing until the clothes are found," I said. "In fact, the best way to sell it is to do nothing until the news breaks. Then, we act as we would if Scotty was dead."

"What about the anonymous tip?" Tristan asked.

"The cops already have it," I said.

"How?"

"I called it in."

"*You?*" Brandon asked incredulously. I knew his disbelief stemmed from my high pitched and feminine voice.

"You forget I'm an actor," I said. Then, I switched to the deeper voice I'd used to call the cops with a tip about Scotty. "I saw him wade out into the river. He went under. I watched, but he never came back up again."

Brandon looked impressed.

"How do you *do* that?" Tim asked. "You sounded nothing like you."

"I'm an actor," I said again and grinned.

We talked a bit more and then our meeting broke up.

"I don't know if this will work, but it's a damned good plan," Brandon said to me just before he left.

Marc and I walked down the stairs and out onto the street, then he drove me home.

"Do you think it will work, Marc?"

188

"It's your plan."

"I know, but do you think it will make things better for Scotty?"

"That depends entirely on his family. If they don't care about him it won't help at all."

"Do you think they care?"

"Yeah, I do. I think in their own messed up way they are trying to do what is right for him. I think they know they are being cruel, but believe they're doing it for his own good. I don't think they are actually bad people. They're just seriously messed up and out of touch with reality."

"I think you may be right. I sure hope so."

"Me too."

Marc stopped his car in front of my house. He kissed me and smiled at me. I climbed out feeling all warm inside. Being loved was the most wonderful feeling in the entire world. I wanted Scotty to feel that.

I didn't know if my plan would work or not, but at least I was doing something. If this one didn't work I'd try another and another until I made things better. I was going to be stubborn about this. I was going to make things better for Scotty or die trying.

***

Soon, rumors about the anonymous tip were spreading through the school. Everyone was talking about Scotty drowning in the Tippecanoe River. New rumors built on the "facts." I heard that Scotty had left a suicide note tacked to a tree by the riverbank. I heard someone else say there was probably a note to be found and they might just go look for it. Some said Scotty stripped nude before going into the river. Some said he went in fully clothed. Some said his drowning was probably an accident. Others said that someone had probably drowned him and then tried to make it look like a suicide. The variations of the tale were many. Only one detail was constant: Scotty Jackson was dead.

I wondered what Scotty would think when he found out he'd died in the Tippecanoe. Hearing that you are dead had to be disturbing news. I almost smiled at the thought, but I didn't. As far as nearly everyone else was concerned I thought Scotty was dead too. I made myself cry a couple times during the day, but I didn't overplay it. After all, it was just a rumor. Nothing was for certain yet. I had to play this properly. This performance was more important than any other.

Scotty's death was certain by the afternoon. During play practice someone ran in with a newspaper. There was a surprise there for even me. The front page told not only about the anonymous informant, but about the discovery of Scotty's clothing.

The Verona *Citizen* –
Wednesday, April 13, 1983:
SEARCH FOR MISSING YOUTH'S BODY BEGINS

Scotty Jackson, 17, a junior at Verona High School, has been missing since last week. Searches by authorities yielded no results, until last night. Acting on an anonymous tip, local police began a search of the area where an unnamed witness saw Jackson wade into the river and disappear. Articles of Jackson's clothing were found in bushes near the riverbank, leading authorities to believe Jackson's death may be accidental.

"We think he might have gone for a midnight swim and underestimated the currents of the river," stated Sheriff Brad Easton. "His clothes were placed on bushes near the riverbank. Had they washed off his body they would have been far downstream or likely not found at all. We believe Jackson disrobed before entering the water, which indicates he planned to come back for his clothing. Foul play is not suspected at this time."

Jackson's parents aren't so sure. Earlier, a family spokesman informed the *Citizen* that Jackson "had been hanging out with a disreputable crowd" and that "his parents believe this unsavory element may have tempted Scotty into participating in unwholesome activities and are likely responsible for his death." After hearing the news of the discovery of Scotty's clothing Mr. Jackson stated, "We aren't sure whether Scotty's death was accidental or intentional, but we believe he was not alone on the night of his death. We are very suspicious about certain individuals and their names have been turned over to the police."

When asked about the family's accusations, Sheriff Easton stated, "We found no evidence that anyone but Jackson was on the river bank when he went into the water. Only one faint set of footprints was discovered. If anyone else was present they were not near the riverbank. Jackson's clothing was found not far downstream from a public access point at a location that is popular with swimmers. The river is too cold at this time of year for most swimmers, but we still believe Jackson went in for a swim. We're keeping an open mind, but there is no evidence of foul play."

Questions remain. How did Jackson get to the Tippecanoe River? No vehicle was found at the scene. Did he walk such a considerable distance? Is his family correct? Was someone else present? The only hope for answering that question lies with the anonymous caller.

"This is still an open investigation," Sherriff Easton stated. "We're ruling out nothing as of yet. "Divers are searching for the body, but the chances of recovering it are slim. If we can locate the body we may get some answers. If not, Jackson's death will be recorded as an accidental drowning."

One thing remains clear, a young man is dead and his family and friends grieve for him. In a small town like Verona everyone experiences the loss when one of our number passes on. It's especially difficult with one so young. Scotty Jackson will be missed.

But not for long, I thought to myself.

"I guess he really is dead then," I said for the benefit of those around me.

My eyes filled with tears and a single tear rolled down my cheek. My lower lip trembled. Tess wiped at her eyes too. I felt guilty for making Tess and all the others suffer, but I consoled myself with the knowledge that things were going to be better for Scotty when this was all over. I didn't know that for sure, but how could his family not be touched by his death?

The drama crowd was hit the hardest by Scotty's death, but the next day the entire school felt subdued. The atmosphere was a little too quiet and a little too solemn. There was a stillness that didn't seem to like being broken. The day before everyone was talking about Scotty's possible death, but now it had become real. Scotty Jackson was dead and he wasn't coming back.

The next couple of days were hard. I wanted to spill the secret so bad! Whenever I saw someone who looked sad I wanted to take them to the side and whisper the truth in their ear. I knew I could not do it. All of those involved in the hoax would be in big trouble if we were found out. I hadn't thought about the authorities sending in divers to search for Scotty's body. I hadn't thought about all the hours the sheriff's department would be wasting. I was glad Scotty knew nothing about what was going on. When he came back he could profess ignorance with complete honesty.

There was no turning back now. Coming clean would only serve to undo the good we all hoped would come from our stunt. We had to play this to the end—no matter what.

I had no contact with Scotty's parents, of course, but I saw Justin in school. He had a stunned look as his classmates offered him their condolences. I even saw him crying. Witnessing Justin's pain made me feel cruel. Only days before I figured he deserved to suffer, but now that he was grieving over the loss of his big brother my heart went out to him.

I didn't dare approach Justin myself, but I was extremely eager to find out how Scotty's family was handling his death. I did have an in with Justin. He was a soccer player. Marc and Justin didn't get along well. Justin wasn't fond of Brandon and Jon either since they sat at the homo table, but there were other team members...

After lunch, Marc and I trailed Brandon and then pulled him to the side.

"Will you do something for me?" I asked.

"Dorian! Propositioning me right in front of Marc! How could you?"

"Nothing like *that*." I rolled my eyes.

"Okay. What?"

"Is there someone on your team that could talk to Justin and subtly find out how his family taking Scotty's death?"

"My team? You mean straight boys?"

"No. I mean the soccer team," I said putting my hands on my hips and giving Brandon the homo stare of death.

Brandon smiled.

"A secret mission, huh? Yeah. I'll find someone. I think I know just the guy. He owes me a few favors."

Marc raised an eyebrow.

"Just what did you do for him, Brandon?" Marc asked.

"Nothing like you're thinking—pervert. I'll take care of it Dorian. I'll get Trent to talk to him."

"Trent is part of the drama crowd..." I said doubtfully. I'd thought of Trent myself, then dismissed him as a possibility.

"He's pretty tight with Justin," Brandon said. "He can find out what you want to know. He'll do it for me."

Marc started to open his mouth.

"Shut it, Peralta."

Marc laughed.

"Thanks!" I said.

"For shutting Marc up? Anytime!"

Brandon took off before I could respond.

I didn't have long to wait for a response from Brandon. He called me that very night.

"Scotty's parents are devastated," Brandon said.

It sounds horrible of me, but I was glad. Their grief meant they really did care about him.

"According to Justin they are barely functional and I mean barely, as in they eat and go to the bathroom. Trent said that Justin told him his mom won't leave the house. She just sits on the couch crying and repeating, "My baby, my baby is gone.""

I felt cruel and wretched as Brandon spoke, but also hopeful.

"His dad goes to work, but that's it. Neither of them goes anywhere else. Justin is pretty scared. He said their pastor came to talk about Scotty's funeral and they weren't even able to talk about it."

"I didn't know it would be this bad," I said.

"It's bad, but... isn't that exactly how it should be?"

"Yeah, it's just... I hate how everyone is suffering. I wanted to help Scotty, but now I want to help his family too."

"There is no way to help them without ruining everything."

"I know, but..."

"What?" Brandon asked.

I didn't say anything for several moments.

"Are you still there, Dorian?"

"Yeah, sorry. I think there is a way we can help them."

"How?"

"What do you think is the worst thing for a family that has lost a kid, other than actually losing him?"

"I dunno... the funeral, I guess. Seeing him lying in the casket. Having to pick out a casket..."

Brandon paused. He was catching on.

"We will plan Scotty's funeral! We will make all those hard decisions."

"Uh, Dorian... Scotty's parents hate you and all the gay boys. To them you are perverts who ruined their son. They probably blame you for his death."

"They don't have to know we're doing it. Get Trent to talk to Justin again or get him to talk to Scotty's parents. Have him say that the soccer team wants to help by arranging everything so the family doesn't have to do it."

"I don't know, Dorian. I don't know if they'll go for that."

"Just try, okay? If they won't go for it, fine, but I feel responsible. I want to help them."

"Grr, why did I ever get involved with you homos?"

"Because you love us! Because we're more fun than everyone else!"

"Yeah. Yeah. Keep deluding yourself, gay boy. Okay. I'll do it. I'll talk to Trent. I'll have to let him know you and the other homos want to help with the funeral. Scotty was one of you, after all, so Trent will accept that as a reason without knowing the whole truth."

"Good. Thanks, Brandon!"

"You owe me."

"Brandon! I have a boyfriend!"

"Grr! Shut up, homo! I don't mean it like that."

I laughed and then we both hung up.

I went into the living room where Mom and Dad were watching TV and sat down by Mom.

"Are you okay, Dorian?"

"I'm okay, considering," I said.

"It's hard losing one of your friends," Mom said.

The guilt descended upon me again. I knew the death of one person touched many, but knowing it and experiencing it were two entirely different things. My brilliant idea was bringing pain to people who didn't even know Scotty. I just hoped the outcome was worth the price and that the whole thing didn't blow up in our faces.

"I don't really want to talk about it, but I appreciate knowing I can," I said.

Mom smiled at me and mussed my hair.

"Okay, we won't talk about it. How are you and Marc getting along?"

"He's lovely," I said. The smile on my face said even more than my words.

Scotty

Aunt Anne led me inside her farmhouse. We passed through a large, cozy kitchen and into a comfortable looking living room. Everything was nicely arranged and well kept. The overall effect said "home."

A large tabby looked up from his napping place on the sofa and promptly went back to sleep again.

We went up the stairs and into a large bedroom

"This is yours for as long as you want or need to stay."

"Thank you..." I paused. We'd all been calling her Aunt Anne, but she wasn't really my aunt. I wondered if I should call her that anyway or if I could call her Miss or Mrs. Hertwig.

"You can call me Anne," she said, sensing my predicament.

"I really, *really* appreciate you letting me stay with you. Any of my friends would have let me stay with them, but I was afraid my parents would find me and then send me away to be "cured.""

"What nonsense about being cured. That's like trying to cure a cat from being a cat. Utter rubbish. You're welcome, Scotty. I'm glad to have you here. I could use the company."

"I'll be happy to do whatever you might want me to do while I'm here."

"Well, you don't have to pay your way by working, but I may ask for a favor or two."

Anne smiled. She had such a kind smile.

"Anything."

"Make yourself at home. Have a look around. Unpack if you like. I'll be downstairs in the kitchen. You can join me for tea in a while if you like. If you're not a tea drinker I can make coffee."

"Tea is good."

"I'll see you in a bit then. No hurry."

The furniture in my bedroom was antique. I think the style was called Mission Oak, but I wasn't sure. The bed, dresser, desk, rocker, chair, and even the bookcase were all oak with very straight lines. The furniture was very plain in a way and yet it possessed a certain simple elegance.

The floor was hardwood and was probably cold in winter, but being as it was April that wouldn't be a problem. Botanical prints were framed and hung on the walls and there was a large mirror. There were oval hooked rugs on the floor. Three large windows looked out on the countryside. The overall atmosphere of my bedroom was comfort.

I didn't have a lot to unpack so I figured I'd leave that for later. I liked my room. I felt safe here. Anne was kind and there was no way my parent's would track me down here. Anne said I could stay as long as I liked and that made me feel more secure. I was going to do everything I could to be a considerate houseguest and I was going to be of as much help as I possibly could. I was going to have plenty of time on my hands so I figured I might as well put it to good use.

I went downstairs into the kitchen. The wonderful aroma of something sweet filled the air. The kitchen reminded me a little of the 1950s style kitchen in Tristan's house, but this one looked older. There was a golden oak table with lion's paw feet surrounded by four matching pressed back chairs with what looked like a poinsettia design.

Anne was getting plates out of an old fashioned kitchen cabinet. The dishes themselves looked old. There were mostly cream colored, but had little bluebirds on them. Everything Anne owned looked like it was from an earlier time and yet none of it looked too fine or fancy to actually use.

"Is the furniture in my room called Mission Oak?" I asked.

"That's right. I'm surprised you know that. Most boys your age don't know much about old furniture."

"I don't know how I know it. I wasn't even sure, but the name came to me. Everything here is old, isn't it?"

"Including me?"

"Oh, no! I didn't mean that! I meant the furniture and the dishes."

Anne laughed and I knew she had just been teasing me.

"My husband loved to go to auctions and he got me hooked on it too. Other than a few electronics, I don't think there is a new item in the house. Things are usually much cheaper at auction and older furniture is much better made. The pieces in your room were made about 1910. The varnish has darkened considerably but otherwise the furniture is the same as the day it was made. My husband and I bought every piece of furniture in your room at an auction when we were first married."

"It's very nice. So, your husband…"

"He died about three years ago."

"I'm very sorry."

"We were married when I was twenty and he was twenty-five so we had seventeen years together. I was hoping for many more years, but I'm thankful for the years I had with him. That's how you have to look at things. I miss him, of course, but I'm glad for the time I had with him."

"Everything is temporary, I guess. I suppose it's best not to dwell on losing people and things, but be like you instead, thankful for the time you had."

"Let me pour you some tea. Have a seat. I have cookies in the oven. I mixed them up this morning but I waited until you arrived to bake them so they'd be nice and warm. Chocolate chip cookies are always best that way."

Anne poured tea into amber glass cups she had hanging on hooks under the top of her old-fashioned kitchen cabinet. She poured tea out of a pretty cream-colored teapot decorated with a few flowers on the side. I took a sip of tea. It was just hot enough without being too hot and it was delicious.

The cookies were soon done. Anne took a batch out of the oven and lifted them off the baking sheet and onto a kitchen towel covered with waxed paper to cool. She prepared the next batch and slid them in the oven. Soon, a platter full of cookies was sitting between us on the table. They were warm and chewy and the chocolate chips were gooey. They even had pecans in them.

"These are delicious," I said.

"Thank you."

"So, you're Mark's aunt?" I asked for lack of having anything better to ask.

"Yes. Did you know him?"

I shook my head.

"Some of my friends knew him. Most of my friends haven't been my friends for long. I've known Shawn the longest since we both worked in Ofarim's, but I didn't even know him very well. The guys pulled me into their group when they found out I was gay and that I was having some troubles."

"You would have liked Mark. He was a very kind boy."

"The guys told me that you let Mark and Taylor stay here."

"Yes. I told Mark he was welcome to come and live with me permanently, Taylor too. It just wasn't to be. Events moved too swiftly and before I knew it they were both gone."

"Are you mad at him for killing himself?"

"No. I understand why he did it. When my husband died I missed him so much and it hurt so badly that I thought the pain would never end. I never contemplated suicide, but I do understand the pain and despair that comes from losing someone you love. I wish Mark could have held on because there is life even after losing someone who is dear to you. If he hadn't killed himself he might be living with me now. My sister was devastated. Before Mark died I tried to talk to her about being more understanding and accepting but she wouldn't listen. You probably know Mark's father killed himself not long after Mark died. I don't think he could stand the guilt."

"Yeah. It's all around horrible."

"My poor sister lost her son and then her husband. The loss of her son was partly her doing and she'll suffer for it the rest of her life."

"Do you see her much?"

"Not much, but we talk on the phone. We're closer now than we were before Mark died. At first I felt a lot of anger toward her for what she'd done, but it's no good holding onto anger like that so I let it go. Besides, my sister is punished every single day for what she did and what she didn't do. I feel only pity for her now. Mark was a kind soul and I'm sure he would have wanted me to be there for his mother."

"I'm sorry, I shouldn't have brought all this up. I just... I almost feel like I am Mark in a way, except I don't have a Taylor."

"There is no need to be sorry. Such things need to be talked about. Bottling up feelings never works. They will come out one way or another. Trying to hold them in is a terrible mistake. I hold onto the happy times with Mark and Taylor just as I hold onto the good memories of my husband. The boys stayed with me shortly before their deaths and they were happy here. None of us had any idea about what was soon to happen. I think they were happier during their short time here than they had been in a long time. That's what I remember."

Aunt Anne looked at me.

"I know things are difficult for you right now, Scotty, but you just have to hold on. Don't make the mistake Taylor made. He let despair overwhelm him. If he could just have held on a little longer things would have become better and he and Mark would both be alive today."

"You don't have to worry about that. I did think about killing myself. I scared myself and that's why I went to my friends."

"That was a wise thing to do."

"I can't believe how much they've all helped me and just knowing they care means so much. Brendan showed me around IU yesterday. We went out and had pizza with his friends and had a great time. I'm sure he was trying to show me that there are good things in life, even when life is hard. Whether or not that was his intention, that's what I got out of it and it was just plain fun. I can't wait until I can go to college. I'm going to IU. I've already decided."

Anne smiled.

"There are always good things in life and there are always bad things too. You may never have a time in your life when you have no problems. There is always something to worry about. The trick to being happy is to dwell on what is right with your life instead of what is wrong."

"Like staying here with you and eating these incredible cookies."

"Exactly. If you can take pleasure in the good things in life the bad things don't matter so much anymore. Being happy is largely just a matter of deciding to be happy. That's what I do with my life. I chose to be happy."

"No one can be happy all the time."

"No, but one can seek happiness all the time. There is nothing like looking if you wish to find something. If you look for something to worry about, you'll find it for sure. If you look for something to be happy about, you'll find that instead."

"I've got plenty to worry about without looking, but I see what you mean. I sort of feel like my situation is hopeless, but I know it's not. I know that my life will continue even if I can never go home again. I am going to college and I'm going to IU. I may have to get a GED instead of finishing high school and I may have to work a few years before I can afford school, but I'm going. Nothing is going to stop me."

"I think you're going to be just fine," Anne said.

"Yeah. I just don't like the idea of never seeing my family again." I felt myself edging toward tears, but I wasn't going to let myself cry, not just now anyway.

"Don't give up on the idea of being with your family again. You never know how things may change. I don't know your parents, but if I were them I'd be plenty worried right now. Maybe that will make them see things a little differently.

"Time changes things too. We aren't the same people we were a year ago. In another year we won't be the same people we are now. Don't assume that you've lost your family. There is plenty of time for the situation to improve."

"Thanks."

We finished our tea. I liked Anne. She felt like a kindly aunt.

"Do you mind if I go out and explore?" I asked.

"Of course not. There's not as much to see as there once was, but I still have a few chickens as well as two horses. The horses are friendly so don't worry if they come toward you. They'll be curious."

"I love animals. I'll be back in a little while. I'd better take a cookie with me just in case."

Anne laughed.

"You can help me feed the chickens a little later if you want. I like to give the horses a little grain too, although they have plenty of grasses to graze on at this time of year."

"That sounds like fun. See you soon."

I departed with my cookie. The late morning sunshine was wonderfully warm and I was glad to be outside. If I was in Verona

I'd be sitting in a classroom. I almost pitied my friends back in VHS. They were stuck inside while I had a farm to explore. I just wished they were with me. I missed them.

I walked across the yard to a small wooden gate in the fence. I entered the barnyard, being careful to latch the gate behind me, although the chickens pecking around near the large barn didn't look like they had any thoughts of getting into the yard. They seemed quite unconcerned as I approached, but I didn't get too close. Most of the chickens were a golden color, but a couple had dark feathers and a couple of others white. I had no idea what kind of chickens they were, but I guess it didn't matter.

I stopped and gazed at the barn. It was old, wooden, and painted red. I could catch the scent of hay from inside. I thought about going in to have a look around, but instead turned to a large gate that separated the barnyard from the pastures. I climbed over and followed a grassy track that led off into the distance. Beyond the fences surrounding the pastures were large newly plowed fields.

The grass in the pasture was a green than seemed greener than the grass back home. It looked good enough to eat, not that I was up for a taste. I took a bite of my cookie instead. I could eat my weight in Anne's cookies!

I stiffened when two horses galloped toward me, but they slowed as they neared and eyed me cautiously. I slowly walked toward them and they moved forward as well. One was a white-gray with a black mane and the other was light brown with a white patch on his face. I didn't know their names. I wished I had thought to ask, but we'd just have to get along without names for now.

"Hey there," I said, slowing reaching out to the white horse and stroking his muzzle. He whinnied and the other horse drew in close, obviously wanting some attention too. I reached out with my other hand and stroked the muzzle of the brown horse.

"You guys are friendly, aren't you?"

I was glad they were friendly. Up close horses are big! One kick from a powerful leg could easily have killed me, but I was completely at ease standing there. One look at their big, brown eyes told me I had nothing to worry about. I petted and talked to them for a few minutes and then they wandered off. I guess their curiosity about me was satisfied for the moment.

I walked on until I came to the fence and gate at the southern end of the pasture. Beyond the gate the grassy track continued between the fields. I climbed over and kept on walking.

I thought of Ethan. He spent his days in a place like this; driving a tractor, taking care of horses, sheep, and chickens, and doing all kinds of farm things. I didn't think I'd make a very good farmer. I didn't know anything about it for one thing. Being outside all the time would be awesome, but then again not all days were like this one. I didn't think I'd want to be outside when it was 90 and humid or when it was only 20 and the snow was blowing. It might be worth it if I could have a body like Ethan's but then again maybe not. I didn't think I could hack farm work. It sounded way too hard.

I guess it didn't matter. I had no plans to be a farmer. I did enjoy myself as I walked between the fields. The weather was just about perfect; warm without being hot. There was a pleasant scent on the air. I couldn't identify it. The best word to describe it was "green."

I wondered what my parents were doing and what they were thinking. They were probably furious that I'd run off. Were they worried too? I wondered if Justin was worried about me or if he was just enjoying having a bedroom all to himself. I think my family cared about me, but they had a weird way of showing it. In the days before I left I didn't feel like they cared. All I sensed was anger and disappointment. All they cared about was forcing me to be something I wasn't. Why couldn't they understand that I couldn't change? Why did they have to treat me like I had a disease that needed to be cured? I wished my parents cared more about me more than they did their church. That's what it came down to. The church was first. Justin was second. I was third... maybe.

I wanted to go back, but I didn't think I could. My parents would never stop trying to change me. They would never stop acting like something as wrong with me. They would never stop being disappointed in me. I wondered how long it would be before they stopped loving me. I felt like they still cared, but I was becoming increasingly uncertain. One reason I left is because I was afraid they would send me away to be "cured." I'd heard too much about those horrible places to risk being sent there. How could my parents even think of sending me to such a place if they cared about me? That's what made me wonder if they cared or not. I feared they would only care about me if I became what they wanted me to be. If I tried to be myself they would toss me out and forget about me. I probably just saved them the trouble by running away.

How depressing. My life really did suck, but there were good things in it too. Brendan had shown me that, and Anne had told me exactly the same thing. I wasn't going to dwell on my parents and the fact I couldn't go home. Maybe Dorian and the others would find a way to help me. I didn't think they could magically make everything okay, but any improvement would be welcome. I didn't think there was anything they could do, but maybe they'd come up with something. They were an inventive lot. Even if they couldn't help I wasn't giving up. I wasn't going to wallow in self-pity or let myself become depressed either. I was going to seek out reasons to be happy and I was going to find them!

I took my time walking between the fields. I followed the grassy track to its very end. There I discovered a lake, not large, but too big to be called a pond. There was a gentle breeze that sent little waves lapping quietly on the shore. I sat down and drank in the beauty of the water sparkling in the sunlight. It would have been a beautiful place for a picnic. I wished I could bring Jeff here. We'd eat cold chicken and potato chips, drink Cokes, and then make out on the grass. We'd strip naked, explore each other's bodies, and then I'd let him do to me what Blake had done, only this time my brother wouldn't interrupt!

It was a nice little fantasy, but I wasn't sure Jeff was a picnic kind of guy. I didn't know if he could be romantic or if he was like Blake, only interested in getting it on without delay. I didn't know Jeff well, but I did know there was more to him than Blake. For one thing, he made out with me, which made me think he might be into taking long walks and having a picnic with his boyfriend. Blake would never have a boyfriend. He was all about sex. I wasn't sorry for hooking up with Blake, not at all. I was only sorry we got caught. Still, there had to be more than sex between two guys. As good as sex was it didn't last that long. Even if it went on for a couple of hours, what did two guys do with the rest of their time? Most of the gay boys in Verona were paired up. I wanted what they had.

I sighed. I could forget about finding a boyfriend for now. As much as I liked Jeff, he was a college guy and I was still in high school. That worked for Brendan and Casper, but they knew each other before Brendan went off to IU. For now, I was living on Anne's farm, but I had no idea how long I would be there. It might only be a few days. More likely it would be weeks and perhaps months, but who knew? My future was uncertain, but a boyfriend was something I could eagerly anticipate. It was another reason to live.

I wondered where I'd find my boyfriend or if he'd find me. Had I already met him or was he going to be someone completely new? How old would he be and what would he look like? Would he own a dog? Maybe he'd be an artist like Tristan or a jock like Shawn. Maybe he was even somewhere right now wondering about me; the boy he didn't know who would one day be his soul mate.

I threw a rock into the lake and laughed at myself. What would Brandon or Jon say to me if they knew I was sitting here thinking about my future boyfriend? I was sure that whatever they said it would be funny and likely rude. I missed those guys even though I hadn't known then long. I missed all of the Verona boys. I felt lonely so far away from them. At least Brendan was close by and so was Jeff. I'd give them a call sometime soon. Brendan had promised to bring me back to Bloomington too. I couldn't wait!

I stood up, brushed the dried grass off my jeans, and then gazed out over the lake. Near the edges were cattails. Among the reeds I could hear unseen frogs croaking. On the opposite shore was a forest. It came nearly down to the water. I thought about walking around the lake and exploring the woods. It wasn't far for the lake wasn't that big, but I thought I'd save that for another day. I didn't have to see everything at once. I wasn't sure how long I should be gone either. I didn't want Anne to worry about me. I didn't want to cause her any trouble. She was doing me a huge favor. I'd say I couldn't believe that she'd taken in a boy she had never met before, but after meeting her I could believe it. She was truly a good person.

I turned and wandered back the way I'd come. I was surrounded by beauty. I wished I had someone to share it with, but I would not let what I didn't have ruin what I did. That's what both Brendan and Anne had been telling me, each in their own way. I knew I would be much happier if I could make myself look at life that way. I was already beginning to do so. I'd even done it without thinking about it at different times in my life, but now the philosophy was much clearer in my mind. I had to choose to be happy.

"Are you hungry?" Anne asked as I entered the kitchen. She was rolling out dough on the counter with a rolling pin.

"Not really. I had a big breakfast and I kind of pigged out on those cookies."

"I'm going to fix us a nice supper to celebrate your arrival, but if you want anything before that help yourself from the refrigerator."

"You don't have to go to any trouble for me. I'll eat anything, except liver, and I'd eat that if I had to."

Anne laughed.

"I promise not to make you eat liver. I always found it disgusting myself. I won't cook too many big meals, but I like having someone to cook for. It's hardly worth the trouble with just me."

"Do you need any help?"

"No. I get along best by myself when I'm cooking."

"I met the horses. I'm glad you told me they were friendly. They came rushing toward me. I was a little frightened anyway because they are so big! What are their names?"

"The gray is named Flair. The other is Fallah. You can ride either if you like. I don't ride anymore myself, but I like to have them around. They're a part of the family so I wouldn't think of getting rid of them."

"I don't know how to ride and I think I might be afraid to climb up on a horse," I admitted.

"It's not for everyone. I rode when I was younger, but I find it a bit too uncomfortable. If you decide you want to give it a try I can show you how."

"Thanks, but I think I'll stick to just petting them. They seemed to like that."

"Yes, they love attention. I spend a little time with them each day, brushing their coats and, of course, feeding and watering them, although they mostly feed themselves at this time of the year."

"I'll be glad to help you with that."

"Wonderful."

"I'm going to run up to my room and grab a book. I thought it would be a good time to read outside."

"Oh, yes. It's a wonderful day for that. Just make sure you're back by five. We'll have supper then or soon after."

"I'll be back. In fact, I'm thinking about just sitting under the big oak in the yard. It's huge."

"I love that tree. You go enjoy yourself."

"Thanks."

I went up to my room, retrieved the book of poems by Robert Frost that Tristan had given me, and walked outside. I sat down on the grass and leaned back against the trunk of the oak. I could see the barn, the pastures, a grove of pines, and some outbuildings I had not yet explored. I took a deep breath. Maybe it was just my imagination, but the air smelled cleaner here.

I turned my attention to the book. I wasn't big on poems. When we read them in English classes I was usually bored by them. Most of them didn't even make sense to me. A few Haikus were kind of cool, but I didn't get most of them either. Tristan obviously thought I'd like these poems and he was a smart guy so I figured I might as well give them a try.

I began reading *The Road Not Taken*. The poem reminded me of exploring the farm. There was plenty to see, but I'd had to make some choices about what to look at and what to save for another day.

The poem was short, but I kept reading a little and then looking up and thinking about the lines while I took in the beauty of the oak tree, the grass, and the daffodils that were springing up near the fence. The last two lines made me think the most; "I took the one less traveled by, And that has made all the difference."

Maybe I wasn't getting it, but I thought that the poem was talking about more than what it seemed. Poems were sneaky like that. That's something I didn't particularly like about them. Often, poems left me feeling stupid because I didn't get them. I thought I did get this one. Robert Frost wasn't just talking about the joy of exploring somewhere most others passed by. I think he was talking about taking a different path in life. Maybe he was talking about becoming a poet instead of getting a more traditional job. I think he meant that going his own way and not doing what everyone else did made his life better.

I felt like I was on the road less taken. Most people wanted to fit in. They hid whatever was different about them. They went along with what everyone else wanted instead of making waves. True, I had not come out to my family or to most people by choice, but I had come out to Dorian and then to the rest of the gay boys back in Verona. I'd made a choice to go my own way and be myself rather than do what my family and my church demanded; fit in and be exactly like everyone else. My plans for the future had been kind of vague and yet I had planned to come out to everyone at some point, probably while I was in college. Maybe I wouldn't have told my parents about me until I was finished with school, but I had chosen to be the real me. I think that was the road less taken and I felt good that I'd made that choice. Maybe that's what Robert Frost meant. Maybe the choice I made would make all the difference.

Maybe I was reading something into the poem that wasn't there. Like I said, I often don't get poems. Maybe it didn't matter that I was reading something into the poem that the poet didn't intend. I was still getting something out of it. Maybe that was what poems were all about. Maybe each reader was meant to get his or her own meaning out of it.

I liked *The Road Not Taken* and that surprised me. I went on to the next poem and then the next. I read each one slowly and then put the book in my lap to think about what I'd read. I gazed up at the dark green oak leaves above me and ran my fingers through the soft grass. I closed my eyes and felt the breeze on my face and listened to the whinny of a horse carried to me by the wind. I let my eyes wander, taking in the barn, the outbuildings, and the chickens scratching at the dirt in the barnyard. I sat under that great oak tree and just lived.

I bet a lot of guys would think reading poems was gay, but then I was gay so it didn't matter. I grinned. I didn't think I liked the poems because I was gay. I liked them because I was me. I still didn't care for poetry in general. I didn't like most of what I'd read previously, but maybe I just hadn't found the right poet before. Tristan was right. I did like Robert Frost. Perhaps there were even other poets I might like.

Another poem I really liked was *Nothing Gold Can Stay*. It was a very short poem and I felt like I got it. The meaning was in the title itself, but the rest of the poem illustrated the point. The poem meant that wonderful times were fleeting. It meant that things change and that nothing is permanent, especially good things. My time with my family before I realized I was gay was golden. I didn't know it then, but that time was not to last long. My time being a part of the cast of Willy Wonka was golden. I missed that so much! It was a golden time. My time on Anne's farm was golden and I'd be wise to enjoy it and get all I could out of it instead of focusing on my problems. The poem was telling me to enjoy all that is good in life because none of it will be staying around for long. The poem was sad in a way and yet not. Golden moments faded away, but there were always more to come. The trick was to enjoy each one when it came.

I didn't read all the poems. The book was thick and I took my time. I barely got started, even though I sat there for an hour or more. I had a feeling poems were meant to be read a few or even one at a time. I didn't think I'd get as much out of them if I sat and read a bunch of them. In school, I hadn't cared much one way or another. Poems had been something to endure; something to get through as quickly as possible. These were different. These I enjoyed.

I closed the book and stood up. My butt was getting tired. I walked off toward the pine grove, enjoying the warmth of the sun. Wild roses grew in the fencerow that separated the barnyard from the yard. The blooms were small and white with just a touch a pink. They didn't have a scent, but they were beautiful. I wondered if they had just grown there or if they'd been planted on purpose. If the fence broke the rose bushes themselves would act as a fence. There was no way to get through them.

There was a little vegetable garden by the fencerow. There were a couple of tiny tomato plants, a few small vines that might be squash or pumpkins, a row marked "green beans" and others marked "peas", "marigolds", and "zinnias." Everything was just beginning to come up. I leaned over and sniffed the tomato plants. Most people didn't care for the scent of tomato plants, but I liked it. It was the scent of summer. At one end of the garden were several heads of Romaine lettuce. They were the only plants of any size, but then it was just April.

Between the garden and the pines was a grassy area. It wasn't a mowed yard, but the grass wasn't too thick and only came up a little past my ankles. There was so much space here! That grassy area was bigger than our whole yard in Verona and here it was just an unused space surrounded by acres and acres of fields and pastures!

I walked on under the pines. Most of them were huge, but there were smaller pines along the edges. The ground was completely covered with a bed of pine needles and the air was, not surprisingly, filled with the scent of pine. The pine trees whispered to me in the light breeze as I walked under their branches.

I hadn't noticed from my spot under the oak, but there were little hills and valleys in the pine grove. I crested the first hill and then walked down into the small valley between it and the next. I was just low enough to cut off the view of the farmhouse when I sat down. I could see nothing but pine trees in every direction from that position. The grove was probably no more than a couple of hundred feet wide in any direction, but I could sit there and imagine it was a huge evergreen forest that went on for miles and miles. I bet the trees were beautiful covered with snow. I wondered how much snow made it to the ground.

I lay back on the pine needles and closed my eyes. It was warm and pleasant under the trees. I felt safe and cozy. Without meaning to I drifted off to sleep.

I dreamed about the golden time when I was younger, before I even thought about having a sexual orientation. I'm not sure what age I was, but Justin was in the dream too, only he was almost the age he was now. Mom and Dad were in the dream. That's what the dream was about; family. I don't remember specifically what was going on in the dream, only that we were all together and we were happy. The dream shifted about and then Justin and I were both our current ages. Everything was still fine in the dream. My life with my family was golden again.

I awakened. I don't know if I had other dreams or not. I usually didn't remember any of my dreams, but I had a sense I always dreamed when I went to sleep. It's like I lived this whole other dream life that I mostly didn't know anything about.

I remembered only bits and pieces of my golden dream when I awakened. I was disorientated for a few moments. I wasn't accustomed to waking up in a pine forest. My memories quickly came flowing back. I lay there for a while; thinking about my dream and savoring the pleasant feeling it left behind. I felt as if I was back with my family and everything was okay. I wondered about the last part of my dream for I sensed it was taking place in the present or the near future. Was it a sign that somehow things were going to be okay? I hoped so. I was going to go on with my life one way or another. I was going to have golden times whether or not they included my family, but I wanted my family to be a part of my life.

The pine boughs swayed in the breeze above. The sunlight made the branches a brilliant, bright green. I wondered if Robert Frost had ever written about pine trees. I bet he did. I'd find out sooner or later. I planned to read the whole book of poems Tristan gave me. It might take me months to finish since I planned to read only a few at a time, but I'd read them all.

I stood up and looked at my watch. It was almost 4:30! I wasn't sure what time it was when I lay down and drifted off to sleep, but I was surprised it was so late. I guess I was more tired than I thought. I smiled when I thought of what Jeff and I had done in his bed the night before. He wore me out!

I crested the small hill and there was the farmhouse and barn. It took no time at all to walk back. When I walked into the kitchen wonderful aromas wafted toward me. I could smell dressing and potatoes and some kind of berry pie. My stomach rumbled.

"The whole kitchen smells delicious."

Anne smiled.

"Supper will be ready in just a few minutes. Would you set the table? The plates are in the top of the cupboard as are the tumblers. The silverware is in the left drawer."

"Sure."

I walked to the old kitchen cabinet, or cupboard, and pulled out two plates with little bluebirds on them.

"These are old, aren't they?" I asked.

"Yes. I think they made those back in the 1920's, although I'm not sure."

I put the plates on the antique oak table and then pulled forks, knives, and spoons from the drawer and placed them on the table.

"Get us each a small plate and a bowl too. We'll need them."

I nodded and continued my short task. I liked the old plates with little bluebirds. They were really pretty.

"Is that a berry pie I smell?" I asked.

"It's a blackberry cobbler. It's like a pie, but rectangular and deeper."

"It smells so good."

"It is, especially with a little vanilla ice cream on top."

"Mmm."

In just a few minutes the table was filled with wonderful things to eat; chicken and dressing, mashed potatoes, green beans, and fresh-baked yeast rolls. The blackberry cobbler cooled on the counter.

We sat down and began eating. The chicken and dressing was delicious, as was the mashed potatoes. I even liked the green beans and I wasn't big on green vegetables. The yeast rolls were downright heavenly.

"I hope you like leftovers. It isn't possible to make a little chicken and dressing. That's why I rarely make it for myself."

"Don't you dare throw any of this out," I said and grinned. "It's all so good I don't want to waste any of it."

I had to force myself to eat slowly. Everything was so delicious I wanted to devour it. I didn't want Anne to think I was a wild boy and I also wanted to savor the taste. I almost felt like moaning with pleasure as I put the chicken, dressing, and mashed potatoes into my mouth.

Anne put a kettle on the stove before we finished. By the time we were ready for dessert hot tea was ready.

"Would you like ice cream on yours?" Anne asked.

"Yes, please."

Anne set a big bowl of blackberry cobbler in front of me with a large scoop of vanilla ice cream on top. The ice cream began to melt quickly. I tried a spoonful of cobbler and melted ice cream.

"This might be the best dessert ever," I said.

"Thank you."

"I'm a big chocolate freak, but this is even better."

Anne poured us both cups of hot tea.

"What kind of tea is this?" I asked.

"Famous Edinburgh."

"It's really good."

"It's one of my favorites."

I loved the sweet blackberries, but the crust was the best part. It was soaked in blackberry juice and had a glaze of sugar on the top. Mixed in with the ice cream, the cobbler was Heaven on Earth.

"What did you do with your time this afternoon?" Anne asked.

"Well, I went to explore that little pine grove, but when I got there I lay down to look up at the trees and I fell asleep. I slept almost the entire time I was gone."

"Oh, I love a good nap myself. Dasher likes to curl up with me. It's comforting to feel him beside me and I think he feels the same way about me."

"I think I'd want a cat or dog if I lived alone. I've always had to share a room with my brother. Well, since he was born, and he's not much younger than me so I don't remember having a room to myself."

"Cats and dogs are a lot of company. I love both. Cats are lower maintenance and they sleep 16 to 18 hours a day."

"Wow. I think I want to be a cat in my next life."

"It doesn't look like a bad life to me either."

We finished our dessert and then I helped clean up. Tidying up wasn't difficult because Anne had a dishwasher. It was disguised as an old cupboard, which is exactly what I thought it was until she opened it.

We walked into Anne's living room, which she called a sitting room. It was a comfortable place with two overstuffed sofas and golden oak furniture that matched the table and chairs in the kitchen. An old pump organ stood in one corner.

We sat and talked about nothing in particular. Anne didn't pry into what brought me to her, although she knew the basic details before I arrived. She just told me things about herself and her late husband. I talked quite a bit about touring IU and

Bloomington with Brendan. Anne was familiar with most of the places, which lead to stories about some of them.

As it grew dark, Anne left the lights off and illuminated the room only with candles and lamps. Dasher rested on her lap, but when she got up to light the lamps he moved over and sat first beside me, then on me. He felt furry and warm. Stroking his fur made me feel content. I didn't know what awaited me in the near future, but for the moment at least I was in a safe place and I was content to remain there.

Dorian

"The answer is yes," Brandon said as we sat alone in his car after school. It was one of the few places at VHS we could talk without being overheard.

"Really?"

"You sound shocked."

"Well, I am."

"If you thought it was so unlikely that Scotty's parents would agree to someone else making the funeral arrangements why did you bother trying?"

"It never hurts to try. So they really said yes?"

"No, I'm just saying that to build your hopes up so I can crush them."

Brandon smacked me on the top of the head.

"Oww!"

"Stop being so blond."

I giggled.

"Scotty's mom is so distraught Justin didn't dare ask her about funeral arrangements. He was afraid she'd freak out. He told his dad that some members of the soccer team had offered to make the arrangements for Scotty. He told a white lie or two about their parents lending a hand, but Justin said his dad barely listened. He just stared out into space. He's really taking this hard. He wouldn't even answer Justin until Justin pressed him and told him that everyone would expect a funeral. His dad just nodded and slid his checkbook across the table."

"What if he doesn't remember he agreed?"

"He will remember. He may regret it, but he'll remember. I think this will ease Justin's mind. He doesn't know what to do with his parents acting so crazy. He told me that he thought he was going to have to arrange everything because they wouldn't. He didn't have a clue about where to start. He's very grateful the soccer team is taking care of it."

"The soccer team will do a very good job," I said.

"Now, get the hell out of my car. My girlfriend will be here soon."

"Okay. Thanks, Brandon."

I went back inside for play practice. I gave Marc, Dane, and Tim the thumbs up. I think they were shocked Scotty's parents agreed. I hadn't really thought about it when the idea came to me, but the whole planning-Scotty's-funeral thing was pretty crazy. It's probably a good thing I didn't think about it much or I wouldn't have even tried.

Play practice went smoothly. Everyone was still upset about Scotty, but I think that's why things went smoothly. Acting is an escape. Actors are someone else when they are performing. Their own problems and worries fall away. I've often stepped off stage after a scene and been shocked to discover I wasn't Tom Sawyer or Dorian Gray. I bet it's like that for others too.

After practice, Marc, Dane, Tim and I walked out to Marc's Camaro. None of us said a word about Scotty until we were in the car and the doors were closed.

"They really agreed?" Tim asked the moment we were safe from being overheard.

"Why does everyone sound so amazed?" I asked.

"Because it was an insane idea," Tim said. "No parent would let someone else plan their kid's funeral."

"They would if they're barely aware of their own surroundings. Justin thinks they might be in shock," I said.

"So, we're really doing it? We're really planning Scotty's funeral?" Dane asked.

"Yes," I said. "Tim, can we meet at your place tomorrow evening, say about 8:30?"

"Yeah. I'm sure Shawn won't mind."

"Good. Marc and I will gather information. I'll make a list of what I think we need to do. This is my first funeral after all."

"Maybe you can be a professional funeral planner. This could be the start of something big for you," Dane said.

"I think not!"

We dropped Dane and Tim off at Tim's place and then Marc took me to his loft. He got us both Cokes while I sat at the table with a pen and a notebook.

"We will need to visit the funeral home," I said. "I'm sure we can get a lot of help there. We need to figure out a time for the visitation and the actual funeral."

"Um, do we need a visitation?" Marc asked. "There is no corpse to visit."

"Visitation isn't for the dead. It's for family and friends. The same with the funeral."

"I don't want either when I'm dead. Just stick me in a garbage bag and leave me by the curb," Marc said.

"Absolutely not! Besides, you aren't going anywhere. I'm not done with you, mister."

"Yeah? You have plans for me? Does it involve messing around in the shower?" Marc asked hopefully.

"Later. We have to get this done. We need to pick out a casket, write an obituary, put an announcement in the paper... Oh, who knew there was so much to do?"

"I think you're enjoying this."

"How often do you get to plan a friend's funeral?"

"Not very often, I hope."

"Let me rephrase that. How often do you get to plan a friend's funeral knowing that he's alive and well and hanging out on a farm?"

"Um, once?"

"Exactly. Now, I think we should try to keep expenses down seeing as how Scotty isn't really dead, except I think we should splurge on the casket. They can probably use it later, can't they?"

"Sure. They can just pop it in storage until Scotty needs it or perhaps use it as a coffee table."

I rolled my eyes.

"Hmm, what am I forgetting?"

"Flowers."

"Family and friends send flowers. Don't you know anything about funerals?"

"I don't know about planning them. I've never been to one. I have a rule about weddings and funerals that keeps me away from them."

"What's that?"

"You come to mine, then I'll come to yours."

I banged my head on the table.

"Oh why did I get involved with a jock?" I said to the air.

"Probably because of my big, hard..."

"Tombstone! We'll need a tombstone!"

"That's not where I was going."

"I know where you were going, but we need to think about *this* now. We can't leave it all for tomorrow after play practice."

"Why not? Procrastination is a wonderful thing. Never put off until tomorrow what you can do next week."

"I've heard that somewhere before and it doesn't quite make sense."

"It doesn't have to make sense. I'm a jock, remember?"

"Get over here and help me."

"Oh! I love it when you get dominant."

Marc and I sat down and put our heads together. We made of list of things to do. We sat there a surprisingly long time getting it all sorted out.

"That's it. Dying is too much trouble. I'm not doing it," Marc said after we'd been planning for a good, long time.

"Well, it's fine with me if you live forever," I said.

"Are we done now?"

"Yeah, I think we're done until tomorrow after practice."

"Good, come on."

"Where?"

"The shower. Remember?"

"Oh yeah!"

Marc pulled me toward his bathroom. We pulled off each other's shirts, jeans, underwear, and socks then climbed into the shower. The water was hot and Marc was even hotter.

We made out, then soaped each other up, and made out some more. Marc's body was smooth and hard. I loved his muscles. The sight of him shirtless always drove me crazy. Naked, he was so hot I couldn't control myself. Luckily, I didn't have to. I kissed and licked down his torso and then got on my knees and made him moan. That was only the beginning.

You know how shower scenes in movies and porn look really hot? Well, the real thing is even hotter! We must have stayed in the shower for an hour, filling the bathroom and the loft with our moans and groans. When we climbed out and dried off we moved to Marc's bed and started all over again! It was nearly eleven when Marc drove me home. I would have stayed all night if I could, but I was expected home by eleven on weeknights.

Marc kissed me again in his car when we stopped in front of my house.

"Can't you get enough?" I asked.

"Of you? Never."

"Good," I said and kissed him back.

I climbed out of the car and went inside. I couldn't wait until tomorrow evening. At last we were going to plan Scotty's funeral!

I was almost too excited to sleep, but Marc had worn me out. I stripped and then climbed into bed. My mind was racing with ideas, but within only a few minutes I was snoozing away.

It was hard to keep up my grieving act the next day at school because I was excited about planning Scotty's funeral and, of course, Scotty wasn't dead. I managed to look properly downcast, but on the inside I was hopping up and down.

Marc and I spread the word about the planning session that night. Tim had already told his brother and that meant Tristan knew. It took most of the day to tell everyone because absolute secrecy was needed.

I spotted Justin and Brandon walking together between 3rd and 4th period. Brandon was an incredible guy. He was a popular jock, the very type that picked on gay boys at my old school, but Brandon helped out everyone. He was always there for the homos and now he was helping Justin deal with the loss of his brother. I felt the urge to tell Justin his brother wasn't really dead, but we had to play this through to the end or risk making the whole exercise pointless. It was absolutely necessary that Scotty's family, and everyone who had been unkind to him, feel the pain of his loss so they could see the error of their ways. I bet Mark and Taylor's parents would have given anything to find out their sons weren't really dead after all. I couldn't help Mark or Taylor's parents, but I could help Scotty's family. The more I learned about the grief of Scotty's parents and brother the more I felt for them and the more I wanted to help them. Before, I just wanted to kick their asses for being so stupid and cruel. Now, I realized that they needed help as much as Scotty, perhaps more so.

Scotty's funeral wasn't the only good news. Marc was growing increasingly more comfortable in the role of Charlie. I'm sure he secretly hoped Scotty would return in time to resume the role, but Marc was slowly losing his fear of performing in front of an audience.

I was amused that my sexy, jock boyfriend feared to stand upon the stage when I didn't fear it at all. I wasn't physically strong like Marc. I wasn't boisterous. Yet, it was easy for me to perform in front of hundreds of people. I think my lack of fear came not so much from experience, but rather because I was on public view every minute of every day. People noticed me because I was androgynous. I didn't fit what they expected from a boy. I dressed in very tight pants and fabulous clothing. I had a high-pitched voice. I didn't bother trying to be something I wasn't. All that, and likely more, meant that I was up on stage every moment of every day. Anyone who was near was my audience.

Marc drove me to the Miller Funeral Home right after practice. Marc's presence was comforting. It was kind of creepy inside the funeral home. There were no dead bodies lying around, but it was cold, too quiet, and a sweet scent, like flowers but not so pleasant, lingered in the air.

"Can I help you boys?" said a man who came out of a side room. He was dressed in a black suit and kind of looked like he should be lying in a casket himself. His face was too pale.

"Um, yeah. We need to plan a funeral," I said. "We're handling the arrangements for Scotty Jackson's family. His parents... aren't up to it."

"It's a tragedy when one dies so young. I am Mr. Miller and you are?"

"Dorian and this is Marc."

"Follow me and we'll get started."

Mr. Miller led us into a large room off to the left. I was immediately creeped out because there were eight caskets on display around the edges of the room. Mr. Miller led us to a seating area with two love seats and a low table. Marc and I sat close on one of the love seats.

"We've never planned a funeral before," I said.

"Don't worry. I can handle all the details. My job is to make things as easy as possible for the family. Were you friends of the deceased?"

"Yes. Scotty was in our drama class. He was going to be Charlie in the spring play, *Willy Wonka and the Chocolate Factory*."

"I'm sorry for your loss."

Mr. Miller still creeped me out a little, but I was sure his calm and compassionate manner helped put those who really were grieving at ease.

"Usually, there is a visitation one afternoon and evening, followed by the funeral the next morning."

"We would like it soon, but we'll need time to plan," Marc said.

"I think we should make everything brief," I said.

"You can set whatever hours for the visitation you wish."

"Perhaps 2-8 for the visitation the Saturday after this one? With the funeral and burial Sunday morning at maybe 10?" I asked.

"We can accommodate that quite nicely."

"Great," I said, a little too enthusiastically. Marc looked sideways at me. "Great," I repeated, more calmly.

"I believe the body has not yet been recovered. Were you thinking a casket or an urn?"

"A casket. I think Scotty would have liked that," I said.

We definitely wanted a casket. It was so much more dramatic than an urn!

"Very well. I'll show you the models we have on display here. We also have a brochure. We can have any casket you like here in a day."

The truly creepy part came next as Mr. Miller began showing us caskets. The first was closed and I dug my fingers into Marc's arm as Mr. Miller opened it. It was irrational, but I was afraid someone was going to jump out at me.

The casket was black with fancy brass fittings. Two wooden poles formed the handles on the sides. Mr. Miller pulled out the white velvet and draped it over the side of the casket.

"This model is 18 gauge steel. The interior is velvet and includes an eternal rest adjustable bed with matching pillow and throw."

I could see Marc trying not to smile out of the corner of my eye. I hoped he didn't start laughing. Mr. Miller sounded as if he was trying to sell us a bed set.

"There is a memory and record tube for including personal items and written information if the family desires."

"Written information?" I asked.

"Yes, some families like to include a short biography, newspaper clippings, and other information about the deceased. Others like to include poems they have written, letters, and etcetera. It's purely a matter of personal choice."

I nodded. I had no idea there was so much to a casket.

"There is a locking mechanism and a full rubber gasket seal. All of our models fit in standard burial vaults."

Mr. Miller showed us the other caskets and described each one. There was a white casket, a blue one, a gold one, and even a rose one. I particularly liked the silver casket. It was so shiny! There were a couple of wooden caskets too. One was cherry and another oak.

"Here is a brochure you may take with you. It includes all the models we have on display here and more. I'm sure you'll want to take some time to decide. I'll leave you alone for a moment and get the necessary paperwork."

Marc and I sat on the loveseat again. I opened the brochure and browsed.

"Ohh! This one! I love this one!"

"You're too loud," Marc whispered.

"Sorry. What do you think?"

I pointed to the purple casket in the brochure.

"Um, no. There is no way Scotty's family will want him buried in a bright purple casket. It's way too gay."

"Oh, I guess you're right. Wow, I want this casket when I die. I didn't know they came in purple!"

Marc giggled. I smiled. I was getting way too excited.

"If you're very good, we'll buy you a purple casket, but only if you promise not to die until you are 100."

"Deal," I said. "Okay, if I can't pick the purple one, I want the silver one."

I pointed to the casket over in the corner.

"I think that one will work."

"Good. I hope everyone else agrees."

Mr. Miller was back.

"The contract will need to be signed by whomever is paying the bill. You can take it with you, read it over, get it signed, and bring it back with the deposit check. I will need it tomorrow as well as your choice of casket so we can proceed with the arrangements."

I nodded.

Mr. Miller went through more details with us and offered helpful suggestions. He made things much easier than I'd expected. I was clueless about the whole process.

"What about a headstone?" I asked.

"Headstones are handled separately and usually after the funeral. A small temporary marker will be placed on the grave and will be replaced later by whatever monument the family chooses. In the packet I'm giving you is a list of local monument dealers. There are only two and I recommend them both. They take care of creating the monument and placing it."

I guessed we didn't need to worry about that then.

We were finished only a few minutes later.

"There's a lot to it, isn't there?" I said to Marc as we climbed back in his Camaro.

"Yeah. People really should take care of all the arrangements before they need a funeral. Could you imagine dealing with all that when you've just lost someone?"

"It's no wonder Scotty's parents can't face it," I said.

"How are we going to get that form signed?"

"I'll give it to Brandon to give to Justin. I think we can be more direct now since the "soccer team" is planning the funeral and Brandon is on the team. Justin doesn't seem leery of Brandon anymore either."

Marc nodded. I leaned back in the seat and grinned at my boyfriend as he drove down Main Street. We were on our way to Shawn and Tim's apartment. Shawn was cooking supper and then we were all going to sit down and plan Scotty's funeral. I couldn't wait! It's not often you get to plan the funeral of one of your friends and I was looking forward to it. I was already thinking about what music to play. There would be none of that horrible organ music at Scotty's funeral. After all, it was the ultimate going away party and I knew Scotty would want to go out with a bang. I wanted to get Scotty the shiny, silver casket I'd spotted in Miller's Funeral Home. It was sweet! I just hoped the others would go along with my ideas. I figured I had a right to have the biggest input. It was my idea to kill Scotty after all. Without me there wouldn't even be a funeral. Sure, most of my friends helped kill him, but it was still my idea.

Marc parked down the street from Café Moffatt. Shawn and Tim had their own apartment right above the café. Shawn worked there part time, as well as at Ofarim's. He sure had a short commute to Café Moffatt!

I gathered up all the paperwork and carried it up the stairs. Marc knocked on the door and Tristan let us in. Several members of the gang were already there. Tim and Dane were wrestling on the couch. I could smell spaghetti sauce and garlic and was suddenly very hungry.

"Tim, get off Dane and get out the plates and silverware," Shawn called from the kitchen.

Tim reluctantly climbed off his boyfriend and went to help his brother. I wondered what it was like to live with an older brother instead of parents. Shawn and Tim's dad was alive, but they had moved out months earlier because he was abusive. They didn't know if their mom was alive or dead. She'd left when they were younger and they hadn't heard from her in years. I couldn't imagine having no idea where my mom was or even if she was still living. Shawn and Tim got on very well, but I was sure it was rough getting by. I was impressed that they managed it. They seemed happy, so I guess that's what really mattered.

There was a knock on the door. Tristan answered and let Ethan, Nathan, and Casper in.

"Sorry, we're late. The tractor conked out on me and it took a while to get it going again," Ethan said.

"We're just getting ready to eat so you have arrived at the perfect time," Shawn said.

Soon, we were all seated, some of us at the antique counter that separated the living room and kitchen and others at the table, which was located in the living room since the kitchen was small.

"This is really good," Jon said. "I love your spaghetti."

"Thanks," Shawn said.

"The key to good spaghetti is the boiling of the pasta," Tim said.

"Which means Tim did that part," Tristan said.

"Shawn could never make it without me," Tim said.

"I'm willing to try. Does anyone want a slightly beat up younger brother?"

"Yeah, like you'll get any takers on Tim!" Brandon said.

"I'll take him!" Dane yelled.

"There's a shock," Marc said.

"I don't think your mom will let you have a pet, Dane," Shawn said.

"Ruff!" Tim said, then panted.

We talked and laughed all through supper. We had a great time, but then why not? We had gathered to plan a funeral!

Everyone pitched in to help clean up after we finished eating, so it wasn't long before we were all seated about the living room. Dane sat on Tim's lap to "help make room" as they put it. It was difficult finding enough seats, but Dane and Tim could never be pried apart for long.

"I think everyone knows why we're here, but just in case someone is clueless..." I said.

"Like Brandon," Jon said.

"Shut it," Brandon retorted.

"We have gathered to plan Scotty's funeral. Marc and I stopped by the funeral home and made some of the arrangements, but there are still decisions to make and things that need to be done. First, we need an obituary for the *Citizen*. Does anyone want to volunteer to write and submit it?"

"I will," Nathan said.

"Cool. We need to think about music for the visitation and the funeral. We don't want any of that sad organ music."

"I'll pick out some music, maybe some upbeat classical," Tristan said.

"How about some hard rock?" Shawn suggest, although I think he was only kidding.

"Noooo!" Tristan said. "That's why I'm picking the music. Who knows what you or Brandon would choose?"

"Something completely inappropriate I'm sure," Casey said and laughed.

"Yeah, and there will be people there besides us," Tristan pointed out.

"We also need to keep Scotty's parents in mind. We want them to like what we choose," I said.

"You are being very thoughtful about Scotty's parents all of a sudden," Dane said.

"They're a lot more upset than I thought they'd be."

"Justin is calling the shots at his house now," Brandon said. "According to him his parents are only borderline functional. Scotty's death has hit them HARD."

"Good, then maybe they won't be such bastards when Scotty returns from the grave," Jon said.

"Has anyone talked to Scotty?" I asked.

"Yeah, he's doing well on Aunt Anne's farm but he misses everyone. I told him we were working on a plan so he could come back," Casper said.

"I hope you didn't hint that we'd killed him," Brandon said.

"Hey, I'm not stupid."

"Eh-eh," Brandon said flipping his hand back and forth. Casper stuck out his tongue.

"If you make a blond joke, you die," Marc said. "We're already getting a casket. We can pop you in just before the burial and no one will know the difference."

Brandon put his hand on his chest and looked shocked as if he'd never make a blond joke. We all knew better.

"Speaking of caskets," I said. "I'll pass around this brochure and everyone can have a look, but if you love me, you'll let me get the silver one."

"It's so shiny!" Nathan said as he took the brochure and spotted the silver coffin.

"Well, we know why Dorian likes it then," Brandon said.

"Actually, that was his second choice. He loved the purple one," Marc said.

"Ohhh! Let's get the purple one then," Casper said, looking at the brochure with Nathan.

"I don't think Scotty's family would approve," Marc said.

"It is rather... gay," Ethan said, taking a look.

"I promised Dorian he could be buried in it, if he lives to be 100," Marc said.

"Why wait?" Brandon said. "Let's bury him now. We can probably get a group discount."

I shot Brandon my most menacing look. He didn't seem frightened.

"I like the silver one," Tristan said. "Besides, I think Dorian should get to pick since he came up with the idea of killing Scotty."

"That's what I was thinking!" I said.

"Works for me. Who cares what a casket looks like anyway?" Jon said.

"I do! It's a fashion statement," I said.

"With you, everything is a fashion statement," Brandon noted. I couldn't argue with that.

"The silver one is cool. I think Scotty would have liked it," Shawn said.

"We can ask him after he comes back from the dead," Casper noted.

"It will already be buried then," Marc pointed out.

"He can dig it up and have a look. It is *his* after all."

"Congratulations, Dorian. The silver casket it is," Marc said.

"Yes! Unless anyone wants to go for purple?" I asked.

"Forget it. If you suggest purple again we're getting that hideous green one instead," Ethan said.

"I would never bury Scotty in that travesty of a casket! The silver one it is," I said.

We moved on to other details. With everyone there it was all falling into place. We brainstormed and split up the tasks. This was going to be the best funeral ever!

"We really have to throw Scotty a kick-ass wake after he comes back," Brandon said.

"The deceased can deliver the eulogy," Ethan said.

"The eulogy! We forgot it!" I said.

"You can do it, Dorian," Marc said.

"Yeah right. Scotty's parents would both die on the spot if I did it or they might kill me."

"Well, call the funeral home and see if they offer a bulk rate deal," Brandon said. "I'll spring for the purple casket if you promise to use it within a week."

"Not a chance!" Marc said.

"Seriously, who can we get to do it?" I asked. "It can't be any of us gay boys."

Everyone looked at Brandon and Jon.

"Let's get Devon to do it," Brandon said.

Everyone just stared. Brandon *hated* Devon. He'd even tried to kill him once.

"Don't look at me like that. It makes perfect sense. Devon goes to Scotty's church so we know he'll be acceptable to the family. Devon is on the soccer team and he knows Scotty. They weren't friends, but they weren't enemies until Devon found out

Scotty was gay. He will have to do it if asked. Otherwise he'll look like a jerk. Besides, I like the idea of using Devon as a tool. "

"Ahh, that last part makes sense," Jon said.

"I always thought of Devon as a tool," Ethan said, then laughed.

"Who is going to ask him?" Marc asked. "He'd probably just spit on most of us and I know he won't do any favors for Brandon."

"Why not? I do him a favor every day by not kicking his ass," Brandon said.

"Have Trent ask him," Jon suggested.

"Yeah, he'll do it," Brandon said.

"Okay, that's settled then, if Trent agrees," I said.

"Jon and I will make plans for the wake," Brandon said.

"We will?" Jon asked.

"Yeah, I just volunteered you."

"Um, okay. That's very generous of you to volunteer *my* time," Jon said.

"I give 'til it hurts."

We left the talk of caskets, funerals, and eulogies behind. Tristan and Shawn made cookies and we sat around and talked while we snacked. I was sorry Scotty couldn't be there with us, but then he could hardly be present while we were planning his funeral. Hopefully, we could include him in all our group activities when he came back from the dead.

The party broke up. I gathered up my papers and notes and Marc drove me home.

"That was fun! We should plan a funeral for a friend more often," Marc said. We looked at each other. "Um, I guess not."

Marc stopped the car in front of my house. I leaned in and kissed him on the lips. The kiss deepened, but we pulled apart after a few moments because we knew we'd end up doing it in the car if we didn't. While getting in on in Marc's car was not without appeal we were both very tired. I yawned.

I gave Marc a peck on the lips and then climbed out of the Camaro. I walked inside, pleased with how well the plans for

Scotty's funeral were coming along. He was going to have the best funeral ever!

Scotty

"You friend Brendan called," Anne said. "He had some very good news for you."

"Yeah?"

"Your friends back home think it's time for you to return."

"Really? So soon? It's been less than two weeks."

"Brendan said that your friends thought it would be safe for you to return."

"Did he say why?"

"No. I didn't ask, but you can ask him when he comes to get you tomorrow. He told me he will pick you up after his last class and you'll spend the evening and part of the next day with him in Bloomington before heading back home."

"That's great!" I said, but then my mood fell. "I'm going to miss you."

Anne smiled.

"Well, you are planning to attend IU, right? That means you'll be in Bloomington for four years. I'll only be a few minutes away. You can visit as often as you like. You can come out and spend some weekends with me."

I gave Anne a hug.

"I hope you won't be lonely without me."

"I managed well before you came so I'll be just fine after you leave. Don't forget, I have Dasher, the chickens, and the horses. I'm far from alone. I have immensely enjoyed having you here and I will be looking forward to your visits."

I hugged her again.

"What would you like for supper?" Anne asked. "This will be your last evening here so I want to fix you something special."

"Well, what I'd really like is another blackberry cobbler, but for supper I'd love biscuits and gravy and maybe bacon."

"You aren't just saying that to save me work, are you? Biscuits and gravy are easy to prepare."

"I don't like creating work for you, but I really would love biscuits and gravy and don't forget the cobbler!"

Anne laughed.

"I'll get started on the cobbler then. It will take much longer than the rest since it has to bake a good long time. We'll have to wait a while after supper to eat dessert."

"Sounds good to me!"

I headed back outside since Anne liked to be alone in the kitchen. I'd offered to help out more than once, but she never took me up on my offer. I would likely have only been in the way since I didn't know anything about cooking.

I opened the gate that lead into the barnyard and closed it behind me. The chickens pecked and scratched in the dirt and grass near the barn. I could hear crickets chirping loudly somewhere off in the tall grass and a woodpecker pounding on a dead tree in the distance.

I climbed over the gate and dropped down into the pasture. Flair and Fallah galloped toward me, but I wasn't afraid.

"How would you two like a little grain? It's my last evening here if you can believe it."

Flair snorted and Fallah whinnied. I took that to mean yes. I turned toward the barn. I entered through the open doorway and walked into the large area reserved for the horses. There was straw on the floor, but I'd never seen Flair or Fallah in there when they weren't being fed. No doubt they spent more time in the barn in the winter. I imagined it was cozy inside when the doors were shut.

I climbed over the half-wall and took the scoop off a post, then opened the old feed bin and scooped out some grain into the tough for the horses. I knew how much to give them because Anne had shown me. I gave them fresh water while I was at it.

"There you go," I said.

I climbed back over and stroked the horse's necks as they munched on grain. I suspect it made a nice change from grass although they seemed to like that well enough. I wondered what grass tasted like to a horse.

"I can't believe I'm leaving here so soon. I feel like I just got here. I'm going to miss you guys."

I was pretty sure the horses understood every word. I walked out of the barn, leaving them to their grain. I wandered about aimlessly, lost in thought.

Why did the guys think it was safe for me to return? What could possibly have changed in such a short time? To be honest, I'd never had much hope that the Verona boys could do anything to make my life better. I knew they wanted to help and would try, but what could they do? My parents were not going to change. They believed they were doing the right thing. If they had forced me into one of those places that claim to cure gays they would have truly believed they were doing what was best for me. I was plenty angry with my family, but I knew they weren't trying to make my life difficult. Dad was a control freak at times, but he wasn't a bad person.

My biggest fear was that my parents would stop loving me. As twisted as their point of view was I thought they still loved me. I'll admit I was no longer sure. It's kind of hard to think someone loves you when you fear they'll send you away to be tortured so that you'll become what they want. That's what they did in those treatment clinics—mental and physical torture. Brendan had told me.

I wasn't sure my parents still loved me. Running away probably just made things worse. I had no choice, but it showed my parents that I'd been lying; that I had no intention of changing. They wouldn't react well to such defiance, especially because it went against their religious beliefs. My church preached that gays were an abomination. How could my parents accept that I was an abomination and that I was determined to remain one? I knew there was absolutely nothing wrong with being gay, but my parents thought it was a sin. I knew how much my parent's beliefs meant to them. I thought the church they forced me to attend was borderline evil, but that didn't mean I could expect my parents to change their beliefs. Religion was supposed to comfort and help people, but it had destroyed my life, at least life as I knew it.

How could anything have possibly changed back home? What could my friends have done? I trusted them not to lead me astray. They'd gone to a lot of trouble to set up my escape and find me a place to hide out. I didn't see any way they could have changed things enough that it was safe for me to return and yet they must have done something. I guessed I'd find out everything from Brendan tomorrow.

I looked around at the farm. This place hadn't been home long, but I was going to miss it. Anne had been so kind to me. She had been accepting in a way my family never had been.

I was going to miss sitting and talking with Anne in the evenings. I had found myself spilling out all my problems and she listened. She sometimes offered a suggestion or a new way to think about a situation, but even just knowing that she was truly listening helped. Mostly, we just talked. She told me a lot about her husband and their life together. She told me about the rough times right after he died and how she'd managed to go on. She told me how she'd found happiness again and how she felt that he was still with her. Anne really was happy in this place with her memories, her cat, her horses, and her chickens. She really was not alone here even though there wasn't another person around that often. Anne did have friends. Two had even stopped by. I was glad she had friends. As much as she loved her animals, she needed human company sometimes.

As sad as I was to leave the farm, I was excited to be returning to Bloomington and Indiana University and more excited still at the prospect of being able to go home. It seemed too good to be true, but who knew? Well, I guess Brendan and the Verona boys did, but I wasn't going to get my hopes up. Maybe the guys had somehow convinced my parents not to send me off for treatment. Maybe that was all there was to it. Maybe everything else would remain the same. I didn't know if I could live like that, but maybe it would be worth a try. I didn't think I could stand not seeing my friends or being able to go out, but at least I'd be home. I'd have to think on it.

I was wasting my time thinking up scenarios. All I had to do was wait a few hours and I'd know what was up. The waiting was going to kill me! I just knew it!

I wandered around visiting familiar sights. It was amazing there were familiar sights on Anne's farm, considering how short a time I'd been there. I hadn't even explored some parts of it. There wasn't enough time to explore now. It's weird how I thought I had all the time in the world to explore when the days I had left here were few. I guess life was like that. Death was too. It was weird to think that I could die and be buried in the ground a couple of days later, but it happened to people all the time. One just never knew when there would be no tomorrow.

The biscuits and gravy and bacon that Anne made for supper was the best ever. There were extra biscuits with strawberry jam to go on them. I love breakfast foods like French toast, pancakes, omelets, and biscuits and gravy. Back home we only had breakfast food at breakfast. Mom or Dad probably thought it was a sin to eat pancakes for supper or maybe Mom just never thought of breakfast for lunch or supper.

After supper, I help Anne clean up and we sat in the sitting room as we often did and talked. I was going to miss sitting and talking with Anne and I was sure she'd miss me too. At least she had Dasher. He was good company.

Later, after the cobbler was taken out of the oven and allowed to cool for a while, we went into the kitchen. Anne made us hot tea just as she did my first night and most nights. She dished out big bowls of hot, blackberry cobbler and put vanilla ice cream on top. I loved Anne's cooking, but I was going to miss her blackberry cobbler the most.

That night, I lay in bed wondering what was to come in the next couple of days. I was sure Bloomington would be fun, but as for what happened after I wasn't at all sure. I wasn't going to worry about it. I took comfort in the fact that I could come back to the farm if things didn't work out. Anne said so.

The next morning Anne made blueberry and pecan pancakes for breakfast, as well as bacon. She was spoiling me for sure. Part of me wished I could go right on living on the farm with her and not just because of the food.

The morning passed too quickly. I spent it mostly with Anne instead of wandering around the farm. For lunch we had bacon and tomato sandwiches and for dessert there was still blackberry cobbler!

I packed my few belongings after lunch and tidied up my room. I didn't want to leave a mess for Anne. I went out and said goodbye to Flair and Fallah. I said goodbye to the chickens too, but unlike the horses they didn't pay much attention.

I spent the remainder of the time I had left sitting on the porch with Anne. We talked, drank iced tea, and swung back and forth on the porch swing. Anne's farm was beautiful, but I wondered how she lived there year after year with only the company of her animals and a few visitors. We had made a couple of trips into Kroger in Bloomington, but other than that we hadn't gone anywhere. I wondered if Anne ever went out just to eat. I kind of figured not. If I had a car and was free to drive into Bloomington whenever I wanted I might not have minded living on the farm too much, but I preferred living in town where something was always going on. I had the feeling Anne wouldn't like town life at all. I think she was exactly where she wanted to be. She was happy so that's all that really mattered.

Brendan arrived at three. Anne invited him to stay for some blackberry cobbler and Brendan eagerly accepted. I guess that proved that jocks weren't stupid after all.

Brendan told Anne about playing football for IU while we ate. I wasn't terribly hungry, but I think I could eat blackberry cobbler with vanilla ice cream anytime! I just sat, listened, ate, and enjoyed myself.

Soon, it was time to go. Anne walked outside with us and I gave her a big hug.

"Thank you so much for everything!" I said.

"Thank you for visiting. You are welcome to come back anytime—to stay or just to visit."

"I will definitely come back to visit. I'll keep in touch. I plan to go to IU so I'll be living in the neighborhood for at least four years."

"You let me know how everything works out," Anne said.

"Oh, I will."

We hugged again and then Brendan and I climbed in his Cutlass. I felt a sense of sadness and loss as we drove away from the farm, but I'd meant what I said about staying in touch and about visiting.

"So, why is it safe for me to return to Verona?" I asked when we were barely out of the drive.

"I can't tell you that."

"What not?"

"It would ruin the dramatic effect."

"I don't understand."

"Of course not.

If you understood that would ruin the dramatic effect too."

"But, it is safe for me to return? My parents aren't going to send me away to one of those places?"

"I would not take you back if I thought that was a danger."

I was confused.

"So, I can go back home... as in to my parent's house?"

"I don't think that will present any difficulties."

"Will I be able to go out when I want? Will I be able to hang out with the guys?"

"I can't say for sure, but I have the feeling you'll be able to do all that."

"How? I don't understand. I've been thinking on it since I got your message yesterday, but I can't figure how the guys could have done anything to change my parent's minds."

"Come on, Scotty. You know what a devious and resourceful lot they are."

"So, they did do something to make it safe for me to return?"

"Yes."

"But you won't tell me what it is?"

"No."

"Was it illegal?"

"Probably."

"You're driving me crazy. Do you know that?"

"Yeah. I look at it as a fringe benefit."

I growled.

"Come on! Just tell me!"

"Nope! I'm not telling so you might as well not waste your time. You'll just have to wait until tomorrow."

"I'll find out what they've done then?"

"What did I just say? Yes. Tomorrow you will know exactly what they have done and I'm not saying another word about it."

"So... how's Jeff?"

"You mean your boyfriend?"

"He's not my boyfriend!"

239

"I'm just teasing you. Jeff is... Jeff. He's been sarcastic, blunt, and a smartass. In other words, he's fine."

"Can we go out again with Jeff?"

"I thought I'd introduce you to Gabrial."

"The quarterback? Really?"

"Yes. I believe I mentioned introducing you to him before. We hang out a lot and I thought you'd enjoy meeting him. Maybe you can seduce him."

"Yeah, right!"

"Well, he is interested in guys."

"Really?"

"Yes."

"Since he's the quarterback I bet he can have almost anyone he wants."

"Almost."

"So, why would he want me?"

"Take a look in the mirror sometime. You will see the answer to your question."

"I bet he's hot."

"He's very hot."

"Have you guys ever... never mind. You wouldn't cheat on Casper."

"You're right."

We were back in Bloomington in no time. I'd missed it! Brendan drove to the stadium and parked his car.

"We'll take the bus to Forest Quad. Gabrial will be driving this evening. You'll love his car."

"Yeah?"

"It's a cherry red Trans Am and it is sweet."

We joined a line as we waited for a campus bus. In about five minutes one appeared. I followed Brendan on, but he gave me the window seat. We didn't talk as the bus moved around campus. It made several stops so the trip was a lot longer than it would have been in a car. I didn't mind. Each stop gave me a chance to get a good look at a dorm or some other campus building. It gave me a chance to check out guys as they got on and off too. There were so many good-looking guys!

Brendan smiled at me when he caught me checking out a cute skater with longish blond hair. He was carrying a skateboard as well as a backpack. He was soo cute! I could feel my face grow hot when I noticed Brendan grinning at me, but he didn't tease me.

We climbed off the bus with a handful of others when it reached Forest. I followed Brendan in, although I thought I could probably find my own way now. Soon, we were back in his dorm room.

"Hey, Scotty. Welcome back," Jeff said.

"What? No greeting for your roommate?" Brendan asked.

"Oh, sorry. I didn't see you."

"Yeah, right."

Jeff smirked at Brendan, but smiled at me.

"I hear you'll be spending the night again," Jeff said.

"Yeah."

"You can sleep with me if you want. Brendan snores."

"I do not snore."

"He might also molest you in your sleep."

"Jeff keeps hoping for that," Brendan said.

"As if."

"Scotty knows he'll be molested if he sleeps with you," Brendan said.

"Which is all the more reason for him to sleep with me."

"It's a date," I said, then boldly leaned over and kissed Jeff.

"Now you'll have to have your mouth disinfected. Who knows where those lips have been," Brendan said.

"I keep telling him jocks shouldn't try to be funny, especially blond jocks," Jeff said.

"I'm not blond. My hair is light brown. I happened to know some very intelligent blonds," Brendan said.

241

"Like your boyfriend?"

"Yes."

"I like Casper, but he can't be too smart since he hasn't dumped your sorry ass," Jeff said.

"Don't make me hurt you."

"Brendan is into rough sex. He's always coming onto me like that," Jeff said.

Brendan just shook his head.

"You can forget sleeping with Scotty. We're going out with Gabrial in a bit. Once Scotty sees what a real stud looks like he'll forget all about you."

"I'm unforgettable."

"Don't you mean unforgivable?" Brendan asked.

Jeff flipped him off.

"You can come with us if you must," Brendan said.

"Can't. I already have plans. In fact, I'm going to be late if I don't leave right now." Jeff turned to me. I'll see you later."

"Later."

"Jeff definitely likes you. He's never that nice to anyone," Brendan said once Jeff was gone.

"I think he's great!"

"That's it! We're not talking about Jeff anymore. If you can't say anything nasty about Jeff, don't say anything at all. Come on, I have something I want to show you."

We walked out of Forest Quad and headed over to Jordan Avenue, then turned north. After a short time we turned west and followed a sidewalk that led deeper into campus.

"The building on the right, in case you don't remember, is the IU Auditorium," Brendan said.

"It's big."

We walked around the front of the auditorium and there was a large fountain. Brendan pointed out the Lily Library on the left and the Fine Arts building on the right. We had walked through the area on my first visit to campus, but I couldn't remember all the names of the buildings. Brendan and I followed the sidewalk to the next building on our right.

"This is the IU Art Museum."

I wasn't particularly excited. I liked art okay, but I didn't know how long I wanted to spend looking at it.

"We don't have a lot of time, so I'll show you the best part," Brendan said as we entered a revolving door.

We walked across a large atrium. I looked up to the glass ceiling three stories above. I followed Brendan as he ascended the stairs and entered the gallery on the second floor. In a few moments we were standing not by a painting, but by an ancient Egyptian sarcophagus. It was only the lid, but it was amazing. It was covered with hieroglyphs and figures of Egyptian gods.

"Cool, huh?"

"I was expecting a painting, but this is much cooler. A mummy really lay under this thing?"

"Oh yeah. Come look at this. It's not as impressive, but I think it's even more interesting."

Brendan led me a short distance away. I peered through the glass for a moment and then read the tag; "Model of a combined bakery, granary, brewery, and weaving shop. Ca. 1991-1782/3 B.C." The model was almost 4,000 years old!

"Look at the little figures," Brendan said. "That one is kneading bread. That one looks like he's grinding grain. This was placed in a tomb so that whoever was buried there would never run out of bread or any of the other things that are being made in the model."

The model kind of looked like a toy. It was made of wood and painted. Most of the figures were shirtless and wore white skirts like I'd seen in ancient Egyptian tomb paintings in books. They all had the same long hairstyle. It must have taken hours and hours to make the model and to think it was made just to stick in a tomb where no one would ever see it.

"I want to show you something in the Greek section."

I gazed in case after case as Brendan led me into another area. There were Greek vases everywhere. I paused to look at an especially cool vase. The tag said it was a red figure krater from

450 B.C. The painted scene was of Achilles killing the Amazon Queen. It was absolutely beautiful.

Brendan led me to what looked like the top of a small tombstone made of marble. Carved on it were some Greek letters I couldn't read and a nude boy.

"This is my favorite piece. I find it haunting. It is the funeral stele of Apolexis from the mid 4th century B.C. I think it's a beautiful piece. It gets to me. It's a tombstone for a boy who died over 2,000 years ago. When I look at it I wonder who he was and what his life was like. I feel a connection to him."

I looked at Brendan, then at the stele. I kind of got what he meant.

"It's hard to imagine what life was like back then. His death must have been hard on his parents. How old do you think he was, maybe ten or twelve?" I asked.

"I don't know. The stele doesn't say and it's hard to judge."

"I bet he never thought that anyone would be looking at a carving of him over 2,000 years after he lived."

"Probably not. There is something else I want to show you. It's over in the Roman section."

I followed Brendan past busts and pieces of pottery displayed in glass cases. He led me to a large mosaic on the floor. It must have been ten feet wide and twenty-five feet long at the least. Most of it was geometric designs and there were three large circles. In the left circle was what looked like ducks feeding in a pond. In the right was a water bird with a long bill, and in the center was a rabbit.

"This is really cool. I never thought of all this stuff being in an art museum."

"There are some cool paintings on the first floor, but I like the upper floors better. The university has an incredible collection."

I read the sign near the mosaic. It said it was from the Bath of Apolausis and was 5th century A.D. Roman. The mosaic was from a site near Antioch in modern Turkey and was on loan from the J. Paul Getty Museum.

Brendan handed me a large laminated pamphlet that told about the mosaic and had pictures of it when it was discovered. It was only one of a few mosaics that formed the floor of a large structure. It was really cool to think that the mosaic in front of me had been buried for centuries and then excavated by archaeologists.

"I like to come to the museum now and then when I want to get away from Jeff and my books," Brendan said. "I usually focus on only one gallery. I like to take my time. It's too bad we're rushed today, but I wanted to give you an idea of what's here."

Brendan let me wander around for the time we had left. I went back to the Greek section. I think the Greek pottery was my favorite part of the museum, although it's hard to top an Egyptian sarcophagus. The pieces I liked best were the kraters. They were painted burnt orange and black. The figures were nude males running, fighting, and wrestling. The images were kind of homoerotic, although I don't know if they were meant to be that way or if I was just seeing them that way. I was amazed that I was standing only a few feet from pieces of pottery that were thousands of years old!

We walked back outside and headed back the way we had come. Students were walking all over, alone and in groups. There were all kinds, from jocks like Brendan to artistic types like Tristan and everything in between. The more I saw of the campus, the better I liked it. I imagined college campuses all over the U.S. were like this. I could probably have gone to Ohio or California and found the same atmosphere, but I liked it here. A lot of my friends were going to come to IU and that was a big plus. I wanted to meet new people, but I liked the idea of already knowing a few people on campus.

We walked around campus with no particular destination. I had no idea where we were most of the time, but then I'd recognize something I'd seen before. Then, I'd get lost all over again. I liked looking at all the buildings, the trees, the flowers, and most of all the boys!

"Let's head for Forest Quad. Gabrial will be arriving soon," Brendan said.

We walked east, passing yet more students and older people who were strolling around campus. Brendan took me in front of the Simon Music Library and we watched the fountains for a couple of minutes. We crossed the street and I could see Forest Quad up ahead. I wondered how long it took new students to learn the campus. I wondered how long it would take me when I became a freshman.

We waited by the parking lot to the north of Forest for only a few minutes before a cherry red Trans Am pulled up. Brendan was right. The car was sweet! Brendan opened the door and I slipped into the backseat.

"Hey, this is Scotty," Brendan said as he got in and fastened his seatbelt. "Scotty, this is Gabrial."

What I noticed most about Gabrial was that he was extremely good looking and that his arms were well muscled and beautifully shaped. I couldn't see the rest of him well, but he was definitely hot!

"China Buffet?" Gabrial asked.

"Sounds great," Brendan said.

"It's one of Brendan's favorite places," Gabrial said. "He always gets the same things. Just watch. There will be peanut butter chicken and General Tso's chicken on his plate for sure."

"Hey, it's good!" Brendan said.

We didn't drive far at all before Gabrial pulled into a strip mall. I could see College Mall across the street and we weren't far from Forest Quad so I pretty much knew where we were. All three of us got out of the car and I got my first good look at Gabrial. All I can say is WOW!

Gabrial was even better built and hotter than Brendan and that is saying something! I felt downright ugly beside them. Gabrial was about 6'3" with broad shoulders and a thick chest. He was all muscle. I would have paid to see him without a shirt. I tried not to stare, but only partially controlled myself.

I made sure to walk behind Brendan and Gabrial as we headed for the restaurant because I wanted to check out Gabrial's butt. It was fine! I enjoyed the view as I walked behind the two studs. I almost couldn't believe I was hanging out with two IU football players and one of them was the quarterback!

I couldn't identify the scent as we walked into the China Buffet but it was yummy! Brendan paid for me since I was broke. I felt a little guilty about that, but I'd pay him back someday when I wasn't on the run. Maybe soon. I sure hoped things were okay back home. I wished Brendan would tell me what was going on, but I'd find out soon enough.

Brendan picked us out a booth on the right, not too far from the buffet. He put our ticket on the table and we all headed for the buffet. There were a lot of different choices on three small buffets tables. I picked sweet & sour chicken, rice, crab Rangoon, mashed potatoes, and pork dumplings. I took my plate back to the booth and then got myself a Coke.

Brendan and Gabrial's plates were heaped up way more than mine, but then they were bigger and they were football players. I was seated next to Gabrial. I must admit I enjoyed being near him. He was so sexy!

"What did I tell you?" Gabrial said pointing to Brendan's plate. "Peanut butter chicken, General Tso's chicken, and, what a shock, crab Rangoon!"

"So I get the same things every time. I like them! Scotty, you have to try this," Brendan said. He forked a piece of peanut butter chicken onto my plate.

I tasted it.

"This is really good!"

"See?" Brendan said. "I pick the same things because I know what is best."

"I like variety," Gabrial said.

"That means he's a slut," Brendan whispered as if Gabrial couldn't hear him.

"I just try to allow as many as possible to have the Gabrial Diaddio experience."

"Like I said, slut."

"Hey, I'm very selective!"

We spent most of our time eating. The food was delicious. There were quite a few college boys in the China Buffet, but many others as well. It was a popular place and I could see why.

Gabrial looked at me often as we talked and ate. I almost could not believe he was checking me out. He smiled at me a lot and asked about my life back in Verona.

When Gabrial went to refill his plate, Brendan grinned at me across the table.

"What?" I asked.

"Gabrial was flirting with you."

"Was he?" I asked. I thought he was, but I wasn't sure. I couldn't believe a guy that hot would flirt with me.

"Oh yeah. If you weren't leaving tomorrow I bet he'd hit on you."

"Maybe I should stay for a week!"

Brendan laughed.

"Sorry, you have to go back tomorrow."

I grinned. The hunk of a quarterback was actually into me. Wow.

I headed for the buffet again, refilled my Coke, and got a few pieces of peanut butter chicken. It really was tasty!

Brendan and Gabrial did most of the talking and, of course, they talked football. It was interesting listening to them, although I got a little lost at times. Brendan and Gabrial had a great rapport. As I sat there with them I began to think how they would make a good couple. They were both jocks, both into football, and they were a good physical match. Gabrial seemed a much more logical choice for a boyfriend for Brendan than Casper. I wondered if Gabrial ever tempted Brendan. Gabrial was one of the hottest guys I'd ever met. He was hotter than Blake York by far and Blake was smokin'!

I was willing to bet Brendan was tempted by Gabrial, but I would've bet just as much that Brendan had never cheated on Casper. I hadn't observed Brendan and Casper together much, but what I had seen told me all I needed to know. Casper was one lucky boy, but then so was Brendan. If Casper was single I would have dated him. I just hoped I could date guys before college. I wanted a boyfriend or at least regular sex.

All of us got some ice cream for dessert. I had a scoop of vanilla and a scoop of chocolate with chocolate and strawberry syrup and peanuts on top.

After the ice cream, Brendan and I got some hot tea and Gabrial got coffee. Everything was included in the price, which I thought was really cool. I could see why the China Buffet was such a popular place. I was going to make sure I remembered it when I moved to Bloomington someday.

Brendan and Gabrial told me a lot about IU. We talked about dorms, classes, life on and off campus, and more. I couldn't think of many questions to ask, but they answered all those that I did ask. I had a great time sitting there with them talking. It made me yearn for college life. It was too bad I had to finish high school first! One really cool thing is that I didn't think once about my problems back home as we sat there. I'd experienced times like that on Anne's farm too. Sometimes, I enjoyed myself so much that my problems just floated away. Such times were reminders that life went on even though all was not well.

Gabrial was definitely flirting with me. I wondered if anything would have happened between us if I was around for a bit longer. Maybe Gabrial just enjoyed flirting. I guess I'd never know, but it didn't matter. The mere fact that a guy that hot was flirting with me made me feel more attractive than I ever had in my entire life.

While Gabrial and Brendan were talking, Gabrial put his hand on my leg and began to idly rub it. I couldn't tell if he was even aware he was doing it, but I was instantly aroused. It was a good thing I didn't want to go back up to the buffet just then because I sure couldn't have. The front of my jeans would've had a very noticeable bulge.

Gabrial ran his hand to my inner thigh, while still talking to Brendan, who didn't seem to notice. I had to stifle a moan when he groped the big bulge in my jeans. Gabrial looked at me for just a moment and grinned.

Gabrial kept groping me while he talked to Brendan. I was glad I didn't have to speak because I could not have kept my voice even. Gabrial's hand kneading my bulge was driving me insane. He kept groping me as I got closer and closer to losing control.

Then, it happened. I was on the edge. I was about to lose control and then Brendan looked at me and grinned. He knew exactly what was going on! I couldn't take it a moment longer. I moaned and soaked my underwear. A moment later I turned completely red. I had never been so embarrassed in my life and yet it was so hot!

Brendan crossed his arms and stared at Gabrial.

"What?"

"I just can't take you out in public, can I?"

"I'm so embarrassed," I said and buried my face in my hands.

"Don't be. You have excellent control. If you were here a few days longer I'd see just what else you could do. I'm going to get some more ice cream."

Gabrial left the table. I looked at Brendan.

"Was he serious?" I asked.

"Oh yeah. Gabrial never says anything he doesn't mean."

"Wow." I was lost in thought for a moment, but then my embarrassment returned. "You won't tell anyone will you?"

"Of course not. Gabrial has a sick sense of humor. I would have told him to stop but you looked like you were enjoying yourself."

"I'd have been pissed off if you told him to stop," I said.

Brendan laughed.

We stayed in the China Buffet almost until closing time, then Gabrial drove us back to Forest Quad and dropped us off.

"He is soooo hot!" I said the moment we were out of the car.

"You should see him naked."

"You've seen him naked?"

"We're both on the football team, remember?"

"Oh yeah! If I was good enough I'd try out just to see Gabrial naked every day."

"I don't think you'd like it. Practices are brutal. My first practice made me puke and I wasn't the only one running for a trash can."

"I don't think I could handle that." I paused. "I can't believe that just happened."

"The under the table handball?"

"Yeah."

"It happened." Brendan laughed, but I wasn't so embarrassed now.

We headed inside and upstairs. Jeff was on his bunk, listening to music, but he pulled out his headphones when we entered.

"So, did the jocks bore you to death?" Jeff asked.

"No, it was fun. Gabrial is so hot!"

"If you like the built, jock type," Jeff said.

"Like you wouldn't lick him from head to toe if you had the chance," Brendan said.

"I might give him a little lick."

"Uh huh."

I looked at Brendan, but he gave no sign of telling Jeff what had happened. I was relieved, but I already knew I could trust Brendan.

We sat around and talked until I yawned. I hoped we'd go to bed soon, not so much because I was tired but because I wanted to mess around with Jeff. The action with Gabrial only made me need more. I just hoped Jeff was up for it. Brendan smiled at me as if he could read my mind.

"I'm turning in," Brendan said.

Brendan stripped right there in front of us. Of course, with such a small room there was nowhere else to strip. I couldn't help but check him out. Damn! What a body!

"Goodnight guys," Brendan said, climbing into his bunk. He pulled the sheet up to his waist and turned his back to us. It was as close as we could get to privacy with him still in the room.

"Goodnight."

Jeff motioned toward his bunk with his head and pulled off his shirt. We undressed, then climbed into his bunk, and began to make out. Jeff's tongue was wet and silky. He tasted a little like peppermint.

We made out for a long time. Just like last time, making out with Jeff was hotter than having sex with Blake. Guys who didn't kiss really missed out. Kissing worked me up more and more until I was so aroused I couldn't stand it.

I climbed down out of the bunk for a moment and searched through the pockets of my jeans. I returned to the bunk and handed Jeff a condom.

"I want you to, but... will you go slow?"

Jeff grinned.

"You sure?"

I nodded.

I lay on my stomach and looked over toward Brendan. He still had his back to us, but I didn't know if he was asleep or not. He could turn at any moment and see what we were doing. He had a pretty good idea of what we were doing without turning around. He knew that before he climbed into his bunk.

I was a little turned on by the idea of getting caught. Maybe that's why people had sex in public places. They liked the thrill. I thought back to Gabrial in the China Buffet, but push him out of my mind. I wanted to focus on the present, and Jeff.

I felt Jeff on top of me. I was scared, but also incredibly turned on. I did my best to relax, but I was afraid of the pain. Jeff eased inside me, but I still hissed. It stung! Jeff held still, then pushed against me more. He was being careful and gentle and that helped me to relax. The more I relaxed, the easier it became to let Jeff in.

I let out a little moan when Jeff was all the way in. The pain was still there, but so was pleasure. Jeff took it easy until I told him not to. By then, I was ready for it. We tried to be quiet, but it was difficult. I looked over at Brendan now and then, but he gave no sign he was awake.

Jeff's pace increased along with his breathing. After a while, he pushed himself all the way in and moaned. I could feel him experience his orgasm and it made me feel closer to him. He lay on top of me for several moments after he was finished and then climbed off. I turned over and Jeff immediately leaned in and brought me to a climax in only moments. I moaned way too loud, but I couldn't help it.

Jeff took me in his arms and held me. I knew we couldn't be boyfriends, but what Jeff and I had shared was special to me. It wasn't just sex. It was something more.

I slept better that night than I had since the last time I'd slept in Jeff's bed. I liked feeling him close to me. It made me feel secure. Any time I awakened in the night he was there, sometimes with his arm over me and sometimes just pressed up against me. I wished I had someone to sleep with every night. Someday I would. That was another reason to keep on living.

It was past ten when I woke up the next morning. Brendan was just returning from the shower. I was glad I woke up in time to see him nearly naked. He looked so sexy wearing nothing but a towel.

"You can use my shower stuff again. I'll put it all here on the desk."

"Thanks."

Brendan didn't say anything about what he might have heard last night. I still didn't know if he was awake or asleep when Jeff and I were having sex. I felt a little sore, but I guess that was to be expected. Sex with Jeff was amazing.

Brendan pulled off his towel and I was treated to the sight of his bare butt. He had such a hot ass! It looked as hard as his biceps. Brendan turned to get some boxers from his drawer and I had the chance to check out what he was packing. Damn! I wondered how Casper handed that. Brendan was big. It seemed almost unfair that one guy be that good-looking, that built, and that hung. Brendan was a truly nice guy so I guess if anyone deserved it he did.

I climbed out of bed, slightly self-conscious, not because I was naked, but because my body wasn't that great compared to Brendan's. I wasn't as hung either. I was just average. Sometimes, I worried that I was a little on the small side. Brendan didn't pay much attention. I wrapped a towel around my waist, gathered up the shampoo and other shower supplies and headed to the bathroom.

A really tall boy was coming out of the shower area wearing only a towel when I entered. He was just plain looking and was skinny, but he had the sexiest abs! There were hot guys everywhere at IU!

I hung up my towel and took a shower stall. I lathered up while I enjoyed the hot water streaming down over my naked body. I'd done a good job not worrying about my return to Verona. Supper with Brendan and Gabrial and then sex with Jeff had kept me too busy to think on it. I tried to prevent myself from thinking about it now, but I was returning this very day and I was nervous. I wished Brendan would tell me what was going on. Not knowing was agonizing. One thing that set me at ease was my trust in Brendan, Dorian, and all the other guys. I knew they wouldn't put me in danger and if they said it was safe to return then safe it was. What if they were wrong? What if they had made a mistake or had been tricked? I had to stop thinking about it. I was probably worrying about nothing.

I did my best to get my mind on other things. I thought about last night with Jeff. I thought about Brendan's incredible body. I thought about supper with Brendan and Gabrial *and* what happened under the table. I thought about Anne and my time on her farm. I had certainly had an adventure.

I thought back to what had started it all—getting it on with Blake York in his car. I wished we hadn't been caught, of course, but even more I wished that I'd saved my first time for someone else. Blake was smoking hot, but I found myself wishing that my first time could have been with Jeff instead. I had no illusions about Jeff. We couldn't date because we lived too far apart and we were at different places in our lives. I don't think we would have dated even if I was attending IU. I don't think Jeff was seeking that kind of relationship. Even so, Jeff and I had a relationship. We weren't in love but I knew he cared about me. Both times I'd slept with him had been wonderful. That's why I wished my first time could have been with him. It would have been a far more pleasant memory than doing it in the back of a car *and* getting caught.

I couldn't change the past, but if I had recent weeks to do over again I'd make different choices. Of course, if I didn't hook up with Blake I wouldn't have been caught, wouldn't have come to Bloomington, and wouldn't have met Jeff. I guess there was no need to think about it. I couldn't travel into the past and doing so would probably be a mistake anyway.

I rinsed off and the stepped out of the stall and grabbed my towel. There was no one else in the bathroom and I passed no sexy boys on my way back to the room, but I guess I couldn't have everything.

It was a little after eleven by the time we were ready to depart. Jeff woke up in time to say goodbye. He gave me a hug and even kissed me. I felt so sad as Brendan and I walked downstairs that I almost thought I was going to cry. I was going to miss Jeff!

"You okay?" Brendan asked as we waited at the bus stop. I guess my sadness showed.

"Don't laugh at me, but I miss Jeff."

"Hmm, it is hard to think about anyone missing Jeff," Brendan teased.

"I like him a lot."

"I gathered that. You bring out a kinder Jeff than I'm used to seeing. He's nicer to you than anyone. He obviously likes you too."

"I like being with him."

"I know. I heard you moaning."

I turned completely red. I was glad no one else was there to see. Brendan laughed.

"You don't think I'm a slut, do you?" I asked.

"No. I think you're taking advantage of your first taste of freedom."

The bus arrived soon and I gazed out the window during the ride. There were so many dorms and buildings at IU!

In just a few minutes we got off the bus at the stadium and walked to Brendan's car. We got in and headed for Verona.

"I guess you still won't tell me what's going on," I said.

"Not a chance. If it makes you feel better you're not the only one I'm keeping in the dark."

"What do you mean?"

"You'll find out... later."

"Argh! You just like torturing me!"

"Well yes, but everything is going to be okay, Scotty. It really is."

My mind raced. I didn't understand how everything could be okay, but there was no use trying to figure it out. I would just drive myself crazy trying.

We stopped at a Burger King and got burgers, fries, and drinks to go. Burger King really did have great burgers. I think it was my favorite burger place.

"I want to pay you back for all the money you've spent on me," I said.

"No. I don't want you to pay me back. I have lots of money."

"Well, I'd still like to."

"If you want to do something for me, be a good friend to Casper. That's worth a lot more than money."

"I'd do that anyway. I like Casper. He's been very kind to me."

"I love him a lot, so if you're nice to him that's all I need."

"I really appreciate all you have done for me. I thought you were just giving me a ride to Anne's farm, which would have been favor enough, but you've done so much more. Even if things aren't okay at home, I feel like I have a reason to live, several reasons."

"Wow. Jeff must be incredible in bed."

"He is, but that's not what I meant!" I said, turning red again.

"I'm just teasing you. I know what you mean. I wanted to show you that high school and Verona isn't the whole world. When I was in high school I had trouble seeing beyond it. It was my world. Even switching towns and high schools didn't change that. I knew there was life beyond high school, but it was hard to envision. Part of me felt like my life would just go on and on exactly as it was. I knew better, but that's still the way I felt."

"Yeah. I always knew I'd graduate and move on, but it is hard to imagine anything else, or rather it was until this trip. Now, I've seen another world and I can't wait to move on to it!"

"Don't be in too much of a hurry to leave high school. This time in your life will never come again. College is great, but there is no reason to rush. I love IU and I love playing football on a college team. I'm living my dream life, minus having Casper in Bloomington with me, but I can't tell you how much I miss hanging out with the guys at VHS. Some days I would give anything to go back and listen to Brandon and Jon go off on each other."

I laughed.

"They do that *all* the time! What's up with that?"

"I think they do it from habit. That's how they interact. You should hear them away from school."

"Worse?"

"I think they have a competition to see who can say the nastiest things. They will say the most horrible things to each other and then start laughing. They are a bit deranged. Feel free to tell them that if you want."

"I hope I get the chance."

"You will. Relax. Everything is going to be okay."

"How can you be so sure?"

"Because I know things you don't know."

"Come on, tell me! I'll do anything you want, just tell me!"

"Scotty, I have a boyfriend!" Brendan said, pretending to be scandalized, but I could tell he was kidding.

"That's not what I meant. Just tell me. Please."

I used my best puppy dog eyes. I even tilted my head to the side.

"You are pathetic."

"So, you'll tell me?"

"No."

"Argh!"

Brendan laughed.

"We will be there in a couple of hours. You can wait that long to find out."

"I'm scared of what's going to happen. What if you and the guys only think everything is going to be okay? What if you're wrong? What if..."

"You're like a truffling pig, only instead of truffles you're looking for things to worry about."

"I can't help it."

"Relax. Everything is going to be okay. As for what is going to happen remember that I will be there. I won't let harm come to you, not that it will anyway."

"Thanks, Brendan."

We talked all the way to Verona. I asked a lot of questions about college life, classes, and college boys. Brendan asked me about what I did on Aunt Anne's farm. It was easy to talk to Brendan. He made me feel comfortable and relaxed.

I figured that Brendan would drive me to the Selby farm first, but instead he drove right into town. I thought maybe we were going to Shawn and Tim's loft over Café Moffatt or maybe to Dorian's or perhaps to Marc's place, but no... I was totally confused when we pulled up near Miller's Funeral Home. Brendan looked around and then we got out.

"What are we doing here?" I asked.

"You're about to find out."

My heart clutched in fear. We were walking toward the funeral home. Had something happened to my parents? Surely, the guys wouldn't... but no. Maybe there had been an accident. I didn't want my problems with my parents to end like this. My lower lip began to tremble. I tried to get a look at the sign that told who had died, but Brendan blocked me. No matter how hard I tried he kept me from looking.

I looked at Brendan; my eyes were filled with fear and grief.

"It's going to be okay," is all he said.

I followed Brendan into the funeral home. My lower lip trembled, butterflies fluttered in my stomach, and my knees felt weak. Now that I was about to find out why Verona was safe for me I wasn't so sure I wanted to know.

Dorian

Marc and I waited until about 2:30 p.m. to go to Scotty's visitation. We wanted to blend into the crowd as much as possible since Scotty's parents would probably not be pleased to see us.

Marc and I had both dressed up. Marc looked delicious in a white button-down shirt and black slacks. He was even wearing a deep blue tie. He was so handsome I wanted to rip his shirt right off him, but then I usually wanted to rip his shirt off and sometimes did.

"You look mischievous," Marc said.

"I'm always mischievous."

"Mmm, yes, but behave yourself," Marc said.

I matched Marc well. I was wearing a tight, long-sleeve black shirt and black slacks. I wore a gold chain on the outside of my shirt. I looked fabulous, if I do say so myself, but my clothing was suitably dark for a funeral.

Marc and I signed the guest book and walked in. I was overwhelmed by a sense of grief when I took in the scene before me. Scotty's parents and brother were standing near the silver casket I had selected. Justin was trying to comfort his mom as she cried not entirely silent tears, but his own eyes were red. Scotty's dad wasn't crying, but he looked hopeless and sad. A picture of Scotty sat on an easel near the closed casket. I knew Scotty wasn't in there, but tears rimmed my eyes and threatened to spill out.

There was a big crowd. A lot of kids from school were there. I recognized some as Marc's soccer teammates and others I knew from my classes. I spotted several of the gay boys of Verona. Brendan was supposed to be coming home for a visit, but I saw Casper standing alone and Brendan was nowhere in sight.

I trembled slightly as Marc and I approached the casket. I wondered if it wouldn't be better to come back when Scotty's family wasn't standing there. I was afraid Scotty's mom might start screaming at me. I wanted to veer off and disappear into the crowd, but it was too late for that. Scotty's dad had spotted us and was watching.

As we approached, Scotty's dad extended his hand to Marc. I don't know who was more shocked, Marc or me, but Marc took his hand and shook it.

"I want to thank you for all your help. We..." Mr. Jackson stopped speaking for a moment and his eyes filled with tears. "This has been very hard for us and we appreciate all that Scotty's teammates have done for us. Justin tells me that you and your... boyfriend made many of the arrangements yourself."

My eyes widened. How did he know *that*? I couldn't believe my ears either. Did Mr. Jackson just say boyfriend without going berserk?

"Well all... um... Scotty was... a good friend. Dorian picked out the casket."

Mr. Jackson actually smiled at me. I didn't know what to do so I smiled back at him for a moment. I felt like a deer caught in the headlights of a car. This was not the reaction I had expected. I thought Marc and I might have to beat a hasty retreat after checking things out.

"It's lovely," Mrs. Jackson managed between sobs.

Those two words cost her. Mrs. Jackson broke down and Mr. Jackson had to lead her out of the room. Justin watched them go. Tears streamed from his eyes. Scotty's family was suffering terribly. I had never felt so bad for anyone in my entire life. I also felt extremely guilty. All this was my idea. Maybe my plan had worked too well. Maybe I'd made a horrible mistake.

Marc put his arm around Justin's shoulders and squeezed. Justin didn't flinch or draw away. He just cried. He looked at Scotty's picture.

"I was the worst brother *ever*," Justin said, still crying.

"I..." Marc began, but grew silent. What could he say? Justin *was* a crappy brother.

"It's true. You know it as well as anyone. The worst part is that I'll never have the chance to make things right."

I almost smiled. I fought to urge to tell Justin he would have his chance to make things right. Soon, we'd be able to send for Scotty.

"I'm so worried about Mom. I don't think she's going to get over this. Dad isn't much better. Maybe after tomorrow, but..."

"They will get better, Justin. It will just take time," Marc said. There was an awkward pause. "There's a ton of people here."

"Yeah, everyone liked Scotty."

"I don't see any kids from your church here, except Devon," Marc said, and then swallowed hard. He was probably wondering if he'd said the right thing. I looked around. I didn't notice any of the Anti-Christians either.

"It's not likely you will. Dad told the pastor off and then the whole church. I'm surprised you didn't hear about it."

Marc shook his head.

"You should have seen it," Justin said. He grinned for just a moment. "The pastor started in on this anti-gay sermon. I noticed Dad's face getting red. Mom didn't notice, but then she couldn't notice because she was too busy crying. The pastor kept going, talking about the sins of homosexuality and Dad got up and accused him of killing Scotty. He said we'd all killed him because of what we'd said and done. He said we should have loved and supported him, but instead we were cruel to him. Then Dad started crying and said he was the guiltiest of all. The pastor started to speak, but Dad said he would have nothing to do with a church that preached hatred and wouldn't accept his son. He walked out. I followed and pulled Mom out with me."

"Holy shit!" I said, a little too loudly. I put my hand over my mouth and looked around, but only a few people were looking at me.

Justin grew silent for a few moments. Vivaldi played in the background. It was suitable and yet hopeful music. Tristan had chosen well.

"None of this means anything," Justin said. "Me being sorry, Dad telling off the church... None of it means anything now because it's too late."

"It means something," I said. It meant a whole lot more than I could say. Oh how I wished I could tell Justin how much! I could not wait to call Scotty and tell him it was time for him to come home.

"It won't help Scotty." Justin looked around to make sure no one else could hear before he went on. "I don't think his death was an accident. I think he killed himself. I think he killed himself because he thought we didn't love him, but I *did* love him! I didn't even know it, but I did!"

Justin began to cry. Marc held him and I put my hand on his shoulder.

"This is all my fault!" Justin said loudly. "I said the nastiest things to Scotty before he died. I told him he was disgusting! I told him I hated him and I wanted him to die! And he did die! He killed himself because of me!"

Justin totally lost it. Everyone was looking, but trying not to look. Justin's mom and dad hurried back in. Mr. Jackson took his son from Marc and held him.

"Don't blame yourself," said Justin's dad. "It wasn't you. If it was anyone, it was me, son. I..."

There was a gasp from the crowd. I didn't know what was going on for a moment until I looked up the aisle between the chairs and then I gasped too. Marc and I looked at each other, our eyes wide.

"He's alive!" someone shouted.

Chaos broke out as friends and family rushed toward Scotty. He was standing there, looking dumbfounded. I swallowed hard. This was not part of the plan!

"Scotty?" Mr. Jackson said.

Suddenly, Marc and I were alone by the empty casket. Scotty's family rushed toward him, crying with relief. Everyone made way for them as they hugged and kissed the son that moments before they believed to be dead. I was so happy I began crying. Marc put his arm around me as we both watched. Marc leaned in close to my ear and whispered.

"I think your plan worked."

I grinned through my tears. I watched as the Jacksons fussed over their not-dead son. Scotty's mom was all over him, hugging and kissing him. Justin was crying and laughing and jumping up and down. Mr. Jackson hugged his son and put his hand on his shoulder as he spoke to him. Scotty smiled as I'd never seen him smile before.

Scotty looked in our direction with a question his eyes. I shook my head and he nodded. I hoped he understood. If we were found out we would all be in big trouble, especially Marc and me.

A little part of me didn't care, but most of me was just plain scared. Even so, being up to our necks in trouble was worth the scene before us.

There had probably never been so much noise in the funeral parlor before. Everyone was talking at once and staring at Scotty in shock. Scotty's arrival had created chaos. Scotty was totally overwhelmed. He almost looked as if he might pass out.

I laughed for a moment and then I spotted Brendan. Brendan was smiling at me across the room, grinning a little too broadly. I began to suspect that Scotty's arrival during his own funeral was no accident.

"Come on," I said to Marc and pulled him away from the casket and toward Brendan.

'You did this, didn't you?" I asked quietly, although everyone was paying too much attention to the resurrected Scotty to notice the three of us.

"Me?"

Marc looked at me and quickly caught on. Brendan was trying just a bit too hard to look innocent.

"You did!" I said.

"I hate funerals. I didn't want to sit through a boring sermon. Besides, I've always wanted to create complete chaos."

Brendan had done that for sure. Some people were rushing out of the funeral home, probably to spread the word that Scotty wasn't dead. Most everyone was excitedly talking whether anyone was listening or not. Poor Mr. Miller was running around unsure of what to do. I bet it was the first time the deceased ever showed up at his own visitation.

"You may have just got us all in a ton of trouble. What if Scotty..."

"Relax, Dorian. I didn't tell Scotty anything because it would have ruined the surprise. I'm sure he knows who is behind this, but he won't betray us. As far as his parents will know he ran off on his own with no help from us."

"You're just a little bit evil, Brendan," I said.

"I'm glad someone finally noticed."

"Brendan!" Casper said as he hurried over and gave his boyfriend a hug.

"Did you know about this too?" I asked.

"Know about what?" Casper asked.

"Casper didn't know. I wanted to surprise him too."

"Surprised! I almost wet my pants!"

Marc laughed, but my face went white as I stood there.

"I just thought of something! There will be questions about his clothing that was found on the riverbank," I said. "We have to talk to Scotty before..."

"Relax, Dorian. You're so excitable! Give Scotty a little credit. He's not an idiot. We will fill him in as soon as we have the chance," Brendan said.

I nodded and calmed down.

"You know, you might have let the rest of us in on your plan," I said.

"That would have ruined it for you. You should have seen the look on your face, Dorian."

Brendan laughed.

"A lot of work went into planning the funeral..." I began.

"Most of the work went into the visitation. The funeral would have just been playacting. I know you love to act, Dorian, but I think you get enough of that on the stage."

"Well, I'm a little ticked off, but I am also enjoying the drama of all this. It's very theatrical.

"I am a *god*!" Brendan said, grinning to himself.

"You're a conceited..."

Marc put his finger to my lips and grinned at me. He pointed toward Scotty, being fussed over by his family. I grinned then too. I think my crazy plan to make Scotty's parents realize how much they loved him worked.

The whole gang was present and I was glad. I would not have wanted anyone to miss out on Scotty walking in on his own funeral. One advantage of Brendan keeping us all in the dark is that none of us had to act surprised. We were all just as shocked as those who truly thought Scotty was dead.

Marc put his arm around my shoulder and we just stood there and watched. Everyone was grabbing Scotty and hugging him, when they could get him away from his mom that is. She kept hugging him and crying. Scotty's dad and brother hugged him and patted him on the back and smiled through their tears. If I was reading lips correctly, they were telling him they loved him. Tears well up in my eyes and I started crying. Marc looked over at me and laughed, but it was a laugh filled with kindness. He knew I was crying because I was so happy.

Before long, a reporter arrived from the *Citizen* and took a picture of Scotty standing beside his beautiful silver casket. My grandfather had told me that back in the old days they used to take photos of dead people in their caskets, but I bet no one had ever had their picture taken standing beside their own casket before!

It was too crowded in the funeral home. Even people who hadn't come to the visitation were squeezing in to get a look at the boy who returned from the dead. Scotty's family led him out of room. Scotty looked at me when he passed. He had tears in his eyes, but he was grinning. He nodded at me and I smiled back.

I was crying as we followed the crowd out onto the street. Scotty and his family climbed in their car and drove off. Everyone waved and cheered. Even after the Jacksons were gone everyone stood around and talked excitedly. Scotty walking into his own funeral would be the talk of Verona for years to come.

I motioned to Tristan and Shawn to follow me. Silently, the gang separated from the main crowd and walked down the street. Everyone started to ask questions.

"Let's go to my place so we won't be overheard," Shawn said.

Shawn and Tim's apartment was only a few blocks away, so we walked there as a group. Those who had driven left their cars at the funeral home to come back for them later.

We freely talked about our shock at Scotty showing up unexpectedly. Such talk helped us blend in. I noticed Brendan grinning. He was pleased with himself.

Once we were all inside Shawn and Tim's apartment the questions began. I pushed Brendan to the center of the room.

"This is the guilty party," I said. "Brendan decided to bring Scotty home for his funeral without telling any of us."

"Not even his own boyfriend!" Casper said.

"I didn't want to ruin the surprise for you," Brendan said. He leaned down and gave Casper a lingering kiss. That ended that argument right fast.

"So, how much does Scotty know?" Shawn asked.

"I'm sure he's figured out we faked his death, but I told him nothing," Brendan said.

"I think we should let Dorian tell Scotty the details," Marc said. "It was his idea to kill Scotty, after all."

Everyone cheered for me. I grinned and turned red.

"This has to remain an absolute secret among us and Scotty," Tristan said. "Some of what we did was almost certainly illegal."

"Agreed, although it is kind of a shame to keep it a secret. You know this stunt would make us all legendary," Brandon said.

"You're already legendary. Someday, you'll be known as the world's oldest virgin," Jon said.

"I'll have you know...." began Brandon.

Marc and I exchanged a look.

"We're out of here," Marc said. "The rest of you can stay and listen to Brandon and Jon bicker.

"You guys should just get married already," Dane said to the arguing pair as we left.

"Listen, you little punk..."

Brandon's voice faded out and Marc and I walked down the stairs and onto the street.

"I guess I don't have to perform in front of a crowd now that Scotty is back," Marc said.

"I hadn't thought about that! It's kind of a shame Scotty didn't return just a little bit later, although I'd hate for him to miss out on playing Charlie."

"I'm a little sorry I don't get to perform, but mostly I'm relieved."

"We've had a lot of fun practicing," I said.

"We have a lot of fun, period. Hey, why don't I buy you supper?"

"Yeah! Why don't you? Ofarim's?"

"The Park's Edge. We need to celebrate. Your crazy Lucy and Ethel plan actually worked."

Marc leaned over and kissed me.

The Park's Edge was only a few blocks past the funeral home, so when we passed Marc's Camaro we kept on walking. It was a beautiful day for a walk anyway.

"Soon, it will be summer and I'll take you to the beach," Marc said, after we'd walked along in silence for a while.

"That's where we met, remember?" I asked.

"Of course I remember. I thought you were a beautiful boy."

"I bet you thought I was a girl when you first spotted me. Be honest."

"Well, you are too pretty to be a boy, Dorian."

"You did! I knew it!"

"Yeah, I did, but you were shirtless so I caught on to the truth pretty fast. I also thought you were way too young for me. I didn't know you were my age."

We were nearing the Park's Edge. It was right across from the park, hence the name, and right next to the Paramount Theatre. Soon, Marc opened the door for me and we stepped inside.

The Park's Edge was fancy, with linen tablecloths, candles on the tables, and too many forks. The host led us past a fountain and gave us an enclosed booth. It was like having our own little private room, only one side was open to the restaurant and there were so many plants that it was hard to see very far.

Our waiter arrived and took our drink order; a Coke for Marc and a Diet Coke for me.

"Like you need a diet drink. There isn't an ounce of fat on you," Marc said.

"And you would know."

Marc wiggled his blond eyebrows.

I looked at the menu.

"Don't order the cheapest thing. Order what you want. We are celebrating," Marc said.

"But..."

Marc leaned over the table although no one else could possibly hear us.

"If it wasn't for you, Scotty might well have ended up killing himself."

"I don't think he..."

"Shh, no arguments," Marc said, putting his finger over my lips. He leaned back in his seat.

I browsed the menu. It was too expensive. We should have eaten at Ofarim's. I wanted to say so, but when I looked up Marc gave me a warning glance. I smiled.

"The eggplant parmesan does sound good," I said.

"Order it then. I'm leaning toward a fried chicken hoagie. I love those things, especially with extra honey-Dijon. Mmm."

We ordered when our waiter returned with our drinks. Then, we sat and talked. That's what I liked best about having a boyfriend, just being with him. Don't get me wrong, the sex was intense and I wanted to do it often, but I love just being with Marc, whether we were naked or clothed.

"I can't believe this school year is almost over," I said. "We have the play coming up in a week and in a month we graduate. Can you believe it? We are almost finished with high school."

"It doesn't seem real," Marc said. "I think I'm going to miss it."

"I know I am. There was a time, before I came to Verona, that the end of high school could not come soon enough, but now I will miss it. I'll miss being in the plays and mostly I'll miss hanging out with the gang at lunch."

"You'll be in more plays, just in college instead of high school, and then who knows?"

"Yeah. Who knows? I'm really going to miss everyone. I know I just became a part of the group a few months ago, but I feel like I've known them forever."

"I wonder who will be sitting at the homo table next year," Marc said. "Brendan and Ethan graduated last year and now Brandon, Jon, Nathan, Casey, you, and I are leaving."

"That leaves Casper, Shawn, Tristan, Tim, Dane, and Scotty. There will be quite a few of the old gang left."

"I bet Scotty will join us now," Marc said.

"I sure hope so."

"There is no reason he shouldn't. I don't think his parents will object."

I smiled and looked around the restaurant.

"This place is beautiful, but it's too expensive to eat here often," I said.

"We'll save it for special occasions."

"Hmm, who do we know who is single?"

"Huh?"

"I think Scotty needs a boyfriend."

"He might not be ready to take that step. He did just come back from the dead. He probably needs some time just to get used to living his life again. Besides, don't you think Scotty can find his own boyfriend?"

"He is going to need some guidance. He is new to the gay scene," I said.

"I didn't know there was a gay scene in Verona. When I think of a gay scene I picture clubs and circuit parties."

"I just mean hanging out with the gay boys, hooking up, and like that."

"I guess he doesn't know much about any of that, although he did hang out with us in drama class and play practices."

"True, but it's not the same as just hanging out."

"So, you're going to play matchmaker?"

"I would if I could think of anyone. The problem is that everyone is paired up."

"Yeah, I guess we were the last out gay boys running wild in Verona," Marc said.

"There have to be a few more in hiding."

"Or maybe one will move into town. Have you ever noticed how gay boys keep moving here? Just think about it—Ethan, Brendan, Casper, Taylor, Tristan, Dane, you, and me. Verona is a magnet for gay boys."

"Maybe Verona will become the homo mecca of Indiana," I said.

Marc laughed.

Our food arrived. The eggplant Parmesan was delicious! Marc and I ate and talked and enjoyed our time together in Verona's most expensive and fancy restaurant. I couldn't stop smiling. I almost couldn't believe my plan had worked!

Scotty

The first thing I spotted when I walked into the funeral home was Mom and Dad standing by a silver casket. I almost burst out crying because I thought Justin was dead. He hadn't been a model brother, but the thought of him lying in that casket was too much to bear. Just as a sob was working its way up my throat I caught sight of my brother. Mom, Dad, and Justin were all alive so who dead? It was at that moment I noticed the large picture by the casket. It was a picture of me! *I* was the one who was dead! *I* was in that casket! This was *my* funeral!

Tears of relief ran down my cheeks. I don't think I quite realized how much I loved my family until just that moment. There was a gasp as someone spotted me and the quiet funeral home exploded into chaos. Brendan! I wanted to kick his butt, but I also wanted to hug him. I couldn't believe it! I had walked in on my own funeral!

My mind was spinning with confusion. Friends and classmates who a moment before had thought I was dead quickly surrounded me. Mom cut her way through the crowd and hugged me. She was bawling and almost hysterical, but she was obviously happy. She kept kissing me and I thought she might kill me for real by smothering me. Dad and Justin weren't far behind. They were crying too.

My mind was reeling. I was in a state of shock. I couldn't believe everyone thought I was dead! I hugged my mom tightly, then my dad, and my brother. I never thought I'd get to hug any of them again. I had feared I was dead to them. Even when Brendan told me it was safe for me to come home I didn't let myself dare to hope that everything would really be okay.

I think I cried harder than my parents. An enormous weight had been lifted from my shoulders. I knew my friends would look out for me. I knew I could go back and live with Anne, but I had been so afraid that my family wouldn't want me. Now, they were hugging me and kissing me and telling me they loved me. Even Justin!

Everyone was talking around me. Everyone was patting me on the back and telling me how happy they were that I wasn't dead. A photographer came from the paper and took my picture by my casket, but it was all a blur. Mom and Dad guided me to the exit. My eyes locked with Dorian's for a moment. I smiled and nodded. He had done this! I didn't know how, but Dorian and the others had made all this happen!

I climbed in the back of the car when Mom was finally able to force herself to let go of me. Justin climbed in the other side and Mom and Dad got in the front. Justin grinned at me.

"You're not dead!" he said as Dad pulled away from the funeral home.

"I think that much is obvious," I said laughing.

"I'm so sorry I was such a jerk," Justin said.

"Justin, it's okay."

"No. It's not. All I've been thinking about since I thought you drowned was how horrible I'd been to you and how I'd never have the chance to tell you how sorry I am. I have that chance now and I'm so, so sorry."

Justin began crying and it made me cry too. I had my brother back. I had my whole family back.

Soon, Dad pulled into our drive. There was the familiar home I'd grown up in. I'd missed it so much. We all went inside. Once there, Dad hugged me like he'd never hugged me before.

"I thought you were dead," he said and cried.

There was a lot of crying for a while and I was hugged more than I'd ever been hugged in my entire life.

"Are you hungry?" Mom asked.

"Yeah."

"There is tons of food. Everyone has been bringing things for us."

We went into the kitchen. There was loads of food all right. I told Mom what I wanted and she loaded up a plate with too much lasagna, baked beans, and macaroni and cheese. Everyone else sat down and ate with me, not in the stuffy dining room, but in the kitchen. I was so happy right then I almost couldn't stand it.

"You're going to be famous at school. You'll be the only guy to have ever come back from the dead," Justin said.

"About that... I didn't know you thought I was dead. If I'd known, I would have come back sooner but then again..."

"Go on," Dad said.

"Well, I might not have come back because... I wasn't sure you cared."

Dad was hurt. I could tell. It wasn't my words that hurt him so much as the reality of what I'd said.

"We have a lot to talk about, but I want you to know that we've always loved you Scotty. We've... I've made some terrible mistakes, but there was never a moment when I didn't care. I'm the one who is sorry. I'm sorry that I made you think I didn't love you."

"Well, part of me always felt that you did love me, but... you were so harsh and demanding and then I got afraid you were going to send me away to one of those places where they would try to change me."

I began to cry.

"Scotty," Mom said, taking my hand. "Scotty, we will never do that. Don't worry about that for a moment. Your father and I have done a lot of soul searching. We realize now that we've made some horrible mistakes. We weren't listening to you. We weren't listening to reason. We didn't mean to be bad parents. Your dad and I have always been taught... but that's no excuse. You should have come first. We hurt you and we are so sorry for that. I hope you can forgive us."

I nodded. I didn't think I could speak without crying louder. When I got myself under control I said something that had to be said.

"I am gay. It's not a choice and I can't change it. It's not a sin or an abomination. It's what I was born to be. I want to stay here, but I can't if things are going to be the way they were. If you can't accept me for who and what I am I'm going to leave again."

My heart pounded in my chest. Despite everything, I was afraid.

"It's difficult for us to change our way of thinking and turn our back on the teachings of our church," Dad said. I began to lose hope as I listened to him. I feared he was going to start quoting the Bible to me, but I was wrong. "But, I have done some reading and I've learned that many believe sexual orientation isn't a choice."

273

I noticed Mom looking at Dad. She obviously didn't know he'd been doing any research.

"I'm inclined to believe that it is not a choice," Dad said. "I've also been spending a lot of time reading the Bible. I noticed that the words "homosexual" and "gay" are not found there. I also came across something that stuck me. Jesus said that we should love each other as he loves us. He didn't attach a condition to the love. There was no "if" or "but" or "unless." He simply stated that we should love each other. I realized I hadn't been doing that. The church has taught me to tack on provisos and to make that love conditional, but that's not what Jesus said. That's why your mother, Justin, and I have left the church."

I nearly choked on my lasagna.

"We've been looking and we're hoping to find a church that more accurately reflects the teaching of Jesus. When we find one, we'll begin going to church again, but I think that you and Justin should make the decision about whether or not you wish to attend. I forced you both to attend church because I thought I was doing the right thing, but the church led me astray."

"When you find a new church, I'll give it a try," I said.

My dad smiled.

I didn't mention anything about hanging out with my friends, performing in the play, or having the freedom to do what I wanted after school. As important as all that was I figured we could discuss it later. So much had happened already. So much had changed and all the change was for the better.

After supper, I went to my room. Mom wanted to follow me, but Dad held her back. I was relieved. I needed a little breathing room. Justin came with me. Everything was just as I remembered it.

"I guess they didn't start giving away my stuff yet," I said.

"Mom wouldn't even come into the room. I think she would have had a complete breakdown if she'd tried sorting through your stuff. It was bad while you were gone, Scotty, *real* bad. Mom lost it and Dad wasn't a lot better. I felt like I was the parent."

I looked around my room. It felt so weird to be back. I almost felt like I really had returned from the dead. When I noticed Justin again he was gazing at me. Tears rimmed his eyes.

Before I knew it was coming my little brother grabbed me and cried on my shoulder.

"I'm so sorry. I'm so sorry."

I held onto him and almost cried too.

"Can you forgive me?" Justin asked when he pulled away. "I promise not to be such a beast anymore."

"Don't make promises you can't keep. You'll always be a beast."

"Jerk," Justin said.

"I forgive you. Think you can deal with having a gay brother?"

"Well, I love you and you are gay so I have to deal with it. I don't quite get it, but I'll do my best."

"There's not much to get. I just like guys instead of girls."

"I can't imagine not liking girls, but I'll try to understand."

"Maybe I'll meet a boy who has a hot sister for you."

"Now you are talking!" Justin grew quiet. "I really caused a lot of trouble, didn't I? I should have just kept my mouth shut. What you do is your business. I guess... No. I know I saw ratting on you as my chance."

"Your chance for what?"

"To come out on top. I always feel like I'm not as good as you. You get better grades and you don't cause trouble like I do. I know Mom and Dad love me, but I've always felt like they love you more. I saw my chance to change that and I took it. Look what happened."

"I'm glad you did."

"Why?"

"I wasn't glad at the time, but look at how things have turned out. Mom and Dad would probably have found out about me sooner or later. There would have still been trouble and maybe things wouldn't have worked out nearly as well. I could have even ended up killing myself. I don't know."

"Don't ever do that. I thought I lost you once. I don't want to go through it again. I didn't realize how much I'd miss you until you were gone. I didn't realize how much I loved you until I thought you were dead and then it was too late."

"Only it wasn't too late," I said.

"I'm so pleased you aren't dead," Justin said.

"I'm glad *you* aren't dead either. For a moment, when I saw Mom and Dad standing by that casket... I thought you were inside. I started to cry but then I spotted you."

"I guess I'll have to be extra nice to you now," Justin said.

"Don't be too nice or I'll think I'm dreaming."

"Funny!"

Justin's expression saddened.

"I've been a really horrible brother. I'm sorry."

"Well..."

"I have been. There is no denying it."

"You have been pretty terrible lately, but that's all in the past. Let's forget about it and start all over."

"No. I don't want to forget about it. I don't ever want to be like that again."

I didn't know what to say, so I said nothing.

I looked at my desk and there was my script for *Willy Wonka*.

"You think Dad will let me do the play now?" I asked.

"Are you kidding? He will probably let you do anything you want. I wish everyone had thought I was dead. Do you have any idea what you can get away with now?"

I laughed.

"I bet you get away with plenty all the time," I said.

"What Mom and Dad don't know won't hurt me."

I shook my head; Justin was still Justin, only now I liked him better.

"I bet you were already planning how to organize the bedroom since you'd have it to yourself."

"Well..."

"You'll get it. You just have to wait until I go away to college. I've decided I'm going to IU..."

Justin and I began talking about the future. He seemed more like a brother than he had in years. I hadn't lied when I told him I was glad he ratted me out. If he hadn't, none of this would have happened. I felt more hopeful now than I had in a very long time. At last I had a future.

Dorian

I didn't hear from Scotty over the weekend, but I wasn't surprised about that. His parents probably didn't want to let him out of their sight. It was entirely likely that his mom hugged him the entire weekend. Needless to say, I didn't mind that he spent all his time with his family.

I spotted Scotty on Monday morning. Classmates, who were no doubt asking about his wild adventures on the run, surrounded him. I wondered what he'd tell them and what rumors would spread. Scotty looked up as I passed and smiled at me. He looked... happy.

When lunch rolled around I received a wonderful surprise. Maybe it wasn't exactly a surprise, but it was wonderful at least. Marc and I were talking when I heard a voice behind us.

"Mind if I sit here?"

I grinned.

"Scotty! You can sit right by me!" I said.

"Yeah, if you want to risk getting groped," Brandon said. "You should probably sit by me."

"I think Brandon has a crush on someone," Jon said.

"How 'bout I crush you?"

Scotty laughed and sat down.

"So... how are things at home?" I asked.

Scotty looked like he was going to cry and for a moment I was worried, but then he smiled.

"It's wonderful. Mom and Dad are like different people and Justin has been so nice to me. Mom and Dad want us all to go to family counseling."

"Counseling?" Casper asked, alarmed.

"Mom brought a stack of books home from the library on Saturday. She found a guide for parents of gay teens and it suggested family counseling. It's to help them understand me. My parents haven't found a counselor yet, but they're looking.

"We had some talks over the weekend. Mom and Dad are trying to be understanding and accepting. It's hard to shake off what they've been taught in church, but they both have an open mind now. They're looking for a new church, too, one that isn't prejudiced and anti-gay."

"You can come to my church," Casey said. "It's wonderful. Maybe you can all come as my guest this Sunday."

"Watch out. I think Casey's church is a cult. They'll probably shave your head," Brandon said.

"Don't make me come to your end of the table and beat you," Casey said.

"I guess violence is accepted in Casey's church," Brandon said with a smirk.

"No, but in your case I'll make an exception."

"Keep going, Brandon. I want to watch Casey kick your ass," Jon said.

"No, I believe in religious toleration. Even for cults," Brandon said under his breath.

Casey gave Brandon the evil eye, but didn't say more, and didn't kick his ass. It was too bad really. I loved dinner theatre.

"Justin and I played soccer together like we used to when we were kids," Scotty said. "He said he was sorry for being a beast. He even asked me some questions about being gay. My whole family is trying to understand. It's not that everything is perfect now, but it's soooo much better."

"That's wonderful, Scotty," Tristan said.

"Yeah, I guess when my family thought I was dead it made them think."

Scotty looked around the table. I almost laughed because everyone was trying to look innocent.

"I think we need to talk after play practice," I said. "I have some explaining to do."

"Care to do any explaining now?" Scotty asked.

"Uh, we had better wait until after school," I said, looking around.

"About play practice... I'll be there," Scotty said.

"Thank God!" Marc said. "The first performance of *Willy Wonka and the Chocolate Factory* is Friday night. If you hadn't returned I would have had to go on as Charlie!"

"Maybe you still will. Mrs. Cook might not let me rejoin the cast."

"Of course she will! You never left the cast. You just took a little vacation," I said.

"Yeah, you were dead. She can't blame you for that," Shawn said.

"Did you bring a note from your mom? Something like, *Please excuse Scotty, he was deceased*," Tim asked.

"Hmm, I wish I had thought of that," Scotty said.

"Note or no note, you are playing Charlie this weekend," Marc said.

"You could have done it, Marc. I know you could," I said.

"Yes, but now I don't have to do it. I'll stick with soccer."

"Soccer is way more important than a boring old play," Jon said.

"Boring! Boring! This play will be fabulous!" I yelled.

"Calm down. Don't be such a spazz," Jon said.

"You'd better be there, Jon Deerfield," I said.

"Uh oh, he used your last name. You'd better not skip out on the play or Dorian will have a hissy fit," Brandon said.

"I'll be there. I'm taking my girlfriend."

"Is that the blowup girlfriend or the other one?" Brandon asked.

"I don't have a blowup girlfriend. That's you."

"No, I only have a real one. We will be there too."

"We'll all be there," Tristan said.

Scotty looked pleased. Marc looked relieved, but also just a tiny bit disappointed.

People kept coming up to Scotty during lunch. He was a celebrity. I don't think anyone at our school had come back from the dead before. Hmm, did that make Scotty a zombie?

"I'm not used to all this attention. I kind of feel like hiding somewhere," Scotty said.

"It will pass. You're the topic of the day. Coming back from the dead will do that for you. Tomorrow, everyone will be back to talking about what a god I am," Brandon said.

"When has anyone ever talked about that?" Dane asked.

"All the time!" Brandon said.

"We discussed this, Brandon. There's fantasy and then there is reality," Jon said calmly, as if speaking to a mental patient. "You being butt-ugly is reality. Being a god is fantasy."

"Reverse those last two sentences and you've got it right."

"Okay. Being a god is fantasy. You being butt-ugly is reality."

"Yeah, that's... Hey! That's not what I meant!"

Jon patted Brandon's hand. Brandon glared at him.

***

Scotty was immediately and completely surrounded when he walked into the auditorium for our last period drama class. Tess grabbed him and hugged him and she was only the first. The girls passed Scotty around like he was a rag doll. Scotty had a huge grin on his face. I don't think he realized how much everyone cared.

Marc surrendered his role cheerfully. I missed being on the stage with my boyfriend, but I was thrilled to see Scotty step into a lead role again. He hadn't forgotten anything. It was as if he'd never left. The performances were going to be awesome!

We couldn't talk freely between drama class and play practice, but after practice Marc offered Scotty a ride home.

"Let's go to Marc's place so we can talk," I suggested.

"Sounds cool."

Scotty laughed.

"What?"

"I think aliens have replaced my parents. Mom told me to call if I was going to be late getting home from practice, but Dad told her I was seventeen and didn't have to report in unless I was going to be *really* late. It's amazing how much they have changed. Dad said he's glad they left the church. I never thought I'd hear him say that. Of course, I never thought my parents would stop going to that church."

We talked about the play the rest of the way to Marc's place. Once there, we went inside and Marc fixed us all sodas. We took seats around the kitchen table and Scotty stared at me.

"So... start talking."

"Just promise me you won't tell anyone what I'm about to tell you. Marc and I and several others could get into a lot of trouble if you do."

"I promise."

"As you've probably figured out, we faked your death."

"I knew you must have, but... that's just so..."

"Insane?" Marc offered.

"Yes!"

"It was Dorian's idea to kill you."

"Yeah, everyone thought I was crazy when I suggested it, but once I explained my reasoning they went for it."

"We weren't at all sure of what the result would be," Marc said. "Dorian was hopeful, but most of us weren't so sure. We figured it wouldn't hurt to try and how often do you get to plan a friend's funeral?"

"The actual funeral was going to be cool, but Brendan decided to bring you back in time for your own visitation *without* telling any of us. I feel like beating him," I said.

"I couldn't get him to tell me what was going on. When we pulled up in front of Miller's Funeral Home I was afraid one of my parents had died. Then, I walked in and there was *my* picture by the casket! That was so freaking weird. I had this irrational thought that I might actually be lying in the casket!"

"Did you check to make sure you weren't in there?" Marc asked.

"Uh, no."

"I had second thoughts about my plan after we got going with it," I said. "I wanted to force your family to think about life without you, but your death hit them even harder than I hoped it would. Your mom was a basket case and your dad wasn't much better."

"Yeah, Justin told me. He said he had to take over. They couldn't even go out and buy their own groceries. Dad went to work but... it was bad. What made you think of this whole thing?"

"Mark and Taylor. Marc and I were checking out the memorial to them by the soccer field and it hit me. I thought of all the pain their deaths caused and how their parents would probably do anything if they could have them back. If we made your parents think you were dead..."

"Your plan worked," Scotty said.

"We have to keep it a secret. We have to let everyone believe they jumped to conclusions. A lot of people were hit hard by your death. If they figure out we faked your death they will be pissed!" I said.

"We might have even broken a few laws. We're not sure about that, but we want to play it safe. The police were searching for you and even dragged the river trying to find your body," Marc added.

"I won't say anything."

"If anyone asks you went swimming in the Tippecanoe and left your clothes behind," I said.

"Come again?"

"We planted some of your clothes on the riverbank to make everyone think you'd drowned," Marc said.

"So that's how I died. Justin mentioned drowning. Hey, how did you get my clothes?" Scotty asked.

"You showered at my place. I told you to leave your dirty clothes and Mom would wash them. Remember? They were still in my hamper," Marc said.

"Oh yeah!"

"We needed to fake your death and we obviously couldn't come up with a body so..."

"You decided to drown me. You know, that's a nasty way to go."

"There was already a rumor that you'd drowned in the Tippecanoe. We decided to make the rumor sort of come true," I said.

"I never thought I'd say this to anyone, but thanks for killing me."

"Any time," I said.

"I think once will be enough. I did have a nice funeral, or rather visitation, didn't I?"

"Yes, you did," I said.

"Dorian put a lot of work into planning your death and your funeral," Marc explained. "He picked out your casket."

"It's beautiful. I almost can't wait to use it." Scotty laughed.

"You'd better wait a long, long time to use it," I said.

"I'll try to hold off. It wouldn't be fair making everyone go to two funerals for me so close together."

"Did you like the music?" I asked. "Tristan picked it out. We wanted to make sure you didn't have any crappy organ music."

"It was great, although I would have preferred rock."

"We were afraid your parents wouldn't go for that," Marc said.

"Today, everyone kept coming up to tell me how sorry they are that I'm dead. I told them that I expected to get better. I wonder if this is my fifteen minutes of fame."

"You have more fame coming up this weekend," Marc said.

"About that, I talked to Mrs. Cook. Since there are two performances on Saturday and since you know the part as well as I do, I think you should do one of the Saturday shows," Scotty said.

"Me?" Marc asked.

"Of course, you. Who else? Did you think I meant Dorian? He's good, but even he can't play Willy Wonka and Charlie."

"I couldn't do that. It's your part. I was more than a little nervous about doing it anyway."

"Well, too bad. You're doing one of the Saturday performances. Mrs. Cook and I decided."

"People are so bossy when they come back from the dead," Marc said to me.

I knew Marc was nervous about performing in front of a crowd, but I also knew he was secretly pleased he would get to do a performance.

"Guys, I really appreciate what you've done for me."

"It wasn't just the two of us. It was a group project. It *was* Dorian's idea. I don't think anyone else would have come up with something so crazy."

"Are you calling me crazy, Marc?" I asked, trying to pretend I was mad.

"No. I'm calling your idea crazy."

"Well, it worked, didn't it?"

"Yeah, it did," Marc said.

"When I left Verona, I wasn't sure I'd ever come back again. I knew you guys said you were going to fix things so life would be better for me, but I didn't see how you could possibly do that."

"Until Dorian came up with the idea of killing you we didn't know how we were going to do it either, but we were all determined that we would make things better for you."

"You have. Things aren't perfect at home, but they are a whole lot better. I'm not only allowed, but encouraged to hang out with the other gay boys. There is one thing, though..."

"What?" I asked.

"Mom and Dad would like to meet some of my gay friends. They want to know who I'm hanging out with and I think they just want to see what some other gay boys are like."

"Ethan and Brendan definitely have to go," I said. "When two jocks show up it will blow their minds."

Scotty laughed.

"I would very much like you two to come and meet my family. You're... well; you're the ones who have been there for me the most. If it weren't for you I probably would be lying in that casket right now. I think I would have cracked under the pressure.

If you hadn't spirited me away from Verona I think something very bad would have happened."

"You're welcome," I said.

"If things ever do get bad..." Marc began.

"You'll kill me again?"

"Um, no."

"I'll know who I can come to," Scotty said, grinning. "If you guys ever need a friend I'll be here for you, thanks to you."

"You know... we've already met your parents. We met them at your visitation," Marc said.

"Yeah, but I want them to really meet you. You will come, won't you?"

"Of course we will," Marc said.

We all went quiet for a bit.

"If Brandon was here he'd make some comment about us getting sappy," Marc said.

"Yeah, but I saw tears in his eyes while he was watching Scotty with his parents at the funeral," I said.

"Yeah?" Marc asked.

"Yeah."

"It's almost too bad we can't tease him about that, but we'll find something else," Marc said.

"Yeah, it can't be that hard. He is straight. He can't be too bright if he prefers girls," Scotty said.

"Oh, don't let him hear you say that," I said. "On second thought, do!"

"I should probably head home, guys. I sure my mom is worried about me. She's so clingy now. I don't mind so much. It's a big improvement and I figure she'll chill out eventually. I kind of like being home now."

"I'll drive you," Marc said.

"Marc needs to take me home anyway. I have a ton of homework and I definitely won't have time to work on it this weekend."

"Yeah, you'll be too busy being a star," Marc said.

"We'll all be busy being stars!" I said. I put my arms around Scotty and Marc's shoulders and we walked downstairs and out of the barn to Marc's Camaro.

When we dropped Scotty off, I saw the curtains move in one of the windows. I was willing to bet it was his mom. I was glad she was worried about him now. It meant she cared. Of course, she wouldn't have been a basket case when she thought Scotty was dead if she didn't care. I wondered what it was like for her to discover her son was alive after all.

"You look thoughtful," Marc said as he pulled onto the street.

"I was just thinking about Scotty's mom. We put her through a lot. I feel guilty."

"We caused her a lot of pain, but look what we did for her. If we hadn't caused her pain, Scotty might have killed himself, then he would be dead for real. Even if he didn't commit suicide, I don't think they would have ever had much of a relationship. They may not even have spoken to each other. Look at what she has now. I'd say it is worth the pain. Scotty's mom is lucky you were around to mess up her world. Otherwise, she might be like Mark or Taylor's parents now—their sons are never coming back."

"I just wish his parents could have been like mine from the beginning."

"Yeah, but they had their own road to travel. They had to learn the hard way."

"I know, but it would have saved Scotty a lot of pain."

"True that."

We were soon sitting in front of my house. I slid over and Marc and I hugged and kissed. We made out for a good ten minutes.

"I wish I didn't have so much homework," I said.

"Me too, but we'll have time together soon."

"I can't wait."

"Me either!"

Marc gave me one more kiss and then I climbed out of the car. I watched him drive away and then went inside.

***

I peeked out at the audience from stage right. It was Friday, the opening night of the play. I spotted Shawn, Tristan, Ethan, Nathan, and a few other friends before my eyes fell on whom I was seeking. Sitting very near the front was Scotty's parents and his brother, Justin.

The play began. Scotty was magnificent as Charlie. I didn't appear in the first scene so I had a rare chance to just stand back and watch the others perform.

"He's wonderful, isn't he?" a voice whispered in my ear.

"Almost as good as you," I said and then gave my boyfriend a peck on his lips.

"You look magnificent in your costume," Marc said.

"Thanks!"

I loved my costume, especially the long, deep purple coat and purple top hat. The pants were lavender and so was the shirt, but the shirt had a pattern of little candies in every color. I was holding a fancy walking cane in my right hand. On the top was a purple gumdrop. I really felt like Willy Wonka.

Mrs. Cook called me over to touch up my makeup and a few minutes later I was offstage, waiting for my cue. Then, the moment came when I ceased to be Dorian Calumet and became Willy Wonka. I slowly made my way down the red carpet, leaning heavily on my cane. I pretended to stumble and then turned my stumble into a perfect roll and hopped to my feet. Charlie grinned at me as I spoke to the holders of the golden tickets. I turned and lead the group into my factory to show them the wonders inside.

After the play, the cast lingered in the hallway outside the auditorium. We were all dressed once again in our street clothes, but the magic remained. Brandon was teasing me in front of his girlfriend when Scotty walked up.

"Will you come and talk with my family?" he asked.

I nodded and we walked together to where they waited.

"Mom, Dad, and Justin, you've met briefly before, but this is Willy Wonka, who we usually call Dorian."

"Dorian, Scotty has told us so much about you. He told us how much you've helped him and how you have been there for him when he needed you. He said that without you..." Mrs. Jackson's voice broke and she very nearly began crying, but after a few moments regained control. "I just want to say "thank you." I'm so glad that Scotty has such a good friend."

I could tell she actually meant it. I knew then that everything was going to be okay.

I was excited about Saturday night's performance. Marc was playing Charlie. It was the third performance of *Willy Wonka and the Chocolate Factory* and the second for that day, but this performance would be special. It was likely the only time I'd perform with Marc in front of an audience.

"How do you feel?" I asked Marc, only minutes before we were set to begin.

"I think I'm going to throw up."

The stage lights came on. I led Marc to the curtain.

"Take a peek at the audience," I said.

Marc hesitated.

"Go on."

Marc looked through the curtains.

"I can barely see anyone with all the lights."

"Exactly. Remember what I told you before? The performance isn't like practice. With all the lights shining on the stage you won't even be able to see the audience. It's like they aren't there. You'll only see me and the other actors. You know the part, Marc, and we'll all be out there with you. It will be fun. I promise."

Marc smiled at me nervously. I pulled him into a dark corner and kissed him. Soon, he forgot his nervousness. Minutes later, the play began and there was no time for anxiety or fear. Marc became Charlie and he was fabulous.

"So?" I asked, when we'd taken our bows, the final curtain had come down, and we had a moment alone.

"Maybe we should bump off Scotty again so I can take over his role," Marc said.

I laughed, then hugged my boyfriend.

The final performance was Sunday afternoon. After the show the cast gathered backstage for the cast party. We all stood around drinking punch, eating cookies, and laughing about our small screw-ups on the stage. Scotty looked happier than I'd ever seen him. For the first time in his life he didn't have to play a role and I'm not talking about his role as Charlie. Never before had Scotty been able to truly be himself. Now, his family accepted and supported him. He could finally be the Scotty he was meant to be.

After the cast party, Scotty piled in Marc's car with Dane, Tim, and me. We drove to Marc's place where another party awaited.

"What's all this?" Scotty asked as we walked into Marc's loft to find it filled with music, streamers, and friends.

"It's your wake!" Brandon said. "We couldn't let you die without throwing you a kick-ass wake!"

"Yeah and you have to deliver the eulogy!" Ethan said.

"Speech! Speech!" Tim and Dane yelled.

Scotty was pushed to the center of the room. He looked around at all of us and grinned.

"Scotty Jackson was a man among men," Scotty began. "Every boy either wanted him or wanted to be him."

"I think the guests should be allowed ten minutes for rebuttal!" called out Brandon.

"Quiet down, the deceased is talking," Shawn said.

"We will all miss me. We will miss my wit, my handsome face, and my incredible charm."

I could see Brandon rolling his eyes, but he remained silent.

"If I was alive today, I would tell each of you how important you are to me, how much your friendship means to me, and how much I appreciate all you've done for me, especially you, Dorian. Thank you for killing me and giving me a new life."

"I'm going to miss him," Nathan said, putting his arm over Scotty's shoulder.

"It will be okay, Nathan," Ethan said. "It's almost as if Scotty is still with us. I can almost hear his voice and feel his presence. He will always be with us."

"Unless we can find a way to ditch him," Brandon said.

Scotty stuck out his tongue, then laughed.

"Well, if I'm not allowed a rebuttal, let's eat!" Brandon said.

Scotty laughed again. He laughed a lot now and it was good to see. Tim and Dane led him toward the big table loaded with cold cuts, potato chips, barbequed cocktail wieners, chocolate chips and snacks of all sorts. Brandon had gone all out.

Later, we turned up the music and danced. I was happy. More importantly, Scotty was happy. Later, the music slowed and I put my head on Marc's shoulder. I looked over to see Scotty dancing with Casper. He noticed me watching him, smiled, and mouthed, "thank you." I threw him a kiss and grinned back. I knew Scotty's new life was going to be a whole lot better than his old one. Tonight was only the beginning.

Epilogue
Scotty

I sat in the crowd with my friends and watched as Marc, Dorian, Brandon, Jon, Nathan and Casey graduated. I almost couldn't believe so many of my newfound friends would not be returning to VHS next year. I almost couldn't believe I was now a senior! In another year I'd graduate. Then, I'd go to Indiana University in Bloomington. I couldn't wait and yet I could because I wanted to experience all VHS had to offer my last year of high school. I was impatient to get to college, but there was no reason to rush.

Someone else graduated too. Devon. That was one guy I was not going to miss. I could easily do without his sneering face. I was sure the others who were returning to VHS would be glad to be rid of him too. He wasn't all bad, but there was something seriously wrong with that boy.

After graduation, we all went out to the Selby farm for a big graduation bash. Marc, Dorian, Brandon, Jon, Nathan, and Casey were there, of course, as well as family members and tons of others from VHS. There were a whole lot of older people I didn't know, but I figured they were parents and relatives of the graduates. The entire gay crowd was there, including Casey's girlfriend. Even my brother was invited. Justin and I had been spending more time together and he'd met my gay friends. What's more, he liked them.

Brendan was home from school since the spring semester at IU had ended about the first week of May. I talked to him a lot about my plans for coming to IU. Even if Dorian and the others hadn't killed me and improved my home life dramatically, my life would still have been better because of Brendan. He showed me that life was worth living and he gave me plenty to eagerly anticipate.

"Before I forget, Jeff says "hi." He also said you're the best corpse he's ever slept with," Brendan said.

"I hope I'm the only corpse he's ever slept with."

"You never know with Jeff, do you?"

293

I laughed.

"He also said to give you something."

"What?"

"This." Brendan leaned over and kissed me on the cheek. I grinned and turned just a bit red.

"Okay, that's enough of Jeff. Let's eat!" Brendan said. We turned and joined our friends.

There was tons of food! You name it and it was there—hamburgers, hot dogs, fried chicken, cold cuts, slaw, baked beans, mashed potatoes, corn—the list was endless. There were big galvanized tubs filled with ice and soft drinks. My favorite was the dessert table. There was a huge sheet cake in the school colors of blue and white with all the graduates' names on it. There were chocolate brownies, chocolate cake, chocolate chip cookies, cupcakes, cherry, apple, and rhubarb pie. My favorite was the blackberry cobbler. It reminded me of my time on Anne's farm. I had been writing Anne letters and she was delighted that all was well.

Hours later, after most of the crowd had cleared out, I sat around big bonfire with all my friends. Most of the guys were paired up, so Justin sat by me. We talked and laughed and remembered all the funny things that had happened throughout the school year. I hadn't been a part of group for most of the year, so most of the stories were new to me. I was sad that so many of my new friends had graduated, but happy that many of them would be returning to high school with me. I was happy that I'd have another year at VHS. I was happy that I could look forward to attending IU. I was happy that my family loved me. I was happy, period, and all thanks to my friends.

The Gay Youth Chronicles
Listed in suggested reading order

Outfield Menace

Snow Angel

The Soccer Field Is Empty

Someone Is Watching

A Better Place

The Summer of My Discontent

Disastrous Dates & Dream Boys

Just Making Out

Temptation University

Scarecrows

The Picture of Dorian Gay

Scotty Jackson Died… But Then He Got Better

Someone Is Killing the Gay Boys of Verona

Vampire's Heart

Keeper of Secrets

Do You Know That I Love You

Masked Destiny

Altered Realities

Dead Het Boys

This Time Around

Phantom World

Second Star to the Right

The Perfect Boy

The Graymoor Mansion Bed and Breakfast

Shadows of Darkness

Heart of Graymoor

Yesterday's Tomorrow

Boy Trouble

Fierce Competition

Christmas in Graymoor Mansion

A Boy Toy for Christmas

Also by Mark A. Roeder

Homo for the Holidays: Mostly Gay Christmas Tales

Ancient Prejudice (This is an early version of *The Soccer Field Is Empty*, which is recommended by the author instead of *Ancient Prejudice*.)

Information on Mark's upcoming books can be found at markroeder.com. Those wishing to keep in touch with others who enjoy Mark's novels can join his fan club at http://groups.yahoo.com/group/markaroederf ans.